THE DREAMERS

THE DREAMERS

Ellen Bromfield Geld

Doubleday & Company, Inc., Garden City, New York, 1973

ISBN: 0-385-06473-X
Library of Congress Catalog Card Number 73-79669
Copyright © 1973 by Ellen Bromfield Geld
Printed in the United States of America
First Edition

To Manasse, who thinks things out so carefully and is yet a Dreamer.

THE DREAMERS

CHAPTER 1

Malachai Kenath sat in a rocking chair on the veranda of the fazenda's big house, his sculptor's hands folded across his slightly protuberant middle, practicing what he called "the sweet doing nothing."

It was a habit he had acquired in Italy during his self-imposed exile from Rumania and the beginning of his search for a place where one could live and think in peace. There they had called it "la dolce far niente;" in Brazil it was referred to as "a doçe fazer nada." It made little difference.

Here, seven thousand miles away and twenty years later, Malachai had come to the final conclusion that peace was unattainable. Still one could perform "the sweet doing nothing" in a place such as this better than anywhere else. And during those moments when one sat with one's hands folded across one's middle, rocking gently, one could think backwards and forwards to the wars and revolutions and times of peace, and the dark ages that descended periodically upon the earth. One could contemplate the events that were great in people's lives, but small before the destructive impulses of the world, and come close to feeling immune.

He had been sitting here almost without interruption since the day before yesterday, when he had arrived with the others for the weekend and when the great coffee flowering that Josh Moran had been predicting each spring for the past four years, had finally occurred. Each spring—if the south wind didn't blow too persistently, if the rain came in time, if after the rain, there was no frost, or the drought didn't last too long . . . This year it had happened. After weeks of hot, dust-laden August winds, the clouds had banked over the northwestern hills, just at the spot from which the coming of rain was God's irreversible certainty, and performed their miracle.

Josh and his wife, Lia, had immediately gone trudging out over the hills, trailed by a stream of exuberant people and dogs, and come back hours later, soaked to the eyelashes, carrying hatfuls of mushrooms.

"Now wait and see," Josh had said. "Tomorrow will be the day."

And true to Josh's word, the next day, when the sun warmed the earth and shriveled the mushrooms on the leeward side of the hills, every branch on every coffee tree had burst into a galaxy of white stars.

If the flowers took and there was coffee, after the harvest, Josh said, they would buy that extra piece of land, increase the herd, perhaps take a little trip to Europe. Lia had always wanted to rent a house in Brittany just to spend a month contemplating an old and civilized landscape.

Malachai sighed heavily, wary still of unforeseen circumstances, aware that life had a way of slapping down people who had the audacity to persist in their dreams. He was glad it was Josh's coffee and Josh's fazenda, not his.

Still it had been fun, just the same, to see Josh drink to all the great flowerings in history, and dance till he collapsed in his chair in joyous oblivion so that Lia had been obliged to haul off his boots and leave him where he was for the few hours left until dawn. They had all drunk and danced and acted foolish, sharing Josh's optimism over the spectacular event of the flowers; ignoring for the moment the fact that a chill wind might come tomorrow and scatter the flowers like snow.

It was nearly dusk now. Clouds had piled up again on the western horizon, promising a dazzling sunset. In the strange amethyst light that bathed the hills, red cattle grazed in pastures that had turned overnight from wind-scorched brown to a lush tropical green.

There were children everywhere. On the lawn, where the casuarina and flamboyant trees gave way to wide open spaces, a soccer game was in progress, its goals staked out between somebody's old boots. Portuguese epithets in the high voices of choir boys rose in the jasmine-scented wind. Through the screen door that led onto the veranda smaller children and dogs passed in a steady parade, the door creaking and banging in rhythmic protest. In the center of the lawn, perhaps to lure those small children out of hearing, a pup tent had been erected. Though it had not succeeded in its purpose—for there were no children near it—the tent was nonetheless occupied. Protruding from either end, Malachai observed the solid legs of two full-grown men.

One pair, bare, brown and athletic where they emerged from faded bermudas, were unmistakably those of Duncan Roundtree, Josh's friend and associate in what seemed to Malachai an endless procession of never quite crystalized schemes. The other pair, in the same boots that Lia had, cursing, removed the night before, were unmistakably Josh's.

Beneath the canvas an animated conversation was going on, punctuated by sporadic gusts of laughter that caused the tent flaps to quiver responsively. Malachai stopped rocking, lit his pipe and, placing it between his teeth in the spot worn smooth by its stem, watched the tent with small, bright, perceptive eyes.

He knew what was going on under there. It was what they called a "board of directors' meeting." One week it was real estate; another, great herds of cattle in Mato Grosso; another, endless fields of wheat and soybeans in Rio Grande do Sul. Always it was going to be the big deal, the *grande negocio* that would make of them at last independent men. That would enable Duncan Roundtree to give up being vice-president of one of the most powerful banks in America—a position Malachai could see no practical reason to want to give up, considering the ease with which Duncan fulfilled it, alone and unhindered by "the great father bank far away on the northern continent." Too, as a result of the *grande negocio*, Josh would be able at last to buy enough land to allow him to live from farming alone; an area that would evidently have to be the equivalent of a small nation. For despite lush pastures and handsome red cattle and thousands of coffee trees, what he owned was not enough. Like Duncan, Josh had a job; in his own words, a cushy one, with some obscure agricultural agency of USAID that nonetheless provided him with imported cars, paid vacations for all the family, and such delectable items as untaxed whiskey and little smoked oysters in cans.

When there were so many in the world who would find such positions enviable, it seemed to Malachai not quite right that these two should be scheming so incessantly to bc free of them.

Incessantly and yet with a curious lack of seriousness. What were they laughing at under there? Did they really think that even this great land of opportunity, Brazil, could provide them with a fortune if they treated it all as a joke?

It made Malachai nervous to think of the consequences—not so much for Duncan, who, despite an attitude that lacked conventional reverence, was not in as much of a hurry to give up the vice-presidency as all that. Not, at least, until some sign of a fortune was evident. But for Josh, who ever since Malachai had known him had seemed to have a certain proclivity for climbing out on limbs and applying the saw. Last night, for instance, before sinking into oblivion, hadn't Josh's final words been, "And what's more, I've written my last stinking report. I'm quitting. From now on, all reports up AID's asshole. Nobody reads them anyway, that's where they belong."

Quitting! Leaving it all; the cars, vacations, schooling for the children—everything. "Then what will be left?" Malachai had leaned solicitously over Josh to ask. But Josh had already departed from the realm of the conscious, leaving Malachai to answer his own question. "Nothing but a lot of unreliable flowers."

"And that." Once again Malachai squinted down a Jewish nose the size and shape of a wilted turnip, at the tent which threatened, at any moment, to emit one final guffaw and collapse. He was thus absorbed, his emotions growing all out of proportion to his role as a detached observer, when a violent threat from within the house announced the approach of Lia Moran.

"One more child through that screen door and I'll put the lot of you through the meat grinder—not once but twice—do you hear?"

"But we wanna get through," a small voice replied, unintimidated.

"Well, get through, dammit, and stay through. Have you no sense of decision? I want peace."

This last Lia uttered with a contrastingly subdued laugh as she sank into the chair beside Malachai and crossed her sandaled feet upon the table before her.

"My God, what I wouldn't give for a great crashing, thundering storm."

"You just said you wanted peace," Malachai reminded her, glancing sidewise at the finely made, sensitive face which could be one moment furious, the next gentle and solicitous, the next, oddly remote and dreaming.

She looked at him uncomprehendingly. "To me storms *are* peaceful. After a long hot day they fill me with relief."

"Don't they frrighten you?" Malachai said, his Balkan *r*'s rolling richly.

"Why should they?"

"Well, the possibility of being struck by lightning is very real. I think I should warn you. I speak from experience. It happened to me in 1938." He leaned backward and puffed on his pipe reminiscently. "I was fleeing over the Alps into Switzerland. There was a storm, and there was I huddled against the leeward side of a barn. I ask you, how could I have known that the seat of my pants was attached to an ungrounded lightning rod?"

Rather than a sense of caution and respect, Malachai's warning aroused only a burst of unsympathetic hilarity. "Oh, Malachai. If it had been anyone else, I wouldn't believe it, but you."

Malachai did not respond. There was a certain poignant truth in her reaction that he preferred not to think about. Indeed, he was about to switch the subject to Josh and his intentions when something landed in his lap.

It was the size of a small bear, had rings around its eyes, a ferreting nose and formidable claws. "Help," said Malachai. The ferreting nose was going for his tobacco pouch.

"That damn coati," Lia murmured regretfully. "He was such an irresistible funny little thing a month ago. Don't move. Just sit still."

"Move? I'm paralyzed!"

"Well, don't be that either. Just relax. Fear encourages him." Kneeling agilely beside his chair she put out her arm. "Come, Nikki . . ." Muttering and twittering, the creature removed its snout from Malachai's pocket and scrambled up onto Lia's shoulder, where it balanced, clinging with its murderous claws until she crossed the lawn to a flamboyant tree and, leaning suggestively against a convenient limb, persuaded it to make its departure.

She was back in a moment, propping her feet on the table again.

Malachai moved his rocking chair an inch to the left. "You're almost as dangerous to sit beside as a lightning rod. Couldn't you have taken the creature a little farther away?"

She shook her head despondently. "Only if we turned him loose in the Amazon and then only if we dropped him from a plane, but Josh wrecked the last plane he flew, remember?"

"I am not familiar with that period in his life."

"It was fun, but this is better," said Lia, looking out over the hills.

"Which reminds me," said Malachai, taking up where he had left off before she appeared, "what's all this about Josh giving up his job?"

"All? It's quite simple. He's given it up."

"Do you mind my asking why?"

"Because they want us to move, leave the fazenda."

"And you couldn't do that? Even temporarily?"

Lia didn't answer immediately, but he could sense her spiritually digging her heels into the ground. From her look he realized he might just as well have asked a dedicated Zionist to give up the thought of Israel. "Nothing"—she spoke each word with exaggerated distinction as if to make sure he need never ask again—"is worth doing that."

"But there is a matter of making a living."

"Ah well," Lia tossed her head and laughed again with the same sublime confidence with which she had lent that horrible coatimundi her arm. "Josh will come up with something, he always does."

Malachai's eyes rolled upward toward the tiled roof and fixed themselves upon a pair of swallows darting and swooping in to feed their clamorous young in a nest under the eaves. By comparison the birds' attitude toward life seemed so stable, balanced and sane. But then who knew? Perhaps Josh *would* come up with something. Perhaps in a moment the board of directors would emerge with a solution, a means of making a fortune, buying more land, living without a job. Then all of them would celebrate again, Duncan, Josh and their women, Malachai's Clea, not the least of them, Malachai himself, who adored a celebration, raising their glasses as they had done yesterday to the flowers. And who could truly say that it might not work out? After all, wasn't it a phenomenon peculiar to Brazil that things seldom turned out as badly as one expected them to? "*Em fim tudo dá certo*." It was a sort of national attitude that suited people like Josh perfectly, kept them optimistically sawing off limbs as they went along.

He shuddered nonetheless. "To tell the truth, I am not surprised at this move. It is *typical*."

"What do you mean by that?" said Lia, who was not at all fond of the word typical.

"Did you ever think of why you really came to this country?" said Malachai.

"Of course," she answered, shifting so that she might better see the sunset over her land. "We've always known what we wanted."

"But why come here?" Malachai insisted.

"Because," she said impatiently, "we thought it would be easier to start in a frontier country."

"And has it been?"

"Not really."

"And yet you are still here."

"One becomes accustomed to everything," she said, using another old Brazilian dictum.

"Accustomed . . . nonsense." Malachai shook his head. "If you can't be honest and tell me the reason, I will be compelled to tell *you*. It is not because of the land Josh came here any more than Duncan Roundtree came because he was sent by the bank. He would have gotten here some way, mark my words. It is because you are dreamers, all of you. You couldn't bear to live in a place where all the jobs had been done a thousand times over and all the questions answered. Is that not true? Perhaps, you are thinking, are you not?—here the answers will be different. There *is* that element of wonder, of suspense."

He didn't turn his head as he said this, but looked at her sidewise, catching a smile that reflected inward and told him he had struck a note always present but seldom touched; which caused her in turn to say at last, "Well, and you? What are you here for? What are you after, come from Rome to this mecca of art, eh, Malachai?" She said it chidingly, still she listened intently, for there was something about the pronouncements of this person who spent so much time watching and thinking that made them unsettlingly prophetic.

"I?" for some reason he seemed now reluctant to reply. "What can I say about the answers? I am not a good judge. I have spent far too much time—centuries actually—escaping across borders in the night. I find it all very interesting this pursuit of dreams, but I tell you I haven't the energy left for it. For me it is enough to sit on the sidelines and see how it turns out."

"Nice, if you can do it." Lia smiled again, this time as much for him as for herself.

Dusk was beginning to fall. A chill south wind had arisen, dispersing the heavy scent of the jasmine that climbed the veranda posts and dispelling Lia's hopes for a storm. The shadows all but covered the lawn. Before their deliberate advance, the soccer game had given way, the boys seeming to dissolve in thin air as they did periodically, disappearing without one's notice to crystalize again noisily at some other hour.

With an upheaval of poles and flaps and strings, the board of directors appeared. As he made his way across the lawn, the last light of day reflected from what Duncan Roundtree called his Ton Ton Macoutes glasses. But even these dark glasses could not fully detract from the appearance of an American thoroughbred; the kind of relaxed good looks that suggested Ivy League, and would be at ease amidst those who considered themselves to be the right people anywhere. And yet here he was crawling out of a pup tent with Josh Moran, who, though tempered in midwestern steel mills, reminded Malachai of Russell's sketches of plainsmen, lanky and strident and not very respectful of fences; a good man to have around all the same when one found it necessary to shoot a rattlesnake quickly.

"Drinks," Josh said commandingly to Lia as his booted foot touched the first step of the veranda. "Time to celebrate. We've just formed a new company."

"Another?" Malachai looked distressed but not surprised.

"Hah," said Duncan, baring his long teeth in the smile of a schoolboy who had something horrid in his pocket.

"Hah, what?"

"Chicken in the basket."

"Ooh," Malachai moaned, horrified. This was worse than anything he had expected. "Fast foods—could you have chosen anything less in keeping? Are you trying to change a whole nation's personality?"

"Well, more or less fast," said Josh, reminding Malachai of his talent for adaptation to local conditions.

"But Brazilians don't even like to eat sandwiches without a knife and fork, let alone chicken."

"They'll learn," said Duncan. "It's modern. *Para frente.*"

"Come," said Lia, "don't be depressed. You'll have nothing to do with it, remember?"

"*Graças a Deus.*"

"There now. What will you have?"

"Scotch on the rocks, please, and some of those smoked oysters, as, for us, they will soon cease to exist." So saying, Malachai Kenath sank more deeply into his chair and tried not to listen as from somewhere amidst the foliage in the garden there came the muttering, twittering sound of the coati.

CHAPTER 2

Malachai was right, of course. They had come to this out-of-the-way place because they were dreamers. Yet if he had been fully aware of the events that had surrounded Josh's plane crash some five years earlier, he would have been less inclined to classify him as a dreamer, than as a fanatic, or perhaps even a maniac.

But then, probably only Lia knew the full story of why Josh had allowed himself to be talked into flying over the Brasilian Pantanal during the time of the "*bruma seca*." A time, each year, when, trapped in that vast, shallow bowl of rivers, jungled islands and dried swamps, the wind rages, turning dust over smoke and separating earth from sky with a near impenetrable cloud of darkness that can make safe return to earth, once one is above it, a near impossibility.

It was on such a day and at such a time that Josh had left Lia at the landing field in the border town of Pirapora, saying, "Just sit tight. It's my one chance to really get to know this guy McGuiness. You know, don't look blank. He's the head of the Research Institute. Hell, if I can impress him, Lia, I just might come back with a job that would put us on the ground for good."

So she had "sat tight" because if there was anything she'd wanted then, it was to get Josh onto the ground for good. And even as she sat years later, talking with Malachai and watching the sunset, she knew that her reason for saying so airily, "Oh Josh will come up with something," was the same now as it had been then. For perhaps more than anything she had always been tied to Josh by her faith in his ability to act, to jump when the moment was crying for it. It was a faith that had made her feel safe with Josh Moran ever since she had first come to know him.

The odd thing, whenever she thought back on it, was how long it had taken to get to know him, though they had lived in the same town of Elmira, Ohio, and gone to the same school all the years of their childhood. It had been his brother Johnny she had known, first of all, just as everyone had known him, for Johnny had a real flare for the limelight.

He was a troublemaker in the old-fashioned sense of the word, who drank too much beer and tequila and liked to skip school with the girls in his souped-up jalopy; who was generally suspended from school on Tuesdays and reinstated on Fridays because on Friday night the football team couldn't do without him.

Johnny Moran. She laughed inside herself and loved him still a little whenever she thought of him and all the boys like him who lived in the soot-stained frame houses in the lower part of town. The houses were noisy and crowded and smelled of rabbit stew and hot peppers, and the boys—the apples of their mothers' eyes —came swaggering out of them each day, handsome, uncouth, cocksure, forbidden, romantic. In high school all the girls were wild about them. They seemed to know so much more about life than the boys who lived in the orderly, white houses in the shadows of old trees in the high part of town; the boys, whose parents had planned them, indeed planned everything so that there was no mystery, nothing forbidding or exciting about them at all.

The girls were mad about the boys from the gray houses and the girls' mothers considered them a menace and prayed nightly (though without quite saying so to God) that their daughters might avoid getting knocked up by them long enough to go to college and settle down to "reality."

Like a great many others, Lia had been Johnny's girl for a while. She'd ridden in his souped-up jalopy and even gone to his house that smelled of peppers and rabbit stew and been received with warmth, and a degree of suspicion scarcely less intense than that which her own parents felt for Johnny.

But she had never paid much attention to Johnny's older brother, Josh. Josh was peculiar; always reading or studying or locked up in his room "conducting"—waving his arms like a madman, as Johnny, who peeped through the window, reported— some symphony or other that came over the radio on Sunday afternoon.

Or he would be off, walking; where, nobody quite knew. Nor did anybody bother to ask.

Victor Moran, his father, who had come from Hungary when he was fourteen and had worked himself into the position of head foreman in the steel mill, thought it best to leave well enough alone. Johnny gave him plenty of trouble, Josh gave him none. Besides, he was studious. Victor Moran worked and saved, and allowed his eldest son to go his way, never doubting that one day he would go to college and become a lawyer or some kind of high-class government employee. It was Victor Moran's dream.

But on the day Josh graduated from high school he went into the United States Air Force as a volunteer. The trouble in Vietnam was just beginning and Mrs. Moran, who had seen war sweep over Europe in her childhood, had wept until she could weep no more, which was an accomplishment close to drying up the Nile. Victor Moran turned his brawny back and waved a calloused hand and shouted, "Go get killed, go ahead, be a goddamn hero. I ain't got nothin' more to say about nothin'." From then on, however, he had begun to feel old and think about retirement, for work's no fun, nor is anything else without a dream.

Nobody had known much about Josh or ever really bothered to ask. But Johnny, acting smart and making jokes one day, said his brother's peculiarity dated back to the summer he had worked on a farm and been hit on the head with the trap door to the hayloft. "He's never been the same since—" Perhaps only Lia, three years later, would discover how close to the truth Johnny Moran, acting smart and joking, had really come.

Josh came home a few months before he was ready to muster out. Lia was in the "going to college and settling down to reality" stage of her development and not doing very well at either. She was a trim, poolside-brown eighteen with hair the color of dark honey and eyes that were blue on sunny days and gray when it was cloudy, and irreverent all the time.

It wasn't that she still cared about Johnny, who, having graduated from the football team, sat over his beer waiting to be drafted and talking, as if life were already over, of the "old times." But she was even less inspired by the boys from the brick houses and shaded lawns who talked about cars and joked self-consciously about the summer jobs that their old men gave them so that they could play at "working their way up." Chrysalises in cocoons, bored and boring, who would one day strike out, though without ever knowing quite why, at the dullness of their planned lives.

Lia had a summer job in the bookstore. She sat behind the counter or, better still, back amidst the shelves, where it was quiet and cool, reading Salinger and feeling like Holden Caulfield.

Then Josh Moran, whom she'd never bothered to look at before, came in one morning and requested everything she could find on Australia, New Zealand, Nigeria, Rhodesia, South Africa, Brazil, Argentina and Uruguay. For a moment she stared intently, as if she half expected him to pull out a gun or fall in a fit on the floor. But he just stood there leaning on the counter, looking patient but intransigent, so she began her search. After forty-five minutes of looking under Australia, Africa, America and South, she returned with one dusty volume on poisonous snakes and a plea. "None of those places exist, how about Peyton Place?"

"That's why I want them, because they don't exist."

"You thinking of going AWOL or something? What's your racket?" She felt oddly elated and curious. Somehow, she didn't want him to go away. As he leaned on the counter, holding her with a gaze that proffered friendliness, yet somehow lacked mercy, it seemed to her she'd never seen eyes so full of life. Not restless and impatient like Johnny's, but alive with thought and a curious look of expectation. He seemed to be not just looking at her, taking in her features, but thinking about her, considering.

"If you'd really like to know my racket, I could explain it to you —but it would take time."

"You think I'm retarded or something?" Her overdeveloped chin thrust forward in an expression of belligerence.

He narrowed his eyes thoughtfully, "Probably not. But to understand my racket, you'd have to spend at least a day with me, way out in the country—" He must have noted a certain hint of alarm in her expression, something that said, "Ye Gods, even his own parents never knew where it was he went," because, of a sudden, his own expression changed. It became reassuring. One would have felt one could go anywhere with him, anytime. "I assure you, if you go," he said, "you'll be as safe with me as you want to be."

CHAPTER 3

They borrowed Johnny's car because Josh didn't have one and
Johnny didn't know who Josh was driving out into the country
with. They drove to a place where an iron bridge girded a stream
and, leaving the car, they jumped down from the concrete wall
that supported the bridge, landing on the sandy embankment below. Then they walked, sometimes along the bank, where flutelike
bamboo reeds and marsh marigolds grew out of the soft, damp
earth; sometimes down the middle of the stream itself, jumping
from one jutting rock to the next, wading into deep pools formed
by the swirling currents in a bend in the stream, wetting their
clothes and scattering sunfish like bright swift darts of light.

Lia Cunningham had been on trips to Yosemite and Yellow-
stone and had stood in a group with the camera she'd gotten for
her birthday feeling awed and a little tired because so many people
seemed so intent on seeing so much majesty at once. But today it
was different. It was as though she had really left the town and
come into the country for the first time, and all her senses were
alive as they had never been. Overhead was an August sky, intensely blue and clear at the center, with the clouds piling up over
themselves on the horizon, blackening, threatening storm, then
dispersing with a wind from somewhere that touched their cheeks
for an instant and was gone. The sun was hot on her head and
back and the water wonderfully cold and strong as it splashed over
her sandals and rushed against her legs. She could smell its cool-
ness and the scent of the grass in the pasture above the banks,
wilting and dusty in the sun.

They scarcely spoke. Only now and then Josh would say something like, "Look out, a river monster," as a crayfish slid around a
rock, or a turtle dropped off a log into the water . . . They said

very little, but once in a while, Josh caught her hand and the warmth of it and strength of it were greater than the warmth of the sun, or the strength and coldness of the river or the hardness of stone beneath her feet.

There was a curve in the stream where a great tree had fallen and driftwood and rock, caught in its branches, had formed a dam, hollowing the sand into a deep pool here, piling it up to form a beach there. A couple of birch trees rose out of the bank, stretching their gray and white patched limbs over the beach of sand and pebbles. Here they sat with their backs resting against the smooth thick birch roots that rose out of the eroded earth, their feet stretched out toward the dappled light that shone through the branches and leaves.

Not far off some Angus cattle stood round a salt lick in the shadow of some maple and oak trees, chewing their cuds and dozing. But at the sight of human beings, they lifted their heads and their ears came forward in curious, wondering unison. Lia started up, but Josh pulled her against him and made her sit still. "Don't move, and don't be afraid. They have an irresistible curiosity, you'll see." And so they sat, not stirring until the boldest heifer, keeping as far as she could and stretching her neck until her eyes seemed to bulge with the effort, touched Josh's arm with her wet nose. He didn't move, so she tried him with her tongue —and after a time another heifer came and then another, blowing through their noses, tasting the salt of Josh and Lia's hands with hesitant sand-papery tongues, until Josh flung up his hands and shouted, "Blhh!" and they rocked backward on the short Angus legs, alarmed, but not very, moving to a safer distance, but not far.

Lia had never owned a dog or a cat. They messed up the furniture. And so this touching of these animals was strange and wonderful too. She leaned close against this Josh whom she had never known and felt exultant and conspiratorial like a child who had run away from home and was never going back. And suddenly she felt very much like talking.

"We're here," she said, "in the country and we've walked a long way and I feel as safe as I want to. Now you're supposed to tell me what your racket is."

"All right," he said, "spread out the food and we'll talk."

She took out the sausage and the cheese and the black bread

and put all together in large thick slices. They ate ravenously and drank of the wine, and while they ate, he told her the simple straight thing he had never told anybody because sometimes the simplest, straightest things are the hardest to understand.

He told her about how he had come to this place in the beginning as a boy of fifteen. "I couldn't get a job in town that summer, so my father gave in, even though it seemed degrading to him, and let me look for a job on a farm. He regretted it ever afterward because, according to him, it was after that I began to act funny—"

"Take walks out into the country?" Lia smiled remembering Johnny's smart-alec comments.

"I suppose he was right in a way," said Josh. "I've never been very realistic since. I mean, I could have gotten a scholarship and studied to be a lawyer or an economist or something. That's what he dreamed of. But I learned so much that summer on the farm that I've never been able to unlearn since. It was different from anything I'd ever done. I'd shined shoes and been a delivery boy. This was much harder. By the end of the day you were hot and filthy with dust and sweat—so dirty and hungry and tired, you couldn't tell what you wanted to do first, wash, eat or sleep. But they were all good feelings—I suppose because you could see the empty wagon, and the hay bales piled in the loft, or the cattle blowing around in the feed and feel as though you'd done something. Do you see what I mean?" He looked at her quite anxiously, as if he only half expected her to, but she nodded, thinking of the river and the sun and the cattle with their rough, curious tongues.

"I think I do."

"So," he went on, looking relieved, "I used to walk out here on Sunday and sit like this and think about what it would be like not just to do these things for somebody else. Oh, I'd get tired of that —but on land of my own—"

"Is that what you never told anybody?" Lia stared at him, half relieved, half astonished. "Why?"

"It sounds all right to you, huh?"

"Why, it's the greatest."

"That's what I used to tell myself, but when I thought of saying something like, 'I think I'd like to be a farmer someday,' I could see my father." Josh gave an imitation of Victor Moran, slapping his forehead and groaning, " 'That what I put you through school for?—to become a slave, a peasant?' Or someone like your father, Lia, tell me. What would he say?"

Lia thought she knew. She narrowed her eyes and looked grave and suspicious, " 'What's that Josh Moran in on, some speculation scheme? Can't be tax evasion, doesn't have any money.' "

Josh laughed and Lia noticed, in spite of his being so young, how many and how deep were the lines at the corners of his eyes from laughter and squinting in the sun. "You've got it. To want to own a farm a half a century ago was a legitimate dream. Now, at best, it's something funny. Why hell, even dishonest."

"And so," Lia said, baffled and genuinely sad, "you decided to give it all up and join the Air Force."

Josh shook his head, his fine light eyes filled with amusement. He was enjoying himself. He didn't dare think how happy it made him to say the things he thought and have someone understand them—especially this girl who moved with such confidence and ease like a fine filly. Whose sun-streaked hair cast its shadow across lightly tanned skin in such a way that he wanted to know every inch of it—that skin.

"Don't jump to conclusions. It's a bad habit. Remember the books I asked for?"

"Will I ever forget?" Lia groaned.

"Books like you said about places that don't exist for most people—big stretches of country that have never been touched, that are begging to be put into crops—cotton, peanuts, sugarcane, grass . . . Can you imagine? Acres and acres, a sea of grass . . ."

"I follow you about the books and the grass," said Lia, "but what about the Air Force?"

"Money," Josh interrupted her. He wanted no more questions till he was finished, till he'd laid the whole complicated picture before her. "Even in places like that there's no use dreaming if you haven't got money. First, you've got to get some, and while you're getting it, you damn well better have something practical to offer. So that's where the Air Force comes in. Do you see? In places like that, where there are no roads—"

"Surely," said Lia, laughing, caught up in this sweeping scheme as if in a windstorm, "surely there'll be a need for someone who can fly a fighter bomber—"

"Not a fighter bomber"—he faced her now, his expression turned serious and a little wary, as if perhaps she wouldn't understand after all—"but a bush plane. I've gone into it, studied the situation, Lia. Bush pilots are rare animals. You can make a pile, and in the meantime . . ." His voice fell, suddenly full of disgust. "You don't see it," he said with finality. "Let's go wading."

Josh Moran had a mania for wading, it seemed—now he was stripping off his shirt, plunging in as if he were literally on fire and the only way to cool his vexation was to douse it, soak it, wash it away.

"But I do see it. Of course I do." She stood a moment on the water's edge, rejected, indescribably miserable, left behind, and then she plunged in after him. The water in the depths of the pool in the shadow of the trees was colder than it was in the sunlight. She surfaced, shivering, and he, with a hard angry look still, pulled her toward him. Through the wetness of her clothing, she could feel her breasts hurting against him and the warmth stealing over her again as it had when he had caught her hand walking up the stream. It was warmer, colder, cleaner, better, a thousand times better than anything she had ever known in her life.

Under the birch trees, safe and hidden in a hollow of roots and earth, the earth and sand and roots hurting her back, they lay together, pressed tightly along the length of their bodies. And with the cattle not far off, lifting their heads at the whisperings and murmurings of man on earth and under heaven, she became passionately, gratefully as safe as she would ever want to be with Josh Moran.

CHAPTER 4

They returned often after that, though Johnny would never again lend Josh his car. They returned to watch the cattle and wade in the stream and sit and draw maps in the sand imagining great herds now in the African veld, now on the edge of the Australian desert or the *pantanos* that bordered the rivers that flowed from the Andes down to the sea. And always these games of dreaming and speculation ended with their lying in each other's arms.

Sometimes their love was gentle and seeking like a quest for something bright and shimmering in the waters of the stream and it pleased her. Sometimes it was like some thundering wave, unrestrained and uncontrollable, against which she rebelled until her rebellion became in itself an infuriating ecstasy. For Josh was as absolute in his living as in his dreaming. To him it was all one, all good. There were no measures if you loved someone, no boundaries—only love to be given richly and completely, or withdrawn.

At times like these it didn't please her so much. Despite what she told herself, it seemed to her that there *were* boundaries. Without wanting to she found herself looking into those unabashedly glazed and passionate eyes with a certain repugnance, seeing there a look more raw and unbridled than anything she had ever known. Against her own will, something inside her, born of centuries of Puritan gentility, discretion nurtured within white houses beneath ancient trees, quivered and withdrew. Then, as she sat on the sand by the water's edge, thinking of the rough, angular figure who sat beside her, the disturbing thought would come to her that it was perhaps only an idea—a fantasy of wide open spaces and unconquered lands she was in love with and not a man.

What if suddenly he should say, "Look, I've decided I really want to make it here. Study something, go to an ag. school. The department of agriculture has all kinds of opportunities for a realistic young man"? What if suddenly with those keen, challenging eyes, he should turn to her and say that? But of course he wouldn't. If he did he wouldn't be Josh Moran. The man and the idea were inseparable.

That was why there by the river everything was different. She no longer felt trapped in a kind of glutinous suspension—like one of those things her mother called a "cold shape," in which every canned peach and pear had its exact, inert position until the moment of devouring. There by the riverside, the maps in the sand were as real as Josh's assurance that, come the day of his mustering out—now, then and forever, there would be thought, decision. Whatever happened in life it would be the result of a move.

Still she was a person with a will of her own and so this thing of Josh's always having his way bothered her, caused her to awake at night, wanting to run to Josh and plead, "Not always, in everything. It can't work that way." But that wouldn't have done either. So one day just before it was time for Josh to go away, as they sat beneath the birch trees, figuring, talking and thinking, she said,

"I'm not interested in Africa. If it's Africa, you'd better count me out. I couldn't stand the feeling of being one of a few, trying to hold everything together by sheer force."

"What difference would that make?" said Josh, not believing her. "We'd live our own life in Africa or anywhere."

"No." She felt good at her own stubbornness. "It's an irreparable situation, tragic. I don't want to begin my life in the midst of something that's just plain against nature."

"All right, count you out of Africa." He shrugged impatiently and she could see he was angry, hurt and disgusted. But this time she couldn't say, "All right, I see, I do see." It was quite impossible.

After that, in the days that followed, he became strangely considerate and, at the same time, detached—as if he were pacing around inside himself, thinking, and hadn't decided to come out yet.

It was terribly cold, outside the world of consideration and detachment. So cold that on the night he went away, just at the moment of parting she said—she didn't know why, perhaps just to see if the jab could penetrate—"You know, Josh, I think Australia would be a bit of a drag too—too socialistic."

He gave her a painful little smile and held her very tight for a moment and kissed her very hard. But what he meant by it, she couldn't tell. And when he was gone, she felt herself sinking back into the jelly.

If there was anything in this world she resisted, however, it was being made a fool of. So she sank cheerfully, playing tennis and swimming in the pool and being suntanned and trim and witty and social. And her mother, who had been frightened out of her wits, said with noticeable relief that Lia was a peach.

"Oh, God."

Perhaps she shouldn't have said that about Australia. It was being a bit perverse. Besides, she hadn't really meant it. She *could* stand Australia—oh, Lord, even Africa. She had no idea how many letters she started that said, "Look, Josh—Listen, Josh." Melodramatic trash, torn into tiny, mother's-curiosity-defying bits.

Then the telegram came, saying, "Brazil. Not socialistic, not tragic. Not nothing. Your choice."

International Beef Incorporated, that possessed packing houses and land all over the world, had hired Josh to fly their brand-new Cessna and operate out of Pirapora. Wherever that was, it was where they were going.

So Lia was not a peach. Mrs. Cunningham took it back. She was a deceitful, ungrateful little (idiot was not a harsh enough word but she could use none that was).

"Those Moran people—oh, they're decent, hardworking—you don't have to tell me, John. But how does one hold a conversation? A pilot. And with what sort of background? Hungarian immigrants. He hasn't even got a degree. What are they going to talk about?"

And Josh would never become a lawyer or one of those people who wrote reports for the government. "Nowhere. It's nowhere they're goin." Mrs. Moran knotted and unknotted her handkerchief. "Lord God, we just got *here*. We just began to live decent. It's that girl, she don't know what it's like in other places—she ain't never done anythin', been without nothin'."

It was useless to try to explain, impossible to understand. For the rest of their days, the Cunninghams and the Morans, each in their own way, would consider their children traitors to a town, a country, a way of life. Failures before life ever began. It made Josh and Lia sad, but there was nothing to be done.

CHAPTER 5

Pirapora was in the midst of endless open country. On every side the land was gently rolling, hill upon hill, covered with forests of fire-blackened tree trunks around the roots of which grew cotton and peanuts and children—sallow brown—coming out of shacks built of palm and thatch. Or grass, tall as sugarcane, in the midst of which herds of white cattle roamed almost as lone and savage as wild creatures of the veld. Something about the big, open country must have had a disconcerting effect upon those to whom it belonged, for the owners of the land all lived in town. Indeed, they seemed to find peace in the sight of high walls and windows that looked onto the square where the loudspeakers blared rock and roll, gaucho ballads and announcements for Eno salts and society balls. In the square the girls walked in a circle one way, the boys the other and the trucks roared steadily by, belching the smoke of burnt oil, constantly reminding the married women who leaned on the windowsills that they were not far, not far—

"From what?" Lia used to ask.

"From São Paulo, the center," they used to answer.

"And what about the land?"

"Oh, it is too empty, too far, the sounds of the crickets and frogs in the night are too unbearably sad—"

No one could ever understand what Josh and Lia were doing in Pirapora when all anyone wanted was to learn English and see the world.

It was no use trying to explain here either. So Lia gave the ladies English lessons and learned Portuguese and how to make delicious dishes with African seasonings from the northeastern country; and listened to the hearts of these women who lived on the edge of the frontier.

These women who spent the afternoon two days a week at the Salon Paris manicuring their hands and pedicuring their feet and stiffening their lovely black hair with lacquer. Who kept the backwoods servants under surveillance and saw that both the tiled floors and the children were spotless and shining. The servants lived under the surveillance of the women and the whole world lived under the surveillance of the old mothers and aunts in black who walked each morning to the church to say a mass for the dead and sat each afternoon on the veranda crocheting and embroidering little shirts for the poor; storing up treasures in heaven, keeping vigil on earth. Perpetual mothers, these kind and patient women, to their children, to the fathers of their children, who, raised by perpetual mothers, had never quite grown up themselves.

In the evenings the men came home from the big open country to bathe, eat largely and sit on their narrow verandas behind high walls to talk endlessly of cattle and land. Josh spoke of what he knew, but this was another world, where cattle were giant and lanky and wild—the farther out you got, the wilder. So mostly Josh listened, for he had everything to learn and he was in a hurry.

Amidst the eternal mothers, Lia became a mother twice herself in the space of three years—for, never admitted, watching the skies was an anxious occupation. And each time Josh touched down on the airstrip outside of town, the moment was suffused with a celebrant air that made caution more a matter of principle than behavior. Children born of exultant relief, whom she walked to the church in the square to entertain with the crocodile that crouched, docile and awed, at the feet of the Virgin Mary. Whom she took to swim in an arroyo on the edge of town away from the hot barren streets.

Then one day Josh didn't touch down before dusk. A bad day, hot and still with a heaviness in the air you could almost lift in the palm of your hand, and the sun hanging like a ball of molten lead above the town until it faded in the coppery darkness of smoke and dust.

She went through the motions of feeding and bathing and putting the children to bed. Then she went out onto the porch and sat watching the sky, though she knew it was too late for him to come. The women brought sweets she couldn't eat and made coffee, and the men came to give their solidarity. And feeling awk-ward at the sight of her, began to talk amongst themselves—their conversation turning inevitably toward *bruma seca* and plane wrecks, until the women, knowing the pain of dread, nudged them onto something else, for a time.

It didn't really matter. It was kind of them to be there, no matter what they talked about. But she was scarcely aware of them. Dread is something no one can share, let alone unburden oneself of. It is there, a weight in the stomach that holds all one's attention. If she moved, it was the better to see the sky, though there could be nothing there to see. If she listened, it was for the nothing there was to be heard.

All through the next day the dread remained hideous and fascinating, until toward dusk she heard his voice alive, exuberant over the radio. And the only thing she could say in return was, "Shit! Where in hell?" and then a tremulous, "Over."

"Over. Listen, I'm at Fazenda Jabaquara on the Rio Negro. Sorry I couldn't get home last night, but I flew into a flock of urubus. Over."

"Over. You drunk or something? Over."

"Over. Not this time. Look, I'll be home in about two hours. Then I'll tell you all about it. But listen, are you listening? Over."

"Yes. I mean, damn this bloody machine. Over. Yes, I'm listening. What? Over."

"Well, I got the job on the ground, do you hear?"

CHAPTER 6

So Josh had achieved what he had set out to do when, on that morning prepared to take off into the bruma seca, he had told Lia to "sit tight." Dr. Harry McGuiness had been determined, as usual, despite the danger, to complete a study which, once the rains had begun in the Pantanal, would have ceased to exist beneath the rising waters. And Josh, the bush pilot, though he could have refused on grounds of personal safety, had been more than willing to fly him into the dust and smoke.

At the time, Josh had been as sick of flying as any man could be. It had served his purpose; gotten him where he wanted to go, given him a chance to become familiar with the big, wild country and the men who coaxed or tore a living from its earth. But by then he had wanted to get down to that earth, own a piece of it himself, and instinct, logic and optimism had told him that Harry McGuiness was the key. For if, as Josh had heard, the Institute had just completed a contract to spend some of USAID's money on research, surely there would be jobs in the offing. What kind of a job would require Josh's services, he could not exactly say. But surely someone who had spent the past five years roaming this vast and complicated country . . . ?

And so there they had been, the one ruminating over the resistance of *Braquiaria decumbens* to drought and flood; the other wondering if his own dissertations on that and related subjects had been sufficiently impressive to cause Harry McGuiness to consider him employable. Indeed, Josh had just about gotten up the nerve to speak on the subject when the flock of urubus had appeared in the sky before him. Without any forewarning, there they were, perhaps fifty, perhaps a hundred broad-winged black vultures circling in the yellowish haze, no doubt taking one last reconnaissance themselves before the bruma seca gave way to the darkness of the night. There'd been no time to avoid them, only time to break rudely into Harry's thoughts on grass and cows and rain with, "Bend over and put your head between your knees, Harry, we've just sucked an urubu into our propeller."

With Harry thus transformed into a 170-pound fetus beside him, and blood, guts and feathers streaming past the window, Josh had started scanning the ground for somewhere to land. It was insane how calm he felt, ridiculous how sure. He'd cut the motor immediately to avoid fire. There'd been no time, not time at all between the plane and the earth; and the earth had been advancing toward him in a hideous monotony of spreading treetops. Still something in Josh's mind kept repeating, "This is not the time, not the time. There is going to be a place." Then the place had been there, the size of a small bed sheet when first he'd seen it; the more thickly abundant in cattle and tree stumps the closer he came. He hadn't cared. He'd blessed it, loved it, this ridiculous clearing. And just as he'd told himself he would, he'd gotten himself onto it, unbelievably missing stumps and scattering cattle as he touched earth. It was only when they were on the ground and still rattling forward that the real trouble had begun; that, had it not been for a scrawny bull charging in defense of his territorial prerogative, might have ended in something far worse than it did. For it was then that the plane's left wing had struck a stump. Swerving wildly in the opposite direction, the tail had collided with another stump, ripping open the fuselage. As the aircraft had swung back again, like a top in a game of skittles, the bull, charging in blind fury at the floundering metal-winged monster, had lunged into the rear of the plane, causing the flapping halves of the fuselage to close, trapping the bull and bringing the disastrous swinging and swerving to a miraculous, lurching, groaning end.

Then another miracle had occurred. As shakily the two men had lowered themselves toward the ground, eying the trapped and bawling bull in stunned disbelief, a human being had appeared as if sprouted from the very earth on which he stood. Focusing somewhat dizzily upon this apparition, Josh had seen that he was a bugre, of Indian blood, a woodcutter, no doubt, small and sinewy, malarial of eye and slightly drunk.

It was the bugre woodcutter who, with a man of the forest's

calm acceptance of all occurrences as natural phenomena, had helped them disentangle the bull; provided them with shelter; and taken them personally, a day's journey in his dugout canoe down the Rio Negro to the nearest fazenda, where there had been an airstrip and a radio with which they had rediscovered the world.

The boat trip had given them rather more time than Josh had bargained for to talk. And this could have led to further disaster, for, except for their willingness to take a risk, one might have said of Josh Moran and Harry McGuiness that they had literally nothing in common. The scientist, McGuiness, was a dry and dedicated man who had little desire or aptitude for making himself amicable to his fellow men. There was a touch of Navajo in his veins and this, combined with a spartan nature, had molded his features into a perpetual hawklike grimace, that had earned him the title, amongst his subordinates, of "Big Chief Totem Face." The title was apt, unshakable. His awareness of it caused this introverted man to smile with greater pain than ever, to speak sparingly and generally only as much as was necessary to get a job done.

Perhaps his infinite shyness was the reason for Harry's caring so little about anything but his work, or perhaps it was the other way around. However it was, he was very different from Josh, who loved to listen and to talk; who felt that, whatever work he did, it was only a part of a great deal more.

Josh's interests and desires were as boundless as Harry's were few. There were priorities on his list of necessities in life, one indeed which he held high above all the others. Still, though he might kill himself by accident in pursuit of those desires, he would never work himself to death for any of them. He was willing to gamble, but never to sacrifice.

On the other hand, Harry's life had been a series of hard sacrifices for the sake of his work. To him a gamble was repellent, irresponsible. He would walk into a noose if duty so demanded, but never attempt to dive through it. That was the difference between them.

In such a case, it would seem that, if Josh Moran desired employment under this man, the most logical approach would have been to express knowledge and ability but no opinion. And this, during the day preceding the wreck, Josh had striven diligently to do.

But the wreck had changed all that. Now, thanks to Harry's willingness to sacrifice and Josh's willingness to gamble, the two were sitting together in this boat with a bottle of lemon juice and *cachaça* between them. Now, drifting along, guided by the river-seasoned hand of Seu Salvador, the bugre woodcutter, the shock and pain of aerial disaster nicely steeped in raw rum, they found themselves saying a great many things they would otherwise never have said. In fact, during this strange, suspended moment, in which the world and their lives seemed to be something they observed from a distance, they embarked on an argument which would continue on between them, in one form or another, for the rest of Harry McGuiness' life.

It began by Josh's replenishing the two halves of a cottonseed oil can which served as their drinking vessels, taking a sip and saying, "You ever think about how you got down here in the first place? I mean, not here in the middle of the mato"—there was something of the unrepentant brat in his grin—"we both know that—but Brazil."

"Hell, Brazil?" said Harry. "Simple enough. I was sent here."

Josh looked doubtful, "No other reason? Like wanting to come here? Liking it?"

"Like? Never thought much about it. A job is a job. One place is as good as another as long as I can work in peace."

"Really? You mean you could be just as happy working in Podunk, Illinois, or Sumatra or Afghanistan?"

"Why not?" In Harry's severely drawn countenance, specifically in the sharp black eyes, Josh witnessed an encouraging light of humor. "What're you doing here, flying around in a smoke screen, crashing into urubus? Don't tell me it's your favorite way to fly. You were sent here too, weren't you? Don't tell me you chose this place above all others."

"I did," said Josh. "That's wha. I learned to fly for—so I could get here."

"But why *here?*" Harry leaned forward so far that Josh had to lean backward to balance the boat.

"To be on my own. To have a piece of land that belongs to me, something I can do anything I damn please with. Didn't you ever have such a desire?"

"Never." Harry waved the suggestion away with a sweep of his hard hand. "God forbid—don't give me any problems. I just want to think and work in peace. That's all a man needs to mess up his life—something of his own to worry about."

"Can't a job mess up your life?" said Josh. "Just when you think you're beginning to get somewhere, can't someone say, 'We don't want to study pastures anymore'? We." Josh threw up his hands to show his disdain for the "we's" of the world.

"So you do it on your own," Harry countered, "and the whole damn thing falls through and you're broke. Who's going to pick up the pieces?"

It was thus that while Seu Salvador guided his boat around islands of yellow flowering ipê and between banks edged by somber, impenetrable forest, they argued back and forth, passing the bottle between them to keep pace in their mental equilibrium—about whether independence was security or security was a job; whether it was better to risk being destroyed by one's employers or pursue ruin on one's own.

It could hardly have been considered the ideal discussion to be carried on between a potential employer and employee, and yet, by the time Seu Salvador announced that the promised fazenda was around the next bend, Harry McGuiness had offered Josh Moran the job.

Later on, although both swore the cachaça had nothing to do with it, Harry McGuiness would claim temporary madness—a kind of hysterical gratitude for being alive, such as a patient feels upon awakening after an operation to discover that the doctor hasn't killed him.

But Josh remembered the conversation becoming fateful at just the moment when he said, "McGuiness of the Institute, I'll admit, it's remarkable—you've been here fifteen years and nobody's bothered you yet. How long do you think your luck can hold out?"

"As long as someone forks out the dough. I'm entrenched," said Harry, just a little too defensively for one entrenched. "Ever hear of the Joint Participant Program?"

Josh struggled to keep cool. He might have said, "Hell yes, why do you suppose I flew yesterday, thinking to myself, maybe I can quit flying now, quit leaving Lia—maybe there's something in this for me—not for long, of course, but long enough?"

Instead, he said, "Sure. Who hasn't? USAID is coming in with one of those governments-matching-funds deals, I hear."

"The Institute has got itself a Joint Participant Contract." As he said it Harry's stiffly carved features betrayed uncertainty as if he weren't quite sure whether the thing the Institute had gotten was benevolent or malignant.

"Which will mean what to you?" Josh pulled on his cigar, and because he didn't want to look at Harry, watched a pair of egrets sweep over the water upstream and disappear, two flashes of white amidst the flowering trees.

"Why, a lot of things, money, equipment, more technicians—"

"More headaches?" said Josh at length. "How's the money to be parceled, who are the technicians?" It was at that moment that the expression in Harry McGuiness' black eyes—which Josh was learning were the key to everything—became thoroughly candid and Josh knew that over these last few days, Harry had been thinking of him as much as he had been thinking of Harry.

"College professors," said Harry, "who may know their stuff, but don't know Portuguese and don't know Brazilians and don't know their asses from an armadillo hole. I'll tell you, Josh. There's a lot they could do and I hope they can do it . . ."

"But?"

"But—you know damn well but what—I want them to do *their* work, but I want to be able to do *mine* too." He regarded Josh once more as if summing him up for the last time, and then plunged ahead. "Look—you've been here a long time, flying around this big crazy place, talking, listening. I'll tell you something, I don't know exactly how, but I've an idea, if you'd be interested, the Institute will be needing someone like you to sort of help keep us all from losing our minds."

Josh had a face that was at once tough and what Brazilians would describe as "*simpatico*," which in turn was something more and something less than sympathetic. A lean, angular face with lines of laughter and sunsquint around eyes the color of autumn before the leaves really change. When he wanted them to, those eyes could express everything he thought. When he didn't want them to express anything, they could become as veiled as an

Eastern merchant's. Now, as he tried to forget that he was a man without a plane and no doubt as a consequence, jobless, they expressed very little.

"It would depend, of course. To make it worthwhile, I'd need more or less the same deal as the other Americans."

Years later, thinking back, he could still remember the weightless sensation as if the boat were sinking away from beneath him as Harry McGuiness stared in vague wonder at this man who either had no sense of values, or had lost his mind.

"You suffering from the heat or something? Why hell, they're all masters and Ph.D.'s and you don't even have a degree!"

Josh allowed the slightest smile just to show that he was suffering from nothing, or, if anything, it was Harry who was suffering from amnesia. "You don't need any more guys with degrees, you just said so yourself. You need someone who's been flying around, talking and listening—who *does* know Portuguese and Brazilians and the difference between an armadillo hole and his ass hole," Josh said conclusively, and sat looking out over the water again, watching the bubbles made by fish spread out in circles and disappear, like time. It was hard to ask such a price of Harry McGuiness, who came, as he did, from a world where a diploma was almost a man's entire worth. But here there were other things that weighed; he had just enumerated them. Besides, it was the price he thought he was worth and if he didn't ask it now, he might never ask it of anyone again.

A silence had fallen as both men sat thinking about the things they had said and all that was at stake. It remained as heavy and oppressive as the mosquito-ridden air about them until Seu Salvador the woodcutter broke it by announcing in his garbled tongue and sing-song voice that the fazenda was in sight. Then, though his face was still stiff as polished gumwood, the brief humorous light flickered in Harry's eyes again long enough for Josh to catch it and never forget it.

"Okay, Josh," he said, "if you want this nameless job, it's yours. We'll discuss the details once we get our feet on the ground."

CHAPTER 7

The job never had acquired a name. Its duties were too elusive. In the main, they had consisted, as Harry McGuiness had suggested, of trying to keep everybody from losing his mind. It had been a job of explaining: American technicians and Brazilian counterparts to each other; the Institute to USAID; USAID to the Ministry of Agriculture. And then of trying to explain the whole thing to himself when the Director of AID, over his PX whiskey at a cocktail party, rumbled self-righteously, "The state of São Paulo is rich, what does it need assistance for?" And thus inspired by his own perspicacity, signed an order the next day that scattered funds and assistance as thinly as sand in a windstorm.

Josh had taken part in the game for four years, watching the money come in at the beginning of the year and, because of the bureaucratic infighting of two governments, only become allocated at the end. Then because you couldn't spend money on seed and fertilizer when it was already harvest time, watching it go for some bizarre creature of modern efficiency like a computer for crop cost profit analysis which nobody could use since there'd been no money to plant the crop in the first place.

By the end of it, he was more convinced than ever of his side of the argument with Harry, that if you ever want to try and carry something to completion, you'd better do it on your own. Still, he'd kept the job long enough to earn the money to buy himself a piece of land, stock it with cattle, build himself a house. And all this during a time when the country was in a greater state of chaos than it had ever known in all its history. When Jango Goulart, then President, fascinated by the powers once attributed to Argentina's Peron and longing to imitate him, would gladly have sold his country's soul in exchange for the dictatorship.

It had been a time when people were putting their money into Swiss banks and had advised Josh to do the same. But he hadn't. He had spent it all on the land instead. It had been a good gamble. The Revolution of '64 had ousted Goulart and had given the country the great breathing spell in which to work and build that it now enjoyed. And instead of just a job, Josh had himself a fazenda.

Wherever he was, whatever he was doing, it was always in the back of his mind. The sun at the center of the universe could hardly have been more real than this land which began on a high bluff and swept away toward the river Atibaia. Grassy land with patches of wood along the edges of the creeks and the river, and coffee, dark green and vigorous against the red earth of its hills. And halfway between the bluff and the river, an old house with a low veranda and windows deep set in thick walls.

It was there. Even before he owned it, it had been there, at the center of *his* universe, giving meaning to his flights through the drought-hazed skies or whatever else he did. The thing had been to find it, make it his own. Now that this was done, now that he had become familiar with every corner, gulley and hollow, how much more inseparable it was from him. It *was* Josh Moran. Everything he had done on it was himself, from the greenness he had coaxed from the abandoned earth, to the cattle he had loosed upon that greenness to the last child—a special child—begotten under the faded tile roof, through the cracks of which Lia could see the stars.

Sometimes it appalled him to think of all this. He wondered if others hadn't this same deep longing, and if, since every man could not own a piece of land, this obsession was not, at the least, absurd, at the most, insane. But whatever it was, it was undeniable. All things had meaning because of the land, and it sickened him to think what meaning anything would have without it.

For four years now, he had driven almost daily to the town of Campos, some ninety kilometers distant, where the Institute maintained its headquarters, there to do his best to help Harry McGuiness keep his sanity, while he himself earned the money to pay for his fazenda. To tear out old coffee trees on his land and plant new. Now the new coffee had grown and begun to bear fruit. Now it was the spring of 1966, and the Monday after the great coffee flowering, witnessed by Malachai Kenath with such ambivalent feelings. And Josh was about to quit the last job he ever hoped to have.

CHAPTER 8

On this particular Monday morning, by the time the bell in the church tower had rung the eighth hour, the town of Campos de Santana was alive and full of purpose. The boy from the bakery had come by on his bicycle and the children carrying steaming buns stuffed with mortadella sausage were already straggling into their classrooms. While professors rapped on their desks for attention, storekeepers rolled up their corrugated iron store fronts and trucks, groaning under their cargoes of fresh fruits and vegetables, rattled into the market square.

Everyone, even the beggar, leaning against the church wall and arranging his stumps in appropriately pathetic positions, seemed to have some goal in mind; everyone, everywhere, except perhaps in the offices of the Roosevelt Institute of Agricultural Research. Here things were in that melancholy state of flux that had become chronic ever since the Institute had signed its contract with USAID and become a joint participant.

On the ground floor of the old colonial house in which the Institute was installed, secretaries sat winding Turkish embroidery on their pencils in none too subtle protest over the fact that their monthly wages had not been paid. There seemed to be some administrative debate over which participant of the Joint Participant Program was supposed to provide the funds this month.

Teodoro de Todos os Santos, whose mission it was to get to the bottom of such uncertainties, was diligently trying to contact Rio on the subject; but this morning the telephone system was decidedly working in favor of evasion. In response to his persistent gentlemanly inquiries, the operator's reply was, "Patience, *meu senhor*, we are making providence."

"Providence, ah!" Even Teodoro, whose patience was notorious, found his hands twisting little hangmen's loops in the telephone cord. His walleyes, over which he lost control when excited, were beginning to go berserk.

Upstairs things were hardly any better. Dr. Samuel Epstein, the legume specialist, stood by the window of the office he shared with Professor Sleighbaugh, the animal nutrition man, soliloquizing over the fact that *they* had plugged his 110-volt protein analysis machine into a 220 socket, thus reducing its $5,000 copper coils to ashes. "The damned, underdeveloped, incompetent . . ."

Professor Sleighbaugh didn't hear. He was old and a little deaf and had troubles of his own. Rumor had it that, in spite of the fact that this was classified a "hardship post," the "participant program people" were about to be deprived of their PX privileges. What Mrs. Sleighbaugh bought in the PX that she couldn't get in the supermarket down the street, he didn't know. But her parting words, "It's a breach of contract, Henry, what are you going to do about it?" still rang in his ailing ears, making it impossible to think of anything but the coming evening, when he would arrive home to report he'd done nothing.

In the entire building there were perhaps two who sat behind closed doors, ignoring, as best as possible, the seething atmosphere, and, like the people in the street, pursuing some sort of purpose. One was Harry McGuiness, the Institute's research director, who sat bent over his annual report with the absorption of a man who loves his work above all else.

The other was Josh Moran, who was also polishing up his report. But while he sat, scattering such requisite phrases as "intergovernmental co-ordination" and "institutional developmental impetus" like seasoning amidst the data, his mind was elsewhere, carefully considering various next moves.

This was his last report, of course, heralding the end of his job. Though the thought of never again receiving a salary gave him a somewhat weightless sensation in the pit of his stomach, he could not say he felt regret. He simply thought of it as inevitable.

The modern neurosis for mobility had caught up with him. In the queer, collective thinking of large organizations, to stay in one place and put down roots, was somehow questionable. If you weren't willing to "transfer" there must be something wrong with you.

There was "something wrong" with Josh. He was well aware of it. He had found his place and was going to stay in it. Still, the place—the land—was far from ready to pay for the privilege of Josh's remaining. And if the inevitable future of any job was to "transfer," then there would have to be another way. So that was why, ever since he had bought the fazenda, he had been preparing for the day when he would be asked to move and he would have to say, "Sorry, Campos is far enough. I can't go any farther."

The preparations had been diverse and extremely complicated. One of them had consisted of enlisting Teodoro de Todos os Santos, who was presently downstairs struggling to contact Rio, as his partner. Teodoro, with his spastically rolling eyes and simian features, was probably the ugliest man miscegenation had ever put together, and one of the sharpest.

Long before Josh had ever come onto the scene, he had made himself indispensable to Harry and the Institute by letting it be known that if there was ever anything to be done that required waiting in line or knowing the district attorney's brother-in-law, he was willing and ready and knew every district attorney's brother-in-law who had ever existed. His elevation in life from that time on, then, could be attributed to his ability to use such phrases as "*excellentissimo*" and "Sr. Doutor" without gagging, and behave toward dyspeptic little men who stamped documents as though their function were of some earthly use.

It was a rare man who could perform such functions and maintain his dignity, not to mention his humor. And certainly Josh did not want to perform them himself. And so when Teodoro had expressed to him the desire to detach himself from the atmosphere of apathy and Turkish embroidery that pervaded the Institute, Josh had embraced him.

Since then, a large part of both men's activities had consisted of putting on a tie during their lunch hours and hurrying from bank to bank, generally one agile step ahead of their creditors. It had been rather like a game of "step on my shadow" and perhaps they would not have made it so far had it not been for a convenient Brazilian predilection for bank holidays. Thinking on this, Josh couldn't help grinning, the fine lines of amusement fanning out from the corners of eyes that were at once knowledgeable and impious. Fourteen official holidays and sixteen saints' days over the past two years had most probably been the salvation of the enterprises of Moran, Roundtree and Todos os Santos, which otherwise would have ended in bankruptcy court for want of an extra day to cover the last check.

As it was, while Josh and Teodoro stood on the brink of severance, their lunch hour machinations—Josh sensed it under his skin—had reached a kind of turning point.

Selling feed to chicken farmers, exchanging bankrupt fazendas for apartment houses in Campos, was not enough. No. Conspiring together through cigar smoke in lunch bars during the week, and in the shadow of the trees on Josh's lawn during the weekends, the partners had conceived still another idea.

"Exchange feed for chickens. Roll the birds in a 'special formula' and exchange them, southern fried, for cash. Not fazendas, or apartments or promissory notes, but cash."

"The fast food business." Teodoro, whose manner of expression invariably suggested earth-shaking inevitabilities, said the idea would be a turning point in Brazilian history, like the supermarket and the Revolution of '64. Unlike Malachai, he didn't seem to fear that the national personality was in danger. In fact, he never gave it a thought.

Duncan suggested that in a few years they'd all be able to buy titles from the Pope. Josh merely and urgently reckoned that, this way, he might never have to have a job again.

Whatever anyone thought, there was really no turning back now. Things had gone too far. For instance, at this very moment Dr. Horace Lindquist, the Institute's newly arrived Chief of Party in Participant Co-ordination, was sitting in Rio struggling to "make do" with what he'd brought in his suitcase, while he fumed ineffectually over—where in hell his unaccompanied baggage was—

If anyone, Josh, who almost daily replied soothingly to his frantic telephone calls, could have put Dr. Lindquist's worst fears to rest. But how was Josh to tell him the stuff was on the docks in New York awaiting the arrival of two deep-fat chicken fryers, suspiciously larger than would seem necessary for use by a middle-aged, childless couple. He couldn't. Dr. Lindquist would just have to suppose, as Josh suggested, that it was the inefficient New York dock workers or delay in the Caribbean. Or a storm off Recife, where the South Equatorial and Benguela currents came to grips, a dangerously far-fetched idea but one Josh couldn't resist suggesting.

When the baggage finally did arrive in Rio, no doubt Teodoro de Todos os Santos' last service to the Institute would be to meet the shipment and "sort out the household goods." At least it better be.

Josh stretched his limbs, and rested a moment before putting the final touch on his report. No, there was no question about it. He'd sold five young bulls to pay for *his* part of those machines. Certainly there was nothing to do but go ahead.

"Therefore"—he leaned forward again, seized with a final paroxysm of inspiration—"through the careful collaboration of its members, the Joint Participant Program has this year contributed substantially to the developmental process of new and promising institutions." Ripping out the last page, he clipped it to the rest. Rising, he opened his door and crossed the sea of discontent that separated Harry McGuiness' office from his.

CHAPTER 9

The lines in Harry McGuiness' face were few for his approaching sixty years. They had not increased in number since Josh had known him, but simply deepened, making the totem face more rigid and formidable than ever. Yet Josh had come to know that face well, and the small black eyes that, veiled by severity and shyness, lived a life of their own. Once one had penetrated that veil, the humor and sadness and comprehension of this queer world that one discovered therein, were wonderful, and sometimes appalling to see.

Outside of their work, Josh and Harry saw little of one another —for outside of his work, Harry was a lonely man who had little in common with anyone. Yet for Harry, Josh bore an admiration and respect he held for few other men.

He knew that Harry McGuiness wanted to go to Rio no more than he did. That the move was just one more step toward being taken in, dissolved until the Institute became a part of one big liquid Joint Participant Solution. Liquid spreads to take the shape of its container, and in a country the size of Brazil, the whole thing was getting shallower and dryer by the minute. But Harry had half a lifetime involved in all this and he would stay until there was nothing left to stay for.

Josh, as Harry well knew, had never intended to make this or any job his life. Still, it was not as easy as Josh had thought it would be to walk in this morning and place the report on Harry's desk. Harry glanced over the report and looked up, those eyes that lived a life of their own, mirroring a certain profound cynicism.

"From the looks of this, we're changing the world so rapid' there soon won't be anything left to do."

Josh laughed and felt better. "Think anyone will read it?"

"Hell no. If I worried about things like that, I wouldn't be here, would I? I write my reports for myself—But, uh"—the dark eyes became uncomfortably stern in their shyness—"I presume you won't be writing any more of these. Isn't that what you came in to say, Josh?"

"That's it." Josh was grateful for Harry's coming to the point immediately and getting it over. "I'm sorry. It would be impossible for me to go to Rio."

"Sorry. Huh!" Harry's laugh was short and dry. "Do you think I expected you to do anything else, the way you've dug yourself in here?" Though Harry had obviously been aware of Josh's lunch hour enterprises, it was the first time he'd ever mentioned them.

"Sorry about that too," said Josh.

"What the hell for? You've been against the rules from the start. Don't you think we'd have fired you if we hadn't needed you?"

"You had plenty of opportunity," Josh conceded.

Harry allowed a grimace that could actually, if you knew him, be counted as a smile. "It's not going to be easy without you. Not to mention Teodoro. And for Christ's sake, don't say you're sorry about him or I'll throw up on your report."

Josh grinned. He really couldn't say he was sorry about Teodoro de Todos os Santos' decision to leave the Institute and become his partner.

It was a big step, nonetheless, for a man like Teodoro; bigger and more illogical in a way than it was for either of his partners. It was rather like a good sailor who safely earned his living on the mail route between Genoa and Palermo being invited by Columbus to embark on the Sea of Darkness. Josh knew this, and so did Harry, a fact which now brought a hint of accusation into Harry's sad and knowing eyes. "Teodoro was asked to go to Rio too."

"Teodoro has a good reason for staying in Campos," Josh replied, for the first time somewhat defensively. "The last operation on his daughter's eyes was useless. She can't see at all now. You know that, don't you?"

"I know, I know," Harry conceded grudgingly. "And a big anonymous city like Rio is no place for a girl like her. All the same" —he gazed hard at Josh, still unconvinced—"Teodoro has dreams of glory and you know it. What do you expect of him, Josh? A man with a fourth grade education?"

"A hell of a lot. He's smart, he's ambitious and he's got the resistance of a mule. Even on our own, we'll still be tangling with bureaucrats . . . Look, we've talked about all these things. He came to me because I could be as useful to him as he could to me. If a guy decides to take a chance, then he has to take it, doesn't he?"

There was nothing but truth in what he was saying, still a certain bluntness in his tone caused Harry to be that much more adamant. "One hell of a big chance, if you ask me. The feed business, that's one thing. You've got a reliable American company behind you there."

"Behind me or on top of me," said Josh.

"But the rest"—Harry ignored his comment, and waved his thin, precise, sun-wrinkled hand expressively—"it's poetry."

Josh grinned, glad to seize an argument that had continued on and off between them ever since the day he and Harry had fallen together from the sky. "I don't say that it isn't poetry. I never did, did I? I've only always said, if you want to make poetry, the way to do it is on your own. In the end, if you don't, just when you're in the middle of something, someone ups and decides to send you off to Rio. Isn't that the way it is?"

He hadn't meant to wound his old antagonist, he had only meant to poke him slightly; get back at him for the parsimonious attitude concerning Teodoro. But for a moment the deep lines in Harry McGuiness' face seemed to deepen even further with a sudden look of untold weariness.

"Rio. Ya—that's what I like to be, close to my work. If they'd just give us the money and leave us alone, eh? That way I would never have needed you in the first place—"

Like a general on the battlefield, however, who dares not allow too great a glimpse of his despair, he gave Josh a tough, sour smile. "But never mind, let them. Let them mess the whole thing up, but good. Then they'll say, 'Well, Harry, perhaps *you* have a suggestion?' Ahh, don't worry, we'll all be right back here where we belong in six months. They won't be able to stand us in Rio."

"Right back where you started," Josh couldn't resist saying.

And Harry couldn't resist answering, "Just you hope that's not where you'll be in another six months. At least I'll have a job, but, brother, what'll you have?"

Josh laughed and held out a Dunhill cigar, "Here's to both of us then."

Harry took the cigar, accepted Josh's offer of a light, drew deeply and then raised the cigar in a salute. "I suppose you've quite a store of these things?"

Josh shook his head. "I've smoked the lot. I never was any good at saving things." He rose. "Do you know, it's damn near lunch time?"

Harry rose with him, arranging his face at last into a businesslike expression. "Look, uh—just for the books. I take it you'll be staying till the end of next month?"

"That's right." Josh too looked businesslike and just a little bit overly conscientious. "I want to leave everything in the best order possible, of course."

"Uh huh," the totem face was stiff now, as if it had been freshly carved from the most resistant of woods. Only the eyes showed something in their near impenetrable blackness that only Josh and a few others dared recognize as amusement. "And everything, I suppose, also includes Dr. Lindquist's baggage?"

CHAPTER 10

Duncan Roundtree leaned back in his folding canvas chair and turned his face toward the sun. The varied sensations caused by sunlight, depending upon where and when one encountered it, never ceased to impress him. This Florida sun, for instance, had made him feel differently the last time he'd been under it. His sensations then as assistant golf pro at the Tropical Gables Winter Paradise had been those of delightful irresponsibility. He hadn't known a thing about golf, but skimming Ben Hogan between forays onto the no-man's-land of the course, and using his infinite capacity for aping the pros in any profession, he'd managed to remain bathing in the Florida sun's luxuriant rays through an entire winter season. It was the nearest he had come to being a kind of drifter with nothing behind him, nothing ahead, having come from nowhere and having nowhere to go.

But now, ten years later as he sat by the pool of the Miami Palace Hotel, each time he closed his eyes, the Florida sunlight became the sunlight on a carioca beach which could make one feel at once sensuous, careless, ambitious and optimistic. The vision behind his closed eyelids in turn made him feel like a penned pigeon, desperate to get home.

"Home?" Bertrand Skinner, the president of the bank, had said to him over cocktails in New York, taking a couple of steps backward and looking at Duncan again. "Heh, heh—sounds as though you're going native, Duncan." Obviously to Bertrand Skinner home was a house you'd bought on "the Cape" to live in when you were eighty-four. As if to confirm it, he went on, "All joking aside, it's rather hard in most businesses to put down roots anywhere nowadays, don't you think?"

"Oh, I don't know." Duncan had felt captive at this unnecessary cocktail party, and therefore rebellious. "Some people stick to the same job all their lives and keep changing addresses, others stick to the same address and keep changing jobs."

Bertrand Skinner had chuckled as if Duncan had made an inappropriate joke and left it at that. Nor had Duncan tried to pursue his thought. In spite of a quirk that made him "say things," Duncan realized that someone who had spent his entire life allowing himself to be shuffled and shifted from one place to another until he reached the ultimate plateau of the presidency would never understand someone who preferred to remain in one place as assistant vice-president because he liked the place and felt alive in it. Skinner was not the kind you sat down with and talked to just for the pleasure of it; or ever reached the point of confiding, "I have a friend called Malachai who could explain the reason why."

Yet the longer Duncan had been in New York, the more he realized the truth of so many things that Malachai Kenath, watching, thinking, reading, remembering, had to say. The more time he had spent "checking in" with the New York head office, the greater had been Duncan's sense of suffocation, the feeling that he had entered a great glass-walled labyrinth from which there was no way out. Just an endless series of conferences behind closed doors which ended with, "If it were up to me, but you know how it is," or, "A road from Belém to Amapá? Where's that? It seems to me the entire thing has to be gone into in greater depth," or, "Now, Duncan, when I studied economics at Harvard, we had this visual process of elimination called 'the decision tree.' "

"Which all adds up," Duncan thought, each time the individual on the opposite side of the desk leaned back and carefully touched his fingertips together, "to calculating the risks and deciding not to stick one's neck out. But if you keep on doing that in *this* world how do you expect to survive?"

"Now, don't get us wrong, we expect to move eventually, but we have to move carefully. You must realize this isn't one of those fly-by-night California outfits. It's an old and respected firm—"

"Which," Duncan went on thinking, "has done all the jobs and heard all the answers so often it's gotten constipated. For God's sake, has anybody opened a window around here since this mortuary was built? And by the way, what's the name of one of those California outfits?"

Anything, even the New York sidewalks that absorbed heat like the black cloth of widow's weeds, was refreshing by comparison. As if in search of comic relief, each time he had found a door in the glass wall that opened outward, he had rushed to a booth to phone Josh's New York contact about the fryers.

Wherever it was, it seemed, Josh had a "contact"; some individual mad for excitement, willing to perform all manner of antics for no apparent reward but the possibility of being caught and losing his job. The New York contact was Marion Gibbs, the Roosevelt Institute's office manager, a slender, elegant young woman with more laughter and warmth in her clear brown eyes than one would generally expect of a person of her profession.

In Duncan's experience, office managers were generally female impersonators with budding mustaches and a profound distrust of laughter, to whom every rule was a mainstay of society, a defense against erosion. Marion was different. Apparently she was aware that a lot of rules were asinine. If she'd been Socrates, Duncan thought, she would certainly have "blown that pop joint" without a second thought.

Muffled laughter came over the phone. "*You* should try to convince these people in Decatur. They've never exported anything, let alone two hotel-sized machines marked 'household equipment' to someone called 'The Chief' in a foreign country with a New York address."

"For Christ's sake, Marion, did you explain to them that boats don't wait? Don't they want the money?"

"That's what I told them. You'll get your check in advance. Let *us* worry about the address. But, Duncan dear, you can stop fretting about the boat. Haven't you looked at this morning's papers?"

"As a matter of fact I overslept—"

"Well, if you had, you'd see we're in the midst of a dock strike—"

"Dock strike? Why, that means—gee, Marion, that's the best news I've heard since I hit New York. Are you free for lunch? We ought to go out and celebrate."

They ate clams on the half shell and broiled lobster, had sherry before, brandy afterward and wine with the meal, and became very festive and gratifyingly candid.

"Marion, you could lose your job."

Her frank brown eyes regarded him unperturbed. "Do you know what I was doing when Josh Moran radioed the other day? Spending the morning helping the African botfly specialist's wife adjust to the thought of Senegal. Mrs. Bot Fly is just deliberating over whether she should take a year's supply of Heads Up shampoo and Discreet Toilet Tissues to Africa when the telephone rings and it's a radio call from Brazil through someone's patch in Cherokee, Nebraska. 'Okay, Marion'"—she deepened her voice in an imitation of Josh's—"'it's all set. The cookies are on the way. Now all you have to do is get those frying pans into the Chief's bag.'"

The image was very clear. Duncan's grin widened. "Cookies, huh? I'll have to put that in my speech to the Conference on International Investment."

"So," Marion continued, with an expansive gesture of her slim, competent hand, "I figure if some gland type can clog the mails to Africa with half a ton of duty-free toilet paper, why not a couple of frying pans to launch a budding enterprise? Why, the chief should be gratified."

"Not all individuals," said Duncan, lowering his voice as if the waiter leaning over them with the wine had a bugging device in his necktie, "are as open-minded as we are. Besides, I'd say it would depend a lot on how many changes of underwear the poor guy took along to Rio in his emergency suitcase. Josh tells me he has to wash his jockeys out every night and wear them damp to work every morning."

Marion's laughter tinkled gaily above the sound of clinking glasses and the buzz of conversation. She raised her own glass. "Here's to Moran, Roundtree and Todos os Santos. And remember, if you ever need an office manager, I'm ready to brave the culture shock. People don't laugh enough in this city."

He would never be able to explain it, unless it had something to do with extrasensory perception, but on the day the 40-cubic-foot crate from Decatur arrived at the docks in New York, Marion had another miracle to announce: "Strike's over! Look in this morning's paper."

"It's unbelievable!"

The Mormac ship *Argentina* was scheduled to depart at noon. He and Marion went down to the docks and, while the Chief's luggage was being hoisted below, had drinks with Brazil-bound passengers aboard. Later, over lunch, he helped Marion compose a telegram to the USAID office in Rio. "Strike over. Personally accompanied Chief's baggage aboard. All's well. MG."

He took a night plane to Miami and the next day he gave his talk to the conference.

No doubt the talk he gave was that much more of a success because of the morning's experience. Certainly he'd felt an irrepressible euphoria, as if all the business opportunities he described were his; as though he moved under some benevolent star; as though things could only go well for Roundtree, Moran and Todos os Santos.

Still, even though he often professed his primary pursuit in life to be a quest for the sun, he would not have been able to speak to the conference if he hadn't known his stuff. If, wherever he sat in a folding canvas chair, there was not beside it a brief case full of financial literature to be absorbed with alternate sips of ice-cold beer. And if the business dealings of the world were remarkable and vital to him, the game of investment in Brazil was even more so. It was like a puzzle the pieces of which were an official predilection for roads, hydroelectric plants, schools, the size of coffee crops, the price of cattle, the cash available for Galaxies or Volkswagens. Fit the intricate elusive shapings together and you came up with the answer as to where to put the cookies. But only if you knew the officials, the investors, the farmers and the bankers and were able to sort out the gossip; if you possessed an instinct for judging whether conversations would ever come to anything but just conversation—

His audience could not have been aware of all these essentials as he stood before them looking businesslike and impressively eastern. But his own knowledge of them lent an authentic ring to a talk that would have otherwise been damn difficult going.

The talk had been roundly applauded and the question and answer period had extended beyond the stipulated half hour. There had been no containing it. Duncan had gone back to his hotel feeling warmly euphoric and longing for Caroline. Direct, outspoken, questioning Caroline, who knew the truths about Duncan and the reasons his speech was a success. Whose enthusiasm for life and capacity for celebration were like no one else's he'd ever known or, he was sure, ever would know.

But Caroline wasn't there. And so gradually the euphoria began to give way to a familiar skepticism about the things he had just said and the effect they would have upon the people who heard them once they returned to the slots from which they had emerged. The hours that followed had done nothing to relieve his mood.

The bank's regional manager in Miami, Bob Guthries, had lived in Rio for a while, but try as Duncan would to steer the conversation in some other direction, it always returned to the Gavea Golf Club and how cheap the caddies were there.

Bob Guthries had no other interest in Brazil, nor did it take Duncan long to reach a conclusion as to why. In all the time he'd been there, he had never made an important decision for the bank any more than had the men who listened to Duncan's talk, or for that matter Duncan himself. Then why had Guthries *gone* to Rio? Why was Duncan here? Why had Duncan given the talk and what had all those international representatives listened for?

Bob gave Duncan a smile of cheerful complacence—"You know how it is"—and offered him another drink.

But if Bob was complacent, his wife Sybel made up for it by being the opposite. Bob, despite his golfing, had a young paunch that made him look rather pregnant under his summer sports shirt. Sybel, on the other hand, had religiously kept her proportions in line. They were nice proportions and she would have been an attractive little piece if she hadn't been so damn serious.

"Sybel never goes with me on my trips." Bob looked at her with a certain wary indulgence. "She's always too involved."

Her latest involvement, it appeared, was something *now* called ecology. Did Duncan know that for years farmers and chemical manufacturers had been deliberately killing the world by slow poisoning?

"Oh, I don't think it's *deliberate*, do you?" Duncan ventured.

"Don't they *know* they're using poisons?" Sybel responded indignantly. "Why, even the meat"—suddenly the rather nice roast beef on Duncan's plate seemed to take on a devious appearance—"you can't imagine the trouble I go to to get *unadulterated* beef.

And then there's the oxygen problem, but we're working on that one." A note of conspiratorial joy came into her voice. "This year nobody's buying live Christmas trees."

"But, Sybel"—Bob looked sidewise at Duncan and laughed nervously—"Christmas trees are like crops, they plant new ones every year."

"And what do we do while they're growing?" Sybel gave Bob a look that plainly said, money-grubbing traitor. "Every little bit counts, you know. And now"—rejecting her husband, she turned appealingly to Duncan—"they're going to chop down the Amazon forest."

"Not all of it," Duncan said encouragingly, but was ignored. Sybel was determined to put across her point in continental dimensions.

"Do you realize that twenty per cent of the oxygen we breathe in this hemisphere comes from the Amazon? Are Brazilians aware? Are they doing anything to prevent this disaster?"

Duncan struggled to swallow a mounting sense of hysteria along with a morsel of rocklike bread made from *pure stone-ground flour*.

"I'm afraid it would be rather like saying, 'Don't go West, young man, it might affect my bronchial tubes.'" Seeing she didn't think it at all funny, he gave Sybel one of his most appreciative, sympathetic looks. "It's a good thing someone thinks about these things, but I don't know how you sleep with all this on your mind."

"Oh, I have my therapy, didn't you see my organ?"

"I don't know how I could have missed it," said Duncan, thinking, "Perhaps I *am* going mad." But there *was* an organ, a Hammond one, and after dinner, with several miles of artistic jewelry clanking over the keys, Sybel, warmed by his understanding attitude, gave him a special rendition of "Brazil." He sat, his malleable features pleasantly attentive, and when it was over, his face aching from smiling, he made his excuses.

"I'm exhausted, terrible storm on the way down from New York. Plane dropped two thousand feet at one whack. One guy had a heart attack and died. Yes, very depressing." It was all a lie, but Sybel, with her involvement and her organ, was a nice little woman. He didn't want her to think he was leaving because he couldn't bear to hear an encore featuring "Tico Tico."

Back at the hotel, he sat at the bar and tied one on all alone. Couldn't see anyone he'd wanted to drink with. Been a long time, in fact, since he'd seen such a lot of fat, unattractive people. They all looked as though they ate compulsively and must have "America, love it or leave it" stickers on their cars. He loved America but he had left it and perhaps that was one reason why. Did everything have to be advertised?

The last drink, a brandy, he had alone in his room. He fell asleep, respectfully holding the "essence of the angels" upright on his chest, a friend in Caroline's absence, a guardian against the encroachment of a world that seemed to have lost its sense of humor.

His hand with the brandy was still in the same position on his chest when he was awakened the next morning by the telephone. Still not spilling a drop, he placed the glass gently on the bedside table and picked up the receiver. It was Bob Guthries, still being dutifully thoughtful, suggesting Duncan spend the day with himself and Sybel at the golf club.

"Thanks, thanks a lot, Bob, but I never *did* learn how to play golf. Besides, I've got a pile of figures I have to look into between now and when I hit São Paulo tomorrow."

"That's too bad." Duncan could imagine Guthries' eyes rolling relievedly out of sight even though he managed to keep his voice solicitous. "Is there anything I can do? I can easily skip the club."

"That's good of you, Bob, but no, really." Duncan experimented with just the right tone of vice-presidential martyrdom, "there's really nothing you can do. Have a good day." So saying, he hung up and immediately called for some strong coffee before heading for the pool.

Half an hour later, leaning back in his deck chair beside the pool, if there were any figures to be checked upon, they were behind those closed eyelids. With the distant sea in his ears, he could imagine them; dusky mulattas endlessly parading, the salt water glistening on their skin, sprinting figures, lean, wiry and brown in a perpetual game of *futebol*, *molegues* hawking pineapple ices and racing the wind with wide winged kites. If nothing else, underdevelopment certainly had a favorable effect on the appearance.

He wondered what was happening *there*. No use looking in the papers, Brazil was never in the news unless it was for poking a kidnapper in the balls or devastating the oxygen supply.

Lying here it was hard to believe that tomorrow night he would be home, having dinner with Malachai and Francisco Cavalcanti, the engineering genius. Francisco had done something in his spare time, made a little design of a drive-in fried chicken restaurant for his friends. Or maybe he'd had his office make it. Didn't matter, just for fun—a pleasure. It all seemed so remote. When you'd been away for more than a week, you began to suspect that, except in your imagination, such a place where people did things for fun, didn't exist at all.

CHAPTER 11

Malachai took up his pipe and his new lighter, principally because he was nervous and wanted something complicated to do with his hands. His friend Inzy had brought the lighter back from Rumania, an old-fashioned gadget Malachai had remembered from his childhood. It had a gaily colored wick almost a yard long that drooped from one's pocket like the peasant's answer to a rich man's watch chain. The original model had had a flint and a stone which, when manipulated with a peasant's skill and patience for a good half hour, finally produced a triumphant flame. But the lighter was no longer the same. Like everything else, the communists had managed to mess it up so that now each time the flint and stone reached their climax some plastic shoe-button affair descended and snuffed out the flame as if fearful it might escape.

"Communist modern, pah!" He tossed the thing aside disgustedly, fished in his pocket for a Brazilian safety match and struck it. The flaming head shot across the room like a meteorite and plunged into a pile of cushions in the corner of the sofa. Malachai pounced to beat out the sparks, striking his shin on the corner of the coffee table as he did. At the sound of his howl, Clea flung open the kitchen door, her expression predicting the worst.

"*O che passa, che passa?*" she trilled in Italian, the language reserved for passion and disaster.

"*Niènte, niènte.*" Malachai sank into his chair, nursing his bruised shin. "It was a match." He gestured weakly toward the cushions, from which arose a faint odor of scorching. "I struck a match."

"You, of all people"—Clea's voice dropped an octave, became relieved and scolding—"ought to know better."

"It was a *safety* match," Malachai expostulated weakly.

"Uff." Clea flung up her hands and, turning her back, disappeared again whence she had come, closing the door on a tempting aroma of spaghetti sauce made with mussels.

Malachai sat forward and lit his pipe, this time successfully, shielding the match with a shaking hand. Clea was right, he reflected gloomily, the usual precautions others took to avoid disaster only seemed to lead him to it. This evening's dinner, for instance, at which Francisco Cavalcanti would appear to present "the plan." Even though he had to admit it was Clea who had set the whole thing in motion, destroying the peace of a Sunday afternoon under Josh's trees with a, "You're not going to *pay* someone to design a restaurant are you? Francisco will do it in a moment, and get such a kick . . . Come now, he needs a distraction every now and then, poor duck."

"Francisco Cavalcanti," Malachai had protested, "is a builder of roads and dams. What in heaven's name does he know about designing restaurants? Dams must be stark, mighty, impassive. Restaurants must be intimate, warm, appealing. The aesthetics are diametrically opposed."

His plea, however, had fallen on deaf ears. The board of directors at the thought of getting a design for nothing had become oblivious to all other considerations. And so he, Malachai, had had to say to Francisco a few days later, "Want to do something funny—in your spare time?"

"Well, now it's done," Clea had reminded him an hour ago. "So no use fussing. We'll just have to face it, whatever it is." Malachai groaned inwardly. Perhaps it had something to do with opposite poles. Disaster attracted him. His marriage to Clea was a perfect example. Not that it was a disaster, not by any means. It was just that Clea got these ideas, and before you knew it, she'd plunged you into them as if into a great wave. And then the wave receded and you were left like a fish, flopping and gasping on the shore.

It had been so, indeed, ever since he'd known her; ever since that fateful night at The Globe in London when she had appeared as a mermaid and someone had stepped on her fishnet tail with catastrophic results. There'd been something so merry in her look as she'd sprinted off the stage, switching her tail as though she'd still had one. It had seemed she might split apart what was left of her costume, laughing. Malachai, young and exuberant and a little bit drunk, celebrating the bust he had just been paid for by the fashionable Mrs. Hugh Henry Haye, had been quite overcome.

In their early days together, he'd painted Clea's portrait, committing to canvas the perpetual conflict of staunch English romanticism and aggressive Italian enthusiasm that raged in her blood. The high, noble brow, the large, straight Roman nose, the sharp cheekbones and droll, hazel eyes, the severe Anglican mouth with its reserved smile that could so easily give way to bawdy laughter, setting the whole face in motion, tears streaming, eyes askew. It had been perhaps the most exacting and exciting work he'd ever done.

Just a few days after they were married, war came to England. And there had been Malachai, an alien, qualified for nothing. The best he could have done was sit quietly and without involvement, observing the holocaust to its end.

If they hadn't been short of money, it might have been quite simple, but the need for a few shillings had caused him to make a clay Scottie dog. And to alleviate the tedium of his task, he had painted a red collar on the thing. Then he'd given it to a friend to sell in the Hay Market.

There'd been thousands of such little clay horrors at that time, lurking amidst the phlox and delphiniums of lower-middle-class London gardens, but none with bright red collars. The horrible Scottie had created an immediate, insatiable demand among a citizenry with money but nothing to spend it on.

Clea had become beside herself. "It's a perfect gold mine."

"But, Clea, the materials, they are strategic! And on top of that, I'm an alien. I could be put before a firing squad!" He'd shut his eyes and gritted his teeth.

"Nonsense, a little dab of red paint can't be *that* strategic. Come on, I'll take the blame. You make the dogs and I'll paint the collars."

So they had baked the Scotties every morning; and every afternoon, Malachai had sat on a bench in the park before their subterranean apartment taking orders for clandestine deliveries.

The demand had soon grown beyond their most extravagant dreams.

"I can't keep up with it. It's a physical impossibility. If I get another oven, who's to stoke it?" He'd sagged piteously at the thought but Clea had already found a solution.

"Deserters," she'd replied as if nothing could be more obvious, "we'll get deserters."

"What?"

"Italians, you dunce. They're coming in by the droves, standing on every street corner, poor darlings."

So they'd added another oven and put the Italian deserters to work. Malachai had continued "sunning" himself in the park and stuffing his pockets with shillings, which he'd brought home every evening for Clea to ensconce in the bottoms of a growing collection of flour tins. Difficulty had indeed begun to arise as to where to put the flour, but even more upsetting had been the ominous approach of summer.

In their flat, in the cellar of an old Victorian house, the ovens were in a back room and artfully concealed behind a door covered with royal purple velvet, in the center of which had hung an inviolable painting of King George. Even the policeman on the beat, whom Clea had occasionally invited to tea as a kind of preventative measure, would never have questioned such an arrangement. Everything would have been beyond suspicion had it not been for the fact that heat rises.

In wintertime the flat above had been toastily pleasant without its occupant's ever having to put as much as a ha'penny in the register. But with the coming of warm weather, things had begun to get uncomfortable. Moreover, the linoleum that covered the floor had begun to make odd squishing sounds with every footstep. It had been inevitable that the occupant, a small, suspicious gentleman called Mr. Abernathy, who dealt in unsavory lawsuits, should one day lift a corner of the linoleum and discover a "positive lake."

"There's got to be something wrong with the water heater. One should imagine your flat to be a furnace, Mr. Kenath." Mr. Abernathy's sharp little eyes had bored into Malachai's with a questioning stare. "P'raps one ought to mention it to the management."

That was when Clea, the originator of the magnificent scheme, had first sensed panic. "I can't bear it, Malachai. Everytime I see Abernathy come out the door I expect to see fungus growing on his cheeks. And this money, Santo Dio, where are we going to put it next?"

Then, just when it had seemed there could be no solution, the war had come to an end. Even though it was summer, the abrupt change in temperature had caused Mr. Abernathy to shiver in his bed. When they'd taken the flour off the top, they'd discovered 50,000 pounds underneath.

Part of it, they never knew how much, had been spent on a glorious trip through France. Another slice had been spun out of grasp by the roulette wheels at Monte Carlo. The rest? Ah, the rest. Malachai, remembering, drew deeply on his pipe and gazed dreamily at the ceiling. One night they'd wandered into a small dark boîte in Paris. There'd been a Brazilian combo with a guitar, a flute and various savage-looking instruments. A tragic, dark young woman had sung something called "Apêlo." Though she could scarcely understand a word, Clea had been overwhelmed with sadness, though not for long.

In another moment, an ebony-colored hand protruding from a white sleeve had begun to tap on a matchbox. The woman so tragic a moment ago had begun to oscillate and quiver. There had seemed to be rhythm in the very tips of her fingers. There was rhythm in the tips of Clea's fingers too.

Back in London, the Brazilian Consulate had informed them stuffily that Brazil was a country devoid of racial prejudice, the world's largest coffee exporter, and the setting for the fastest-growing city in the world, São Paulo.

To Clea, with the dark fingers still tapping on a matchbox in the back of her head, this was the answer to everything. "The fastest-growing city in the world, Malachai. Just think of all those tropical gardens begging for sculptures beside reflecting pools."

Malachai had deliberated. He had thought of Rumania and the Balkan countries fenced off from him forever by a treaty of "peace." He had thought of Israel, its dedicated farmers and artisans surrounded by the most intense hatred the Jews had known in their long history. The thought of London, on the other hand, had brought to mind regiments of clay Scotties amidst ruins. There was something menacing and heavy hanging over the entire European scene that even the joy of victory seemed incapable of dispelling, as though no one would ever believe in it himself. But in a place as remote and uninteresting to the world as Brazil, there might be a certain respite. So if Clea thought this was the answer, why not?

São Paulo. Who could have told them that the fastest-growing city was growing *so* fast, that Brazil was *such* a country of the future that scarcely anyone knew what a sculpture was? One had to see, it was impossible to imagine, the narrow cluttered streets climbing the mountains, broad avenues ending in canyons of red earth; and civil engineers backing up traffic for miles during the rush hour while they measured the street's width with a string.

Thousands of Baianos clamored over hundreds of edifices like mulatto Lilliputians with chisels and hammers in their hands. Thousands of Paulistas curried purposefully hither and thither, making "fortunes" in real estate, cars, public offices, gimmicks and junk. The junk market was tremendous. If Malachai had wanted to he could have set up a couple of ovens, and made—perhaps clay saints and parrots?

Clea had panicked again, but it was too late. The 50,000 was gone. Still, amidst the noise and dirt and fumes and confusion, there was something fascinating, something that attracted the ambitious and intelligent from the distant old and dead capitals of Brazil; and from the great accomplished and jaded or imprisoned capitals of the entire world.

There were enough people amongst them who, if they didn't know what a sculpture was, were willing and eager to learn. And so, as the great houses rose amidst the incredible growth of tropical greenery, Malachai's brooding stone sculptures came to be glimpsed beneath the *tipuznas* and flamboyants, reclining at the edges of quiet garden pools. It was not so bad. These people were sufficiently interesting to keep Malachai, the observer, occupied for a long time to come. "If only one could observe without becoming involved."

As if to emphasize this last thought, Clea appeared once more in the doorway, this time untying her apron and tossing it aside with disgusted abandon. "Mussels—ugh—nauseating little creatures. Will you slap me into consciousness the next time I get an idea like that? Fix me a drink, that's a duck."

"I prefer that to slapping you into consciousness." Favoring his bruised shin, Malachai hobbled to the sixteenth-century oratorio where the liquor was kept and filled a tall glass with a great deal of ice and Campari and a little soda.

"Ah, that's better." Clea sank back amidst the still slightly smoldering cushions. "Probably the best thing for all of us this evening will be to get absolutely blotto so we can't see which end of that bloody design of Francisco's is up anyway." She took a long, thirsty draught of Campari and stared in front of her, "I can see it all. Francisco's been working on the thing like mad. He's coming here up to his ears with enthusiasm and you're all going to pick the thing to pieces. There'll be nothing left in two seconds flat."

"Either that," said Malachai, "or Francisco won't have done a thing, which is also quite possible."

"*That* would be a relief." Clea's eyes rolled hopefully toward the ceiling.

"Except that you assured Josh and Duncan—"

"Oh balls! I wish I'd never heard of this damned idea of theirs, that's what I wish—"

"But that's just it." Malachai struggled to put things once and for all in their proper perspective. "It is *their* idea, so why worry? Besides, it could be a great success. As Duncan says, Brazilians have a passion for anything modern . . . Noise, gasoline fumes, plastic. Have you noticed those stickers on the backs of cars that say BRAZIL, LOVE IT OR LEAVE IT?"

If she had, there wasn't time to say so, for at that moment the doorbell rang announcing Francisco Cavalcanti with a large ominous-looking roll of draft paper under his arm.

He bowed slightly, an elegant gesture that came naturally to him and went along with the fact that Cavalcanti was an old Brazilian name and that this young man who stood before them bore the look of a tall, thin, rather overbred, perhaps tubercular aristocrat. The dark eyes were brilliant, however, and the hand that grasped Malachai's firmly while the other slapped him on the back causing the draft paper to fall as a consequence, reminded him as it always did of a strange, inexhaustible energy.

Malachai returned the "*abraço*" and looked around and beyond Francisco questioningly, "And Delia?"

"Delia?" It was his turn to look around Malachai. "She's not here?"

"Was she supposed to be?" For a moment there hung between them the image of Francisco's wife, Delia Cavalcanti, professor of philosophy, a small and devastatingly feminine woman who nonetheless had a fire about her that drew attention in quite another way—particularly in the midst of illegal student union meetings and unauthorized street gatherings.

"She was. Could be in jail for all I know." Francisco said it lightly, a little too lightly perhaps. Malachai could never tell how much of indifference or just plain oblivion there was in Francisco's attitude toward his wife's activities. At any rate, in the next moment, he picked up the draft paper, seized Malachai by the arm and charged forward. "Now come along, *meu amigo*." There was a note half jesting, half murderous in his voice. "You suggested I do this thing. Now *you* get me out of the mess I'm in—"

"A drink first," said Malachai, and once more made hastily for the oratorio.

CHAPTER 12

Just as Francisco Cavalcanti sank onto the sofa beside Clea, his long legs sprawled out in front of him, the other members of the evening's gathering, Duncan and Caroline Roundtree, were driving back toward the city from the airport. Duncan, feeling still somewhat unbalanced from having spent the last nine hours hurtling through the air like a sardine in a great jet-propelled can, allowed Caroline to do the driving. She was good at it, unhesitant, and, as one had to be in this game of bluff called traffic, unafraid to take the initiative wherever the chance presented itself. Knowing this, he leaned backward and left it all to her, resting a little before dinner, as he put it, glad to be with her, glad to be back.

It would have been nice, in a way, to have been able to go straight home tonight and be with her alone. But Francisco was bringing the design, whatever it might be, and since this young engineer who often seemed to be shaping the interior of Brazil single-handed was perpetually disappearing into the incommunicable wilderness, Duncan knew the value of pouncing upon him when he was within reach.

Besides, it wasn't as if they were dining with strangers. Like Malachai and Clea, Francisco and Delia were old friends. And though they disagreed violently and volubly on a number of subjects; and though what they had in common was as elusive as the enchantment of the country they lived in, still, theirs was a live friendship oddly stimulated by its wild moments—the kind of friendship Duncan valued highly. Caroline too, for that matter, or there certainly would have been a scene at the idea of their spending these first hours together in the company of others.

Without saying anything, Duncan allowed himself the pleasure of watching her as she leaned aggressively over the wheel. He traced the determined sweeping line of the chin, the wide-set nordic eyes with their smoothly rounded lids and soft streaks of brows, which together with the short, upturned nose gave her the look of a restless, intelligent child. Sometimes in spite of her competence, her obsession with excellence, she seemed to him just that: a little girl who needed desperately his protection.

"Caroline? Why, she can do anything she sets out to do," people had a way of saying. But perhaps only he knew how vulnerable she was; when he went away, how painful were the hours of his absence.

"What've you been doing?"

"Oh, you know—yelling at the kids, taking in a few movies, reading. Last night I went to the opera." A shrug, a compression of the mouth that made it somehow very desirable. "You know."

He reached out and touched the back of her neck and felt her entire being respond to the warmth of his hand. Later they would lie together in the darkness for a long and passionate time, and then—only then—would everything really be all right again.

"No use going home if the kids are already asleep," he said. "I can clean up at Malachai's."

"Good." She gave him a sidewise look. "Listen, Duncan, if you don't like the design, try not to be too biting, won't you?"

"Are you suggesting I'd be sarcastic?"

"Hmm."

"Okay. A minimum of acrimony," he promised, eager to please her, to fill the void of loneliness created by an absence that, when you thought of it, but for getting those machines on board, seemed to have been pretty damned useless.

"So you really saw the machines go aboard," she said, as if she'd read his thought.

"With my own eyes. Now, the next thing"—he peered through the darkness as they turned the corner into Malachai's street—"is to have some damn place to put them."

Francisco had just spread his design on the coffee table and pinned it down with four ashtrays when Duncan and Caroline arrived.

There was little enough time for Malachai to prepare two more drinks with a good stiff extra shot in each, let alone for those drinks to take effect, before they were all gazing at the draft, their vision sadly unimpaired.

Malachai's eyesight, in particular, as was always the case when aesthetics were at stake, was distressingly clear, his tongue uncontrollable. Though good sense admonished him to behave to the contrary he simply couldn't stop himself from saying, "Are you sure you brought the right design? Isn't this an airplane hangar?"

The lead was irresistible to Duncan. Adjusting his glasses and forgetting all caution, he leaned forward menacingly. "This area here"—he twirled his finger in a minuscule circle—"what is it? The broom closet?"

"The kitchen . . ." Francisco found his voice for the first time.

"Ah, I see." Duncan leaned closer and squinted. "Maybe we could hire a tall, thin cook. A Mineira. They're descended from Watusis, aren't they?"

"You *are* a beastly lot." Seizing a pencil from Malachai's desk, Clea began making her own bold lines over Francisco's. "Just take off a little here, add a little here, lower the roof—"

"And watch the whole thing collapse!" Francisco Cavalcanti's long lean frame bent double with laughter. Malachai, who had begun the entire onslaught of criticism had been feeling ever since as though a time bomb were ticking. He should have known better. Obviously Francisco, having tried and failed, now felt absolved. Sweeping the design from the table, he rolled it up again and delivered it into Duncan's hands. "It's yours. I abandon it. At any rate, *Graças a Deus,* I won't be able to do anything more with it because I'm leaving tomorrow."

"Gee thanks, Francisco." Duncan looked bravely politic. "What I'll do is refer it to the board of directors." Taking the drawing, he thrust it as far out of anyone's reach as possible, glad, in truth, to be rid of it and to be free, having caught Francisco in mid-flight, to talk to him of other things.

"Para que lado vai?" He slipped easily into Portuguese.

"Paraná."

He watched the look on Francisco's face change from one of laughter to intense excitement. It was a look they all knew well, that transformed the sallow, almost languid features, made them unexpectedly stubborn—as if all the real strength in Cavalcanti's being was reserved for his obsession of the moment, the dam, high on the river Paraná in the midst of nowhere, for now. But Francisco could see it finished, see the land around it transformed. There was always some such vision for him, it seemed. It was why other things made him laugh so easily, why one shouldn't really trust him to take anything else very seriously—he couldn't help it; there was, after all, only so much seriousness in every man.

"Do you know what I had to do last week?" he was saying. "I had to make them blow up a whole month's work. They didn't have the proper cement, so they used another kind. It might have lasted a year, it might have lasted twenty." He shook his head, his expression incredibly stoic. "It's not irresponsibility as much as ignorance. Or perhaps after all they're the same thing."

"You've a point," said Duncan. "It's rather like telling a caboclo he's going to die of lead poisoning unless he washes that black powder off his hands. He won't believe it. So he dies. So what do you do? Give up your business, go out to Paraná and leave everything here? For how long?"

Francisco gestured expansively with thin, sensitive hands. "A month, maybe two. When there are not enough people who know what they are doing, what can you do?"

Duncan looked dubious. "I just hope it's appreciated. It's been my experience that politicians don't look at things the same way normal people do. Blowing up a month's work when there's some fancy inauguration scheduled might not sit well."

Francisco took out a cigarette and lit it slowly, deliberately. "I didn't get this contract because I was someone's brother-in-law. Would you believe that?"

"I'll try, if you say so."

"I do say so, or I wouldn't have started." He regarded Duncan intently, as if to get the point across. "I got it because I am expected to do a good job. Whether someone gets impatient or not."

"If anyone should get impatient," Clea broke in, "I should think it should be Delia. Two months at a stretch. How can she stand it?"

The remark, typical of Clea, who for all her grand schemes never thought in abstract terms, had the effect of bringing things back to earth, to the room in which they sat and from which the person in question seemed suddenly rather ominously absent.

"Wherever she is, I'm starving," Clea went on with decision, "and I'm going to put the food on. Anybody want another drink while I'm at it?" She disappeared again into the kitchen and, with the assistance of her great gray-black servant Ramira, began the laborious assemblage of the antipastos.

Malachai rose to fetch the drinks. As he did, he dropped the ice once and mixed Duncan's drink with Francisco's; all this because his eyes, beyond control before in their inspection of the design, now could not be kept from wandering toward the door. Delia *was* impossible. Francisco was going away tomorrow, perhaps for months, and his wife couldn't even come in time to meet him here for dinner. Where was she?

The others, even Francisco, who had long ago accepted the fact that she was thoughtless, seemed to have forgotten her again. They were talking, laughing, Caroline describing last evening's opera, in which La Sonambula had taken a step backward and brought an entire Italian garden, painted on a dirty canvas curtain, down upon her head. Malachai chuckled politely, only half hearing, and handed the drinks around with shaking hands.

It was something of a miracle, he knew, that in all his wanderings, he had never been picked up on the street, awakened in the night, accosted at a meeting—to which curiosity overcoming good sense had taken him—and been hauled away. Still, far better than the others, who had never had to flee from anything, he knew these things happened. He knew all the symptoms and like someone oversensitive to cancer warnings, fear gripped his bowels, gave him stomach cramps. While the others laughed, he settled in his chair, tried to look attentive, and perspired. When the doorbell did ring with an urgent persistency, it was Clea, balancing a tray of *fungos e beringela*, who had to open it. Malachai was too weak in the knees.

It was, he would have to admit later on, an extremely successful entrance for Delia Cavalcanti. Though they'd forgotten her a moment ago, the bell had shocked them once more into suspense. How could they help but be all attention as she stormed into the room, cheeks flaming under the olive hue of her skin, great feverish eyes alive with vindictive fury.

"I've just come from Zaga. They've fired him—pff—like that! The *canalias!*" Her voice, spellbinding in its outrage, burst upon them. Malachai hitherto weakened by apprehension, now weakened with relief, would gladly have sunk deeper into this chair, relaxed, let her go on with the "how," but Clea wouldn't have it. She was hungry and not in the mood for Delia's dramatics.

"Come along, Delia. A little wine and fungos to stop you frothing at the mouth. Sit down, there's a girl." She pushed Delia into a deep chair and thrust a glass of wine at her, then came forward with an assortment of antipastos formidable enough to subdue even the entrance of La Gioconda.

"All right now," she said, her own plate filled and her mood more sympathetic. "Tell us. What happened?"

"What happened? What do you suppose, what would you expect?" Despite her outrage there was a definite note of triumph in Delia's voice. "You know his politics."

"Who doesn't? He makes a damn bloody bore of himself with politics." Clea frowned, searching for the reason why. "Principally because he always seems to recite them. One has the feeling he really doesn't know what he's talking about, doesn't one?"

"Doesn't know?" Delia bristled. "Why? Because you don't agree?"

"*Calma, calma,*" Malachai said gently, "no one is agreeing or disagreeing *yet*. You must admit, though, it often happens," he went on in a voice he presumed to be that of the moderator, "that a great artist who is an idiot in politics allows himself to be used by those who are not—"

"Used!" Delia seemed ready to emit another storm, but this time Francisco interrupted her. Whether the others knew it or not, he had been immensely relieved at her appearance and, now *that* was wearing off, was feeling just the slightest bit jealous, because it was always Zaga or some other "fanatic" who took her time, made her late everywhere she went.

"You know yourself, Delia, the moment the news of his dismissal is out, a hundred universities will be begging for him. But not because he's a fine professor of architecture."

"Then why?" Into the circle of faces that was drawing closer together by the minute, Caroline Roundtree's sharp chin thrust itself like a wedge. Malachai drew back and waited. When first he'd met Caroline, he'd thought there'd been nothing much behind her wide, blue-eyed gaze but seductiveness. A few more encounters had taught him that there was indeed an insatiable curiosity, an elephant's memory, a refusal to allow questions to be sloughed over, left unanswered. She concentrated her gaze now on Delia. "I don't know this Zaga but was he fired because of his political beliefs or because he yakked about them in class?"

"Does it matter?"

"It would matter to me"—Caroline's chin came forward a degree further—"if I had come to study architecture under a great master and he wasted my time telling me—"

"Then one is not to have an opinion?"

"I didn't say that! I said he should keep it out of the classroom."

"Oh? And how does one determine where the classroom begins or ends?"

Malachai drew in his breath. Things were getting hotter. Francisco was smiling dangerously. Arguments entertained him, especially political ones. It looked as though there was going to be one of those verbal free-for-alls that caused all the neighbors to slam their windows shut.

"I say," said Clea, sensing the same rising storm, "with all this hullabaloo, you've forgotten the object of the argument, poor old Zaga. I suggest we give him a call and invite him to meet us somewhere. What about the Jogral?"

"An excellent idea," said Malachai, breathing a sigh of relief and admiring his wife for her genius.

CHAPTER 13

Zaga, the architect, too distraught to appreciate its merits, declined the invitation. It was a pity, but it wasn't only for his sake at any rate that Clea had suggested the Jogral. It was a small joint, so impossibly crowded that whenever a poor sufferer could bear it no longer and had to make his way to the head, everyone had to stand in unison to allow him to pass. It was dark, and if there were decorations on the wall, nobody had ever noticed them, for all attention was concentrated on the stage. To become absorbed with what was going on upon that three-meter-square space of floorboard, half of which was occupied by a piano, was to become healed, to be able to laugh, to regain one's perspective, to remember in a sense, what was meant by the word "Brazilian." Zaga had declined, but there were others, Clea had sensed, who could have done that night with an infusion of perspective.

There were musicians at the Jogral who had hunched over their cavaquinhos playing "O Carinhoso" with the same passionate concentration since the world had begun. Pallid and round-shouldered with bags under their eyes, they looked as though they might be bank tellers and janitors in the daytime, but at night, by their music, they were transformed into their own instruments. In contrast to their pallor and discipline, Joaquim, who played the cuica, did so by instinct, clutching the drumlike piece to his breast, contorting himself around it, baring white teeth in a jet black face as he made the thin wire within talk and laugh and sing, become a bird, a man, a spirit.

No one could remember when Joaquim hadn't been there, any more than they could imagine a corner of that dimly lighted stage not having been occupied by Assis, the flutist, whose ebony fingers had worn innumerable pipes to paper thinness. To whom people would say with infinite gratitude, "I've come all the way back six thousand miles to hear you."

Assis would smile in gracious acknowledgment, knowing it was true. For he knew in his dark, mystical being as thin and brittle as the instrument he played, that he represented to them the soul of something and that it was worth coming back to.

So much of the Brazilian soul is black. Many will try to deny it, but it's no use. And certainly it should be a thing to rejoice, this something implanted here and impossible to uproot, which is so powerful it touches us all no matter what blood runs in our veins. And it is this huge portion of the soul, subtle, variegated and beautiful, which gives life here its peculiar tone, makes things different, less serious perhaps, so that one can never quite call the doomsday, never quite predict the future. Its spell touches a child the moment he can stand on his two feet and watch a *"bloco de samba"* pass by in the street. It comes out in the music and lures one, as Clea was lured long ago by fingers tapping on a matchbox. It roots itself through the old black flutist and renews itself out of remote, unheard-of worlds from which new faces arise.

Tonight there was a boy with a viola, tall and thin and yellow, his eyes two black pinpoints close to his long nose beneath a high, troubled forehead. When he sang, the forehead puckered as if all the energy in his being had concentrated behind those brilliant pinpoints of eyes to burst forth in pure joy at his own ability to make music.

Delia couldn't resist for long. Like a great many others in that impossibly crowded room, she had managed to clear a tiny space around her. She was laughing, suddenly transformed, herself, into a joy, her shoulders moving to one beat, her hips to another, with effortless, abandoned grace. Watching her, Francisco—one of those who admitted the truth about the soul—thought, *"Graças a Deus*—as long as there are boys like this, as long as the soul has roots and renews itself . . ."

"Nega with the stiff hair. What kind of comb do you use?" She was singing now too—she and the boy—singing to each other, unmindful of the entire room and yet enveloping all in their sweet ecstasy. When the music ceased, the boy sat staring and smiling with his bright black eyes and Delia sank onto her chair, laughing.

She'd forgotten all about Zaga, her fury of a moment ago. If the originators of Zaga's sad condition had appeared at that moment to remind her, she would not only have forgiven them for what she considered to be an ill-considered act, but probably persuaded them to consider it again. It was all temporary, of course—but such was the effect of this place and its music of purging one of excess seriousness and making one, for a time, whole.

A guitarist had taken the place of the boy with the viola. His hair cropped close to a finely shaped skull, his cheekbones, prominent nose, sharp and thin, his eyes like dark jewels set in pale golden skin. His long sensitive fingers touched the strings as though the instrument were an unfailing part of himself. He sang truthfully without sophistication the sad story of Zelão's hillside shanty, washed away by the rain:

> Everyone understood when Zelão cried
> Nobody laughed, nobody played,
> Though it was Carnival.

Duncan leaned back in his chair, taking in the scene, trying to visualize at the same time the world he'd left behind, but already not succeeding. Perhaps I am too tired, he thought, but actually he knew better. The real truth was that these worlds were very far apart. Jet transportation, telecommunication, hot lines would never make that much of a difference, never cause them to operate on the same frequency—the thought amused and comforted him.

He fell to watching Caroline, who a moment ago had been so inflamed, and now sat moist-eyed and thoroughly absorbed by the enchantment of the music, one mood as profound and real as the other. Caroline, with whom life could be everything but dull.

"It's such a great combination, strings and poetry," she was saying to Delia. "Rather like the music of the Renaissance. It almost tempts me to take guitar lessons, just to know it better—"

"Why not?" Delia still glowed with the exaltation of her dancing. "Is there any reason why you shouldn't?"

Caroline smiled. "Impatience, I guess. I've been a concert pianist and yet I've never found a guitar teacher here who didn't want to start me out with Jingle Bells."

Delia's shoulders shook now with appreciative hilarity. "Ahh, that *is* a sin, but not necessary either. Look here"—she leaned toward Caroline as if suddenly inspired and gestured with her head toward the guitarist. "I know him. He is a student at the university, writing his thesis. Also having a difficult time with money. He gives lessons." She smiled, her bright eyes full of pleasure at the chance to do two friends a favor, one of whom she'd just done battle with for the very reason she liked her—her spirit and outspokenness. "No Jingle Bells. You want to talk to him?"

At this, Francisco, who had been marveling even as Duncan at the facility with which their women slipped from one mood to another, was seen by Malachai to draw his brows together in a fleeting expression of alarm. The look was missed by Duncan, however, who was thinking, despite all his efforts to the contrary, "That's a pretty damn good-looking cat to be giving my wife guitar lessons." He could, in fact, feel his entire being reacting, his pulses rising and thudding ridiculously. But just because it was so ridiculous and because Caroline's face was so beautified with inspiration as she said, "Why not?" he decided to keep it to himself.

CHAPTER 14

Francisco Cavalcanti never did look at his hideous design again. For the next six months or so, he was in fact destined to look at scarcely anything but designs of spillways, cisterns, turbines; the sight of tractors uprooting gigantic trees, excavating; trucks moving the deep red earth; harnessing a wilderness and a great sluggish river; living the camp life, turning an abstraction into reality in the midst of nowhere. Evidently his employers were true to their word. No inaugurations hung threateningly in the air. They wanted the job done. They'd left him alone to do it.

It was Malachai, once the design had been submitted to the board of directors, who redid the whole thing. At one point, baring his teeth in an iniquitous grin, Duncan had suggested, "Maybe we should nab that Zaga fellow before those hundred universities get wind of him. If he's out of a job." But Malachai had turned pale at the thought. So in the end they handed the thing over to him. He made it "intimate, warm, appealing," if somewhat wanting in function. A lot was rented on one of Campos' busiest avenues, a master worker hired and construction begun. In the meantime Teodoro de Todos os Santos had gone to Rio to meet the ship bearing Professor Lindquist's personal effects.

Somehow whenever Teodoro thought of it later, the memory of that day gave him a kind of Mafioso sensation, at once terrified and daring. He'd done some strange things during his career, but this was perhaps the strangest.

Josh, of course, had been in Rio as well at the proper moment to advise the Chief of Party, unseasoned in the customs of the country, that it would indeed be a fatal error to go to the docks and receive the baggage himself.

"Nothing could be worse." He regarded Professor Lindquist

with a look of outright alarm. "Why for all you know, you could end up on a DOPS police blotter. Leave it to Teodoro, that's what he's for. How about some Bahian food? Ever been to the Oxalá?"

Professor Lindquist, who had little experience in anything but entomology and whom each day, since his arrival in Rio de Janeiro, had brought closer to the conclusion that treachery lurked around every street corner and behind every office door, was only too willing to accept.

And so, while Josh and the Chief of Party alternately cauterized and soothed their innards with Bahian spices and beer, Teodoro went down to the docks. Happily he was no stranger to this great rolling, roaring, crane-swinging bedlam on the edge of Guanabara Bay. He had, in fact, often been before to meet the baggage of newly arrived members of the Institute, and long ago as a sensible matter of course, made friends with Doutor Oswaldo, the customs master. So on that day there seemed nothing unusual in his behavior as they stood together amidst the half-naked figures who moved back and forth, staggering under their burdens, or swinging tipsily through the air on the hook of a crane and into the bowels of ships.

Stolidly they went over the inventory of Professor Lindquist's possessions; an incredibly untempting list they had often gone over before, of items apparently necessary to the survival of incoming Americans.

Three cartons Sani-Sure water purifying pills, four cases Wheatina, ten cans Dog-Off deodorant spray, 100 jars Easy Off oven spray, forty rolls Spread On plastic foil, one Easy-Does-It reclining chair . . . the list went drearily on, preparing, it seemed to Teodoro, the most colorless background, a gray lifeless stage upon which there would suddenly appear in a vivid burst of contrast, Two Chicken Little Pressure Fryers. "Each big enough," Doutor Oswaldo was quick to remark, "to fry a cow in." Teodoro tried not to shudder as the customs master, abruptly awakening from his lethargy over the list, stared unbelievingly, his eyes widening, with a disturbing mingling of suspicion and greed.

Somehow Teodoro managed to contain himself. Drawing on twenty years of accumulated knowledge of the folkways and mores of customs officials, he turned to his friend with a look of mild surprise.

"But surely, Doutor Oswaldo, it stands to reason. Professor Lindquist is in fact"—he allowed his voice to become respectfully sonorous—"the Chief of Party."

"*O Chefe do Partido, ah!*" The predicted and prayed-for reaction was immediate. Malachai's barring the policeman from his ovens with a portrait of King George could not have been more effective. It had been as if, over Teodoro's shoulder, the wily old blackmailer Oswaldo had seen the phantom of a political chief, a man as pompous, troublesome and dishonest as himself, only considerably more powerful.

"*O Chefe do Partido,*" he repeated. "Why didn't you say so? *Pois não, Sr. Teodoro.*" With a nervous flick of the wrist and a respectful lowering of the eyes, as if there were indeed no longer any need for further inventory, he waved the rest of Professor Lindquist's necessities through.

Teodoro struggled momentarily to keep from fainting on the spot, and, nodding briskly, followed the entire procession of crates and trunks to where the trucks stood waiting to carry them all away.

The rest was easy. The monstrous machines would obviously not fit into the moving van with the other articles. Teodoro's brother-in-law, Joaquim, who had just received an engraved Parker pen for ten years of meritorious service as the Institute's most reliable chauffeur, backed the extra truck into position. Once loaded and out of sight of the docks, he suddenly ceased following the moving van in the direction of the fashionable residential district of Leblon, made a U-turn, headed southward and out of the city.

Since that day the machines had stood safely ensconced amidst the bags of feed in Josh's store. It was hard to believe at times, but there they were. And here was he, rising every day at dawn to supervise the construction of the restaurant in which he, Teodoro de Todos os Santos, former red-tape lieutenant and messenger boy, was a partner.

He sat now on a newspaper spread out upon the wall of the lot where the restaurant was to be and allowed his mind to wander a little before the day began. Sometimes it occurred to him that his new role in life had not notably changed the duties he performed. It was he who had done the dirty work of renting the lot, acting as mediator in the quibblings amongst the members of a large and indecisive family until he'd finally gotten them to agree enough for each warily to put his signature on the dotted line. Ah, brotherly love. Nothing could bring relatives crawling out of the woodwork faster than a rental contract. Well, he'd taken care of that. Then had come the countless trips to the mayor's office, the standing in line for building permits, plumbing permits, electrical permits; the requisitioning of bricks, cement, plaster; the endless struggle to see that 2,000 bricks were in fact 2,000 bricks plus one hundred for breakage. He'd been doing things like this all his life. The only difference was that now he was doing them for himself.

Harry McGuiness, whom he trusted above all other men, had told him flatly he was insane. "I don't care what half-cocked scheme you go into or with whom. With your problems, a daughter like Marilia, you can't afford to take chances."

But Harry McGuiness, for all Teodoro's admiration of him, could never be brought to understand that what he'd done, he'd done precisely because of Marilia—his daughter whom one operation after another had not been able to prevent from becoming blind.

When that had happened, when the blindness had been declared hopeless, there had been weeping and gnashing of the teeth and morbid speculation among Teodoro's relatives, not to mention a certain ill-concealed shame.

"You're not going to make her go back to school!"

He had not exactly *made* her go. He had simply always known that she would. And so she had gone, setting out in the morning with her dark glasses and a tape recorder, on the arm of a friend.

Oddly enough, it was the friends who had become accustomed most quickly to this novelty, as if they too had always known that one day Marilia would become blind and that she would continue on just the same. There seemed to be friends everywhere, and professors too, who didn't mind speaking a little bit more slowly, sometimes repeating themselves so that Marilia could hear what she couldn't see.

With her tape recorder and her dark glasses and her spirit, she was third in her class, walking to school on the arm of a friend each day. How could she do that in Rio?

At the end of the year she would graduate and become a teacher: a real teacher in a real school. He couldn't help sitting up straighter as he thought of it. So, of course, he couldn't think of leaving Campos even if he wanted to. But besides that, he didn't want to—that was the truth of the matter. For Josh Moran had offered him a partnership and who else would ever do that in a lifetime? He was worth it to Josh, he knew. When they'd spoken of the business he had put it plainly enough. "I've no money, nothing to offer the business but my abilities."

And Josh had put it plainly to him, "I've nothing to offer you but a partnership. Of course we'll pay ourselves salaries, but not much for now."

It was enough, for now. For Teodoro had untold confidence in the future and absolute certainty that there would never be another Josh Moran who was crazy enough, or sure enough, to offer him, an ugly mulatto with a fourth-grade education, the chance of building something of his own. To be a partner in something, that was the difference. It made you think that what Josh said was true. "In this country you can do damn near anything if you want to." And yet for Josh to do damn near anything there were many chances, while for Teodoro do Todos os Santos, there was only one.

"Did you say something, Sr. Teodoro?"

"Who, me? No, no not really. I was just thinking . . ." Teodoro turned to find João Faria, the stone mason, standing beside him, leaning against the wall. João Faria was a country man and had not been away from the "*roça*" long enough to forget the incredible hours at which country people took their meals. It was only eight-fifteen, but apparently Sr. Faria had just finished his lunch. He was preparing himself a cigarette, rolling tobacco in a piece of corn husk with his large, flat-fingered carpenter's hands. He was a big man with a Basset's sad, humorous face, leathery skinned from spending half his life crawling over rooves in the blazing subtropical sun.

"I've been thinking too." He lit his corn-husk cigarette, drawing deeply and then looking at the end to see if it was alight. "Of course, Senhor should know, Sr. Teodoro, but this restaurant we're building. Such a big lot and such a small building. No place for anybody to sit, it strikes me."

"Ah, Sr. Faria." Teodoro, well versed by his colleagues in the matter, bent down to enlighten the ignorant mason. "This is a Drive-In. People drive up, get their chicken in a box and eat it in the car or take it home. Very practical—no maintenance, no dishes to wash—"

Sr. Faria considered a moment and then looked irritatingly unsatisfied. "Who has a car?" he said, obviously thinking of Teodoro and himself, "and if you did, what would you want to eat in it for?"

"It's an American system," Teodoro enlightened him further, "very popular. Don't worry, Sr. Faria, it's all been studied. You'll see. The thing is to be modern, keep up with the times, not let them get ahead of you."

"Perhaps." Sr. Faria still looked maddeningly doubtful. "I hope you're right. I've never been to a real restaurant, mind you, but if I did go I'd certainly not want to take the food home in a box." He dropped his smoked-out cigarette and stomped on it. "Just to be sure," he said, "I must ask you, is the part where they're going to put tables really only going to be five meters by five?" As if to emphasize his disbelief, he looked toward the area in question, in which his two assistants were already busy laying the foundation.

Teodoro breathed deeply in one last effort to contain his irritation and gave the stone mason a confident smile. "I am sure. Absolutely one hundred per cent sure."

"All right, Senhor should know." Shrugging largely and thrusting out his lower lip, João Faria thus replaced all responsibility squarely upon Teodoro's shoulders and headed toward the foundation to take up where he had left off.

So he thought it was funny did he? Teodoro refused to admit to himself that the reason Faria had irritated him so was because the mason had expressed the very thoughts that from time to time arose in his own mind and were promptly stifled as he stifled them now. Faria, he told himself, was after all a very simple, ignorant man. Josh had brought him from São João da Barra in the interior to do the job for that very reason. In his simplicity he could perform the tasks of three men whereas any mason from the city would require three men to do the task of one.

The day Josh had brought him over, Faria had not had time to build a roof on his sleeping quarters before dark. It had rained that night and the mason had slept under a barrel. He hadn't minded it. It occurred to Teodoro that he didn't mind anything, which was fine for getting the job done. But how could a man of such simplicity accept the novelty of a new idea?

Of course he couldn't. Having assured himself of that, Teodoro jumped lightly down from the wall and made his way toward the shed that housed Faria's sleeping quarters, complete now with a cot, a stool, a cardboard suitcase, a cookstove, a store of rice and beans and a bottle of *pinga*; all Faria needed, apparently, to be content on the job.

Attached to these quarters was another lean-to with a roof and clapboard walls that housed Teodoro's "office." He stopped before this structure now, unlocking the padlock that secured its sagging door, stepped inside and thrust open the wooden window to let in the light. "*Graças a Deus*, it's another sunny day," he thought. For when you had to shut that window it was black as pitch in there and, since the electricity permit had not yet been signed, the only light was a kerosene lamp hanging from the ceiling, which gave him nostalgia for his childhood in the "roça," but not for long.

Pulling back a chair, he sat down behind the old kitchen table that presently served as a desk and quietly performed a ritual. It consisted of sitting back and concentrating on a point in front of him until he saw an office building in São Paulo that occupied an entire city block. Every time he went to the city, in fact, he managed to find some reason to pass that building and gaze through its tinted glass walls upon a hundred agents interviewing a hundred clients whose cars clogged the traffic of the narrow street outside. Clineu Rocha . . . the largest real estate firm in South America. As he thought of it, his own "office" took on an aspect of genteel elegance. Its brick floor became covered with wall-to-wall carpeting, there was jacaranda furniture and Debré prints graced the walls, while a plaque on the door announced in conservative, tasteful lettering, Intercontinental Limitada, Imobiliaria, and in slightly smaller letters, Teodoro de Todos os

Santos, Diretór. It was a vision he evoked daily as some people might evoke the image of Nossa Senhora de Conceicão. When he'd spoken of it to Josh, Josh had pulled on his cigar and grinned squintingly through the smoke. "Duncan and I have thought of that too, but I think we should start out with something more concrete. Still, any business you can rake up on the side—"

There was a slight divergence of opinion between himself and his partners, he would admit, as to what was more concrete—real estate or this bottomless pit that was being constructed brick by brick just outside. Nevertheless that was just what he was doing, "raking up business on the side." This last thought brought him abruptly back to the realities of the day. In a few minutes he would have to rush down to the mayor's office again and get in line to have the requisition signed and stamped so that he could *then* get the permit to plug in the light. After that he'd have to rush back to a very important meeting; a matter of a tract of land that could bring them 11,000 cruzelros in commission money . . . a nice nest egg if he could preserve it from the bottomless pit and keep it for the real estate business. But first he'd have to swing the deal, and for this he had to persuade Josh to play an important part. Thus galvanized into action, Teodoro looked down at the pile of requisitions on his desk and realized he couldn't make them out. Actually they were covered with a film of dust blown in through the cracks in the wall, but he thought it must be his glasses. He took them off to wipe them and immediately the office with its metal filing cabinet and a calendar tacked to the clapboard wall whirled crazily about him and out of sight as his spastic eyes rolled upward beneath his lids. For an instant he knew what it was to be totally blind. It had happened before and was the only sensation that truly terrified him. For what would he do? What in God's name?

Frantically he fumbled for the handkerchief where his wife Clarisse had put it neatly folded in his pocket the night before. Hastily he wiped his glasses and put them on again and for another moment sat very still as gradually the cabinet, the calendar and board walls, swung back into their proper positions. "*Mãe de Deus,*" he murmured, "let this deal go through." Then, appealing to a number of other saints of incredibly varied origin, he rose and walked across to the grocer's, where there was a phone, to call Josh and tell him his plan before setting out on his morning's pilgrimage to public offices.

CHAPTER 15

Almost every day at just about the hour when Teodoro spread his newspaper on the wall of the lot, Josh pulled into the market square in the shadow of the great seringueiro trees that had grown with the town from its beginning. Once the appearance of the Chevrolet Impala, a relic from Josh's "cushy job" which Malachai had renamed the American Bathtub, had created something of a stir. But novelties cannot last and now Josh with his feed and farm supplies was just another of the many who, hawking cheap clothing, patent furniture, candomblé potions, vegetables and fruits, cheeses and salamis, did their business around the square.

This morning, easing the bathtub over the curb, he found his place in the parking lot amidst the countless trucks of varied portage and vintage, and, climbing over the protruding roots of a seringueiro tree, he made his way to the store. As he entered, the cheeping of baby chicks, set in a coop in the doorway to lure customers, mingled with the clacking of typewriters and adding machines of the office boys, who had already begun the battle of the papers. Many people crossed themselves every time they passed a church. Josh, without moving his lips or changing his expression, cursed bureaucracy every time he passed a public building. It was just a little tribute to the boys in the back of the store.

Opposite the counters behind which the boys sat smoking and figuring, the rest of the store consisted almost entirely of bags of feed for laying chickens, fattening chickens, gestating cows, growing calves, fattening steers. Atop a stack of bags marked, "*Reprodutina*" for active boars, the Negro boy Helio lay in a state of sublime oblivion, his long lean body draped as loosely and comfortably over the sacks as that of a sleek panther.

He was very handsome, this Helio. The purity of his blackness, the sharpness of his features were remindful of the fierce nomadic tribes of the Abyssinian desert, but there seemed to be no fierceness in his nature. When the other boys banteringly called him "Macaco," he laughed along with them as if it were the most natural thing on earth to be called a monkey. The offense seemed only to offend Josh, really. It was a phenomenon he would never quite get used to. Now, as he passed Helio on his way to the stairs, he decided not to disturb him. Soon enough Orsini, the Italian truck driver, would arrive to slap him on the rear, and with a cheerful, "*Ei, Macaco, levante, vão trabalhar,*" convert his present couch into a burden and himself into a one-man feed bag parade.

Slipping past Helio's recumbent form, Josh climbed the sloping stairs that led to the second floor, a kind of glorified balcony, from which he and his secretary, Dona Michiko, presided rather like the captain and his mate from the upper deck of a ship.

Dona Michiko was Japanese. During the war she had been taught in school to make little paper effigies of Americans and burn them. But all that was long ago and in another world. In this world, where her parents were prosperous farmers, a kind of Nippo-nepotism was gradually creeping into the key positions of Alimen-Tec Incorperada. Her brother Noáki was the store's chief salesman, and her cousin Káoro, the chief accountant who sat shifting the little beads on his abacus and writing down figures all day, while Dona Michiko juggled cash and credit with the dexterity of an oriental acrobat.

There were no lines in her face. Her features were as smooth as the finest porcelain, her smile equally serene whether she was announcing a financial coup or a disaster, so that it was difficult for Josh to define whether he should be jubilant or depressed as she placed the morning's checks before him for endorsement.

The checks with their signatures, some elegantly illegible, others scrawled painfully and punctuated with the traces of earth from hands that were never quite clean, were like familiar character sketches. Josh could read the signature and see the man, Salim Maluf, the industrialist who imported cows by the plane load from Canada and discussed cattle with Josh at the opera. Tacahama, a wrinkled sun-browned Japanese patriarch who, with the help of an infinite number of filial hands, raised tomatoes and strawberries in the winter, eggplant and peppers in the summer, and chickens all the year round.

Turning over the check of one Manoel Azevedo, the largest dairy farmer in the region, Josh felt a certain gratitude for the persistence of Noáki who had spent a year running back and forth with experimental feeding plans, trying to convince the highly skeptical Azevedo of the efficacy of balanced rations. Now Azevedo was his best customer, not simply because he bought feed, but paid for it on time. With Central Feeds demanding cash for every kilo, all the bank credit in Brazil couldn't have saved Josh without a few stubborn Portuguese like Azevedo on the ledgers. He didn't even believe in credit. For him a bank was only somewhere to lock up your money. On the other hand . . .

He looked up to discover the eyes of Dona Michiko upon him as they probably had been all along, waiting for the moment when he would notice that one check was missing. "What about Camargo?"

"*Pois e.*" Her voice was discouragingly stoic. "No money."

"We were counting on him for today."

"We can stop counting on him, Sr. Josh," she said, not unsympathetically. "You know the old story. He sold his chickens Monday but hasn't been paid. Nevertheless, he promises that by Wednesday—"

"Uh-huh." Josh lit a cigar and started thinking. At times like these it seemed to Dona Michiko that his outer visage turned to stone while thoughts must be running around inside in a mad search for a solution. Josh knew the story, all right. How could one fight it, or even be indignant. Camargo worked like a horse, he had real guts, but he worked on a shoestring. And didn't they all? Only Azevedo, who had an old coffee fortune behind him, could afford the luxury of scorning credit. The rest of them, Camargo, Tacahama, Josh himself, for that matter, had to scramble.

He shouldn't have counted so thoroughly on a poor hard-pressed chicken farmer. But what else was he to do? That was whom he dealt with and Central Feeds was waiting. No money, no delivery. He thought of the loan Duncan had been negotiating in São Paulo. A new bank, Beth-El, it was called. Sounded like a temple, but who cared what it was? The money was promised for

Monday. If they could just shuffle a little till then. "If they can't, with a name like that," he reflected, "we can always try prayer." His stone face broke into a grin.

"Dona Michiko, write out a check for today's feed. I'll sign it, but make sure it's not cashed until late afternoon, do you hear? The kites are flying."

Dona Michiko tried not to stare. She knew that, when there was nothing left to do but pray, Josh Moran had a habit of dismissing the need for prayer from his mind. It was a kind of religion in itself, one that he professed to his employees from time to time. But though she would have liked to practice it herself when butterflies began flitting around in her stomach, somehow she could only pretend. So oriental discretion substituting for self-imposed insensibility, she wrote the check and poured him a cup of coffee.

With the cup beside him, he sat back comfortably and took up the newspaper. A bomb had exploded in a car on Rua da Conçolaçāo in São Paulo, blowing to smithereens the car's two occupants rather than the offices of the American Chemical Co., for which it was intended. Due to the earliness of the hour, 4:00 A.M., and the emptiness of the streets, no other casualties had occurred. The remains, scattered across the wide avenue, were identified (somehow) as those of Maeda Okomoto and Florisvaldo de Oliveira, both listed terrorist suspects. Pamphlets later found in Oliveira's boarding house room, declared with monotonous lack of imagination that the bombing against the imperialist, capitalist American firm *which traded on carnage,* was necessary to draw attention to the repression by the military regime of the *true representatives* of the people.

The pamphlet further called for abolishment of said regime; the banishment of all foreign exploiters (that's me, thought Josh); the "nationalization" of industry; redistribution of latifundios among the peasants; and the *"justicização"* (summary execution) of "those responsible."

Well, attention had been drawn, all right. Two of them had blown themselves up, and since an action provokes a reaction, who knew how many others would be hauled in for questioning. Who were these people and what did they really want? Behind his newspaper, Josh could see in his mind the "wanted" posters plastered on the walls of banks and post offices that stated below the pictures of the offenders, "Assassins of the fathers of families." Some of them looked like plain bandits in the traditional sense of the word. Others looked as though their photographs had been taken from a high school yearbook. They looked like . . . Lupe, the clerk downstairs. There was no way of classifying them unless it was by the belief they seemed willing to share that their demands, if accepted, would bring about a total solution. Josh didn't believe in total solutions. Evil sickened, but seldom surprised him. Man was capable of all things. What disturbed and sometimes frightened him was this absurd idea that evil could be entirely swept away. It was an idea that seemed to him to threaten everything constructive that ever had been or was being done.

The thought now made him want to say something to someone, so he said to Dona Michiko, "One of those terrorists was Japanese. What do you suppose?"

"What do I suppose?" Dona Michiko sniffed disgustedly, dismissing the terrorist with a gesture. "Not typically Japanese. If he were, he'd have been working. Look around you, Sr. Josh."

Josh smiled. Her irritation shed no real light on the why or wherefore—yet she was right about one thing. One had only to look around. From where he sat, for instance, the view from the balcony and through the wide open door took in the entire market square below. It was *feira* day. Ever since five in the morning the *feirantes* had been piling fruits and vegetables on tables improvised from packing cases and planks under the trees and before the old brick-walled, tile-roofed building that housed the market. Things were becoming more congested by the minute and, rather than become involved, the police had abandoned the square, leaving every man to defend his own vulnerable position as best he could. A banana truck had just stopped six inches short of barreling into the side of a truckload of pineapples, from which, gates down, an Italian vendor was offering three pineapples for the price of two, twelve for the price of ten. Josh watched as the Italian, teetering on the edge of his potential avalanche, cursed the truck driver's mother, and the driver, a powerful Baiano, clenched his bicep in a sign that said "bananas" or, translated, meant "fuck yourself," and laughing went careening off in another direction.

As unmindfully as possible, amidst this Friday morning chaos, the Japanese stood behind their improvised tables arranging heaps of shining black eggplant, firm red tomatoes, cucumbers, glistening heads of lettuce, artichokes flowering from long purple stems. Once there had been little more than a few diseased bananas, mandioca and rotting papaya, scarcely worth picking over. Now there was a bounty of peaches, plums, avocados, grapes . . . an incredible variety, the result of imagination and hard work in a place where one could grow anything that could be grown anywhere else in the world.

Inside the market itself, enclosed by high white walls and a cool tile roof, Josh could imagine the sight and smell of the stalls heaped with cheeses and hung with salamis, smoked hams and tongues. And where there had once been only a few stringy fly-specked morsels of meat and ancient skinny hens, there were now tender loins of pork, plump broiling chickens and fine red beef.

"Look around you." Dona Michiko with her sharp peasant common sense and Japanese pride was right. One had only to think back a little and remember how it had all once been to know that in a very short time a revolution had occurred, brought about by men who tilled the land; many of them immigrants who, with their ancient knowledge and hunger for land of their own, had come, leaving everything they had ever known behind.

But for them to come, there had had to be land to claim and roads leading to it, farther and farther into a vast, empty interior . . . So while theoreticians sat in their ivory towers the world over cooking up rules for "the new man" to live by, and terrorists robbed banks and made bombs and fairytale manifestos, this other thing was happening every day.

This, Josh knew, was why he liked the feed business as much as he did. For the same men who sold their produce in the market, came into the store; brown-skinned, weathered men with cracked and earth-stained hands, hard to convince yet impossible to discourage, having lived all their lives with the continuous round of bright hopes and hardships on the land. The infinite complexities of plants and earth and animals they dealt with were real. And so when he spoke with them, he also spoke of real things that made him feel himself to be a part of what was happening.

"*Sr. Josh, tem gente.*" Dona Michiko's voice came to him with the prudence of one awakening a sleepwalker. As it did, he realized that for some time he had been sitting behind his paper staring at the words and reading nothing. He hoped the distance he'd gone from the news didn't reflect too much in his eyes as he lowered the paper. If it did, it could only have been for an instant, for all vagueness left him as his glance took in the stranger before him.

CHAPTER 16

He judged the man to be in his forties. Like most of those who came into the store he had the seasoned look of having spent hours and days in the sun. But unlike most, there was no roughness, nothing crude in his appearance. Rather, his features, extremely well molded, seemed combined to produce an unusual balance of strength and aestheticism. From beneath a high brow and thatch of graying blond hair, the dark brown eyes were strikingly intelligent. They met Josh's now with a look both direct and apologetic. "Jacob Svedelius is my name. I hope you'll forgive my barging up here this way. Malachai Kenath told me it was the thing to do. You are Sr. Josh Moran?"

"I am." Josh rose and leaned across the desk to shake hands. "Please pull up a chair. So Malachai sent you?"

"He did." Jacob Svedelius seated himself. "You don't seem surprised. I saw him yesterday at his house in São Sebastião by the sea. He was vacationing there and I drove down from Piruibi to shake off some loneliness and have a little conversation. He's an interesting fellow, isn't he? Full of advice."

"Oh, that he is." Josh thought fondly of Malachai and smiled.

"When I told him I was going into farming, he immediately suggested I talk to you."

"Farming? In Piruibi?" Josh could feel the undulent fever of his curiosity rising. "In that jungled mountain wilderness?"

"Oh, jungles don't upset me," the stranger said calmly. "I am a forester by profession—trained in Denmark." Before Josh could comment on that, he hurried on. "As you might imagine, there's not much original one can do with forests in my country, but here . . ."

"If you have the money," Josh said, looking suddenly old and wise.

"Which I haven't." Jacob Svedelius laughed openly and Josh noted for the first time how faded were the khaki pants and shirt he wore. "But you see, that's what I've come here for. I've been told—"

"By Malachai?"

"Yes, by Malachai, that you have an excellent knack for starting things with nothing—"

"Starting," Josh agreed. "Though I have yet to finish anything." He was about to elaborate, about to say to this stranger, "but that shouldn't stop us from talking," when the phone rang.

It was Teodoro of course. Before the actual words erupted, his tone of voice had a way of heralding things to come—tragedy, catastrophy, a win on the federal lottery. Today his voice suggested an impending great breakthrough.

"*Escuta aqui*. Remember the widow with the three thousand acres near Laranjeiras?"

"*Claro*," said Josh, "who could forget three thousand acres at a time like this?"

"I have a buyer." Teodoro's voice crackled importantly along the wires. "You know the Dutchman who wants to plant gladiolus?"

"Not the one who trains his flowers to bloom on All Souls' Day, Teodoro." Josh's hopes, briefly aroused, sank again to their former level. "We took him to lunch the other day, remember? And after two hours of regimented gladiolus, we didn't get him to budge a centavo above two hundred thousand cruzeiros. The widow wants two hundred and fifty. So I don't see how—"

"Ah, but you will. Listen, are you listening? I tried a new tactic."

"Uh." Josh was well aware of Teodoro's tactics; imminent signs of soil fertility, inside rumors of housing developments. His partner's voice rattled on.

"Just when I thought all was lost. When I was thinking, Teodoro, you've talked yourself out—"

"You?"

"Just then, I said to him, 'It's a pity, Sr. VonFoche,' I said, 'that you can't come to a decision when there are certain Americans who would be willing to pay a little bit less than two-fifty, but in cash.' *Sabe!* When I said that, a miracle occurred. A true miracle." Teodoro's talk was becoming as uncontainable as his excitement, words spilling over one another in a torrent. "He turned white. I tell you, *branco!* And you know that Dutchman is red, like Italian ham. Have you thought, if we do the business it's eleven thousand for us? Eleven thousand cruzeiros novos!" he repeated.

"There's only one catch." Josh was beginning to get desperate to be off the phone. "We don't know of any American, do we?"

"Ah, but now we arrive at the crucial question," said Teodoro.

"Oh?" said Josh.

"The Dutchman. I'm to take him to the widow's at ten o'clock this morning." There was a pause, a clearing of the throat, all ominous sounds that suggested Teodoro was preparing himself for something big, and then it came. "All I need is someone who looks American."

"Huh?"

"Oh not to *do* anything, you understand, but just to provide a kind of background, sitting somewhere in a car. I don't even have to explain him. *Comprendeu?* All I have to say is, 'Him . . . over there? Ah, he's an American.'"

"Oh, is that all?" Josh hoped his sarcasm was strong enough to transmit itself along the wire. This Teodoro was nuts. *Louco!* A few more brilliant ideas like this and—"What do you want me to do? Dye my hair? Knock out a front tooth? Or do you think I have a closetful of Americans just waiting . . ." Even as he said this, Josh's eyes came to rest with a sudden, horrid fascination upon the Dane, who all this time had been sitting reading trucking schedules on a blackboard behind Josh's back and trying—a certain tremor of the lips and hunching of the shoulders to the contrary—to look unaware.

"Nah," Josh dismissed the thought, "he looks too much like he just stepped out of the pages of Isak Dinesen." But then, as the Dane struggled harder still to contain himself, Josh's courage rose accordingly and he thought, "Who knows, maybe from a distance, with a hat . . ."

"Teodoro, wait!" He covered the speaker with his hand and addressed himself to Jacob Svedelius. "Are you in a great hurry?"

"Not really," said the Dane.

"Because something's come up. I have to meet my partner, perhaps we could talk on the way—"

"Well, I suppose," said Jacob Svedelius, feeling a strange sensation that, just sitting there, he had somehow lost control.

He had of course; at least temporarily. He realized it as a few minutes later he found himself sitting beneath the shade of a grove of bright flowering flamboyant trees in the American Bathtub with the windows rolled up and the air conditioner on. Not that it was that hot out of doors, and in fact the smell of the air conditioner made him feel slightly nauseous, but Josh said sitting like that with the windows closed would make him look more American. It also lent to the conversation going on at a discreet distance on the veranda of the widow's house, the peculiar air of a pantomime being performed for his benefit alone.

On one side Josh Moran stood looking grave and sympathetic as if there was nothing he comprehended better than the Dutchman's dilemma. On the other side, Teodoro seemed to have contracted a strange form of St. Vitus dance that kept his arms waving and his mouth working at an almost unbelievable pace. In the middle, the Dutchman stood, large and silent, apparently unmindful of Teodoro's frantic activities, his face set in the heavy, inscrutable expression of a Rembrandt burgomaster behind whose piglet eyes constant addition and subtraction was in progress.

For all his activity, it seemed Teodoro might just as well not have been there, but Jacob was certain that his *own* role had been a real stroke of genius; for from time to time, the tiny eyes fastened themselves upon Josh's car with its occupant and his frown deepened. For one hideous moment Jacob thought he saw the Dutchman lurch in his direction as if in a sudden decision to stride over to the car and have everything—whatever *everything* was—out in the open. But, as instinctively he felt himself shrink beneath the slightly oversized Stetson that Josh had lent him to authenticate his costume, a flash of inspiration crossed the Dutchman's face. Apparently his interminable figuring had at last reached fruition.

The color in his face increased so that Teodoro's comparison to an Italian ham seemed no longer exaggerated. Turning to Josh Moran he allowed a grudging nod, whereupon Josh's partner's eyes rolled out of sight and Josh's hand came forward in a polite, ostensibly disinterested gesture of congratulation.

Afterward Josh, Teodoro and Jacob Svedelius ate lunch together in a bar frequented by truck drivers and loaders next to Alimen-Tec Inc. The dish of the day was *feijoada*: black beans cooked with salt pork and a myriad of smoked meat, bitter cabbage, hot pepper sauce, and mealy *farofa* seasoned with olives and onions. After such a meal, washed down with cachassa and beer, an atmosphere of peaceful somnolence descended upon the square. In the shade of the seringueiros, sleeping forms sprawled atop heaps of potato sacks, in hammocks strung from the chassis of trucks, or simply in the shadow of their own hats. In all the world it seemed as though only Josh and Dona Michiko had business to attend to.

It didn't take very long, either, for suddenly he was able to inform Dona Michiko they would have money in the bank, real cash within a few days. Leaving her thus, her serenity largely enhanced, he extracted the bathtub from amidst trucks and recumbent forms, and with Jacob Svedelius still beside him, headed for home.

On the way out of town Josh bought a bottle of imported whiskey and one of sherry, "to celebrate our first big breakthrough," he said happily. "By the way"—he grinned, his strong teeth clenched tightly around his cigar—"thanks for playing your part so well."

"Oh, it was nothing."

After the morning's drama it scarcely seemed to Jacob Svedelius that he had only known this person, of whom he'd come to ask advice, for a matter of hours. "I quite enjoyed it. If Piruibi doesn't pay off, I might consider the stage. But are you sure my spending the night on your fazenda won't be a lot of trouble?"

"After all you've done for me?" Josh said expansively. "Just think, because of you, twenty Dutchmen will come over and start a new life growing gladiolus to sell on All Souls' Day. Not to mention the fact that my partners and I can breathe easy for a few days. It's good to feel temporarily rich now and then."

"That it is," Jacob agreed wistfully. "Especially when most of the time one feels temporarily poor." As if he preferred not to dwell on such unpleasantness, he changed the subject.

"Quite astute that partner of yours."

"Oh, he's clever all right," said Josh with a sudden renewed fondness for Teodoro. "I guess it comes from having had to be on his toes from the day he could walk. That and a fertile imagination. Dreams of glory all the time. Right now I guarantee you, he's sitting in that shed of an office of his going over the terms of the contract for the widow and the Dutchman and dreaming of wall-to-wall carpeting while he does it. Too bad," Josh said half to himself, "most of that commission has to go into that bottomless pit of a restaurant we're building . . ."

"Restaurant?" said Jacob.

"Yah." An unexpected tone of depression came into Josh's voice. "It's a long story. And since it's the weekend and you're a forester, wouldn't you rather talk about forests?"

CHAPTER 17

It was late, almost dusk, and as Josh drove home, Lia climbed to the high place, walking with the dogs along the trail that led up through the corn and cane fields to the top pasture, edged by the sheltering grove of eucalyptus trees. It was a long walk and she sat down at last on a knoll to rest and watch the dogs thread back and forth, flushing quail in the deep grass, standing stiff and helpless as the quail escaped them in whistling flight.

Down below her on the fazenda, the *colonos* had hidden their hoes from each other and from the *"patroa"* amidst the coffee trees and were gone. Alone at last, she realized that she had been looking forward to this moment all day; ever since early morning, when the first task had been to puncture a tumor on the leg of a six-month-old calf. She had helped Gardenal do that, sitting on the calf's head and holding his legs, as the old man punctured the tumor with a finely sharpened pocket knife that she knew served equally as well for peeling oranges as for performing minor operations such as this. Later on she'd ridden out to see if the rest of the cattle really were in good shape and if Gardenal really *had* put salt in the salt boxes; because if he hadn't, she knew somehow by the weekend, when Josh checked these things, it would be her fault.

The men had been cultivating the coffee with mules and clearing the weeds from beneath the outspreading branches with their hoes; tough work for lean, wiry, enduring men. She knew them all so well: Marino, thin and slack, yet not *so* slack with his insatiable love for large black women; Berto with his plodding ways and childlike wondering expression; Mingo with his fine Indian features and thinly veiled insolence. Knew them and their ways and their vague underlying resentment at taking orders from a

woman. They should have been used to it by now and she supposed they were. Still, they never would quite get over a sense of
scorn and humiliation that made each order hard to give, and a
reprimand even harder. No wonder by the end of the day she was
relieved to be rid of them, almost exultant to be free at last to
walk alone with the dogs.

Josh sometimes said she'd gotten a little wild since she'd come
to the fazenda . . . wild and elusive like a critter taken to
mountain pastures and abandoned for the summer. He said it was
the result of her climbing to the high place and looking out over
the endless country and imagining herself to be beyond and
above the entire world.

Certainly wildness was not the sensation she felt when she came
here, but rather a sense of peace. As if each time she set off toward
the hilltop with the dogs trailing behind her, she was coming to
the end of a journey she had started on a long time ago. She
wanted to go no farther.

On the fazenda below, there was no beginning, no end, simply
a constant renewal in birth of calves, the ripening of the coffee,
the enriching of the earth. From up here she could look down
upon it all and be at once a part of it and yet detached and at
peace. It was a respite, but not a separation. Separation she
wanted no part of. With every day she found less and less reason
to want to leave the fazenda even for a short time. Her only regret,
and sometimes fear, was that Josh, who had brought her here and
given her all this, still shared so little of it. He had once known
well enough why he had come to this place. But sometimes she
wondered if he still remembered.

She leaned back, resting her head in her hands. Above her, cir-
rus clouds swirled and drifted close to the dome of the sky and
urubus glided, black wings spread against the near transparent
blue. She thought of Josh falling from that great height and remaining alive. "Only Josh," she smiled to herself. Then she
thought of nothing for a while, with her back to the earth and
grass and her eyes on the clouds.

Presently there was a kind of rumpus in the grass beside her and
then Sara, the bitch who had to be watched because of her stray-
ing, sidled up, sighing and snuffling in the peculiar manner of box-
ers, perhaps to tell Lia that she was still here and had not

forgotten herself to run off in pursuit of armadillos, guinea pigs
and numberless creatures that dwelled in the shelter of endless
wooded ravines. She wriggled her stub-tailed body as if to say it
was time to go, and Lia sat up reluctantly.

The sunlight was fading slowly over the hills, turning them
green gold at their heights, casting somber shadows in their hollows. Far out the light reflected glisteningly from distant shallow
lakes where, earlier, buffalo and wild ducks had streaked in to settle amidst the reeds on the water's edge before nightfall. Sara was
right; in a moment it would be dark. Lia rose and started back toward the house, the dogs ahead of her, chasing one another,
crashing in mid-flight, tumbling, springing to their feet and racing
on. Their rushing, tumbling flight was as joyous as their hunting
had been. It seemed to say that they had had enough of solitude
and she supposed she had too. Down below, the house would soon
be busily alive again with the arrival of the children by truck from
school and Josh from Campos, converging as they did each night
upon the world she never left. So she hurried now, knowing there
were things to do.

The children were already there when she reached the house.
She could hear the two boys, Ken and Paul, in their room at the
end of the hall, arguing and throwing things around. In the big
middle room by the fireplace, Christina, the youngest, sat surrounded by bits of paper and cardboard making a poster of some
sort, that said "Nosso saude é nosso alegria."

"Nossa senhora!" Lia laughed, planted a kiss on straw-colored
hair and went on into the kitchen.

There the good smell of woodsmoke and beans and "paio" assured her that the kitchen maid had left the stove lit and things
warming before trailing off down the hill to her home. She thrust
a long branch of eucalyptus wood into the end of the brick and
clay stove to make sure its precious fire stayed alight, and then
went into the house to bathe.

There had been no bathrooms when they had come to the
house but there had been four "alcovas das donzelas." These high-
ceilinged, windowless, chaste cells for virgins had horrified Lia so
that she could scarcely pass their doors after dark. So she had convinced the doubting, dog-faced mason Faria that he could extend

pipes to them from the kitchens and open skylights in the roof to alleviate the prison-like gloom of nearly two centuries.

Now in one of these rooms she turned on the faucets of an old-fashioned bathtub on legs and, in a while, lay soaking luxuriantly in the hot water that came rumbling and gushing from where the pipes coiled like fire-breathing snakes in the kitchen stove. It was good after a day of walking and riding and doing the work of a man, to lather oneself thoroughly with perfumed soap. The hot water glistening on one's breasts and settling over the hollow of one's belly made one feel again like a woman and think vaguely and with pleasure of one's man and the night to come. The alcoves had indeed changed for the better. Surely the poor, suffocating virgins would have approved. She rubbed herself dry before the mirror, thinking, as she did, of this direct, unqualified desire of his and wondering why she could not always match it. Why sometimes Josh's love seemed somehow raw and graceless and left her, rather than satisfied, sad and at a loss over her sadness. She loved Josh and yet she could not describe to herself the way in which she loved him. His very boldness and rawness thrilled her; was what indeed had brought her to his side in the beginning and kept her there ever since. Yet sometimes she wished she could feel something painful and sweeping and devastating. How absurd. She smiled to herself, pulling on a cool sleeveless cotton dress, and slipping her feet into sandals, she stepped out into the hall. A row of deep windows were open to the breeze that smelled ever so slightly of rain. The windows were carved deeply in thick clay walls, whitened with lime, that rose to beams of solid peroba under a roof of tile.

It was good to live in such a house, made of the earth and trees that had surrounded it, its rooms built spacious, high and cool with a sense of the semi-tropical world in which it existed. But for a fireplace to take the chill of Brazilian winter from the walls of the great middle room, she had done scarcely anything to change it. Like the fazenda it seemed eternal to her and made her feel at peace.

She was sitting in the bedroom, brushing her hair, when she heard the familiar, somewhat weary gurgling of the American Bathtub. In the next moment, she was standing at the front door watching Josh and the stranger cross the lawn. They seemed to be loaded down with bottles, and the stranger for some reason was carrying Josh's hat. She frowned slightly and thought, "What's he dug up now?" And then thought again, "But not bad. Very handsome in fact."

"This is Jacob Svedelius," Josh was saying. "He helped us make our first fortune today. We're here to celebrate."

"Good, I love to celebrate." She held out her hand and Jacob shifted the hat to grasp it. "That's my disguise." His gaze was humorous and at the same time politely respectful. "I played the part of the Texas oil man."

"I hope you didn't have to say any lines," she said, noting the sing-song of his talk. "You're Danish, aren't you?"

"Are you a linguist?"

"Ah no, but Danes have a special way. Has no one ever told you?"

"No lines." Josh was ebullient. "Jacob was strictly scenery. Don't you want to hear about it?"

"But of course. Come, give me those bottles and I'll get some ice to go with what's in them. It's already getting chill outside. Josh, why don't you get Paul to make a fire?" So saying, she disappeared into the kitchen, seeing, as she did, that the food was ready and set on the edge of the stove so that the children could have it when they wished. She liked this Dane—he seemed so "straight." She was sure the conversation was going to be good and she didn't want it interrupted by children's hunger pangs.

When she returned with the ice, Paul, the eldest, his lanky, growing body like a half-folded measuring stick, was already crouched over paper and kindling, coaxing them to a blaze, and the dogs had heaped themselves on the rug before the fire in anticipation of the warmth.

Josh went to make the drinks and, because the stranger regarded the shelves of records with such obvious yearning, Lia left the choice of music to him. He put on Brahms' First and Fourth symphonies and set aside a stack of other choices, Bartók, Sibelius, Berlioz, before seating himself in a deep chair opposite Josh.

"Now tell me," said Lia, and laughed richly, spontaneously as they did. Watching her it occurred to Jacob Svedelius that, although greatly amused, she was not particularly surprised by the morning's chain of events, as if they were routine rather than extraordinary, and simply a part of living with this versatile individual who sat now contentedly sipping whiskey, his long legs stretched toward the fire. Yet much as she obviously enjoyed Josh Moran, she seemed neither overwhelmed nor absorbed by his forceful nature. The more Jacob observed her, the more possessed he became with the feeling that, even as they expressed their delight, there was in those clear gray eyes something distant, profoundly discreet that made him think, "Here is someone who lives very much alone and within herself; someone whom perhaps no one really knows."

When the tale was told, he settled back in his chair, listening to the music and looking around him. The house, this room, large and simple and comfortable with its books and music and fireplace, reminded him of the home he had once had and his wife, who had not come with him this time to Brazil—perhaps never would come. It made him feel empty and discouraged and because of this and the fact that he knew the time had come to talk, he began by saying, "You must think it odd, a total stranger coming all the way up the mountain just to ask your advice."

Josh gave a low chuckle. "Malachai can talk anyone into anything. But no, it's not only that. This is a big country, there's so much to do and so little known about anything. God knows everyone's looking for advice. And I'll admit, from the moment you walked into that bear trap this morning, I've been curious. You talked a little about trees on the way here but nothing much about yourself."

"Ah, myself." Jacob looked reluctant, almost as if the subject were a waste of time. "There's not much to tell. Have you ever worked for an international organization?"

"I have," said Josh, "but only long enough to make a couple of down payments."

"Yes." Jacob nodded knowingly. "That, I suppose, is the way to do it. But I didn't. I worked for one for half my life. And so, as you may well know, most of my work is sitting in dusty filing cabinets of UN Agricultural Planning Agencies from here to Guayaquil." He screwed his face up in an imitation of official approval. "'A magnificent plan, Mr. Svedelius. Seems to be just what is needed here.' Then the next day your chief is sent to Italy, your funds are suddenly needed for urban development, a government falls, and vup! into the drawer with you." He gestured wearily. "And that's all."

And so it might have been, except that, even as he dismissed this image with a shrug, the gentle eyes of this stranger became dark with a look of near violent desperation, as if now the thing was begun, there was no more containing it. "Is it any wonder then, that one day a man should say, 'To hell with it,' and decide to take one of those plans and make something of it? Is that so inconceivable?"

The sudden shift of mood in someone apparently so placid, caused Josh to stop and light a cigar, to give himself a moment to think. "Inconceivable? No, I wouldn't say that at all. I only wonder"—he gazed at Jacob through a veritable smoke screen—"why it took you so long."

"Why indeed?" The Dane seemed to have regained his calm once more. "Sometimes one finds oneself in a near impossible dilemma. Do what you want to do and you know you are sacrificing the desires of those you love the most. Have you ever been in such a position?"

Without even looking at Lia, Josh shook his head, so that the Dane felt moved to say, "I can see you've never had to give the idea much thought. Well, at any rate, my children are grown now, nearly old enough to make their own lives. And I?" His smile was sadly ironic. "I've discovered that my old longing still persists, if anything it is even greater. So here I am. A mad Dane who wants nothing so much as to plant *teke* trees in a Brazilian forest."

"So the thing now," said Josh, sensing that there was more to the story but that Jacob Svedelius really was reluctant to tell it, "is to get down to the practicalities. It occurs to me that nobody here knows much about teke. Have you tried planting it yet? What about disease, ants?"

"Ants?" Jacob said defensively, as though he'd heard this question before. "The worst enemy eucalyptus has is ants and it doesn't stop anyone from planting it—"

"In open country," said Josh, "not in the midst of virgin forest. They could devastate a plantation overnight."

As this discouraging interchange began, Lia rose to change the records, renew drinks, call the children to take their supper from the back of the stove. Amidst all these activities, she could hear snatches of conversation that seemed destined to cause Jacob Svedelius to pack up and flee back to Denmark, where there were no such questions to be asked or answered. But still they went on about leaf-cutting ants, limb-sawing beetles, caterpillars, diseases of the jungle and the people of the coastal mountains, who, caught between the mountains and the sea, were more primitive and backward than any bugre in Mato Grosso.

"Oh, come on." She shot Josh a look as she settled in her chair once again, tucking her feet beneath her. "Josh, you act as though you never did anything implausible in your life. There must be something in this for Jacob, if not a fortune, a life." She turned to the Dane. "Tell me, what is it like to live in the Serras do Mar? Quite romantic, I should think."

"Now I see where feasibility ends in this family." In spite of the irony, Jacob's smile held a certain gratitude. "What's it like? Rather buggy to tell the truth. But once I get *that* controlled . . . Have you ever seen one of those old sugarcane fazendas?"

"One or two, they put me to mind of self-contained worlds."

"Ah, so they were once. But now, do you really want to hear?"

"But, of course. What do you think?"

"Well," said Jacob, "the self-contained world only lasted an instant, it seems. But the house still stands there, halfway up the mountain. It's rather like this one, really, only more grandiose and more ruined. There is a balcony that seems to be suspended, held by vines and lianas, above the treetops. From it you can look out over the bay and Piruibi, which is nothing but a fishing village and so, very beautiful. There are islands in the bay, very splendid at sunset—" As he went on, warming to his subject, it seemed to Lia she had never heard a voice quite so enchanting, so musical. She could see with him the house, the great valleys behind it with their ruined sugarcane fields. The jungle below it, with its myriad green mansions beneath the trees, bound by tangled root and threading vine, descending step by step toward the tumbled rock, the white-sanded coves and the sea. He would have gone on and she could have listened longer, for she loved to hear talk of such things, but the talk was presently interrupted by a snore.

Josh had scrunched himself down in his chair in a position very familiar to Lia, arms above his head, long legs dangling over the end of the hassock in a state of total relaxation. At the sound and sight, so unromantic in the midst of this enchanting description, Lia couldn't help laughing. "It's nothing to do with you, Jacob. It's the long drive every day. I forget how tiring it is myself because I do it so seldom."

"Josh"—she gave him a cautious poke—"how about some supper?"

Like the children, they helped themselves from the stove and brought their plates in by the fire and the talk began again. But this time it was of terracing the mountains, planting *cacau* in the lowlands, and higher up, spices and citrus. Of buffalo in the valleys, and a sawmill and the art of getting loans from banks. And the more they talked, the more Josh, who had started out the evening as a thorough skeptic, became excited, throwing in suggestion after suggestion as to how to make this plan of Jacob Svedelius work.

Lia fell silent, watching the men as they talked, thinking how different, despite the adventurousness that united them, they were one from the other. There was Josh, alert and sharp, so quick to seize an opportunity, "Be it to dress a stranger as a Texan"—she smiled again as she thought of it—"or grab a quick nap in the midst of a conversation." A moment after his snoring, hadn't he been fully awake, alive, his look bright and perceptive? His very features seemed to have been carved by this alertness into the hard clean lines that could be warmed, but never softened, even by the laughter in his eyes.

The Dane's features, too, seemed unerodible, but where Josh's had been fashioned by the chance of his breeding—hybrid vigor they called it in cattle—the Dane's seemed to have been fashioned over centuries with infinite care. "Civilized," she found herself thinking, "he is of the people who, while others waged their battles and killed and pillaged, stayed at home and grew and became civilized. And what good will that do him, in this crude world into which he has ultimately plunged himself?"

From the height of his enthusiasm, Lia heard Josh now descend once more toward earth and cold reality. "It can be done," he was saying, "I'm not saying it can't. Every step is logical and possible.

I'd be tempted to do it myself if I had a fortune to spend, but that's where the trouble always lies. Isn't it?"

"Oh, once I get the sawmill going," said Jacob, "and the charcoal kilns—"

"Not enough." Josh shook his head, unimpressed. "Too slow. You need something on the side, something that doesn't cost much and can give you a quick turnover . . . like, down around those beaches . . . ever think of, say, boat tours or something?"

"Boat tours?" Jacob Svedelius laughed aloud, as if the idea were too outrageous. "I?" But his look had become stubborn suddenly, as a recalcitrant child's. "No, no thank you, nothing on the side. I've spent half my life at that."

"And I too." Josh sounded peeved, irritated at last by this person who had come to ask advice but wouldn't face a simple fact. "But I've never been able to find out how else to pay the bills. Maybe you don't realize it, but in this world, producing things people really need is a damn stinking luxury. You've got to make yourself a bloody millionaire to do it. Ever think of that?"

"Maybe so," Jacob Svedelius said doggedly, his expression unchanged. "And no doubt I shall ruin myself financially. But—" He paused, and then said in a quieter tone, "Let me put it this way. May I ask how old you are?"

"Thirty-six," said Josh.

"Yes." Jacob nodded thoughtfully. "That's what I imagined. Well, I am ten years older than that. The time rushes by, and suddenly you realize you've already divided it too much. There's not enough left. Do you see?"

For a while neither said anything, each in his own way feeling thwarted by a truth, perhaps insoluble, that had invaded their dreaming. When Josh spoke again, as if to make up for his bluntness, he became, in the way of his that Lia knew so well, expansive, generous. "I've just the grass for those lowlands. When you're ready for it, come and get a truckload.

"And look, when your wife finally gets here, if there's anything we can do—"

"If my wife *ever* gets here." The look of reluctance crossed Jacob's face once again. "You see, she's never quite changed her mind either. I think of Denmark as an old people's home. She doesn't."

"Oh, but surely," Josh began unbelievingly.

"Surely," Jacob said shortly, "that's what one would think, wouldn't one?"

It was well past midnight when Lia showed Jacob Svedelius to his room. It was in the old slave quarter, shaded by a grove of slash pines, that she and João Faria had converted into a guest house. When she bid him good night and left him, she didn't go into the house immediately, but stayed awhile, sitting with her back to one of the trees.

It was the time of night when even the crickets cease to sing and but for the occasional sharp cry of an owl, there is nothing but stillness. Though it was late and the day had been long, she felt no desire to sleep. She wasn't sure why, exactly, but the presence of Jacob Svedelius and the evening's conversation had disturbed and set her thinking. Now, as she sat with her back to the solid tree trunk, with nothing to do and no one to bother her, she realized that most of the evening she had been irritated at Josh for his insistence on practicality. At times it had seemed as though he were playing some game of putting up obstacles to the Dane's every intention. But then, of course, he wasn't. It was only that the Dane had come to ask advice and Josh had tried to give it. "You've got to be a bloody millionaire—" An exaggeration, but not so great a one. Then why had Jacob Svedelius' response been so chilling? "Time rushes by and suddenly you realize you've divided it too much."

Ah, but this Jacob, who was he to say or to frighten anyone? How could a man spend half a lifetime deliberating and then make such a desperate move? And this, regardless of whether in the end his wife should decide to join him or not. How strange, indeed, that two people could live together for years, raise their children, share a life and all the while be growing apart; so that whether she came to join him or not was of less importance than his remaining in his place on the mountainside. How could they have known each other so well and yet so little? It made Lia feel ill somehow to think of the way he spoke of her, with a kind of tender regret, as if something good was gone and there was no recovering it.

Ah, but what did she, Lia, care? What did it have to do with her? Thank God she and Josh had always thought the same way, wanted the same thing: this land.

Suddenly she felt chilled and very tired. Rising, she crossed the lawn and entered the house. In their room, Josh lay sleeping, his lean muscular frame at rest beneath the covers, breathing deeply. With the look of sleep upon him, he appeared boyish and oddly defenseless. The sight of him gave her a tremendous desire to kiss the white lines in the deep tan of his face that spread clownishly from the corners of his eyes. But she thought better of it, and, undressing by moonlight, climbed stealthily into bed.

She didn't want to awaken him, not tonight. She simply wanted to lie in the safety of his nearness, yet alone with her thoughts until one by one she had reasoned them out, dissolved her strange sense of inquietude into nothing.

CHAPTER 18

Jacob Svedelius went away early the next morning, promising to
return for a truckload of pigs and precious *braquiaria* grass to plant
in the long narrow valleys where, in another century, the slaves of
the Senhores dos Engenhos had planted sugarcane. The journey
on a series of buses beginning in São João da Barra would take a
day, crossing the Piritininga highlands and descending the winding road down the mountains. At São Sebastião, his truck would
be waiting for another two-hour journey over the rutted trail to
Piruibi. "One's got to be a stoic," Josh said, shaking his head as
he and Lia turned and walked back from the bus station to the
car. Lia smiled, said nothing and was glad he was gone.

It was not, she told herself as they drove back to the fazenda,
that she had not enjoyed his company. Obviously Malachai had
sent him for their entertainment, thinking to himself, "Here is
another rare bird to add to that host of dreamers who turn
up periodically at the fazenda to trade their wild schemes." Malachai liked variety in his observation of humanity and certainly, lying in a hammock slung from the veranda at São Sebastião,
talking to this obsessed Dane, he had thought to himself, "I will
send him to Josh and that way, one day we will meet again at the
fazenda and talk of many things."

Well, they had been entertained, recognizing in the straightforward and gentle person someone who, whatever it cost him,
must have command over his own life. In this they felt akin to him,
drawn closer still by his capacity for laughter—at the Dutchman,
at himself, at all the odd little quirks in this Brazilian world of
which they had become a part, that would drive a humorless man
insane, but that for them, made life so pleasurable.

Malachai was right to have sent him. Still, now he was gone, she felt somehow better, safer from the thought, never before expressed, that had come so easily from the stranger's lips. "Time rushes by." Forget it, it was the stranger's thought, not hers. And good riddance. To have spent the day with Jacob Svedelius and his unsolvable riddle would have been tiresome. She liked people and talk, but sometimes she needed more than anything to have Josh here alone, for two days, uninterrupted by eternal arrivals and departures.

"Want to go riding?" said Josh as he pulled the car into the shed beneath the trees.

She could hardly believe herself as she said, "No. I was out all morning yesterday. I'll go with you tomorrow."

"But yesterday you were alone."

"So, *you* go alone today."

He didn't ask her again. Josh was never one to beg. "All right, have some coffee for me when I get back."

He left the car and walked over to the coxeira, where Gardenal had left his horse Guaraná saddled and ready for him. The horse was a *manga larga*, a big-boned cattle horse with a swift running gait and apparently unlimited stamina. A *"Santo Cavalo,"* Gardenal called him, because in the midst of a milling herd of cattle he performed his duty as if the rider's brain were his own. Now, as he paced briskly toward the herd of young bulls beyond the ravine, there was no need to guide him, so sure was he of the way. Josh could allow his mind to wander and think of other things.

Of Lia, and why, when he suggested Jacob Svedelius spend the weekend, she had suddenly been so vehement— "No, for Christ's sake, for once let's just be by ourselves." But then when he'd asked her to go riding . . . She was a moody one, she always had been. Always been a little inexplicable to him too; one who came out and said what she thought, but so seldom told what, deep inside herself, she was thinking. The moods passed quickly though, else Lia would never have gotten through all the strange experiences of all these strange years.

Thinking of this, it occurred to him that, like anyone, probably what she needed was a change of scenery. Himself being on the move all the time, after all, he forgot how much Lia stayed in one place. Everyone else came and went and here she remained. Indeed, when he saw her in his mind it was seldom in any way except against the setting of these surrounding hills. Maybe she really didn't know what was getting into her, but he did. As suddenly as this occurred to him, he made a decision. He'd take her to Rio for a couple of days. Of course, if he had to foot the bill himself, he couldn't do it, but Harry'd been asking him for the Institute. Something about this University to University Program that was gradually squeezing them out. If he could be of help to the Institute and swing *per diem* at the same time . . . The wheels turned rapidly in Josh's mind; things began to fall into place. He felt immediately better. The thing was, he loved Lia so very much. When things weren't right with her, they really weren't right with anything— But there was nothing like Rio for curing one's melancholy. They'd take a trolley up to Santa Teresa, swim, go dancing, drive up into the mountains.

Guaraná was climbing the steep bank on the other side of the ravine. As his hooves dug into the rough, steep ascent, Josh's mind —suddenly at peace—began to move on to other things, to take in the day and the world around him. The ravine that divided his land in half was deep and shadowy and banked by trees; white fig and tall, spreading cedars, and yellow-flowering acacias whose upper branches were bound with vines that formed an arch over the ravine from one side to the other. Countless springs poured into its depths from between the roots of the trees and flowed into a pond that Josh had dug the first year in the heat of summer. From the pond now, whisps of mist rose thinly and dispersed in sunlight, the higher Josh and his horse climbed. The dogs were trailing along as they always did, flushing quail and never catching them. As he watched, he noted with satisfaction that they often were lost from sight in the depth of the grass. A year ago that would not have been so. But the grasses he and the men and his own boys had planted in the contour ditches were gradually creeping out, taking hold, covering even the barest spots on the steep hillside, where before nothing but broom grass and goatsbeard had grown. In another year the land would support half again as many cattle as it did now.

It was a slow process and a hard one and there never seemed to be enough money to do everything you wanted to do. He knew what he'd been saying to Jacob Svedelius last night. It was one of those ironies that in this starving world where people needed more than anything, food, good farming had become a luxury. Even here.

Once, long ago, he had told himself, "One day I shall live entirely from the land." Later on something had told him that such was a remarkable and splendid goal, but that if he ever wanted to work land of his own, he'd better not wait to buy it until he thought he could make a living from it. Now he often wondered if he would ever reach that moment when he could say to himself, "I am a farmer and nothing else."

Who, in fact, had done it? The Japanese with their mud huts and television sets and excursions to Japan every year. Or Lunardelli, who could neither read nor write but had made a fortune tilling the land like a glorified Indian, burning off the best forests, wearing out the best soils and moving on. Josh could imagine neither Lia nor himself living in a mud hut. And, unlike Lunardelli, he knew how to read and write and consequently enjoyed all the wonders those abilities conferred. He couldn't see doing without them. Or without music, good food, drink . . .

So it would take that much longer to reach the goal he'd set himself. But in the meantime, the fazenda was here, becoming richer and more orderly and thus more beautiful every day. And when he looked down, as he did now, to where the young bulls stood flank to flank with their heads in the salt box, thrusting each other aside with sturdy horns and powerful necks, he couldn't help but feel that this was right and that although he spent two thirds of his life scrambling to get the money, it had not been a waste of time.

Near the salt box, Josh pulled Guaraná to a halt and sat looking over the bulls, studying the depth of their flanks, straightness of their backs, the broadness of their quarters. Some of their coats looked a bit rough to him for this time of year; perhaps they needed another worming. One of them, a runty dog of an animal that had been set back by a bout with hoof-and-mouth disease, was still, after months, favoring a swollen, sore hoof. He'd never do and he was spoiling the looks of the herd. Josh made a mental note to have him castrated and fattened for the household.

Hearing the tread of horse hooves, he looked up to see Gardenal approaching on Paul's horse, Estrela. Josh knew that, for Gardenal, there was only one "Santo Cavalo," the one Josh was sitting on, and so when the *padrão* was here, Gardenal always rode with a certain air of suffering that could be discerned even from a distance. Still, though he was old, he rode erect in the saddle like a young man, his whip hand straight at his side. Since they had come to the fazenda no one had worked with the cattle except this old Italian. His mind was a portable filing cabinet for every creature born on the land. He was quite fearless and it seemed to Josh, he'd already lived more than his quota of lives before the gouging horns and trampling hooves of ornery cows. There was no teaching him to be careful. He was stubborn and had his own ideas—born of centuries of ignorance—as to how things should be done. He was extremely crafty too, about covering his misdemeanors and getting around Josh's orders in general. And yet Josh valued him above most men with whom he worked. For quite simply he loved his profession and performed it with pride.

The good thing about loving one's work was that it did away with the fear that haunts so many men that one may be doing too much of it. It gave Gardenal, he knew, a natural dignity that could not be destroyed. As the herder drew near, Josh observed his thin, sharp northern Italian features. The blue eyes were still piercing, but there was a pattern of thin veins across his cheeks, about his nose, that made Josh think, "He's getting old. He'll have to leave soon, the job's too dangerous." And he regretted the thought of how age would come upon him once he was out of the saddle for good. Old riders got thin and died, just like old horses that were no longer ridden.

"We're going to have to cut number forty-four," he said to Gardenal now. "He's no good for anything."

"It's true," the old Italian said regretfully. "Sometimes things just don't heal. Look how I treated him every day."

"Even taking him into the coffee and blessing him with herbs?"

"I? Whoever said?" Gardenal's look was one of outraged innocence.

Josh didn't answer. He wasn't going to say who said. He just wanted Gardenal to know he knew. "Any cows bagging up?"

Gardenal's forehead became a mass of furrows, the portable filing cabinet working furiously away from the subject of unsuccessful acts of witchcraft to secure territory of dates and numbers. "Twenty-two, *puta merda*, remember the monster of a calf she gave last year? Then there's thirteen, bred two days after the death of my wife, and sixteen, three days before—"

"*Ta bom, 'ta bom.*" Josh raised his hand in protest, realizing this recital could go on forever. "Best we bring them all in and have a look."

"*Sim, Senhor, Seu Josh.*" Nudging his horse into action, Gardenal headed him along the ridge on the hill. As his horse broke into a canter and the rider swayed easier with his every turn, Gardenal looked to Josh no older, perhaps even younger than himself.

"Maybe another year," thought Josh. It was funny about men and animals and age.

When he returned to the house at last, Lia was out in the garden cutting flowers: great armsful of geraniums for the wooden *gamela* that stood beside Josh's chair, gaudy bright hibiscus for the stone vase on the mantel, purple and yellow sprays of buddleia and jasmine that hung from the posts of the veranda. She had all the vases lined up on the wall and with an air of concentration was walking back and forth from bush to flower bed to wall. She liked to walk and he liked to watch her. Her legs were strong and well shaped, tapering in at the ankles and again inside the thighs, where so many women's legs continued on with an elephantine lack of grace. Her hips moved rhythmically, as if somewhere, probably in her head, there was some music.

He came and sat on the wall and when she came near, caught her by the bottom of her shorts and drew her near. Her eyes were smiling now, the troubled look gone out of them, swept away no doubt by the sight of the flowers, the clear day, the warm sun on her back. He had been going to ask her why she hadn't wanted to come riding with him, but he decided not to. Whatever had been bothering her was gone. Let it stay gone.

"Let's take the kids to the river," she was saying. "I don't want to eat lunch in the house."

It was amazing how Lia could emanate the most profound gloom at one moment and irresistible enthusiasm the next.

"All right," he said, and did allow, "what're *you* so happy about all of a sudden?"

She frowned. "Do I have to be happy *about* something?"

While she was packing things into the truck, he took care of the payroll, watching her parade back and forth with baskets of potato salad, seasoned meat, bread, oranges, bathing suits, while the men filed up and, with stiffly gnarled fingers, grasped the pen and slowly, laboriously designed their names. He too was beginning to be very glad that once the *camaradas* were gone, there would be no one else . . . nothing and no one but themselves and the children.

It was only in the evening, when they had returned from their day by the river, that Josh brought up the subject of a trip to Rio. They had had a good day, diving and wrestling with the children in the deep swirling waters of the river. Later on, while the children still swam, they had played their old game of drawing maps in the sand. Only this time, instead of Australia, Africa, Brazil, the maps were of the land across the river, or a wild area in the Serras de Bodequena, Mato Grosso, where they would plant wheat and soya beans or raise cattle on *colonião* grass planted amidst the stumps of fallen trees.

It was a game that Lia played with an almost childish eagerness, her entire being warmed and elated by thoughts of rich, wild lands tamed and civilized under their hands. Her zeal at these moments made her seem very close to Josh, as if they thought and lived and breathed with all the same intent. They did, of course. But the nearness and warmth of her at such moments made him wonder all the more if she realized how remote the achievement of all these plans they were making still was for them. So that sometimes he felt, even in the midst of their elation, a sense of deception, a thorn jabbing, that said, "You should set her straight." But then, because he hated to destroy this wonderful mood, he would quieten himself with the thought, "Why should I? She must know." And they would go on, laughing and talking and dreaming and making designs in the sand.

The mood remained with them, even after they returned home to sit that night with the children and dogs by a fire that took the chill out of the winter air and made them feel comfortable and safe and at peace. It was then that Josh looked up from his book with an air of sudden inspiration. "What about a few days in Rio?"

"Rio, now?" The suggestion in the midst of their still lingering afternoon's contentment seemed oddly incongruous to Lia.

Josh sensed this, but, remembering his thoughts of the morning, he went on temptingly, "A little sun and sea, *moquecas* at the Oxalá. I won't be paying," he added helpfully.

"Who will?" She looked vaguely suspicious.

Josh's eyes caught hers. He stared her down mischievously. "The Institute. A little public relations work for Harry. You wouldn't begrudge him a favor, would you?"

"They're paying for you. Who's going to pay for me?"

"Lia, how many square meters of land do you think I'll buy with a ticket to Rio?"

"That's one way of looking at it."

"*My* way." His look became playfully stubborn.

"And the children?"

"Gardenal will stay with them."

She thought of the old man, very much alone since the death of his endlessly talking wife, who loved nothing so much as to sit over a beer and gossip with the children. She knew it was true, they would be perfectly safe with him. It wasn't that. It was something else, a certain scary feeling she couldn't quite put her finger on. "We always seem to have our cake and eat it too. Going to Rio seems so extravagant, so careless."

"So? If we can do it, why not? Is there something wrong with taking a break now and then? I'll have João Faria make you a cross and you can carry it along on your back if it makes you feel any better."

"Oh, you damned maniac." She laughed and felt ridiculous and at the same time suddenly eager to go. Rio, beautiful and thoroughly irresponsible, was a place for breaks, and even the things and places one loved best needed to be left behind from time to time.

CHAPTER 19

So now she sat, with a slight but not unfamiliar sensation of having been kidnapped, by the edge of the pool of the Hotel Gloria. The sun's rays shining through *tipuana* trees that grew out of mountain rock, cast a speckled light on the pool's surface and spread across the flagstone terrace, deserted but for a *babá* and a host of children making fountains in the children's pool, and Caroline Roundtree, who sat on a barstool practicing on her guitar.

After an animated telephone conversation with Campos on Monday morning, Duncan Roundtree, vice-president and sole representative of International Bankers Corporation in South America, had advised his assistant that there was pressing business to be done in Rio and in the company of his wife had taken the Ponte Aérea.

Lia was delighted that Caroline was here. This mercurial young woman was the best, the most enduring female company she knew. When she stopped to analyze the reasons, it was difficult at first to say why. Caroline's intensity was electric, a taut wire carrying a constant stream of messages at 220 voltage to be received with a jolt by the 110 complacency of ordinary folk. Her ego, her desire to achieve and be recognized for it, could turn anything, even a vegetable garden, into an obsession. She was quick: to like, to dislike, take offense, dare. She was also quick to laugh, to give, listen and respond. Of all these qualities, Lia guessed what made her company so enduring was the last two. For how many people were capable of keeping up a two-sided conversation? Some listened with pathetic self-effacement until the *self* was effaced altogether. Others listened and waited again to listen only to themselves. Caroline wanted to know as much as she wanted to tell what she knew. A remarkable quality, especially in one of large ego.

Her obsession at the moment was the guitar, and like so many things with Caroline, it did not come easily. Perhaps her very desire for perfection made it take hours of grimly determined practice to achieve what some street urchin born with the samba in his blood might accomplish with a devastating carelessness . . . Not that even the street urchin could go all the way on carelessness. Caroline's teacher could tell you that. It was just that some had an understanding of the music and a determination to play it. And some had the very music inside them to start with. Caroline had the first two, her teacher had all three, and together they had come remarkably far. So that as she sat on her stool playing and singing *candeias*, the words made oddly more touching by the midwestern Portuguese, Lia could listen with a wonderful, unmindful pleasure. She was enjoying herself and thinking vaguely and gladly, "Caroline's going to do it again."

What she didn't realize was that, as she sat on her stool with her funny look of concentration, Caroline was at this moment thinking less of the music than of the teacher.

Delia had been true to her word that night at the Jogral and when it was time for the janitors and clerks with their cavaquinhos and Sr. Assis with his flute to return to the bandstand, she had signaled to the guitarist to meet them outside, where they could talk and be heard.

He was a student of music at the university, presently on leave due to financial difficulties. Delia introduced him as Dorval. In the pale light of the streetlamp, the sharpness of his features and the dark eyes glowing in the deep hollows of his skull, gave him the look of having a perpetual fever. Those eyes, Caroline noted, regarded Delia Cavalcanti with a look of adoration that suggested goddess worship. When she spoke and explained to him that she had a master's degree in music and therefore would like to start on the guitar without first trying "Jingle Bells," he had smiled with shy amusement and declared that to be a relief. Still, his eyes had remained on Delia, so that Caroline had thought, "I hope the hell I'm not going to be a victim." Nevertheless, later on she had been forced to think ashamedly, "I should have known Delia better. For the boy was a true musician."

He came to Caroline's house promptly at four every Thursday afternoon. No "Jingle Bells." They began immediately with the music of Jobim, Caymmi, Edu Lobo, Chico Buarque. They listened to recordings and, because there was no written music available, picked out the arrangements on their own. Driven by Caroline's incredible resolve, the forty-five minutes sometimes ended in triumphant exhaustion, sometimes unspeakable frustration, but never despair. Whenever Dorval arrived for the Thursday lesson, indeed, it was with a new eagerness, because he found himself discovering things about this music that he had never been aware of. So much so that at times he was forced to remind himself that it was he who was the teacher and this strange, vital young American woman who was the pupil.

Caroline, then, was grateful to Delia and felt fortunate indeed to have discovered such a teacher. But it was for this very reason that at times she felt herself seized with a panic, a despair that seemed to be born of something within herself which had come at other places and other times to destroy the peace of an afternoon.

At first she had attributed to shyness his rather annoying manner of averting his eyes when he spoke to her. After all, unless the profession was prostitution, men were so bad at dealing with women professionally in this country. "I shall be straightforward and, at the same time, very proper and it will pass," she'd told herself. But it hadn't. Still even *that* she could have accepted if, on other occasions when it would have been natural for him to be listening—just listening—she had not looked up to find him watching her: the dark eyes burning with a melancholy intensity.

The look was far from unfamiliar. There was something about Caroline—a nicely proportioned roundness of limb that, combined with the natural warm glow of her super vitality, aroused in men all kinds of disturbing feelings. Sometimes the effect was simply stimulating and amusing and therefore good. Sometimes it was upsetting and therefore destructive. The young man who watched her covertly now was not amused. He seemed, if anything, to be suffering some sort of agony. Whatever the cause—conscience or lack of resolve—it caused Caroline's mind to wander, the chords she had so carefully mastered to be forgotten, stumbled over . . . At length, when her straightforward mind saw no way but to cut through to the heart of things, when it was perfectly obvious that the aesthetic rapport of earlier times was being shot to hell by this staring, she stopped one day in mid-song, put her hand over her guitar for silence, and said, "*Que passa?* Something is bothering you. It is beginning to bother me."

His reaction was instant, melodramatic. He drew himself up, those dark, brilliant eyes stared at the floor, "If Senhora is not satisfied—" Caroline had seen servants whisk off their aprons and stomp out in such a fashion because one had been betrayed by a husband, or another thought herself to be pregnant. Because she valued this splendid teacher more than a servant, and because the situation had become desperate, she said as much.

"Oh, come now, that's what a dumb *empregado* would say."

His response this time was an embarrassed smile of acquiescence and despondency.

"*Esta bom, Dona Carolina.*" He took a cigarette from his pocket, lit it and let the smoke out with a sigh, every action exemplifying, as it had never done before, youthful dramaticism. "It is something I should have told you in the very beginning, but hadn't the courage, I suppose. You see, my absence from the university is not entirely due to financial problems. I have been involved in certain political activities." He drew in on his cigarette and looked at her directly for the first time, searching for reaction. "I am listed as a subversive and am on a kind of probation."

"What?" Caroline laughed aloud with relief. "Is *that* all? You must be kidding."

"It is more serious than I think you realize." His tone was still incredibly grave and now just slightly offended. "I was an agitator, so to speak. My job was to talk to factory workers, act as a kind of link between them and the student." His expression became one of disgust. "I am not involved anymore. It was not what I expected it to be. Still, the connection. It might not be good. It could even be dangerous."

"Dangerous? In what way?"

"Ah." He waved his hands and shook his head as if he were pursued by fantasies and half-truths and was weary of them. "I wish I could say, I can't, truly. I only know"—he became at last subdued and apologetic—"I should have told you. It wasn't fair. But I needed the job—" He stood up, and now having explained his impossible situation, seemed bent upon leaving. But she stood squarely in front of him, her small, neat figure blocking the way with irrefutable determination.

"You needed the job and you have it." She placed her hands in the pockets of her skirt and faced him with all the incredible intensity of her clear blue gaze. "The night Dona Delia introduced me to you we had just had an argument. It came to nothing, as arguments often do with Dona Delia, because I was never allowed to get my point across. But what I was going to say to her then, I will say now to you. I think a person who allows politics to destroy his profession is disloyal not only to his profession, but to himself. Your profession is music. So is mine. That is why you are here. Your time is precious to me because I think you are a fine musician who has something to teach me. Oh, I'm glad you told me what was bothering you, if that was necessary. But listen—I want you to understand that in this room, during this lesson, anything but music, including politics, is just one big waste of time. *Agora, vamos tocar?*" Then because she thought to herself, "You're behaving like Caroline at her most imperious," she gave him her broadest, most enlivening smile.

And that, she thought, was that. Only it wasn't. Because suddenly this musician who was such a fine teacher became a person whom she did not forget promptly at four forty-five every Thursday, and about whom she found herself at odd moments of the day, thinking and wondering.

"Duncan, what do you think about Dorval's having been involved with the MRP?"

"Who's Dorval?"

"My guitar teacher, dammit."

"Oh, him. Just as long as he doesn't subvert your guitar. I haven't even made the last payment."

"Go to hell!"

At length she found herself watching *him*; the sharp sensitive features, the melancholy look that seemed to hover perpetually beneath the surface of every smile, just as sadness lay beneath the laughter of every song.

> Light the candle,
> It's already a profession,

When there is no samba
Then there's disillusion . . .

Until one day she couldn't resist saying, "There's always this underlying sadness."

He struck a derisive, discordant twang on his guitar. "There's much to be sad about."

"You are from the Nordeste, aren't you?"

"*Nordestino puro.*" He smiled proudly now, and put down his guitar. "It's a race. Did you ever read Euclides da Cunha? Indian, Negro and white man in exact proportions always fighting for dominance—Never at rest, never at ease—"

"It's another world, isn't it, from this one?"

"Ah, it is all the music tells you it is. Year after year . . . the drought comes and the people go hungry and they invade the cities. Then the road gangs are organized to keep them alive. Or they climb aboard trucks and flee to the south. Then the rains come and they all hurry back to their land, full of hope. But once the rains begin they don't stop. Every year. Many die, but there are always more born. If one thinks too much, one becomes desperate. Especially"—he gesticulated toward the window and the view, through its iron grillwork, of a shaded street and the solid white walls of large, splendid houses amidst the rich foliage of gardens—"when here everything seems so easy."

"You can't order the rain, can you?" said Caroline, following his eyes as they took in the walls, the greenery and the opulence that they implied.

"No"—he shook his head regretfully—"but sometimes you have a terrible desire, and worse than that, an envy."

"I see," she said.

"No," he answered, "it is too difficult. You only *begin* to see."

And so the conversation grew. About endless beaches and sand so dazzlingly white that the fishermen became blind; about candomblé, and the duel of the feet and knives, *capoeira*, done to the haunting strummings of a *berimbau*. About the jangadeiros, who braved the sea with a raft and a sail. And the cowboy who dressed from head to foot in leather against the thorn trees of a hostile *sertão*, and kept his energy like a dormant seed for the moment when he would need it all to survive.

"The fight is all inside him, waiting. Ever hear of the War of Canudos? A handful of beggars and bandits against the Brazilian Army."

"Baianos? But they are so happy."

"They take life as it is. They sing so as not to think, but the thinking comes out in the singing."

All very informative, very instructive. It helped tremendously to understand the music, so the time was not really wasted. And certainly, it was better than that other, silent watching. But just lately, he had begun the watching again, and now, somehow, those dark, brilliant eyes seemed more haunting than ever.

On the terrace by the pool "Corcovado" began with a soft contagious rhythm that caused Lia to close her eyes and smile, tapping with her fingers on the arm of her chair. Then it stumbled and came to a halt.

Lia sat up straight. "Hey, what's going on? That was so great, what'd you stop for?"

"*Bronng.*" The guitar came down heavily, bumping against the stool. Caroline got down, stood for a moment, a picture of desolation, and then came over and sank glumly into a chair beside her friend.

"I'm fed up. Just goddamn fed up, that's all."

"But why, what about? I don't see it, when everything's going so well."

"Going well? Don't jump to conclusions. You *think* it's all going so well, but you don't *know* how complicated, how goddamn complicated a simple guitar lesson can *be.*"

Lia looked sidewise at her friend and considered. She had a mercurial temper of her own, but somehow it seldom came to grips with Caroline's. She often marveled at how they could talk of everything, diverge so often and yet never explode at one another. Sometimes it occurred to her that this was because they treated each other with the restraint of lunatics who bore respect for the truth and sanity that lay beneath their ravings. "I can't know," she said, "if I haven't been told."

And so the story poured forth and Lia listened, fascinated and wondering herself, until, unable to resist smiling, at length she said, "But aren't you the one who said teaching and learning should be pure?"

"All right." Caroline had a habit of smoking small cigars. She took one, a Schimmelpenninck, and lit it. "So finally one has to admit that it's difficult to draw a line. The things he's told me, there's been so much learning in them. That, oh, that part, heaven knows, is okay. Fine. It's the other thing." Her voice rose sharply above traffic noises muffled in the sultry Rio air. "Don't you see? I started talking to him because I was sick of his staring holes through me. And now it's started again, the watching!"

"Maybe he's planning to kidnap you."

"Shit. What is it, Lia? What gives these guys this goddamn idea? The conductor in Columbus, the art director of that museum I worked in. It's not as if I gave them the old sex play. I can do that when I want to, but there are times when you don't want to."

Lia would have laughed again, but she saw tears rising to the surface, genuine tears of frustration. So she tried to keep serious. "Partially I think it has to do with bone structure. Your eyes, Caroline, somehow when you look straight at someone, they send messages you're not even thinking of. If they were just a little closer together—"

"You make me sound like a Mongolian idiot."

"Maybe you should try acting like one. Oh hell, Caroline, my advice to you is to put that will of yours to work and ignore the watching. After all, he's not going to suddenly throw aside your guitar and dwaang!"

Now they both laughed. It was impossible not to. It all seemed suddenly so ridiculous, here in the dappled sunlight that shone on the pool.

"How did you get here anyway?" Lia asked. "I really only half expected you."

"That's one of the glories of having one's bosses six thousand miles away." Caroline, in a good humor now, blew an artful smoke ring. "You can take the pulse of Rio de Janeiro without having to file a requisition. Really though"—without realizing it, she had lowered her voice—"Duncan's got a very interesting deal cooking. A big irrigation project in the Northeast, the valley of the São Francisco. There's a Brazilian outfit about to invest and Duncan wants the bank to buy in."

"The valley of the São Francisco?" Surprise and the slightest touch of envy came into Lia's voice. "One of Josh's pet dreams: growing melons, grapes, figs—turning the *sertão* green." She frowned. "But isn't that a little 'far out' for International Bankers?"

"Way out. Whoever heard of irrigation, much less the São Francisco River in that mausoleum? Let's just hope Duncan can swing the deal before they find out what he's up to." She stamped out the stub of her Schimmelpenninck. "Let's take a swim?"

And before Lia could answer, as if to exemplify her impatience with life in general, Caroline was on her feet, her restless, energetic body arching into a dive.

CHAPTER 20

Duncan *was* excited. He'd had a long lunch with an extremely interesting young man named Ricardo Soares. It had been one of a
series of meetings over lunch in the city and weekends with Caroline and the children on the Soares fazenda, that looked as though
they would culminate with International Bankers buying into the
Soares family firm.

It was a new firm, built up over the last thirty years. Its very
age gave cause for suspicious head waggings amidst certain vener-
able financial circles; the same circles, Duncan was ironically
aware, that used the weighty aura of tradition as a cover for
senility and general decay. Duncan was not impressed by *that*
kind of tradition and not frightened by the Soares Bank's youth.
He had watched its activities for a long time, even before he had
thought of putting out feelers for International Bankers, simply
because he was interested. Its investments were smart ones: min-
ing in the territory of Amapá, steel production in the state of São
Paulo, irrigation in the valley of the São Francisco River.

This latest scheme, Duncan conceded to himself, was fraught
with a series of Herculean stumbling blocks, not the least of them,
the government ministries involved, scrambling, in their custom-
ary way, to gain a maximum of glory with a minimum of effort.
But they were no worse than ministries anywhere in the world or
any organization that employed more than twenty people, for
that matter. Furthermore, the investment would be guaranteed
by the federal government and that was pretty safe these days. If
that went, just as in Chile, it would all go down the drain in one
big south-of-the-equator, counterclockwise "shlup." So why worry?

And in the meantime, why not get into something exciting?
Manganese in Amapá, irrigation in the São Francisco Valley.

Imagine changing a desolate, drought-stricken wasteland, poorer than India, into a California or an Israel? Ah! Poetry! Duncan, who was at this very moment sitting in a government registry office waiting for some fool to sign a useless piece of paper, shook his thoughts back into practical perspective. The thing was, they'd get their money back at 12 per cent and, since all large projects were inevitably wasteful, there was going to be a lot of money involved.

At any rate, as for getting involved with the Soares firm, it wasn't the project he had so much faith in, but the impelling, confident behavior of Ricardo Soares, in whom, it seemed to Duncan, Brazilian tradition and a new Brazilian outlook were combined in near perfect proportions. Soares took his business seriously, but not seriously enough to allow it to paralyze him.

He had a healthy faith in his country; its riches, its ignorant-intelligent people, its ambition, its greed, its tough, well-intentioned government. "They are generals," he would shrug and say, "and sometimes they behave like generals. But they are holding things together so that people who are not generals are able to act, are they not?"

Duncan was with him on that. Of all the places in the world where one might consider laying down some money—including the suffocating, atticy atmosphere of Europe—Brazil seemed to him the only one worth braving. The only one with a sense of reality; that wasn't ranting self-pityingly over "economic imperialism" while it systematically devoured itself with expropriations and socialistic schemes. And in Brazil, the Soares Bank seemed the most representative of this realism, exuberant and flamboyant as it might be.

He only hoped to hell he could keep International Bankers in tune with this exuberance long enough. So far, indeed, there had been amazingly few prating telexes, hysterical phone calls and demands for sleuthlike investigations.

Could it possibly be that the impression of stuffiness he'd gained in New York had been wrong?

Or perhaps the bank's impression of *him* had not been as bizarre as he had suspected. Maybe, after all, International Bankers had somehow avoided the sclerosis that seemed to affect everything big everywhere in the world. Perhaps, after all, the powers that were, were actually willing to believe that he, Duncan Round-tree, the man they'd sent to do the job, was capable of doing it.

"Nah." Once again he told himself, that was poetry too. The thing was to make haste, before they woke up and discovered he was acting on his own—

And so he was feeling good, in spite of the fact that he had been sitting in a dusty, stale-smelling labyrinth of a registry office since two, waiting for an all-important signature on a document, in literal translation, called "gloves." It was one of an incredible series with various such titles—gloves, pants, sunrises—all of which were imminently necessary, though no one could tell him why, to the ultimate functioning of Frango Frito as an upstanding legal establishment. He was sitting here now because the document's signature depended upon one and only one individual in one particular office in Rio.

When Duncan had entered the labyrinth, a female ogre with a mustache and bulging thighs, tourniqueted above the knees by the elastic bands that held her stockings up, had informed him that Doutor Afonso was "dispatching" and therefore he would have to wait. Familiar with the perverse nature of public functionaries, Duncan had received this information with what he described as his "best shit-sucking smile," and seated himself on a bench along the wall.

Since that moment, Doutor Afonso had appeared and disappeared like a termite boring in and out of the governmental woodwork at least fifteen times. Each time he had managed to walk past Duncan with an elaborate air of disregard as if to impress upon the handsome, prosperous, foreign-looking young man, his utter insignificance in the face of "the law."

Duncan was beginning to feel like a character in a Russian novel: Raskolnikov, patiently waiting in the police delegacy to give himself up as the murderer. Indeed, at last, a murderous sensation was gradually gaining ground on his original good spirits. He had read through *The Economist*, and a 1967 edition of *Manchete*, counted the number of dusty registry books, filled with the meticulous handwriting of green-faced scribes, that lined the shelves before him. These he had multiplied by 350,000 (the number of registry offices in Brazil) and then by 469 (the number of years since the arrival of the great discoverer, Pedro Alvares Cabral). He had attempted ignoring Doutor Afonso, then stuck his feet out to bar the termite's passage, which had only afforded him a frigid and intimidating, "*Por favor?*"

It was getting close to three-thirty, closing time for government registry offices. Now, confirming his worst fears, the fat, mustached woman regarded Duncan across the counter, savoring the power of obstruction with every word. "*Doutor Afonso não asinará mais documentos hoje. É precisa voltar amanha.*"

A water filter stood in the corner, its faucet dripping placidly into a cracked jar. A maniacal desire to seize the earthen, vaselike top of the filter and jam it over the woman's head rose within him and sank again. What was the use? However, the agony of waiting now arousing within him an unusual sense of righteousness, Duncan couldn't resist saying with a pompousness incredible to his own ears, "I only hope Doutor Afonso will be here on time tomorrow. I have important things to do, *minha senhora*, that cannot wait."

With that he rose, seizing his brief case, which, unfortunately, upon putting back *The Economist*, he had forgotten to close properly. It fell open now, scattering over the floor, along with the bank's correspondence and the "gloves," a bathing suit, a tube of suntan cream, a snorkel and a bottle opener.

There was a moment's incredulous silence and then a strange murmur, like laughter under water, as, aroused from their moss-covered lethargy, various green-faced scribes scrambled to help Duncan pick up the wreckage. Placing the brief case on the counter, the better to latch it down over the snorkel, which now seemed to have acquired life and resistance, his eyes once more met those of the rubber-banded obstructionist, and found that they had become oddly human.

She was observing the collection of beach paraphernalia, inspecting it minutely and with obvious pleasure. Apparently the discovery that he was a "*vida boa*" like everyone else had satisfied her in a way that no serious purposefulness ever could. She regarded him now with an almost alarming fondness.

"It is a shame to have to wait," she said pointedly. "Paulistas always have so much to do. Especially when they come to Rio. Be here at ten tomorrow. *Eu vou dar um jeito com Doutor Afonso, viu?*"

"*Um jeito*," of course. There was always a *way* if you had the right approach. He should have let his brief case fall open when he first walked through the door. He realized that now. Delighted, he descended in the creaking elevator and, emerging into the sunshine, decided to walk.

CHAPTER 21

A wonderful fresh breeze wafted in from the sea, stirring the leaves of the umbrella trees in the park along the broad avenue leading to the hotel. He liked to walk along this avenue, observing cariocas in their natural habitat. They were healthier, happier-looking people than the Paulistas. It was the sun, of course, that browned and cheered them and made it impossible to take life too seriously. Just like the episode with the brief case that had so thoroughly restored his humor. Would Paulistas have laughed? He didn't know. Sometimes he thought they were too earnest. Not Brazilian enough. But then when he thought of the rest of the world, he decided that his judgment was a little too harsh.

Caroline, at any rate, would howl at the brief case story. It would put her in the best of spirits. The serious girl with the big laugh. It was as if her very intensity craved a ridiculous situation from time to time as a counterbalance, which was probably why she had fallen in love with him in the first place. Indeed their first meeting had been triggered by one such situation, created, as was most often the case, by Duncan himself.

As he thought thus, he found himself no longer walking along a Rio avenue but in a men's clothing store in Columbus, Ohio, in the midst of what seemed a depressingly futile discussion with a badly dressed customer over the size of a hat. The time involved seemed hardly worth it, especially with a striking blonde riffling, unassisted, through the size forty-five jackets hanging from a rack nearby.

"Would you believe it? I bought the damn thing here yesterday, and now it's too large," the man was saying, as if his head had shrunken overnight. The blonde looked ready to move away.

A sensation of panic and urgency overcame Duncan and caused him to say, "It doesn't look any worse than the suit you're wearing, sir."

The gentleman's reaction was immediate and not unexpected. Mumbling something about "report" and "manager," the customer made his irate departure, leaving Duncan to peer over the rack into the widest, bluest, most direct gaze he had encountered in twenty-five years of searching.

"May I help you?"

"Not if you're going to insult me."

"Oh, I was only advising him to the best of his interests. Besides"—Duncan who was fully six feet tall and had the rather arrogant look of a New England race track dandy, spoke out of the corner of his mouth—"I wanted to get rid of him so I could talk to you. Do you mind?"

"You're going to get fired."

"It won't be the first time."

"Don't you like your job?"

"It's somewhat better than selling rust remover and somewhat worse than being an assistant golf pro. Would you like to hear about my varied career?"

And because Caroline had been in a down mood when she'd come in and the prattling of this maniac amidst the tweed coats made her feel suddenly carefree and a little hysterical, she said, "I'd love to."

"Then let's have lunch," Duncan replied in triumph.

They'd ended up spending the rest of the day and half the night telling each other about each other. They went to a dingy downtown Columbus bar where Duncan found himself gazing at this strangely intense girl over a beer while a jukebox in the background wavered between the atonalities of Stan Kenton and the genuinely off-key wailing of Billie Eckstein. At the moment of their meeting, she had been searching for a jacket to give to her father for his birthday, so she had begun with him: a medical doctor, stern and kindly with a powerful obsession for excellence.

"You should never really want to achieve something," she was saying.

"Why not?"

"Because people don't care whether you achieve or not. They just don't give a damn."

"It's a good thing to discover early in life so you don't waste your time with all that striving," Duncan replied with mock gravity, and then, because he was afraid she'd get up and walk out, and he really didn't want her to, he said, "Don't get mad. I laugh, but it's because I understand, really."

Apparently, despite the belief that one shouldn't, she had followed in her father's achieving footsteps. She had amazingly short fingers, which was probably why, Duncan thought now, she had decided to become a concert pianist. Six years of study, a master's degree; and all the while, with the world's shortest fingers, she had struggled and stretched to encompass an octave while her mind debated such problems as how Bach would have wished his Prelude and Fugue in D minor to be played.

Whether her rendition was to his taste or not, Bach would never tell. But at the end of the recital for which she was to receive her final degree, the director of the Columbus Symphony Orchestra appeared backstage with tears in his eyes to invite her to join his orchestra as a pianist.

It had been the most challenging experience of her life. Only up to what moment of telling? Duncan wondered now—or ever afterward? She had dedicated her entire being to the music and the comprehension of what that particular director had desired from it. The director was an extremely talented man, worthy of response, capable of inducing magnificence from the most reticent of musical souls. He was also middle-aged and the father of three. One day he followed Caroline into the equipment room behind the stage and seized her in a passionate embrace.

"Well, can you blame the poor guy? After all you don't exactly look like Miss Horseflesh, the ninety-year-old cellist. Look here, be honest. Didn't this guy ever make *you* feel, well, let's say, emotional?"

"Of course. Don't be an idiot."

"Then you weren't shocked, horrified . . ."

"Oh no, don't you see? Just disgusted. Because after that we couldn't go on. If the music—my music—had been important enough. But it wasn't." The small hands that had tried so hard, waved it all away with a derisive flick of the wrist. "So what? It doesn't matter."

"So what are you doing now?"

"Oh, just working around. I couldn't bear to go home. In the Art Museum, actually."

"How old's the director there?"

She glared. "You really know it all, don't you? You must have been a jaded old man before you were born." She really would have upped and stomped out of the dingy little bar in which they were sitting if he hadn't said in the gentlest yet most strangely compelling voice, "Wait, maybe you're right. Maybe that's the whole thing." And because curiosity was the other side of the coin with her, she sat back down and listened.

"My father wasn't like yours, for all that's worth. He went off to war and didn't come back, and it wasn't because he died, either." Caroline's look was becoming wary, so he hastened to add, "Listen, I don't mean to blame my parents if I'm an oddball. I just mentioned my dad because you mentioned yours. As a matter of fact, I don't go for that kind of stuff. You don't become a drifter because your parents didn't understand you when you masturbated."

Caroline's eyes narrowed, but she kept her mouth shut.

"I just happen to be one of those who never really felt a desire for this business of reaching for the stars."

"Then what in hell *do* you have a desire for?" Caroline could keep quiet no longer. The immediate answer popped lewdly into Duncan's head but he forcibly pushed it aside. "Oh, whatever enjoyment you can get out of life—there's a lot to be had. But it's never worth kissing anyone's ass for." He looked drolly thoughtful for a moment. "I guess that's my code, if you want it in one succinct sentence. 'Don't kiss anyone's ass; it's never worth it.'"

He'd had his tenth beer by then and somewhat fuzzily, he saw the most amazing color rise in Caroline's smooth, nordic cheeks. "I never kissed—"

He raised his hands in a gesture of appeasement. "Wait, take it easy, don't jump. I didn't say anything about *you*. Obviously you haven't or, oh hell, what I'm saying is, more often than not, I think ass kissing is the price one has to pay. See?" He took another long draught of beer and gazed at her hopefully.

"I see"—the color faded back to normal—"but I can't be quite *that* cynical."

"Heaven forbid." He looked foggily aghast. "I wouldn't want you to be. Besides, I don't disapprove of trying anything if you're ambitious. It's just that I've never seemed to be able to find anything that stirred me enough to want to try that hard.

"You know what my high school college counselor suggested I do? Go to hotel school. I don't know how he came to that conclusion (unless it was by sizing up my general laziness) but the suggestion sounded as good as any, so I went.

"When I got out I managed a big fancy resort in Florida, did a pretty good job too. I even rather enjoyed myself until the owner told us everyone, including myself, would have to go to a Halloween party wearing a tie that lit up and said 'Lover's Haven.' It was a honeymoon resort."

Duncan frowned, searching back in his thoughts through time. "If I remember correctly, I told him to tie the tie around his nuts and plug it in."

"Oh, stop! I can't stand any more." He looked up from his beer to see tears in Caroline's eyes, but this time they were tears of laughter. She was wailing. The whole room was looking.

As a remedial measure, he decided to ask her to dance, and so they did. Oh, closer it seemed than he or she had ever danced with anyone before.

The thing that she liked most about him was his perversity. There was something innately polished and well bred about this young man of Puritan New England background. Yet he was so irreverent. He owned this incredible collapsing MG and wore the most peculiar combinations of clothes that imitated no fashion that anyone could ever have conceived. Dressed in them, he worked in this select haberdasher's establishment with an unsettling air of amused effrontery.

"Liver-colored people should never wear lime-colored sports shirts, sir."

One might have expected his attitude concerning women and sex to be thoroughly cynical and irresponsible. Certainly nothing he said suggested the contrary. And yet one night, the doorbell rang and when he went to answer it, there stood Caroline in blue jeans and an old college T-shirt with a suitcase in her hand. It seemed to him, he'd never seen anyone look so forlorn. As if compelled by a despair that allowed no hesitation, she stomped past him and sank onto the sofa.

"I'm disgusted, just plain damn fed up and disgusted."

"Don't tell me the director of the Art Museum—"

"Oh, shut up. I don't want to talk about it." The red-rimmed eyes she raised to his were so utterly abject. "I don't know what I want. Just please let me stay here and leave me alone!"

And presently, after a brief bout of stifled weeping she settled in. All night long he lay, fitful in his sleep, incredulous at himself, wondering at this strange, immaculate trust that had been placed in his hands. "Why *my* hands?" He'd never expressed to her the belief that man was anything but a weak, rapacious profligate. Yet seemingly she wanted to stay with him and go no further.

He rather hoped that, if this were the case, the austerity of that night, enchanting as it was, was not going to be the rule. For he couldn't remember ever having wanted anyone so much in his life. He needn't have worried. She wanted him just as much, and she was a girl incapable of half measures. What she had withheld from others for the sake of art, she bestowed upon him with all the warmth of her expansive nature.

The more they came to know of each other, the better things got. He was not disappointing. His originality and flare for self-contradiction continued to baffle and surprise her. He asked her to marry him and promptly went off on a two-week vacation to Florida, alone. She told herself he would never come back, but he did. There was something deep inside him that was straight as a ramrod. If she'd have told him he was virtuous and abiding, he would have laughed. But she'd made up her mind that he was.

Once they were married, he suddenly decided to give South America a try.

"We'll go to the language school in Arizona first. Plenty of sunshine there. Then when we've got the Spanish and Portuguese sorted out, I'll offer my talents to some banks."

"Banks?"

"Why not? Banking intrigues me. It must be fun to plot world strategy with promissory notes."

"What do *you* know about it?"

"Nothing yet. But I was a golf pro without knowing how to play golf, wasn't I?"

"Oh, ho-ho, Duncan." He was beginning to become used to her stomach-clutching wails of mirth. She was game. And perhaps *that* was the thing he liked best about *her*.

Her stern, exacting, loving father watched with incredulous helplessness as this being he had wrought, prepared to depart with a capricious haberdasher in a broken-down MG. No use arguing, he knew, with someone who was the inheritor of his own stubborn will.

She had a broken-down MG too, and they set off in both of them just for luck. It was a good thing, because halfway across the prairies they discovered the unresourcefulness of a modern world. At Fish Hook, Nebraska, there was a simultaneous breakdown unrivaled by anything but the collapse of the one-horse shay. There were, of course, no MG parts in Fish Hook. But with a great deal of supervised tinkering by a mental deficient who was nonetheless a genius with tools, they managed to make one car out of two and proceed upon their way.

It was the first leg of a long journey that would not by any means end with the vice-presidency of International Bankers in Brazil. One day, the bank, with a typical contemporary disregard for individual desires, would promote him to some high office— say the South American Bureau in New York, and then, of course, he would have to resign.

In the meantime, though, it wasn't a bad job; its best feature being the fact that it was in Brazil, where you could think of quitting when the ass-kissing level reached the point of absurdity. Where it seemed, with a little knowledge and daring, just about anything was possible—even the spontaneous schemes of his and Josh's that would drive an investment research outfit to *up* its computer.

The schemes were only a vehicle, of course. One day they would make their pile and then Duncan would be what he wanted to be. For at last, from time to time, he found himself surprisingly stirred by an idea. He would like to help people invest in this remarkable country, but he'd like to do it on his own.

All that was quite a distant dream as he walked along the avenue, the traffic rushing by in a frenetic stream on one side of him, white uniformed babás in the parks, gossiping in clusters while the children played under the trees on the other. It was good enough for now to have made it to this point, to have gotten far enough to have just spent the afternoon, sitting, waiting for a signature on his "gloves."

He was near the hotel now. Ahead of him on its pinnacle of rock, the Igreja da Gloria stood, baroque and charming, softening, as did the tropical greenery that surrounded everything, the otherwise starkness of a modern city. Climbing the steps that curved round the mountain toward the hotel, he arrived at the poolside just in time to see Caroline's lithe young body arch into the air over the water. He suddenly felt hot and dry and longed for a drink and a swim himself. He thought of his bathing suit, once again secure in his brief case, and, laughing, hurried toward the pool.

CHAPTER 22

Josh, too, was feeling like a swim, more than anything, perhaps, to wash away the sense of depression, almost of doom, that had come over him upon leaving Harry McGuiness a few moments before.

In a sense, Josh could say he had earned his *per diem* and more. It had been one hell of a busy day. But in another sense it seemed to him he might have been honest in the beginning and said, "None of this is going to make any difference, Harry . . . doesn't matter whom I know." Well, probably Harry had known that, and so had Rod Trimmingham, the Institute's financial director, but no one was immune to hoping that a new light, another angle extremely valid, might open someone's mind.

Josh's mission had begun its course at seven-thirty in the morning, when he'd been summoned to a meeting in Rod Trimmingham's hotel room. The meeting had taken place in the bathroom with the shower gushing its two-faucet capacity.

"What the hell's going on here?" Through the swirling clouds of steam, Josh could barely make out the figures of Trimmingham and Takeo Kanagi, editor of Brazil's leading agricultural magazine.

"Shh"—Trimmingham emitted a swirl of vapor—"shut the door. I think we're being bugged."

Josh slipped inside, closing the door hastily behind him. "By whom?" The fog was so thick he could barely make out Trimmingham's affable, charm school features, but the financial director's voice was incredibly serious.

"I'm not sure. Could be either one or both. Can't take a chance. Look, Josh, the thing is to rally as much backing as we can and as quickly as possible."

"What's lacking?" Josh bellowed.

"I said backing, backing! Shh."

The shower's roar was deafening. How anyone else could hear them when they couldn't hear each other was beyond Josh. Added to that, Trimmingham's six-foot-two-inch altitude was painfully counterbalanced by the Japanese editor's four foot ten. The bathroom was rapidly turning into a howling Hades. Bending down to compensate Takeo Kanagi's height, Trimmingham's skull met Josh's with a crack that reverberated from the dripping walls like some submarine explosion.

"To be perfectly safe," Josh hollered on recovery, "we should be constantly flushing the toilet. No better listening device than a water pipe."

"Cut the comedy if you want to get out of here." Trimmingham's voice sounded distant, aquatic.

The gist of the matter, Josh gathered, was that the new Minister of Agriculture had a new idea entirely of his own inspiration. "Why strain all this research work through the Institute? Why not establish direct contact between the universities? Piracicaba, Cornell, Rio Grande do Sul, Purdue, Km. 47, Rutgers."

"Why not create a tower of Babel," said Josh in answer.

"Obviously. So I thought possibly you could have a chat with Chaves of *O Mundo*, and then trot out to that old farmer Aristedes Arruda to extol the wonders of fifteen years of steady research. Takeo here is willing to write a series of glowing articles."

"All in one day?"

"It's essential that we work fast."

"Especially since none of us is equipped with gills." Josh felt himself gasping and saw Takeo Kanagi swaying hazily beneath his nose. "Who do you suggest I see first?"

"Chaves." Trimmingham flung open the door and for the first time in history, Rio in January seemed cold.

It seemed to Josh for the rest of the day that his lightweight suit would never dry out. When he sat on the leather sofa in Chaves' newspaper office, he fully expected to see a damp imprint left when he rose to his feet.

He and Jose Chaves were old friends, airplane companions from the days when that columnist alone had the courage and interest to try to point out to his fellow countrymen that what their country needed was not an agrarian reform but trucks and roads. Together they had endured the heat and discomfort of a small place, Chaves' huge bulk reminding Josh of a hog in a crate over Mato Grosso, Rio Grande do Sul, Goias; miles and miles of what Chaves described as "no place to sit down."

Now, as they sat opposite each other, it was as if they had only seen one another yesterday and not five years ago. There was no fumbling for common ground but a remarkable directness as Chaves said, "So tell me in a few sentences what's the problem."

"Very simple," said Josh, "and very familiar. The Minister of Agriculture has a new idea. He wants to bring in a raft of professors, make a university-to-university research program and phase out the Institute altogether. Claims the Institute is inefficient, not doing its job."

"Inefficient, eh?" Chaves' heavy lips seethed, eyes bulged with sudden outrage. "Who made it that way? USAID, putting Doctors of Science to cultivate every caboclo's little cotton patch from Bahia to Pôrto Alegre. What they trying to do, make us into India?"

"Would it be too much to ask you to turn off the air conditioner? I spent the last hour in Trimmingham's bathroom having a conference with the shower going. He thinks the place is bugged—"

"Bugged!" Chaves began to roar and shake, tears of mirth rolling down his cheeks threatened to re-establish the damp atmosphere of Josh's former meeting. "Ho, don't be so funny. The Hotel Gloria? One more device in that antiquated electrical system and the whole thing would blow out. Besides"—Chaves' jowls settled into an expression of sad irony—"who knows or cares about the Institute except you and I and Harry McGuiness?"

"After all it's done?"

"After all it's done, meu amigo. You *are* a poet if you think it matters. It has done just about everything that *has* been done in research. You know that and I do, but I repeat, who else knows or cares? University to university, eh? Multiply the inefficiency by hundreds. Scatter professors all over the map with their pocket dictionaries and jealous counterparts. Throw away fifteen years of good organized work. All to gratify a politician's design."

Josh got up, walked over to the air conditioning, turned it off himself, opened the window and stood before it, welcoming the warm, live air from the street. "Hope you don't mind, I was feeling like a corpse."

"No, no." Chaves' eyes rolled comically. "In a few minutes it'll be as if we were back over Mato Grosso in the bruma seca. What a simple life that was, eh, Josh?" His huge body heaved with a sigh as he returned to the subject at hand. "What I can't understand is why. Why didn't Harry say something before? Why wait until the minister started getting inspired with his own idea?"

"Because Harry is stubborn," Josh answered him, "and Trimmingham up there in New York never gets any news unless it's bad news, and then it's too late."

"And what about that USAID fellow? What's his name, Brandenburg?"

"Ah, Brandenburg. He'll only be too glad. The Institute is too practical for him. Their findings never jibe with his theories."

"And so you expect me to try and defend something that nobody wants even to discuss?" Chaves laughed robustly, as if suddenly delighted. "You know that's just the kind of thing Jose Chaves likes to do."

Some hours later, Jose Chaves met him again, in a state of utter gloom. "It will kill Harry McGuiness. It will be the end"—he shook his head knowingly—"but didn't I tell you, years ago? Or was it your friend Teodoro? Ah sim. It was Teodoro. Getting mixed up with a government project, I said to Teodoro, is like purposely swimming too far out to sea. Bom, no use suffering over it now. The thing is to act." His large, shrewd features took on a look of important mission. "The minister is a good friend of mine. No use talking to others, we talk to him." And somewhat stuffily, for all his distaste for governmental figures he said, "I'll arrange an audience."

The minister was charming, affable, knowledgeable and extremely clever. He seemed to have all the time in the world for the journalist Jose Chaves, and his "influential friend" Josh Moran. They sipped hot *cafezinhos* and talked about many things; the great open country of the south; the *chimarrão*-drinking gaucho; the leather-hatted Nordestino; how stubbornly those men love the dry, barren country that starves them. A delightful poetic preparation. Then the meat. Praise for the Institute, its long years of struggle in a field that was so vital and yet in which no one had interest. "The entire country should be grateful, Sr. Josué, for the invaluable work your good friend Professor McGuiness and the Institute have done over the years."

How clearly the minister understood the entire situation. One would almost have believed Harry had made some mistake. Then Josh zeroed in, "But, Sr. Ministro, what about this university-to-university idea?"

"*Pois é.*" From cordial affability, the minister's expression turned to one of excitement, passionate dedication. "The whole program needs revitalization, stimulation—only if we work with the universities can we acquire the best minds."

"But so many minds substituting the same work. Do you really think the best minds will be willing to come here for only two years?" Why, it takes two years just to get the feel of a place like this. And, of course, Sr. Ministro, there is the question of money. Since the Institute linked itself with USAID and the Ministry, it has had no other source of income. This will literally be the end . . ."

The minister didn't seem to hear. A small, energetic man with a colossal idea . . . at least in bulk. "Thank you, Sr. Moran. It has been a pleasure to talk to someone who understands our problems so well. I hope you realize how important I consider the Institute's work to be. *Temos que estudar um jeito. . . . Abraços*" —he slapped Jose on the back—"to Dona Leonora. How are the children? Don't forget next time you are in Paraná, Sr. Josh, my fazenda is at your disposal."

By the time they were on their way down in the elevator, Josh knew that it was useless to see Henry Brandenburg, the director of AID. Perhaps that was why he was possibly a little too blunt, not his usual unflappable self.

Brandenburg was new in Brazil. Though he administered the allocation of funds over a country as vast as his own, he had never visited an experimental station in Rio Grande do Sul, one thousand miles to the south, or in drought-stricken Piauí two thousand miles to the north. He had, in fact, seldom left his air-conditioned office in the embassy except to go to his residence or a cocktail party or the Gavea Golf Club.

But he didn't need to, either, for he had known all about Brazil before he got here. And he dealt with extreme reluctance with this government that seemed to have no intention of holding nationwide, American-style presidential elections in the near future. He was, in fact, ready to pull out, sign up for a post in, say, Czechoslovakia or Poland if things became too unacceptable here.

He leaned wearily on his desk and gazed at Josh through thick horn-rimmed glasses. "Of course you realize, Mr. Moran, everything at this moment is on a very temporary basis."

"Then why these shiploads of professors? Why all this change of policy? There are only a few men who really understand what this place is all about. Harry McGuiness is one of them."

"We have some theories of our own."

"But are they going to pay off?"

Brandenburg shook his head as though at an incorrigible child. "It's all so much more complex than you think—the eco-sociological impact. I'm afraid you can't narrow agriculture down to the science of farming."

"But that's not even what we're talking about, Mr. Brandenburg. We're talking about replacing the Institute."

"Ummm, yes. Exactly . . . you know, the Institute, as a private organization, once backed by Rockefeller, has a slight flavor of, shall we say, economic imperialism?"

Oh, Christ, Josh could feel himself going white around the nose as he tried to contain himself long enough to get out.

He was used to drinking with Harry McGuiness fast and thirstily after a long dusty trek over someone's scientifically planted corn plot; or meeting him in Campos for a quick beer before Harry, in khakis and boots, took off for god-forsaken places that Josh now vaguely missed. He was not used to seeing him in a business suit and tie in a bar with wooden paneling and pseudocolonial decor. His complexion was gray, the deep lines in his face seemed to sag a little. Totem wood, exposed to the wind and rain was never so. It wore away, never sagged. To cover his distress, Josh said, "You look like you haven't seen the sun in a hundred years."

Harry smiled grimly. "I've been spending too much time drinking cafezinhos, talking to important people . . ." There was weariness even in the way he closed his hand around his drink. "Some people thrive on it, but it's not my racket." His eyes met Josh's, piercingly, unavoidably. "I take it you haven't much good to report?"

Josh shrugged. "Chaves is incensed and delighted for the opportunity to be so, he'll go at it like a tornado. He took me to see the minister—"

"And?"

"He knows his stuff, all right. But in this case—"

"I know," said Harry. "Kids want their *own* stuff, not their brother's hand-me-downs."

"I'm afraid it may have done more harm than good, my seeing Brandenburg. I can't understand what a guy like that is here for in the first place. He's a goddamn first-rate Googoo."

Harry grinned wryly. "Oh, come on, Josh, I can see you've been out of it too long. He disapproves of the Revolution, all right, but not enough to want to be knocked off his chair. Not just yet, anyhow." He raised his glass. "All the same, thanks for trying."

"So back to private support," Josh said heartily. "You're better off."

Harry gave Josh a bitter look of wisdom. "Unfortunately it doesn't work that way. Government comes in and private backers back off."

"I see," said Josh. "As bad as that." He tried not to look too appalled. "So what are your plans?"

"My plans?" With an expansiveness all the more telling for its being entirely out of character, Harry said, "Oh, I've all kinds of offers. One in particular . . . big shipping magnate doesn't know what to do with his dough . . . bought land on the Orinoco . . . wants to start cacau and possibly rubber . . . needs an expert."

"The Orinoco?" It was impossible for Josh to hide his distress. They knew one another too well for that. "At your age?"

Harry grinned and, for a fleeting moment, the lines in his face seemed once again carved from the most weather-resistant wood. "It's a job, isn't it? And a good one. That's more than *you* have, buddy."

On the way out, even though he knew he would refuse, Josh

invited Harry to join them for the evening. Somehow he hadn't wanted him to be alone. Now, as he headed toward the back elevator that led to the pool, he told himself firmly, "But that's ridiculous. Harry McGuiness has always been alone."

CHAPTER 23

That night they sat in a sidewalk cafe along Copacabana, drinking sangría, eating shrimp, fried crisply in the shell, and talking. The cafes all along the *avenida* that followed the curve of the bay were busy and crowded, for Rio people are night people who love to sit and talk endlessly on terraces carved out of the mountainside, at sidewalk cafes or on benches overlooking the sea. The pavements, too, were filled with strolling people. Prostitutes, dusky, short-skirted lovelies, ambled in tempting rhythms, their solicitations causing eddies in the flow of aimless wanderers. Beyond the flashing roar of the traffic could be heard the constant breaking of waves upon a beach eerily lighted by the flickering candles of candomblé.

Jose Chaves was with them and Zach Huber of *American News,* a young man, fresh and eager and determined to "get to the bottom of oppression in Brazil." The more sangría they drank, the more vociferous they all became, their voices rising above the hum of the other drinkers and diners to match the shouts of the hawkers in the streets.

"If we are so oppressed, how can we be sitting here shouting at one another about everything?" Jose thrust his big face toward Huber, who strained forward pugnaciously in answer.

"But you'll admit the students are not permitted . . ."

"Tsh, for once they are studying."

"And what about the workers?"

"Working! What would you prefer, Uruguay, where life is just one constant strike? Or Argentina, where the only thing they can think of doing is bring back a Mummy from Spain and put him on display?"

"You're walking a tightrope."

"So is the whole world."

"And what are you going to do when you come to the end?"

"Ah, I see you haven't been in Brazil long enough to know about the '*jeito*.'"

"Ah, the jeito. Of course I know. Compromise," said Zach Huber a shade too righteously. "So that keeps you happy?"

"It has kept us, so far, out of a lot of trouble that a lot of other people have gotten into."

"What has happiness got to do with it?" Duncan wanted to know. "Being happy is simply having something when you want it." This in turn set off a whole new train of thought. Everyone began to speculate upon the definition of happiness over more sangría and more shrimp, of course.

Caroline said it was a moment of accomplishment, nothing more. "Then, crash, back into the doldrums again."

Josh said once the moment of accomplishment came, happiness was already finished. It was the struggle that led up to it . . ."

Lia disagreed. It was having a goal, something you cared about to try for. "What in hell's the use of just struggling if there isn't something really worthwhile, magnificent ahead of you?"

As for Zach Huber, he was of the opinion that it was something to do with being at peace with one's conscience, but then, of course, Duncan said you had to know the rules your conscience was supposed to live by. "After all, some African tribes still believe . . ."

They might have gone on forever had not Jose Chaves risen and, shaking hands and giving abraços all around, excused himself, smiling at Zach Huber as he did and saying, "You're a smart boy, Zach, and I'm sure your innocent black and white view of the world will one day become normally cluttered and colorful."

He left them, then, and while they set off with enthusiasm, forgetting their weighty arguments for lighter things—guitars, soft voices, matchboxes and cuicas—he returned to his home and sat down behind his typewriter, his heavy black brows drawn together with a frown.

"It is necessary to remember," he wrote, "that for all our reasons for euphoria in this country, we are walking a tightrope along which have been placed extraordinary obstacles. Nor can we risk the danger of thinking that, just because we are Brazilians, there is always a way [in Portuguese the word read '*jeito*'] to get around our troubles and go on. We have been able to contain terrorism and chaos so that we might have a breather to work and produce. But part of the price has been a silencing of protest, a suppression of outright healthy dialogue between youth and their elders. The workers are working. They have never had more opportunities for work than they now have. But one day they will also want a better life. This is only a breather. . . . we must make good use of it."

It was a long article, straightforward and thoughtful. He hoped it would be published; he thought it would. And if it were, he hoped that it would be read by Zach Huber and that he, in turn, would examine his conscience as he was always telling others to do. So that he would not take Jose's words out of context and splash them all over the world.

CHAPTER 24

The next day the four friends hired a car and drove up into the
mountains to eat *vatapa* and *moqueca* and drink *batidas* in a place
where they could sit on a wooden veranda, overlooking the jungled valley below. A waterfall poured out of a granite cliff, filling
the air with soft, cool vapor as it replenished a glistening stream.
They were very gay. It was fun to be just the four of them together sometimes. It reminded them of how they had met as the
occupants of the two staterooms on an ancient paddle-wheel
steamer, traveling down the great interior river, the São Francisco,
five years earlier.

It had been a curious journey through the timeless world of
the Northeast; a world green on the edges of the river, where the
water birds swept down, and windswept and parched in the great
empty lands beyond. Together, amidst a strange, enduring people,
they had risen before sunrise each day to stand in the biting wind
on the deck and watch the earth and water awaken and turn to a
myriad of green and henna hues. At night they had sat under the
stars and listened to the sighing and breathing of the smokestack
as they talked.

Anyone who has made this journey down the river knows that
one does not come back exactly the same. It is a spiritual experience, like journeying into a soul and discovering its essence. One
comes back a little moonstruck and with a light-headedness at the
memory of the river that cannot be described but only shared.

"It's our insanity that's kept us together all these years," said
Josh, remembering.

"Speaking of insanity," said Duncan, "isn't it about time we
had a board of directors' meeting?"

They scheduled the meeting for three o'clock that afternoon

and held it upon the sands of Leblon. Overhead *real* kites of bright-colored cloth on bamboo frames, spread their eagle's wings against a vivid sea sky. *Moleques* shaking *reco-recos* to attract the attention of their customers, hawked popsicles, ice creams, pornographic sights entrapped in slide viewers, dropped everything to shoot a few goals in a perpetual *futebol* game, then took up their *reco-recos* again. Caroline sat absorbed in the memorizing of a new song and Lia lay on a straw mat with *Os Sertões* propped before her, of which she had read no more than a page. The battle against the Brazilian Republican Army by Antonio Conselheiro and the mad rabble of Canudos, fascinating as it was, was having difficulty competing with the wisps of discussion that on the gentle sea breezes, wafted across the sand in her direction.

In her mind, she tried to visualize a conventional meeting, sober faces above the gleam of a highly polished table. They might be more soberly stated, perhaps, yet she doubted if the details discussed could be any more real.

"At the going price," Josh was saying, "I figure we've got to turn over at least five hundred chickens a week to survive."

"You think we'll do *that* in the beginning?"

"How the hell should I know? We might not even sell one. But we've got to *believe* it, or nobody else will."

"Aside from this 'faith' we possess in such large quantities," Duncan replied somewhat dubiously, "what other assets don't I know about?"

"You don't know about? Let's see." Josh looked searchingly toward the cloudless sky. "One thing we can thank God for. Central Feeds is willing to finance the neon sign if we put green and white checks around the borders."

"A small cross to bear for being able to keep afloat. Anything else hopeful?"

"Call it what you like . . . Teodoro's got another miracle pending. Ten *alqueres* for housing near the future refinery in Paulinha . . . 350,000 cruzeiros, if he closes."

"If," said Duncan, taking a long draught from the beer bottle he'd just bought from the boy with the *reco-reco*. "There's always this element of suspense. What's the hitch this time?"

Josh cleared his throat. "Brace yourself for this one. Seems the deal has to be discussed with the spirit of the owner's dead father."

"Oh, I see," Duncan sputtered through his beer. "And has Teodoro got anyone working on that?"

"His *mae santa*," said Josh.

"Ummm. Do we mark that down as spiritual consultation?" Duncan looked cautiously over his shoulder. "Suppose anyone's listening?"

"I am." Lia poked her head above the book, fascinated. Perhaps the problems were the same, but the solutions had a definitely original ring to them. "You sound like a couple of lunatics getting ready to take over the stock exchange."

In answer Josh packed a handful of wet sand and flung it, expertly thumping her on the rear end. Then he returned to the business at hand. "Okay, giving the miracle department its due, our real mainstay for a long time, even after we get things rolling, is going to be keeping those credit lines open."

"Which brings us," said Duncan, "to the sobering question of how long we can give ourselves. A year, two?"

"The way I look at it," Josh said calmly, "we've got a lot backing us up that other people don't. The feed business ought to be paying off within a year."

"Then there's my job," Duncan interjected. "It's holding up fairly well. I don't expect to lose it unless they order me to Tasmania."

"We haven't mentioned the fazenda."

"The fazenda?" There was a note of genuine surprise in Duncan's voice, though Josh's became, if anything, steadier.

"Look, it's an asset worth at least 500,000 cruzeiros. If you *do* something, you *do* it, don't you?"

"Yes, well . . . to be frank"—Duncan seemed to be trying to sound as steady as Josh—"I hadn't really thought of using it, except maybe in an emergency."

"We need credit now. To *avoid* an emergency."

"I know," said Duncan. He coughed slightly. "It certainly would open up new horizons. For instance, we could think seriously about getting someone to copy those machines, make 'em Baianoproof and get them ready so that once we start franchising—

But look here, Josh, you must be financing things of your own on that place. I thought you were thinking of—"

"Buying more land? Huh!" Josh's laugh was sardonic. "I cook up some poetry now and then to keep myself going. But let's face it, Duncan. At the present price, if I put everything I had into it, I'd come out with twelve more acres. Nah. That's why I got into this Frango Frito thing in the first place. So okay, first things first."

The book slipped from Lia's hand in the middle of the looting of Jeramaboa. The midafternoon sun on her back somehow no longer seemed so warm, nor the original solutions quite so amusing. Suddenly, lying on this beach in this lovely, luxuriant city seemed hideously unreal to her. She wanted to go now, this minute, back to the land, send the workers away, do everything herself, scratch with her hands.

The two of them continued on. She noted definite relief in their voices and a renewed enthusiasm now this new card was laid on the table, straightforward, irreversible, a sign of confidence they'd both needed.

"The thing, once we've got impetus, is to keep it going."

"After Campos, where to start? In the big city, where the crowds are continually on the street? Or in the small towns, where there's little competition?"

"What about a place like Pirapora . . . small but loaded with dough and desperate to be 'para frente.'"

"Or Ibipiuna?"

"Guaratinguetá."

"Itapetininga."

"Barueri?"

"Ha, ha. Xique-Xique."

So involved had they become, Caroline included, in this litany of exotic names that they hadn't even noticed Lia's rising and walking off to the edge of the sea. She was just as glad that they hadn't. Why spoil their fun? They had enough to worry about, didn't they? It was good that they could laugh and just as well that they didn't see she was suddenly not in a laughing mood. Especially since it was all for the wrong reasons. Good God, they hadn't even gotten a roof over the place yet and already she was feeling trapped by the sudden realization that this little enterprise that had never meant anything to her but more money for more land, could, in the process of beginning, wash their land down the drain. "Xique-Xique, Juazeiro . . ."

She walked along the water's edge, oblivious of the people; voluptuous, spoiled, teen-age beauties in two strips of priceless cloth, ogled by sunbrowned youths and pale hairy old men alike; whole families from the *favelas*, mothers wetting their faded cotton dresses to the bottom of their protruding bellies while swarms of the already born tumbled over one another and the waves in delight. She thought of Josh and of how she had always counted on him to make the right decisions to the point of being near oblivious to any business but the small, everyday, never quite impressive enough business of the land. Now was no time to begin doubting, even if all her instincts seemed oddly, for the first time, to cry out. She wished she could say what it was she felt. Tell it to Josh or to Caroline, who talked about things so easily to her. But she'd never been any good at that. Whenever anything had ever troubled her, she'd always come to the brink of telling it and thought, "What's the use?" Which was what she thought now about the feeling that somehow things were slipping out of their hands, a dream was receding, being lost from sight. After all, it was she who was being unrealistic, not Josh. Fire everyone, do all the work themselves, pull in their belts? Useless.

She turned slowly backward, scuffing along in the water and sand. The sun was making its long fiery path across the sea before setting, bathing the astounding, careless beauty of this city in its warm yellow light. It was magnificent! A moment not to be wasted. Yet she longed, ached to be far from here, in the high place alone and above the world.

CHAPTER 25

The opening of Frango Frito Limitada was, as all associates involved would remember for years to come, a very successful nightmare. Invitations were distributed to a select group of potential financiers and chicken farmers and everybody came with his family, including fourth cousins and in-laws.

The neon chicken in the neon pot hanging over the door looked smugly confident. He could not possibly have been aware of what was going on inside, where his prototypes lay in heaps on a table awaiting the knife and the boiling oil while Lia studied the Chicken Little efficiency chopping chart before her, gallantly hiding the fact that she never had and never would understand charts. Next to her a Baiano, looking cheerfully unconcerned, followed her explicit "agora aqui, agora ali," bringing the blade of his knife down upon wing, thigh, pope's nose and breast with devastating finality.

The coleslaw paper cup loan had gone through in time, but Teodoro, whose last-minute mission had been to scour the town for a chopper, had turned up the night before with parched throat, blistered feet and another knife. One hundred cabbages piled in sacks from floor to ceiling, to which Caroline applied her undying energy, her unconquerable will, challenged the boy who chopped stolidly at her side to a hopeless race against time.

Each time she took a step back, she collided with the refrigerator, a monumental structure of mortuarian capacity, whose creator had gone bankrupt constructing it (because Teodoro was a friend) at a bargain price. In his bankruptcy he had abandoned this edifice seven eighths the size of the kitchen to a free-lance electrician hired for twice the original estimate to complete the job. He was still completing it now, climbing up doors, passing wires over the heads of the others, ordering "*liga, disliga,*" announcing with morbid cheerfulness, "We'll have to break the wall," as the refrigerator heated to Hadean temperatures and the frying machines awaited the signal to come alive, and the hordes drew nearer outside.

No one had ever *worked* the machines; no one except Chicken Little Enterprises in Decatur, Illinois, could confidently declare that they did, in fact, work. Duncan stood before them looking disdainfully assured, his bowels aboil with anxiety. From without he could actually hear the siege approach. Josh at the head of one hundred ravenous grandmothers in the vulture's clothing of their perpetual mourning, hundreds of voracious children ready to cast their pacifiers into the dust; not to mention the in-laws.

Deftly Duncan pushed the panic button . . . A bubbling sound was heard, lights flashed, something that awakened deep memories of the blast that commanded "all men on deck" during his naval career, galvanized him anew into action. The chicken emerged, golden brown and steaming. A take-out box glided mystically on the tips of Josh's fingers above and beyond the scavenging claws of the grandmothers to Harry McGuiness, who gravely tweeked his ear and saluted Josh in grim approval that seemed to say, "Maybe, after all."

Then pure, undiluted motion. Flying take-out boxes on whirling arms and legs, munching jaws, approving grunts, constant streams of relatives transporting vittles, as if this were the last meal before the siege of Jerusalem, to the relatives and in-laws, who—yes, there were even still some who had remained at home.

On the following day, Teodoro called in Dona Bedica the *bençadeira,* who cooked her pot of herbs over a smoking kerosene fire and sprinkled incense in all the corners of the restaurant to cast out any evil spirits that might have sneaked in with the crowd. Then he had installed his brother-in-law behind the cash register, a tall, thin northern Italian, pale to the point of colorlessness, outwardly impassive to the point of causing one to wonder what kind of wheels were turning behind the inexpressive blue eyes. It was the face of the chauffeur he had once been; the same one who had won a gold watch and politely carried off the machine.

Now, six months later, Josh sat behind his desk on the balcony at the feed store and admitted to himself that business was going badly. The thought was not made any easier to bear by the realization that, although he had lived in Brazil for more than fifteen years, their lack of success was due, in large measure, to their "thinking American."

For instance, the parking lot was American in that it was large; Brazilian in that it was empty. João Faria had been right. Who, if he had a car, wanted to eat his dinner in it? Part of the joy of going to a restaurant was to sit at a table and signal imperiously to a garçon for service. And then this business of eating out of a basket with one's fingers. It was modern, all right, but somehow it seemed to give to the Brazilians an uncomfortable sense of latent barbarism.

To make things worse, winter had come that year with a vengeance unknown since the coffee-killing frost of 1955. Just as Clea had predicted, the wind sweeping through the latticed brickwork was comparable to a draft in the Magellan Strait. Teodoro covered as many holes as he could with plywood and posters; installed a traditional Brazilian basin for washing one's hands after meals (tried to avoid the traditional filthy towel). The parking lot would better have been bricked over and filled with chairs and tables and parasols so that people could soak up the winter sun that had shifted to the building's outer periphery. But there was no more money.

Right now Josh was thinking if he could only take some more out of the feed business, but chickens were in a crisis for a change. Half the farmers couldn't pay and all the processes in court could not force them to do what they couldn't. And at any rate, if they were forced to sell out and pay, who would buy the feed the next time around?

Central Feeds, of course, still demanded cash. "Get it from the banks." Josh's legs were tired. He wondered if his appearance—the steady look behind the cigar—still inspired confidence. Was it his imagination or were the bank managers perpetually out of sight these days; no one hurrying across carpet and marble to give him an abraço. Then too, things were tightening up. One could no longer deposit a check in São João de Barra and thank God and the poor postal system that the check took a week to cover fifty miles. Checks had to be confirmed immediately or not released until they were. Added to that, the Central Bank had decreed, "No more bank holidays on saints' days." That was a hard blow. At that news even Dona Michiko looked vaguely as though she'd like to pack it up and go back to Japan.

Nor was the miracle department in any better shape than it had been. Like a great many others, the 350,000-cruzeiro deal for a housing development near the oil refinery of Paulinha had come to naught. Teodoro had even attended a session during which the spirit of the dead father had entered the being of Dona Bedica, his deep, patriarchal voice issuing from her lips with a resounding, "*Não faça negocio.*" And so the son had remained sitting on the land in his rags and bare feet and Teodoro had remained without his commission.

There was a certain splendor, one had to admit, in such filial fidelity. Nothing had been able to persuade the caboclo that three sacks full of money could solve his problems.

"What problems?" he had asked, whether out of ignorant apathy or wisdom, it would have been hard to say. But Teodoro had thrown in the rag, incapable of finding a response. And now even he, the tireless, eternal optimist, was beginning to look haggard and oddly distracted.

"Perhaps," Josh thought, as he sat on the balcony adding up those checks that he knew had funds against those that didn't, "it's Teodoro's eyes." The other day Lia had come in and he'd mistaken her for Caroline. Only when Lia had spoken gently and gracefully, pretending she hadn't noticed, had he realized that she was not. Josh thought of what it must be to constantly fear the loss of one's sight. Then he thought, "God knows, *I* shouldn't feel tired"; and yet he did.

So tired that when he drove home at night, he scarcely bothered to look around him. But perhaps, too, that was because by the time he got back to the fazenda after a long, grueling day, it was too dark to see. He didn't tell Lia how bad things were. What could she do? There were many things he knew, as well, that she did not tell him about the fazenda. Nagging things, small in comparison with what he had to face every day; machinery that was worn out but was too expensive to replace, a bull sold with nothing but a promissory note in return. And she needed the money so badly to pay for repairs, yet she hadn't the heart to ask

Josh for more. She hated owing. He knew it. He was used to this business of being in the banks. She had never been aware of it, never really thought about it until the fazenda was in the banks along with everything else. Even the old magic talk of the land across the river, wheat and soybeans in Mato Grosso was missing from their conversation. It would have been senseless and ironic to talk about that now.

Yet Lia did keep up a certain patter. About how the bulls were looking good enough to show this year. (As if they could afford to support animals at a fair for a week.) Or the idea of planting pecan trees to take the place of the coffee when it grew old. "I'll graft them myself," she'd say determinedly, "and in seven years—"

"For Christ's sake, Lia," he'd once shouted at her, "don't you know we're living from day to day?" And then because she'd looked so devastated, he'd felt more tired than ever and, finishing his meal, he'd gone and slept in his chair till it was time to go to bed.

They told each other less and less, these two who had always told each other everything; their conversation had indeed become oddly stilted, there being so much more weight to what they didn't say than what they did. Sometimes it seemed to him he'd give anything just to be able to buy her those trees. Just so they might be able to talk about something fresh and hopeful that did exist. The desire, so modest for Josh, made him think with a strange new sense of humility, "If someone would offer me a job—right now . . . Harry would smile if he knew I was thinking that, and say, 'My round.' But then he'd probably say too, 'Who would offer Josh Moran a job, who was known for taking jobs, but never seriously? Who would not "stay" if it meant "going to Rio." Who, when there was nothing more he could do about the state of things, did nothing and went to a movie.' "

In fact the thought of going to a movie seemed like a good idea. *Getting Straight* was playing at the Cine Tropical; maybe some real nonsense would restore his sense of humor.

He wrote a check of his own, calmly, authoritatively, as if he knew there could be no difficulty, as if he didn't know Duncan was, that very afternoon, with the worldly air of an experienced international banker, assuring the National Bank of Minas Gerais that it could renew Sr. Josh Moran's overdue promissory.

"*Não, não tem problema.*" Josh could hear him. "A little crisis in the day-old chick market. In another two weeks the day-old chicks will be chickens. *Não é?* Everything will normalize."

"Dona Michiko." He handed her the check he'd written. "Have Lupe deposit this in Central Feeds' account at five twenty-five— no earlier, no later."

"From the Banco Minas Gerais?" Her expression was becoming more inscrutable every day, but she needed no expression for him to understand the meaning of her question.

"*Sim. Se deus quizer,* we'll have funds tomorrow at opening time."

Wordlessly Dona Michiko took the check and placed it in a drawer and then looked up with sudden, undisguisable apprehension at the clatter of footsteps on the stairs. It was not Lupe running ahead of a bank inspector but Teodoro. Nor was it the Teodoro of stalwart, bright cheer who, even at the worst moment, could summon semi-mystic optimism to carry him through the day, but a Teodoro so subdued that had his features not been so distinct, they might have been unrecognizable.

"*E Sr. Harry,*" he gasped as he reached the top step.

"*O' que há?*" Josh rose stiffly, a sick feeling in his stomach, a sudden certainty of what Teodoro's next words would be.

"*Morreu.*" His eyes swung and focused on Josh unbelievingly. "Just this very moment—he's dead."

CHAPTER 26

Later on it would occur to Josh that despite the shock, he had not been surprised. He had not seen Harry for some time, even though he had known that he was "winding up things" here and would soon be leaving for good. The last time they had been together, Harry had grinned ironically as he said, "If you go bankrupt, let me know. Remember, there's always the Orinoco." But there hadn't been much laughter in those sharp black eyes, and it had seemed to Josh that Harry McGuiness was sick of everything, even of their age-old debate; spiritually and physically sick. So, although all thoughts of his own troubles had been swept from Josh's mind the instant Teodoro had appeared, it had seemed almost as if the message Teodoro had brought had been something he'd been expecting for some time: That the running argument with Harry McGuiness had been summarily cut short by death.

It was Teodoro who dressed the corpse and got it to a place where it could be kept until someone decided what to do with it. There was no one else, and as Teodoro said simply, "I have always been the one to dress the corpse." Then he'd gone back to the house, as he'd done on other occasions when Harry had been gone from home just a few days too many, to look after Helen McGuiness.

"And keep an eye on the Missus, will you?" Harry had always tossed the words back at Teodoro gruffly, knowing full well that his red tape lieutenant would understand the intensity of his plea.

It was ironic, unfair, one of those cruel tricks of life that she, who had never been happy here, never, as the Brazilians put it "become accustomed," should be left behind. Teodoro had gone back to the house to take care of the Missus, locking up the bottles

in a cabinet in the cellar as only he could do it, with such absolute compassion.

Josh began working on the consular details: the infinite, pesky,
meaningless details that must impede and hound a person even
in the process of dying and being lowered into his grave. Lia came
over to see what she could do, ashamed that she had not tried
harder at some earlier time to be a friend. But it had never been
easy to be a friend to this woman who was a separate part of Harry
McGuiness' life. Who said, "I'm a Californian, you know . . ." as
if that, in itself, explained her detestation of this remote, unso-
phisticated world.

She was a strange passionate woman who had never quite believed that a man could afford such devotion to his work and yet
have enough love left for anything else. How could he rise from
his bed at 4:00 A.M., leaving the warmth and tenderness of his
wife, to investigate a stretch of cold unresponsive earth, miles
distant, and do it happily? At first it was his work she was jealous
of. Then, as the years stretched by and they remained in this place
that she had always considered a "temporary residence," her jeal-
ousy had gradually become an all-encompassing disease. She had
begun, among other things, to think that her life had been wasted.
She had never been on the stage, and yet Lia couldn't help feeling,
each time she saw her, that she should have been an actress. Her
whole life, it seemed, had been some sort of an act. And yet now,
as she came forward elegantly dressed for the part, it occurred to
Lia that, for her, there had never been a difference between the
act and reality.

She looked warily at the strange group assembled there. Teodoro, who knew everything; Jose Chaves, who had come all the
way from Rio; Josh, Lia. Knowing they already thought her
strange, she'd been certain at first that they'd all come to see the
show. Then, realizing at last that they hadn't, she stood clasping
and unclasping her hands, playing the part to the hilt and yet
being so true.

"You, Lia—what would you do? His sister in Nebraska wants
him back. Incredible, what? But if that's all she has. And what
difference should it make to him? But to get on that plane, get
off it with him . . . dead! Besides, why take him from here? He
always said he didn't care one way or another. But you know,

don't you, if he hadn't cared, he wouldn't have died. Well, that's the truth, isn't it? Good God, don't stare as if I was making some revelation. Doesn't anyone want a drink? Teodoro, somebody's locked up the booze. I swear, in my own house."

"I'll ask the maid," said Teodoro, feeling in his own pocket for the key.

And then when they were all sitting around in the room made so strange by Harry's absence, all feeling grateful for Teodoro's "rediscovery" of the booze, she'd told what just about everyone had expected to hear.

"He didn't have to die. Why, the madman made love to me the night before. That's how strong he was." Her voice trembled with an accentuated rapture, assuring them and herself that he had still loved her. "But he had this pain, in his arm, his side. It was real pain, I could see that. I wanted to call the doctor, but he wouldn't let me. 'Nah, no' "—she brought him starkly into the room with a gruff imitation—"'tuh hell with it.' You can hear him, can't you?

"He didn't care. He just gave up, let himself die. You know that, don't you, Josh? And you know why." There was no avoiding her gaze. She was demanding confirmation. It would have been useless, disloyal to say anything but, "Yes, we all do. That's why we're here."

"Don't dwell on it." The blunt features of Jose Chaves became unaccustomedly gentle. "He lived a good life. He loved his work."

And she, who had never been able to live, really, or accept that other love, said, "Helluva reward, wasn't it?"

It was Teodoro again who stayed after all the others were gone; locking up the booze, taking care of the Missus until they could get her on the plane with Harry, dead, headed for the flat, dry Nebraska plain that had never had anything to do with his life. That had never meant anything to either of them.

It was such an odd thing to do, take him back. Teodoro was convinced that, for all Harry's body might be buried in Nebraska, his spirit would remain here, unable to rest. He said as much. Didn't the sister know? Couldn't she imagine Helen McGuiness, stiff-lipped and alone on that plane? Or hadn't she seen her for many years? And yet Helen now was determined herself to do it— perhaps to prove that she could; perhaps, because in the end, leaving him here in this place would have been like giving in. No one would ever be able to tell. One only wished, suddenly, that there could have been two Teodoros so that Harry's old red tape lieutenant could have continued on keeping his eye on the Missus as long as it was needed.

Driving home after her departure, Lia sat very close to Josh, drawn to him by the feelings they shared and the knowledge, made tangent as it is at moments like these, that they were returning to home and children; that love was within their grasp.

In the back seat of the American Bathtub was the dog, the last thing Helen McGuiness had given up, not knowing where she would go now. He was a boxer, a great gentle creature with a look of distress on his comically wrinkled features. At first he had paced nervously back and forth, barked gruffly, snuffed against the windows. Now, in resignation, he settled down on the pink satin pillow that Helen had provided for his bed. Another symbol of the incongruities of the McGuiness household.

There had been a summer storm, and the clouds, parting and rising, cast shadows that drifted lazily across an exuberant green landscape. On the edges of the woods, there was the damp, steaming look of the tropics after a rain. Here and there, a bougainvillea that had grown into a tree, burst like a purple flame above the treetops; or a lone palm, its fronds still wet and glistening, lent a tall, slender perspective to the wide open, sweeping land. Everything was bright, warm, tropical and alive. Lia thought of Helen McGuiness returning to the cold windswept country she hadn't seen in years and wondered how it would be.

Reaching over the back of the seat, Lia stroked the dog's huge, broad forehead and, thinking of Helen, said, "It's funny. I never thought she understood Harry, but she did, perfectly."

"There's a difference between understanding and accepting," said Josh.

"You mean that business about 'some reward'? Well, it's true," Lia said with a certain bitterness. "He gave his life—you could almost say literally. And who the hell cared?"

"Nobody." Josh's rugged features became still and hard in their thoughtfulness. "But that's not the point to me. He never asked for a reward. He did what he did because he was Harry McGuiness.

He never could have done it any other way. And he took the consequences. It was *him* she never accepted, the way he was. Don't you see?"

"I do." Lia nodded and then said with a strangely exaggerated defensiveness, "But that doesn't mean she didn't love him. She did."

"Yes," said Josh, "I think she did. I think she loved him very much." As he said this, he took Lia's hand and pressed it hard against his thigh as he often did, in a way that he felt must assure her too, more than anything he could say, of the depth and reality of his own love for her.

CHAPTER 27

The dog, Thomas, attached himself to Josh. Used to leash, satin pillow and a lonely woman, he found himself unconfined in the midst of the open country surrounded by other dogs, children, horses, herds of cattle which bore down upon him, snuffing and blowing as he followed at his new master's heels. Then there were days when numerous people sat on the terrace under the pine trees, talking and laughing with drinks in their hands. On those occasions, the dog sat close to Josh and rested his huge head on Josh's knee as if his body could no longer bear its weight. Always Josh's knee, as if some message had come to him from the grave, saying, "Trust this one."

Malachai observed this, as he observed all things, thinking, "This McGuiness must have been a man of strong will and this only similarity between himself and Josh is what the dog senses." Josh had gone off now, the dog close at his heels, to look over the coffee that had been harvested and now lay on the wide brick *terreiro* drying in the sun.

Everyone, in fact, was gone. Clea lay reading in a cool white room in the old slave house. Caroline, full of restless energy that demanded action, had disappeared on horseback, and Duncan, with a patience that he possessed only for such undertakings, had taken his two small sons for a walk. Lia had gone off with a basket somewhere. On weekends, relieved of the man's job of riding, walking, overseeing, she was always off somewhere, exuberant, with a basket doing women's work—picking vegetables or oranges, cutting flowers. Jacob Svedelius, oddly silent and moody for such a contained person, had disappeared altogether. Only Malachai remained under the pine trees on a faded green wooden chair; the other chairs in which they had sat drinking Josh's potent, peppery bloody marys before lunch, stood deserted all around him.

He enjoyed it—this lonely conference of empty chairs. After all the noise, the competition of wits, he could consider his friends at his leisure, recalling each individual to his place without being disturbed by his talk. Still, one chair, deep in the shade, the one Delia, with her innate Brazilian horror of overexposure to the sun's darkening rays, would have occupied, attracted his thoughts more than all the others, because Delia had not occupied it. Malachai's small discerning eyes kept returning to it and each time they did he saw Delia, not seated here in this peaceful, distant place under the trees, but in his apartment in São Paulo, in the middle of everything.

Outside rockets had been bursting like flak, and crowds were swarming by, jubilant over the victory of Santos against Palmerias. They had been watching the *futebol* game on TV and Clea, limp with emotion and celebrational Irish whiskey, had upended before the set and there had remained until Malachai gently guided her to bed. Alone, Delia and Malachai had sat, listening above the noise of the rockets and crowds for Francisco's return from the dam, which was completed, had been inaugurated and was beginning to supply untold energy to a power-starved West.

"Be prepared for what he'll look like when he appears." There had been long suffering as well as indulgence in Delia's tone, as if she were speaking of an incorrigible child. "You may want to spray him before you let him in."

"I? I've already seen him that way a thousand times." Malachai had cautiously fallen into Delia's mood of indulgence. "I like it. It gives me a better sense of what he's been up to, like seeing a boy, still thoroughly happy from playing in the mud."

"Hmm, the mud." Indulgence had given way to a sudden sarcasm. "Just so. Let him play in it. Let him build his dams. At least it does *him* good."

"*Espera uno minuti.*" Malachai's only sign of distress had been a touch of Italian in his Portuguese. "All that electrical power where there was none before, must certainly be of use to someone other than Francisco."

"Ah, Malachai." Delia shook her head pityingly. "You never cease to be credulous, do you?"

"I believe reasonable is a better word. You'll have to admit,

Delia, a lot is being done. This project for irrigation in the North-east. Why, even Duncan, the stalwart cynic, can't keep himself from being excited about it, it seems."

"Excited? I should think so. Imagine the money involved. And think *where* it will all go. Have you seen the plans? THE COMPANY," she said mockingly, "always written in capital letters, of course. Once the government has confiscated the land, THE COMPANY will install the pumping stations, divide up the land and sell it in plots of fifty to ten thousand hectares."

"I believe," said Malachai, as soothingly as possible, "the size of the plots are determined by the kind of crop. You don't need ten thousand hectares for a plantation of melons, for instance, but cotton—"

"Cotton, melons, *porbrezinho*." Delia had regarded him with feigned pity, as if she were speaking to a child. "Wait for some big American firm to come along with the money, and then you shall see how quickly those fifty-hectare plots will disappear and the people with them." At some other point, earlier in her history, her eyes would have lighted now with a hint of amusement, of challenge. But this time they hadn't. "Nothing has changed," she'd said, "nothing will. As long as . . ."

"As long as what?" Malachai had been unable to resist the ex-asperation she'd aroused in him. "Do you think that by changing a system, you are going to change human beings? What tribe of secular saints have you behind your magic curtain, waiting to be revealed? It's energy and ambition that move the world. Must we continually be turning it upside down to see what rises to the surface?"

She had not answered him, as if it were useless to answer. To break her silence as much as anything, he had said, "And so will you be going with us to the fazenda this weekend?"

She'd shaken her lovely head and looked away from him, for fear of what? "No, I think not," she'd said. "I really can't bear their smugness."

Even after Francisco had arrived, dusty, euphoric, famished for a cold bottle of beer, civilized food, and full of talk about the primitive world from which he'd come, his enthusiasm had not served to lighten the oppressive feeling that had come over Mala-chai. Delia had greeted her husband happily enough with a warmth and immediacy that ignored his disheveled, dusty appearance. But while he talked, she had seemed only to be half listening or at times not listening at all, lost in her own thoughts; perhaps, thought Malachai, preferring not to hear.

And they had not come to the fazenda, for all that Francisco's eyes had lighted with a longing to see old friends. It was too bad. Friends unable to keep up an argument, divided by it. It was not right. Not Brazilian. It saddened Malachai whenever he thought of it and, at the same time, filled him with a sense of doom.

Still one could not feel gloomy for long sitting under these trees. The sunlight was warm here and the wind in the high branches sounded gentle and distant like the sea, while all around him, across the valley, he could see the result of man's peaceful work. Corn was yellowing and ripening on the hills, cotton bursting white from its bolls, and in the flatland along the streams, rice was bending with the weight of its grain. He could hear the voices of the coffee pickers. Some sang jubilantly loud and off key, others prattled constantly as their rough hands stripped the branches of berries; others upbraided their children for getting in the way, stepping on the *peneiras*, where the coffee berries lay already winnowed and clean. It was the sound of people not concerned with "the argument," but with day-to-day living: children, crops, harvest, food, drink, rest, work.

From where he sat, listening, reassured by the busy rhythm of life, he now saw Josh standing on the terreiro, where the coffee was spread in the sun to dry. The dog was close by and Josh was bending over to pick up a handful of coffee berries. Placing them on the terreiro's faded brick surface, he crushed the berries under his booted heel, gathered them up again, crunched them in his hands to further loosen pulp from seed, blew the chaff away and smelled.

From the eloquent expression on his face, even at this distance, Malachai could see that the quality of the coffee must be pretty poor—probably Rio Macaco—the sound of the words rather than their definition suggested the taste of monkey droppings. Malachai thought back to the last flowering, that had, like all the others, been celebrated with great expectation. Then forward to the drought that had caused a third of the berries to drop instead of "set" and then on to the exceptional rains in the dry season that had caused the berries to ferment and stew in their own juices, causing the resultant odor, and the look of distaste that could be seen and sympathized with from as far away as the pine trees. Then Josh shrugged and grinned at the overseer, Marino, as if to say, "That's farming." And Malachai shrugged to himself and thought, "Josh is going to make it in spite of the fact that he and Duncan are in debt up to their ears and the coffee harvests never produce their expected bounty." His assumption, he had to admit, was a complete reversal of what it had been in the beginning, when he had thrown up his hands at the idea of trying to persuade Brazilians that it was not only savages and Baianos who ate with their fingers. But things had changed since then, or rather— politically—they had held steady. Whatever Delia thought of it, one could sense the optimism in the air.

It no longer mattered what idea Duncan and Josh had chosen; almost any idea would do. What really mattered was the moment and the people involved. If they could hold out a little bit longer, if the country could resist being smothered, despite its energy and euphoria, by the dark age that seemed to be descending over the rest of the world, Duncan and Josh might possibly become rich. All this, simply because it was the right time and the right place for people such as they, who were ambitious and yet didn't take things seriously enough to become ill at the thought of the risk.

They would make it. If not by farming, which seemed to be, next to sculpture, the most unprofitable profession in existence, then in some other way. Enough to buy five fazendas the size of this. For Malachai, the thought provided, at least temporarily, a comforting counterbalance to the gloom he had sensed at the sight of Delia's empty chair. He felt suddenly secure and peaceful. The pine trees beneath which he now sat, with birds nesting and fighting in their upper branches, seemed for the moment, permanent and safe. There seemed to be time for a nap at least before the dark age descended. Thinking so, he closed his eyes and listened to the wind.

He wasn't awakened all at once by the sound of voices. Rather, they came to him, along with the rustling of leaves, as part of his sleeping, voices and words in a dream. The orchard, just beyond the pine trees, with its oranges, and avocados, was a part of the dream as well as the man's voice, gentle, though a shade too imploring.

"Wait a minute. Stay here. What's the hurry?"

And her voice in reply, a little too abrupt, "Basket's full, isn't it?"

"Why are you always in a hurry?"

"There's always so much to do."

"Not today, Lia. It's Saturday, remember?" Then gentler still and more urgent, "You look wonderful today, did you know that? Fresh and sunbrowned and a part of everything around you."

Lia's laugh seemed unusually brittle. "You've never seen me in my gowns and jewels."

"I don't need to. I know they wouldn't suit you half as well." There was another rustling of leaves, that reminded Malachai of a feeble attempt at escape. The words that accompanied it, feeble too. "What about the things you've planted, the oranges, the tamarinds?"

"They are thriving, despite their battle with the ants."

"Good. She will be pleased to have them when she comes."

"I think not," said Jacob, newly determined. "You see, she is not coming."

There was a silence, long enough to allow other sounds, the cantankerous cry of a cattle bird, to invade Malachai's dreaming, arouse him fully so that he could no longer pretend, even to himself, to be asleep.

Then Jacob spoke again. "You're not really surprised, are you?"

"Not really, only disturbed. It's difficult to imagine."

"How people can grow apart? What can I say? If you don't share life, you become used to being alone. You can imagine that, can't you? And then something happens that makes all reason seem suddenly narrow and mocking." He went on, speaking these words that might have been generalities, but weren't, that made of Malachai a troubled, involuntary eavesdropper. "Or do you think that people are so strong they can surely predict their entire lives?" His voice rose now, became filled with something close to accusation. "You, for instance. Have you never thought your life with Josh could suddenly change?"

178 THE DREAMERS

"I? Oh yes, I suppose so, who hasn't at some time or other?" Malachai had to admire the matter-of-factness of Lia, so determined in the face of this assault. It was maddening. "But Josh and I do share life. It's different, you see."

"How clear. How simple," Jacob said softly. And then in a tone that was somehow challenging in its lightness, "You are a dunce. Look, you've filled the basket so full you can't carry it."

As they emerged from the orchard Malachai endeavored to look asleep without appearing to have been carved that way. He might have succeeded had not at the moment in the swaying green branches above his head, the cattle birds begun to fight over a nest overladen with unidentified eggs. Amid squawks and screeches the black birds tottered and swayed and lurched. Eggs tumbled in all directions; one struck squarely behind Malachai's ear. Before he could bound out of his chair, another struck his forehead. Wiping the yolk away with a pocket handkerchief, he stood watching as the domestic hue and cry from above continued to produce its shower of eggs that smashed themselves on the wooden chair, scattered and rolled over the grass, twenty-two, twenty-three, twenty-four beautiful turquoise eggs, white-patterned as if candle-waxed for a Slavic Easter. To his relief, Lia came up behind him, drowning the squawks of the anús with her laughter, and from the slave house, Clea appeared at an open window to emit a chuckle, at once amused and foreboding.

"God in heaven, Malachai, it's hopeless. You can't even doze under a tree."

CHAPTER 28

That evening, sitting at the head of his table, Josh felt more at peace with himself and the world than he had in a long time, despite his multiple problems, despite the outrage of Harry Mc-Guiness' death, of which he was reminded every time the dog laid his oversized head on Josh's knee. It was an outrage that Harry's will to live had been destroyed by bigness, directionlessness, indifference. But Harry had lived as he'd chosen to live. So be it. On that point they had always agreed and always would. Even after death.

Josh lived as he chose to, and this was one of those evenings when the fact seemed more rewarding than less. Lia and the kitchen girls had outdone themselves with roast pork and applesauce, squash and beans and a salad of fresh lettuce, bitter *rucula*, chives and endive from the garden. Everything was from the fazenda, and serving it all, her sunbrowned arm stretching forth from the cotton knit blouse that molded nicely to her strong young body, Lia seemed in her element. She looked to him assured and happy. There was a special glow about her that he had not seen in a long time and the sight of her now filled him with pride and desire. He was sure her happiness at this moment had—much the same as his own—to do with the sense of permanence they felt, sitting at their own table in the midst of a world they had created themselves amongst friends they had known for years.

Indeed there was nothing Josh liked better than to meet a stranger who seemed interesting; to invite him in, question him, and never invite him again if it wasn't worth it. Yet part of the permanence that he loved had to do with staying in one place long enough for some of those strangers to become deeply familiar, to take upon themselves the special quality of associations that are lasting. A friend is someone who has within his nature, despite all the transformations that occur in his lifetime and yours, something unique to offer you, something that may be hard to define and yet irreplaceable.

It was so that Josh felt about the few people to whom he returned again and again. Caroline, with her infinite ego and passion for living. Duncan, whose amusing cynicism shielded a soul so exigent that it pained him. Clea, the perpetual battlefield of instinct and rationality. Malachai, whose sensitive soul suffered the constant imposition of three-dimensional vision. They were all here tonight. He wished that Francisco were here with his dedication to angles and lines and stresses that seemed to make life so comfortingly uncomplicated. But Malachai suggested that Delia's obsession had reached a stage of illness. That contact was useless until she became well enough to be capable of arguing.

"But she's a friend!" Lia had protested, deeply distressed.

To which Malachai had replied, shaking his head, "Sometimes I wonder if she is who she was."

Among those present this evening then, there was only one whom Josh found intriguing and yet could not really bring himself to consider as a friend. But perhaps, he told himself, that was because he had had little opportunity to come to know him. The Dane came up the mountain from time to time in his battered, sea-rusted truck to pick up root stock and pigs from Josh's breeding lots. But he always departed before Josh's return, wanting to take advantage of the cool of night to transport his grasses and livestock the long distance home. "Jacob was here today," Lia would say of him.

"And how is he doing?"

"Oh, you know Jacob. It's always the same thing. He gets an order for wood and the sawmill breaks down. He gets the sawmill fixed and he can't deliver the wood because the road is washed out. He's not of this world." Thus she would dismiss him, with a strange vehemence that bordered on antagonism, almost as if she considered his charming impracticality some sort of threat. Josh felt not in the least bit threatened by the thoughts and behavior of this rather phantasmagoric figure. He thought of him simply as one of those individuals who asked advice but never took it for fear of compromising some painfully, introspectively acquired principle. It was not that these principles were wrong. They were, on the contrary, so enlightened, so civilized as to be saddening; because they seemed beyond the capacity of any human being to attain. If their understanding of one another never ripened, probably it was Josh's practicality that interfered. Since the day of their meeting they had never seemed to be able to give and take in a discussion, despite all the common ground they had to walk on. It occurred to Josh that perhaps that was the real reason they avoided one another except in a crowd.

Lia had finished serving things but sat now letting her food grow cold, absorbed in a discussion of the supernatural which she herself had instigated by describing Teodoro's distress over the burial of Harry McGuiness in a land that, as Teodoro had put it, meant nothing to Harry's spirit. "He says there'll be no rest," she was saying, "and I'm not so sure there isn't something in it. The dog. You know the look a dog gets when he is being called—not by just anyone, but by his master? I've seen him jump up, out of a deep sleep—"

"Ah, Lia." It was Jacob who was being practical this time. "You *do* have an imagination, don't you?"

"Imagination?" Clea's solemn triangular face loomed mystically in the candlelight. "How do you know which is which? Does one imagine a sensation? Or does he really sense it? The longer you live in this place, my boy, the harder you'll find it to tell whether the thing has come from within or without . . ."

"Oh, come along. I've lived here quite a time, on and off. I wish I *could* blame some of the things that have happened to me on forces beyond my control." Jacob was answering Clea, but Malachai, sitting opposite him, wondered if anyone noticed how intently his gaze rested upon Lia. She looked back at him now, the color deepening beneath the tan of her cheeks. "So everything is a matter of will, is it? Then if everyone in the world decided suddenly that there was no *other* force, would every other cease to exist?"

"Circumstance and timing would still be around," said Jacob. "Isn't that enough to cope with?"

If there was a double meaning to his words, Caroline was not aware of it. "You mean the mysticism, the hocus-pocus? Have you ever been to Bom Jesús da Lapa." She shuddered disgustedly, as if struck by the memory of the grotto by the São Francisco River, beautiful to some, hideous to herself. "The price lists for prayers, beggars begging from beggars, selling their sores. Why, even the Catholics who were with us turned away in disgust, do you remember, Lia? Industry of poverty, they called it. All the evil of Catholic mysticism. And yet—"

"Yes?"

"If someone were very ill—Teodoro, for instance, with his blind daughter—and asked me what I thought of visiting a medium"— her wide gaze seemed infinitely honest—"I couldn't, not for all my Methodist upbringing, advise him against it."

Malachai nodded thoughtfully. "So what Caroline is saying is that it is dangerous to do otherwise." He smiled at Jacob, his heavy lids half hooding his eyes, giving him the look of a Levantine sage, "Perhaps, after all, that is the saving grace of this country, the feeling that man shares his responsibilities with fate. You are familiar—are you not?—with the expression, 'se Deus quizer.'"

"Am I?" Jacob groaned. "It gets in my way every day of the week. Nothing can simply be *done*. It is always, 'if God, *God*' "—he gestured wearily toward the ceiling—" 'wills it.' "

"*There*, you see?" Once again Lia entered the discussion and once again it seemed to Malachai to become personal, something Lia Moran and Jacob Svedelius had argued over intently, more than once. "That is what I've been trying to tell you. If it gets in your way, it exists. Maybe not in Denmark. But then Denmark is so civilized it's dead." She said it with scornful authority. "But here, it is as much a part of everything as the trees you plant, the earth you till. If you don't accept it, it will do you in, I tell you!"

"Control yourself, Lia." Josh was wondering if Jacob Svedelius was aware of how Lia, so often mute on the subject of herself, could nonetheless express herself so exaltedly in an argument. "If anything gets in Jacob's way down where he is, it's climate. Rain, heat, that breed disease and lethargy. Of all the places to choose." Then, reminded of his thoughts of a moment ago, he added, "But I've said all that before."

"I know, I know." Jacob nodded amiably. "The Mato Grosso or somewhere along the São Francisco River, where it's dry and windy. Almost anywhere else but where I am." He threw up his hands helplessly. "I'm doomed, I'm afraid, by a liking for the jungle and the sea."

"Nothing wrong with liking the sea if you can lick the problem of making a living," said Duncan. He had been listening to the discussion with a somewhat stolid expression on his face, having as little faith in mysticism as he had in the human will. "Maybe the thing to do would be set up a grotto in one of those mountainside caves." He looked comically inspired. "We could form a company, hire Teodoro as High Priest, sell fried chicken, substitute a prayer for french fries."

"You know, that's *not* such a bad idea?" said Clea, looking sharply businesslike. "Malachai could make the saints." Everybody roared, Jacob included. "But then why shouldn't they?" thought Malachai to himself. It was funny and they were all in high spirits. Particularly Lia, who behaved this evening with the special grace of one newly adored who has not yet accepted that adoration, enjoying the brief, self-righteous moment in the game of love when everything is in one's favor. Except that such a moment, like a flame, cannot remain arrested.

They rose from the table and went to have coffee and brandy by the fire. While Malachai wondered vaguely how Josh managed to afford the brandy, Caroline fetched her guitar. She played and sang with an appealing warmth for those whom she loved best and for whom she loved best to play. And so the evening went, with Josh, sitting in his chair, his long legs stretched before him, drawing contentedly on his cigar, and Malachai, puffing on his pipe opposite him, afflicted.

Clea, full of expansive enthusiasm, was talking about São Sebastião. "The sea is so clear, the sky so magnificent in January. You must all come."

"If Josh can settle a few crises by then," Lia was saying tentatively.

"Which means you'll *never* come," Clea said with conviction. "Josh lives on crises; if he's settled one, he'll cook up another, mind you. Come whether he does or not." She waved an impatient hand. "It's so good for the children. And when we're all there," she went on, not giving Lia a chance to protest one way or another, "we'll all invade that stronghold of yours on the mountain, Jacob, do you hear?"

"I don't know why you haven't before." Malachai watched the gentlest, nicest, most decent of lonely devils smile humbly, disarmingly. "It's rather monklike, I'll admit. A table, a chair, a single bed."

"Only one?" said Malachai, a sense of exhaustion and comic hysteria coming over him at once. "Never mind, we'll all manage to fit in, if you insist."

CHAPTER 29

Duncan had never known Harry McGuiness, but today he didn't have to in order to believe, as Josh did, that he had died of despair. He was beginning to think that many a man who still had a spark in him by the time he reached McGuiness' age had possibly come to that end. Better to drown the spark, as most of his colleagues who'd been sitting round the conference table almost non-stop for the past two weeks, seemed to have been able to do. But he couldn't. He couldn't accept this gradual fossilization of mind and will that had brought the negotiations with the Soares Bank to a deadlock.

For the past year, Duncan had spent his time talking, listening, studying the field, investigating the investments available. He had sifted out the "traditional do-nothings," the vacillators, the inefficient, until he'd come up with something he was sure of. Then he'd gone to work to convince Ricardo Soares that International Bankers' investment in his firm would be healthy, productive and sensible; and it would have been. Then the heads of the South American Division had come down from New York and allowed a little fart with a Harvard degree to snow them under.

For fourteen consecutive days, weekends included, while Caroline practiced her guitar with a grim intensity that suggested she might kill it, they had sat behind closed doors round the highly polished conference table. They'd sat smoking cigarettes, having coffee and sandwiches sent in while Stanley Heimowitz, Harvard LL.D., whittled. Two or three times, when the quibbling over the wording of a sentence had become stupefying, Duncan had dozed off, awakening just in time to interject with a studious frown, "I definitely think 'fail to advise' is a less offensive phrase and should be used here rather than 'attempt to conceal.'"

Stanley Heimowitz was obsessed with the word oligarchy, out-raged by the manner in which Brazilian law was designed to pro-tect the family.

"Obsolete!" he would rage, with his high forehead, thick glasses, reminding Duncan of nothing so much as one of those beetles that sawed off whole limbs of trees in order to lay their pesky eggs on the stump.

"Nonetheless, it's the law, and this is a family firm."

"Look, buddy, do you haftah remind me every thihty-six seconds that we're dealing with an oligahchy?"

"Maybe I should remind you," Duncan had said in acrimonious tones, "that the guy has already given his fazenda and his real es-tate in the city as a guarantee. Perhaps you'd like his wife, and children too? In the end"—Duncan bared his teeth in a grin that Stanley would later describe as subconsciously aggressive—"you have to decide either to trust the fellow or not. Am I right, or aren't I?"

Well, after ten days of whittling and consultations with the home office, Ricardo Soares had refused to be castrated by the great monolith that desired to buy minority shares in his firm. He had, with perfect Brazilian affability and charm, told International Bankers to go piss in its hat.

"Well," Stanley Heimowitz had said, trying not to look shaken by this incredible turn of events, "thank Gawd I can get back to New Yawk and get a little sun on the roof."

To which Duncan had replied, "You certainly know how to live, don't you, Stanley." And that had been the end of that.

The bank, in Duncan's opinion, had lost out on the best thing going in South America. But what was Duncan's opinion, what was anyone's? The thing was to always do what seemed "safest," and when you weren't sure what was safest, pass the buck until the whole thing dissolved, and there was nothing left to do at all.

He could still see Ricardo Soares, a young man with the whole world before him and nothing much to lose, smiling politely to cover his incredulity.

"You know, Duncan, I have always had a great respect for the hard-working businessman. But I never thought of time as a mat-ter of sitting for hours eating sandwiches and fussing over commas.

I thought it was a matter of making up one's mind at the right moment."

"Do you know how the dinosaur died out?" Duncan had replied. "It got so big it had to have three brains; one in the head, one at the base of the neck and one where his tail connected with his ass. Only all the brains put together could never agree on anything—not even how to eat, digest and fart out a blade of grass."

That was the last conversation he'd had with Ricardo Soares concerning the bank. There would probably not be any more. Not that he cared, he told himself—the thing was to enjoy life, keep pulling down a salary. Only when all you needed to hold a job was a dinosaur's brain, somehow life was not very interesting. In fact it was boring, so damn boring you could scarcely force yourself to go to the office every day. So that was why, when the telex arrived, informing him that the chief of the South American Division would be returning within a week, without Stanley Heimowitz, to attempt a new approach, Duncan merely shrugged and smiled. Then he told his secretary to close the door and reply to all callers that he was "*em reunião*."

That done, he set himself to thinking seriously about chicken-frying machines. Not the machines themselves. There was a crazy Italian whom he was certain could be persuaded to make them. But the idea, the fun of devising a scheme, getting someone to invest in it, finding ways to make the whole damn thing WORK. For the first time, perhaps, he realized that he hadn't taken it very seriously in the beginning. It had been, to him, something on the side, a joke cooked up under a pup tent. Even now, he didn't consider it his final goal in life, any more than Josh did. But as time had gone on, the business had gained an alarming momentum that caused his laughter to be less amused, sometimes, than hysterical. In other words, he was beginning to be concerned about where the damn thing was going to take them all. And this concern, upon emerging from the prehistoric swamps of two weeks in the conference room, was rather like an exhilarating breath of fresh air.

"Look, Duncan," Josh had said the last time they'd met under the pine trees, "how can anyone present a balance sheet at this moment?"

"Why the hell can't anyone?"

"Because it would scare the hair off any reputable firm. What we need is a nice pompous dossier with all kinds of potential expansion charts and some maps with little red buttons indicating areas of potential attack. We'll make up a balance sheet later, when we have something besides losses to show. What do you say?"

In a sense, of course, Josh was right. It was taking a rather Stanley Heimowitz attitude to keep nagging for a balance sheet when they knew damn well how bad it would look.

So now, with the approach of a new wave of conferences in a bog apportioned to a distant corner of his mind, Duncan set to work with words and figures of his own and at lunchtime, instead of going to the Jockey Club to observe the activity, appearance and behavior of São Paulo's "financial community," he took a taxi across town to see the mad Italian.

CHAPTER 30

He wasn't mad at all—really—just disorganized in the Italian manner, a bit of a mechanical genius and very much alive. Alive and in love with life enough to have escaped twice during the war in order to survive. Once from the Russians, who had found him untangling himself from his parachute and had put him behind barbed wire. And then, having successfully reached Italy, he escaped from the Italian Air Force. That time it had occurred to him that he'd never cared much for the war in the first place and that it was about to be lost anyway. So he had decided the best thing to do, instead of testing planes that would never be used but might possibly not survive the testing, would be to take one and fly it across the border into Switzerland.

Of course this final act in favor of life and living had made the idea of returning to Italy appealing only to the nature of a martyr. Therefore he had arranged for a meeting with his father in Marseilles. His father, a hand tool industrialist from Milan who had taught his sons about life by kicking them in the pants every morning as they went to work in the factory, appeared in Marseilles with ten thousand dollars. Administering his final kick, he headed Giovanni in the direction of Rio de Janeiro.

On the ship, Giovanni fell in love with an agreeable young woman from Chile, who helped him to spend the ten thousand dollars in Rio within the space of a year, leaving him once again in a rather desperate situation in a strange land. These recurrent reversals in life had made him extremely adept at pausing only long enough to think, "I must do something quickly." This time he decided to put to use the more practical knowledge he had gathered from his father during his boyhood.

He was a mechanical genius; Duncan repeated this to himself

as he picked his way through the Italian's factory amidst heaps of sheet metal, bolts and nuts in cans, electrical wire that resembled tangled underbrush, amidst which his workers hacked and pounded the most incredible objects into shape. These, in the dust-filtered light that shone from a glass-covered hole in the roof, Giovanni hauled into view: orange squeezers, milk shake makers, hot dog grills, coffee makers, electronic ovens.

"The models are American and Italian." Giovanni beamed. "I import them, legally, if necessary. But even with the tax it is worth it. My copies are half the price before taxes, and simplified, which is more important, so that they can be operated by cane cutters and mule drivers." He tapped his forehead demonstratively. "Have you noticed every restaurant cook is a Baiano? If a Baiano can't destroy it, it's indestructible." He whacked a coffee machine to demonstrate his point; billows of dust mingled with iron filings rose, causing Duncan to sneeze. He flung open a door. Duncan hoped for air. A hot blast of steam and slightly turning meat all but struck him to the floor.

Giovanni stood aside for him to enter. "Who buys my hot dog machines, buys my hot dogs." This time they slithered through slime and vapor, past tables heaped with unidentifiable hunks of cow, bags of something that looked like sawdust. A machine that resembled a one-armed bandit coughed out a steady stream of uniformly sized penises encased in plastic condoms and pinched at both ends. Duncan tried not to breathe.

Before them another gigantic metal door that might have been the entrance to a crematorium stood, framed in an orange blaze of heat. It was held closed by a dirty string, arranged in an intricate combination which Giovanni now undid with a kind of mute and reverent care, as if this string in itself possessed the real secret to success and he was not about to reveal it. Struggling and heaving, he hauled the door open to reveal thousands more of those plastic-encased erections, the color of the sawdust he'd seen in the outer room, roasting now in inferno. Duncan wondered vaguely why the plastic didn't melt. Perhaps it was the kind they used to seal space ships. He wouldn't have put it past the Italian to have thus brought the space age into his "underdeveloped" world.

"Same idea as ours," said Duncan faintly. "Who uses our machines, buys our chickens. But look, Giovanni, I think I'm going to be sick." The Italian let out a cackle of mirth, slammed the door and retraced the intricate combination of the string.

Back in Giovanni's office, Duncan breathed deeply and sipped on beer, surrounded by heaps of dust-covered ledgers, and shelves full of foreign models and Brazilian copies. From his brief case, he produced a picture of the Chicken Little machine. While Giovanni studied the design of the machine's elaborate entrails, Duncan studied the spare, dapper figure of the Italian before him, the lean, clever features converging upon a diabolical chin. There were deep furrows in that face that suggested endurance. He had calculated, acted, survived, and all the while delighted in survival, so that there was a constant light in those level, perceptive eyes.

The eyes met Duncan's now. "Of course it will be unrecognizable, but it will work better. Half these buttons"—he waved his hand disparagingly—"are unnecessary. *Puras frescuras, meu amigo.*" The deep furrows described a broad grin. Duncan wondered, feeling refreshed, when it was he had last negotiated a deal with anyone so frank. "Now what about 'how'?"

"How. Exactly." Duncan smiled back, shedding the last remnant of a prominent banker's air to meet the Italian's clever, penetrating gaze with a look that indicated that he, too, knew something about the world of reality. "In order to get anyone interested in going into this business, we have first to look as though we have a business to go into. You know, the way banks want you to produce a receipt before you've even got the money to buy the stuff?"

"I see, and so you'd like me to make one of these things and hope you can sell it?"

"One for now—hundreds later. It's a bit of a gamble," said Duncan, testing the daredevil in Giovanni, warily watching the effect from behind his glasses.

The gray eyes became glazed. The Italian seemed to have gone into an impenetrable trance. Watching him, Duncan was struck with a vision of him thus, communicating with some personal, unheard-of God before plunging into the Don or turning the Luftwaffe fighter northward over the Alps; saying to the God, "What do I do now?" Then, as if the God had replied, "Something quick," the eyes focused again; not upon Duncan, however, but upon a figure approaching from the far end of the office. Giovanni's mouth dropped open—"*Meu Deus*, the tax inspector" —then formed into an amiable greeting, *Bom dia, Senhor Dias.* Accounting department? *Pois não* . . . up the stairs and to your left."

Duncan watched the man move briskly toward a stairway, the entrance to which resembled, in height, the entrance to a rabbit warren. The inspector was small, but not *that* small. Duncan rose from his chair, a word of warning rose to his lips and was suppressed by Giovanni's hand on his arm and a barely audible, "Tssh." Then, blonk! The tax inspector staggered backward into the arms of two Baianos, who seemed to have emerged as if by magic from the tangled forest of wiring and sheet metal within. In another instant, Giovanni was standing over him, applying a damp handkerchief to a swelling on the inspector's forehead already of turtle's egg proportions.

"*Meu Deus do ceu, que calamidade.* What's the matter, meu senhor, didn't you have any coffee this morning? Hmm. I suggest an x-ray. No, absolutely, I insist. There is a first aid station just around the corner. Pedro"—he stared commandingly at the Baiano nearest him—"call a taxi, *subito!*"

In the next moment, the inspector, groaning, speechless, the egg now resembling that of an ostrich, was gone—gently, solicitously transported through the door whence he'd come.

"*Mãe de Deus!*" Giovanni applied the damp handkerchief to his own forehead and crossed himself. Again, Duncan felt aware of a personal deity. "The blackmailing little parasite. One comma out of place and his hand is there, under the cloth."

"But he'll be back," Duncan ventured, "and not very happy."

"Ah." Giovanni's expression became philosophical. "He'll be back. Or if not him, another. They will always be with us. They multiply like cockroaches. But by then"—he winked pleasurably— "I shall have my commas in order or I'll think of something else. It's all a part of the struggle, is it not?

"Now. About this business. Quite seriously, Sr. Duncan, you think I should trust you, eh?"

CHAPTER 31

That evening Duncan decided to walk home from the office. It was a good three miles, but the traffic was so chaotic that he'd probably get there faster and have a better stomach upon arrival. Besides, he felt like walking and thinking and laughing inside himself over the negotiations with Giovanni. He could imagine Stanley Heimowitz and the executive vice-presidents witnessing such a "business talk"; and he longed to tell Caroline so that she could howl, "Oh no!" as though all the subtle delights of life were suddenly streaming down her cheeks with all the tears of laughter. Yet he didn't hurry, because for once he was enjoying being in the streets. Somehow the crowds of people who filled the narrow sidewalks, impeding the progress of purposeful men, didn't annoy him as they usually did. They were here, after all, like himself to take part in the struggle. Every one of them, from the crippled hawker of lottery tickets in his wheelchair with his merchandise tacked to his oversized chest, to the Arab with his "bargains" in yard goods, to the flat-headed Nordestino plodding along in his ragged work clothes. As one climbed upward from the swirling vortex at the center of the city, toward the broader avenues lined with trees, the people seemed to grow, become straighter, taller, paler. Threadbare cotton, run-down shoes, drooping satin hems, gave way to Argentina wool and English worsted. But still they moved with the same intensity and confidence. Threadbare or comfortably dressed, it was difficult to find a despairing face among them. Preoccupied perhaps, but never defeated, so absolutely certain were they that no matter how bad things were, they were going to succeed. "*Pois logico!* It was the reason why they had come, was it not?"

Sometimes they infuriated him with their patient, undying

optimism—as if just being in the streets of São Paulo was going to do the trick. In the streets and in the way, constantly in the way of everything. But today he felt himself to be strangely in tune with those who struggled, though never too seriously, who laughed at the thought of fate ever turning in their favor and yet, deep inside themselves, never doubted for an instant that it would. In the banking district, nowadays, a guard stood in each doorway and another sat inside in a pillbox with a slit for the machine gun, probably sound asleep, awaiting terrorist assault. Other than these, there was nothing to suggest the state of a city, a country under endless, indeterminate siege. The "Turks" stores stood gaping open with their yard goods and cheap clothing and toys spilling out onto the sidewalks. In a hundred bars along the way, people stood sipping beer or *pinga* or *cafezinhos*, munching on hot fried *pasteis*, filled with savory meat. Record shops blared yei-yei-yei and rock, or an occasional samba that automatically set the women's hips to moving as if in time to their own heartbeats. He stopped in a record shop and bought Caroline a samba, an old one with Noel Rosa's tragic, pinched face that set the words going through his head:

> "When I die,
> I don't want weeping or candles
> I want a yellow ribbon
> Stamped with her name . . ."

Out of the converging threads of narrow streets rose the wide avenue, that bordered the Cemetery of Consolation. In the shadow of the cemetery wall, cars moved bumper to bumper, lurched, collided, their passengers now cursing, now conversing amiably in the interminable lulls between lights. Above the wall rose the statuary of misguided wealth: trumpeting angels in black marble, pink granite pseudo-Corinthian-columned mausoleums, sepulchers that looked like wedding cakes; symbols of the Catholic-Latin terror that, without a hideous monument in the shadow of cedar trees, God and man might forget. Duncan wondered vaguely why anyone *would* remember someone who had to make a monument to himself. At least those granite and marble sculptured caves provided shelter for the weary, the sick who came, so many of them, from so far to be treated in the immense, sprawling hospital across the way, to get well, start anew, or die . . .

"Don't come," the authorities had begun to beg. "There's no room, the city stinks, it's a burning garbage heap, the streets are earthworks. How do you expect us to find you water to drink, a place to rest your head, to walk without being mown down by a million vehicles turned *desperados* in an eternal traffic jam? There's not even time to make a subway." But they came, just the same, and found jobs somewhere and a place to rest their heads, because even the cemetery was more alive than some of the places they'd come from. Patience, optimism. There would be a way.

As it often had before, it occurred to Duncan that someone ought to offer "the church" a cut in the contraceptive business. That would possibly be the greatest occurrence since the original sin.

Beyond the cemetery, he turned away from Avenida Conçolação onto a side street. The farther he walked now, the deeper became the shade of the tall trees. Tropical foliage climbed the trunks of palms, embraced walls, crept through ironwork fences amidst bright sprays of pink and white azaleas in bloom. Dogs barked, maids rocked baby carriages and chattered over gates. It was pleasant walking here, no more crowds, no potholes to stumble into—just shade and tall houses and the roar of the traffic muffled and made distant by the density of foliage.

He began to think again about his encounter with the Italian, Giovanni. About why an hour spent amid the chaotic disorder of Giovanni's workshop should have inspired his confidence. But it had. Perhaps it was the assurance of the man himself that allowed him not a moment's hesitation in flinging open the door on the sausage maker's inferno; or clobbering the blackmailing tax inspector with a door frame, thus consummating every man's hidden dream; saying, "Of course I can do it, only better. And now, do you expect me to trust you?" Duncan's response had been equally precipitous. Their feelings had been mutual. And that was why he had come walking home this evening through the jumbled, dirty, crowded streets, feeling good, knowing that trust was far more a matter of instinct and common sense than bits of paper signed and witnessed and confirmed.

The dogs, the children all assaulted him as he came through the gate, making his progress along the path in the shadow of a gaudily blooming hibiscus hedge, near impossible. They all always seemed to want to pile on his lap the moment he sat down. He seized the baby, George, partly to keep him from getting trampled, and pushed the half-open door with his foot. Today anything went, nothing annoyed him. As soon as he sank into a chair, they could pile up all they wanted, he didn't care. From the depths of the house, Caroline appeared, bringing with her a waft of cinnamon and clove and butter from some frenzied activity in the kitchen. He was going to say, "Okay, that's enough for today. Look at this Jamaican rum I brought you. We've got something to celebrate; let me tell you about this nut, Giovanni."

And then he saw her expression . . . the look in her eyes that had nothing to do with the baking of cakes or anything so simple and pleasant and worthwhile as discovering him home a little early with a good story. From her look, he saw that it had seemed as though he would never come. Her expression reminded him of the first time, when she'd stood on his doorstep, and all the other times afterward, when, without her having to say it, he knew something had happened; something unbelievable that she didn't want to think about alone. It broke from her at last in a low, incredulous whisper. "Delia's been arrested; locked up."

He stood there, not exactly surprised, yet not wanting to believe. As if to fend off the truth a moment more, he said, "Oh come on, Caroline. Where'd you hear that? Who told you?"

"Who told me? Don't be ridiculous, do you think I'd make it up? Malachai told me. He's just been here, looking sick as a dog, as if he'd been arrested himself."

"Jesus." He put down the baby, the record and the bottle of rum he'd brought, all insignificant bundles now. How could one tell a good story, celebrate having met a guy like Giovanni when suddenly in a few desperate words you'd been made to realize that hell did exist not somewhere off in another realm, but near, really quite near. He went into the living room and sat down on the sofa, his elbows on his knees, staring ahead. His mind was working furiously, but it seemed to be getting nowhere. He'd never really felt helpless, as he did now. "Christ," he said, sounding almost prayerful, "there must be something we can do. Where in hell is Francisco?"

"That's the worst," Caroline said with an unusual bitterness. "He's drifting and dreaming on the river. It's impossible to get in touch with him."

CHAPTER 32

Francisco, in fact, *was* dreaming along the river, for what river on earth, if not this São Francisco, born apparently nowhere, winding across a harsh, empty, exasperatingly promising land, could be more conducive to dreams?

It was the dry season and so the journey had been more laborious than usual, taking eight days of intricate crisscrossing and circumnavigation to guide the boat around sandbars and over shallows in sometimes less than three feet of water. A work of experience and instinct more than technical calculation, it had seemed to Francisco, a work of art.

Eight days of sunrises and sunsets that turned the waters to shades of copper and amber, and resedaceous greens that could not have been reproduced upon an artist's canvas without becoming cheap and tawdry. That could only maintain their splendor where *mergulhoēs* and egrets rose in black and white bevies from pale sandspits where the old river wound tortuously between banks of somber trees and dry, ochroid earth.

Sometimes the riverbanks, with their strange, drought-stricken predatory life, filled him with a sense of overwhelming despair. The little towns along the way seemed lost in distances too great to conceive. They were much alike, their houses of clay rising almost simultaneously from earth and crumbling into dust. A cobblestone street, a church painted blue, a bar painted pink in defiance of the parched landscape, bright red cannas in a dusty square. The people who came down to the piers with a few straw mats and clay pots to sell were the color of earth, too. Scrawny, ragged people who asked for nothing, and this cheerfully, but a few centavos. Who, indeed, were not aware that there was anything more to ask for. People of a strangely haunting beauty with agility in their stride and a brightness in their eyes born of playing the game of survival. For how long? Francisco had watched them, standing on the piers, or on the banks beside the neat cords of wood, cut and transported across the dry, thorny plains of *caatinga* for the boat's insatiable devourings. And as the boat pulled away, he had watched them fade into an immensity of brownness that seemed beyond the will or capacity of any man to confront.

But at other times, he had gazed upon the tiny, carefully tended plots of green along the water's edge, watched a woman with an old aluminum washtub patiently splashing water over the lettuce; precious water, shining in the midst of a dry, wind-swept landscape. And he had seen the islands, planted to the last inch with corn and mandioca and beans and the fishing boats, weathered gray with their widespread white and orange sails, and had thought, with a great contraction of the heart, "This could be paradise."

Time was suspended, meaningless on this journey. There was no telling when the boat would arrive. It depended on too many things: where the wood was and how long it would take to load it; how often a white flag should appear on the shore and the boat sidle up to exchange messages, embraces, or perhaps take on a single passenger—a woman with a child on one arm, a bleached sackful of belongings on the other. One night he had watched the Southern Cross heave into sight twenty times between the two supporting posts of the deck before his cabin as the boat heaved and struggled, its boiler groaning, warning bells jingling, to fight the wind that drove them in circles. Once at dawn they'd run aground on a sandbank. Poling the anchor out in a lifeboat and dropping it, they had heaved themselves over the bar.

This evening, just before dusk, they had reached Dobradinha, where the rapids were and where there had been a dam, partly constructed, that had years ago been washed out, along with fleeting hopes, when the river had risen with the rains. Francisco had stood on the forward deck, watching every movement of the pilot, a young, light-colored Negro with powerful features and clear, determined eyes, as he guided the men at the wheel over the rapids. The rapids changed from season to season, day to day. Charts, mathematical calculations played no part in this game.

The instrument of measure was the human eye; the calculator, a sharp, confident mind that could judge, decide, command within seconds. During the entire performance, involving descriptions of rocks, palm trees, guide posts flung in curt commands from pilot to wheel, the captain had stood in the prow, his stern weathered features thrust forward like a figurehead in the wind. Only when the rapids were safely executed did he turn, raise his thumb in a gesture of approval, a grave smile lighting his mulatto face. "That's a new pilot. His first try. Not bad, eh?"

Francisco would have found it difficult to describe the sense of kinship and humility he felt toward these people whose experience was at the opposite pole from his own. How encouraged and inspired he had felt, and, above everything else, assured. It could all be done. The valley could be turned into a paradise. Watching these people, he was suddenly sure of it. More than anything—but wasn't this always the case?—it was a matter of will.

It was sunset by the time they had breached the rapids, and it would be four hours more until they reached the twin ports of Petrolina and Juazeiro, where on the broad flatlands of Pernambuco and Bahia on either side of the river, the project of THE COMPANY was to be begun. On the top deck, Francisco sat talking with a fellow passenger, the young teacher Octavio, who had been born upriver in the town of Xique-Xique and now made, with his wife, Lala, a journey of remembrance. Octavio's father was a *vacqueiro*—a poor knight in leather armor who braved the caatinga to graze cattle on the sparse grasses beneath its merciless thorned branches. By the law of inertia, Octavio should have been one of those people left standing upon the bank. But somehow he had gotten to Salvador da Bahia and educated himself in law. And then he had gone to Brasília to teach.

Of all the passengers on the boat, this one, with his fierce, dark Moorish looks and gentle Brazilian eyes, interested Francisco the most. He admired his intelligence and the tenacity that had lifted him out of this stagnant forgotten world of the river and set him moving. Yet he feared his innocence. He was like so many of his age and time whose curiosity avariciously devoured knowledge, but whose experience was an island, a Xique-Xique, in the vast complicated world in which knowledge and acts never quite fitted together.

"And so you really believe something will happen in this valley?" Octavio sat, his hook nose, full lips and finely bearded chin outlined sharply against the merging colors of the sky. He spoke with a poignant mingling of skepticism and longing. "Here where nothing has ever turned out as it should?"

Francisco smiled, thinking of his feelings as they'd navigated the rapids. "Why not? The land is good; the people, quick and imaginative. Why should they not succeed with some serious help?"

"Serious help?" Octavio reminded him at times of the wild creatures of the valley who indeed had little reason to be anything but wary. "Look at these ministers. I have no patience with them and their trips abroad. How many times have they gone to France, England, Germany? How many times have they come here to see things? What do they know of the Northeast?"

"But listen." Francisco coaxed the wild creature with a morsel of rationality. "That is why I have been sent here. Is it not better that I who shall be helping to change the river, come to know it first? Let them send me here while they take their trips abroad."

"To achieve what? Banquets and dinners and promises and headlines in the newspapers?"

"Perhaps." Francisco was surprised at his own persistence. "But if we produce all these tons of tomatoes and melons and oranges, who is going to buy them unless it is the outside? Our own people cannot afford them; at least not yet."

"Not yet or not ever?" Octavio, the youth, gave his older friend the jaded look of one whose pessimism has been handed down from generation to generation. "What makes you think they will ever reach the point of producing, let alone trading? What was that we just scraped over an hour ago? The ruins of a broken dam. Everything here has always been a broken dam; the money spread out, soaked up, disappeared, like water from a sprinkling can in a desert. Ah, Francisco, you are a Paulista. That's where you get your faith. But this is the Northeast, things here are different."

Francisco shook his head helplessly. "You say that almost proudly, my friend. All right, perhaps so—probably you are right. But on the other hand, you have to have a little faith, don't you, unless you intend to give up in the very beginning?"

It was just then that Lala appeared from below deck, her broad

Indian face full of laughter. "Hurry, you're missing everything. Felicio the head steward is raffling his watch. It looks like something he fished from the bottom of the river. Come quickly!"

Octavio rose. "Are you coming?"

"No, no thank you. I think I'll sit here a while longer. But see what I mean about your people being imaginative? Look at Felicio." Francisco reached into his pocket and brought out a ten-conto bill. "Here, buy me a ticket or whatever it is."

"With pleasure." Octavio laid his hand gently on Francisco's shoulder. "No hard feelings, amigo, perhaps your faith will win you this magnificent watch. At any rate, it will help another Nordestino make a killing."

When they were gone, Francisco sat a long time alone, listening to the sound of the smokestack, a regular breathing sound that gave the impression of an immense lung, as if the boat were a living, pulsating being. With every breath, a shower of sparks rose and drifted on the wind and seemed to mingle with the stars.

He was glad Octavio had gone now, for he no longer wanted to talk. Far off, still several hours distant, the lights of Juazeiro reminded him, with a certain sense of regret, that this was the last of these nights he would spend alone on the top deck, when everyone had gone below, leaving only himself and the *"practicos,"* twin brothers, bronze-skinned and lean-featured, who spun the heavy wheel between them as if they were members of a single body. While they guided the boat along its hidden, devious channel, they talked constantly in low voices. He never heard what they said, but their talk, a cheerful easy murmur, was a human comfort in what otherwise might have been a night so vast and lonely as to be unbearable.

Now, on this last night, as he sat listening to the breathing of the stack and the murmurings of the practicos, he knew that he had gained much more from this journey than simply the knowledge of a river and its valley. Floating upon the slow, strong waters of the shining river in the midst of the great sertão with no schedules to meet until he reached his destination, it was as if a clock had been stopped and the time given to him to do with as he pleased. He had used it all for thinking; but not in the hard, disciplined manner that his work demanded and to which he had been accustomed for so many years. Instead, rather than pour out, his mind had become a receptacle into which new thoughts and understanding had seemed to flow from the very darkness and emptiness around him. A great many things had become clear to him and, without forcing himself, he had come to some of the most important decisions he had ever made in his life.

For one thing, whatever was finally resolved when the technicians and politicians and generals put their heads together; whether they decided to build one great dam or a series of smaller ones, he would work for them. It would mean leaving his business in São Paulo, not for a few weeks or a month, but for years. It would mean picking up stakes and coming out here to live in the town of Juazeiro in the middle of this near desert of a sertão. But he was willing to do it simply because no idea had ever inspired him so much in his life. The vast level land that stretched away to the hills, the endless shining river between high parched banks. The earth-colored people with their clear, questioning, doubting eyes presented an immense challenge, filled with immeasurable difficulties. But he believed in the challenge. And despite the pessimism of Octavio, and his jokes about faith, he wanted to be a part of it, give all aid and assistance to those who had said to him, "Go and see it and then let us know if you would like to try."

And Delia must make up her mind, if she loved him, to come with him. It was as simple as that, though this decision did little to reassure him. Rather, it filled him with a sense of dread, a realization that so much had been broken, that perhaps too many pieces were missing for the whole to ultimately repair.

"Sometimes an experience at a crucial moment can change one's entire outlook, one's life. You should insist that she make this trip with you." Malachai had been disturbingly imploring when he'd spoken of it.

The trouble was, he had never insisted that Delia do anything. Instead, they had both agreed from the beginning that love should demand no concessions. That each should come and go as he pleased, asking nothing of the other. Given freely, thus, with no impositions, their love should have been strengthened. But sitting here, alone, watching the sparks from the stack fly out into infinity, he had come to understand that love was too intricate to be ruled by theories. He realized now, with fear and bitterness, that each had gone his own way until they had grown so far apart there was scarcely common ground upon which to set their feet.

If only at some time when he had returned from something he had done, he had said to her, "Listen, I don't care if you want to hear about it or not. I must tell you about what I have done and what it means to me." Perhaps then they would have found a way to listen more and more to one another, rather than less and less. But instead, foolishly denying the need to give and to possess, each had allowed himself to fill his emptiness in other ways. He had given himself to his work, she to an obsession.

"You should insist." He understood now what Malachai had meant. But he had not really understood before. It was the river and the gift of time it had given him that had made all these things clear. So now, when he returned, he would make her listen, explain, beg, demand that she come and see for herself the life she might choose, in which all the creativeness she possessed could be put to use, rather than destroyed by this obsession with an idea.

"Ideas are pure," he would tell her, "but men never are. You can't abolish our imperfections with rules and creeds and codes. You can't create a new world. Don't waste your time thinking you can."

So many times he had wanted to talk to her in this way. But he had remembered their pact. "Don't argue," he'd said to himself. "Let her think as she pleases." And later, "Don't argue, what's the use? It is her life."

But now he saw how foolish the pact had been. How in spite of it he still loved her desperately. Enough to say, "I am not so demanding, heartless and tyrannical as an idea. If you must give yourself, then give yourself to me."

And thinking this, he was suddenly seized with a terrible sense of urgency. The lights of Juazeiro seemed impossibly far, the breathing of the smokestack, agonizingly slow.

CHAPTER 33

There was, of course, nothing that anyone could do. Neither Duncan, nor Malachai, nor Josh, nor even Francisco, whose father was the director of an important firm, a highly respected businessman with a long record of loyalty and usefulness to his country. "Once it was in the hands of DOPS," came the answer again and again, "no one could touch it. Delia Cavalcanti, professor of philosophy, caught with dangerous and subversive material on her person, was guilty until proven innocent." And the evidence was not encouraging.

There had been a robbery at the Banco de Commercio in the borough of Pinheiros; one of those affairs in which youths, Young Robin Hoods, as the foreign press so fondly chose to call them, appeared from nowhere, brandishing machine guns and ordering everyone up against the wall. Apparently the guard, drugged by boredom and the stuffiness of the pillbox in which he spent his day, had been asleep. By the time he'd been able to get his own automatic through the slit there had been no one to train it on.

On the same afternoon, as the janitor of Delia and Francisco's building had explained it to Malachai, a young girl carrying a suitcase had come by looking for Dona Delia. The janitor had not paid much attention at first, why should he? "Students often came by to talk to Dona Delia. They liked her, she was young and '*muita simpatica*.'" He had raised one eyebrow intriguingly then, to demonstrate that the plot was thickening. "But Dona Delia was not at home. When I told the girl this, she looked very upset, almost as if she would cry.

"I thought from the suitcase she had come to spend the night. People often did, with Sr. Francisco away so much. So I suggested she wait. Dona Delia had gone to the movies, she would be back

soon—surely before dark. So the girl went on up in the elevator.
But she didn't stay, do you see? In a few minutes she was down
again, without the suitcase." The janitor leaned hard and ominously on this last bit of information. "Didn't even say good-by.
Just hurried out the door. In a few minutes the DOPS were here.
Must have been watching from the street. By the time Dona Delia
arrived, they had ransacked the apartment, turned it upside down.
Do you know what they found in the suitcase, meu senhor? Among
other things, the parts of a machine gun."

"A machine gun," Malachai had repeated sickly.

"Pois é—and so they took her away." The janitor spread his
hands and shook his head again and looked at Malachai as though
he had been afflicted by some great deception. "Dona Delia. I
couldn't believe it. She was so . . . so simpatica."

"Are you certain?" The mild eyes of Malachai Kenath had suddenly become inescapable pinpoints. "Are you certain it was not
you who informed the police?"

"God forbid." The janitor clasped his hands dramatically. But
Malachai kept on staring. "Do you realize what happens to people?" The janitor's pale mulatto features seemed tinged with green.
Malachai wondered if he would weep, or faint. What difference
did it make? He had turned his back on the fool and with a sense
of doom that had haunted him such a long time and all but paralyzed him now, he had gotten into his little Volkswagen and
driven down to the delegacy.

"Cavalcanti." The delegate went laboriously down a fresh list of
names, and looked up incredulously. "Of course you can't see her.
She is being held incommunicado." He leaned forward over his
desk, eyes dark and unsettlingly malicious. "You a friend of hers?"
Malachai's heart had stood still, but he had said with a boldness
that surprised him, "Yes. An old and good friend."

There was nothing to be done. The consul regarded Duncan
as if he were some frightening image caused by indigestion that
could nonetheless not be warded away with a Pepto-Bismol. Then
said despairingly and with a certain air of happy inspiration, "What
makes you think this person was not involved?"

"Because I tell you, she is not that kind of person. Articulate,
yes—but, good God, not a desperado, not by any means. I'm will-

ing to vouch anything. But some official plea . . . not for release
without proof, but right of habeas corpus. Perhaps it would be of
help!"

"I'm terribly sorry." The consul's face took on the closed,
sanctimonious look of an official representative; the one that over
the years had saved him from so many decisions. "Our duty is to
protect American citizens. Do you realize, Mr. Roundtree, only
this week the consulate distributed special alarm systems to every
member of its staff. Every member is warned to continuously
change his route between home and office, never personally open
his front door. I suggest you, yourself, consider more seriously how
critical the situation is. It is just a year since the ambassador was
kidnapped; less than six months since Winslow was shot down in
cold blood before his front door."

But he was not alone in his officialdom. The president of the
Commercial Association was an old friend of the Cavalcanti family; also an advisor to the governor. He raised his shoulders and
lowered them with a piteous expression. "How could Delia have
involved herself? It is all so purposeless. Ah, but then, is not every
war? Still, if there were anything I could do—believe me, Francisco—"

But neither the governor nor his advisors, nor colonels, nor generals—not even Teodoro if he really had had a brother-in-law in
DOPS—could put his finger on it.

Relatives could visit the inmates once a month. Business associates with special permission, when necessary. Food and supplies
could be delivered regularly. So about the only thing one's friends
could do was, once a week, bake a cake. And the only thing
one could do oneself was go on living though all one's finest hopes
and dreams seemed suddenly and devastatingly shattered.

CHAPTER 34

Giovanni had made a spectacular machine. Just as he'd said he would, he'd eliminated all the superfluous electrical hocus-pocus, thereby making it virtually possible for any Baiano anywhere from São Paulo to Manaus on the upper reaches of the Amazon, to work it without burning out the electrical system for city blocks. There had been a slight hitch in the automatic lid release that had made it necessary for the factory to be evacuated in the face of a Vesuvian outpouring of boiling oil. But that, Giovanni cheerfully assured Duncan and Josh with a glance that defied questioning, had been taken care of and would never occur again. Now the machine stood shining impressively in the restaurant's kitchen in Campos, cooking a sample batch while Josh stood by looking confident and uttering, inside himself, a silent prayer.

The kitchen had received a new coat of whitewash. The job had in fact been finished just an hour before. Josh hoped the smell of frying chicken would succeed in keeping from his "distinguished visitor," the scent of hastily put on paint . . . for Josh was courting an investor.

The thing had suddenly begun to click. It was difficult to say exactly when. Perhaps it was when, admitting that leisure-loving Brazilians were never in enough of a hurry to eat in their cars, they had covered the parking lot with a brick floor, filled it with tables and parasols. At any rate, after months of juggling checks, bombarding the public with pamphlets and radio spots and flashes on the screen in the local cinema and all the other fruitless nonsense that advertising firms convince their victims is necessary to "conquer the public," Josh was convinced that the thing had "taken hold" by word of mouth. People were there every day sitting under the umbrellas, being "modern," eating chicken with their hands, sipping beer, watching the traffic flash by on the avenue, seeing and being seen.

The visitor was an American, Wayne Merkelson, of the Maximillian Grain Corporation, working out of Des Moines, Iowa, in close competition with Central Feeds of Omaha, Nebraska. He had a crew cut and a manner of polite, yet unswerving conviction. Anything that was good for Maximillian Grain must inevitably be good for those with whom it dealt. With a blind faith as great as that of any twelfth-century crusader, he saw no irony in his words as he said, "Central Feeds doesn't want to go into restaurants, but threatens to take away your dealership if you go into this with us? Rest easy. That's no problem. We'll just switch our dealership in Campos over to you."

Josh pulled on his cigar and gazed in wonder. "I know your dealer. Name's Moretti. He mortgaged everything he had to get that dealership."

Wayne Merkelson looked long suffering. "He's not doing so well."

"Nobody does in the beginning."

"That's beside the point," said Wayne Merkelson with a hint of irritation in his voice meant to remind Josh, without saying it, that he was being presented with a fabulous offer. He drummed his fingers on the table. If this chicken was supposed to be fried in seven minutes, it was the longest seven minutes he'd ever spent. He was beginning to doubt the capacity of these Brazilians to manufacture a decent timer, when a blast like that of a train whistle announced that the crucial moment had arrived.

The chicken was, in fact, delicious, crisp on the outside, tender on the inside, sizzling hot. Wayne Merkelson pursed his lips and looked at the ceiling, his expression mirroring his thoughts. Chicken precooked, stored until its crust was sodden, reheated in instant electronic ovens never tasted like this. He frowned critically. "Umm, just a little different, but not bad. I imagine you'll get the hang of it with time. It's a matter of organization." Oddly enough, Josh could almost feel the hair bristle on the back of his neck. He had never stopped to think before that he could feel defensive about this business he had created.

"We can take care of all of that," Wayne Merkelson went on. "Internal organization, a better accounting system, advertising.

In short, we can give you all our know-how on every aspect. Yes, sir. I think it could develop into a nice-sized industry. Too bad about remittance of profit laws," he said wistfully, and then added righteously, "I mean, here we are, pouring money in, providing know-how, jobs, markets and they only let us take out ten per cent."

"That's something you have to accept," said Josh, at the same time thinking, "you're lucky they let you take any of it out at all."

Josh was beginning to feel oddly suffocated. In a way, Wayne Merkelson reminded him of a Methodist missionary to whom it had never occurred that *his* way just might not be the way to salvation. Perhaps it wouldn't be so bad if just once this guy would smile, even look jaded instead of so sincere as he blandly proposed to swallow you feet and all. Josh smiled for him, his eyes taking on their "Eastern merchant" expression. "So far in all this, we haven't talked about percentage of shares."

"Oh, 51–49." Wayne Merkelson looked vaguely astonished. "We never work on any other basis."

"Fifty-one for whom?" Josh wondered if *he* looked naïve now.

"Why, *Maximillian*, of course. After all, it's a risk—we have to have *some* guarantee."

"And I, in other words, would be fairly well guaranteed with a job, right?"

"No question about it." The president of Maximillian Grain regarded Josh magnanimously.

"Well, that's interesting," Josh said, hoping his voice sounded level. "However, there's a financing company here that's willing to go in with forty-nine per cent of the shares and let *us* run the show."

On Wayne Merkelson's face there appeared an unprecedented look of incredulity. "American outfit?"

"Actually, no. It's Brazilian."

"Ah, well." The director of the Maximillian complex shrugged in a way that dismissed such an idea as beyond the realm of serious consideration. "Anybody else interested?"

"As a matter of fact," Josh went on mildly, beginning now to enjoy himself, "the old Colonel himself has been putting out feelers."

Momentarily, Wayne Merkelson's self-assured, benevolent features whitened. The change in color was followed by a new expression of attention and respect; as for the first time it occurred to him that it might not only be interesting but expedient to snare this Josh Moran and his chicken fryers.

It was a little past noon—good timing. The lunch crowd was beginning to fill up the tables indoors and spill into the sunshine on the terrace. A lot of them would only sit and sip beer for half an hour and go away, having had lunch at home, but they looked impressive. And Wayne Merkelson was watching—his smile no longer self-assured and benevolent but distinctly grim—murderous thoughts of the "old Colonel" and his feelers in the back of his mind. Josh watched him sulk and munch on his chicken for a respectable time and then began asking him about how things were with his wife. Was she suffering from cultural shock?

"Not exactly"—Wayne Merkelson's crusader's face became comically martyred—"but those damn maids sure do drive her nuts and she can't get decent hamburger anywhere. All they keep offering her is filly minion, filly minion. What in hell's that?"

Josh laughed aloud. For a moment, in his frustration, the president of Maximillian looked almost human.

They didn't discuss the business much more that day. Josh indeed avoided bringing it up again, for in truth he didn't want to come to a decision yet. Driving home later, on a road so familiar that it offered no distraction to his thoughts, the scene he'd just taken part in became less ludicrous and amusing than frightening. For, after all, who was "the old Colonel" if not a loud-mouthed promoter by the name of Mike Buchanan, who had flown in from California in search of "investment opportunities"? A fellow who spoke constantly in terms of million-dollar deals but, in reality, couldn't even afford to pick up a tab in a restaurant and charge it to his expense account.

And what about the financing company, headed by Ricardo Soares, that, with the faint reminiscent odor of International Bankers, was still "studying" the little song and dance act that he and Duncan had put together and performed for their benefit? Forty-nine per cent for Soares' firm and 51 per cent for Frango Frito, if they could ever get the damned bird into their hands.

Between these two hung—or loomed—Maximillian Grain and the realization of what 51 per cent meant. That with the signing of *that* contract, no matter what one owned, one became once more an employee. Of course before today's little ceremony, they had already been fairly well prepared for what the offer would be. Duncan, in his usual wry manner, had put it succinctly enough: "It's not so bad for me. I already have a job, so what have I got to lose? But you—"

They had both laughed, but the irony, though always funny, was sometimes painful. It was as if he had gone through the whole wacky business of bonding himself to the Air Force, then flying single-prop nightmares over Mato Grosso, sitting behind a desk for the Institute and plunging finally into "the jungle" only to end up where he'd begun. Was there no escape?

Or was it as Lia had remarked with an unsettling note of bitterness not so long ago? "You don't know where to stop." It had been about the time when they had decided to contract Giovanni to make the machines. "Don't do it!" Her vehemence had been surprising, considering the fact that she seldom talked about the business, let alone thought about it. It was as if suddenly it had occurred to her that she must speak now or never, and whatever the consequences, they would be great, perhaps greater than anything that had happened in their lives. "Stick with what you've got," she'd said, "it's all you need."

"All I need for what?" He had been tired and irritated. He had even resented her words as if, having scarcely ever discussed the thing before, she was suddenly interfering in something that was none of her business.

"To get some more land, buy those cattle, make this place complete." He had never heard such entreaty in her voice. Perhaps he should have heeded it. He knew now, from the guilty twinge that bothered him every time he thought of it, that he should have answered her differently. It was not in her nature to ask, let alone entreat. But infuriated, somehow, he had blurted, "Good God, that worn-out old theme?"

It would have surprised him no end to know that he had touched her in exactly the spot that was hurting. That for some time now it had seemed to her that the fazenda had become for him just that, no longer viable, a kind of luxury, a place to live that he kept—who knew?—simply for her. And this thought was followed by the darker one; that all along, from the beginning, it had never been Josh Moran she'd been in love with, but this place, any place. The land.

"If that's the case," she'd shouted back half in defense against her own terrible thoughts, "sell out. I'm too old for toys." And she'd flung out the door, slamming it behind her, causing chunks of plaster to fall, and had gone, God knew where. It was not in his nature to look for her, so he had stayed behind, iron-willed and unbending. Still he thought how deeply he must have hurt her. And when she'd come back, he'd made love to her, roughly, possessively, for there was no better way for him to express his love.

And afterward, he had talked to her, telling her again all the things he had told her before and had meant. That this land was as much the center of his existence as it was hers. That he could do many things, but if suddenly the land were gone, the other things he did would have no meaning. That she was right, a hundred *alqueres*, a hundred cows. "You damn nut, it's the only figure you've even been able to keep in your head, isn't it? But right now I can't just stop, don't you see?"

She'd said, "I suppose so. Of course. Nothing is ever so simple." But even so, from time to time now when he'd begin a tirade about the weather destroying the coffee crop, or peered into the darkness, saying, "Now what do you suppose that cow is bawling for?" she'd give him a look that said, "Does it really matter?" and he would know that there was a difference and that now perhaps she only half believed.

But he *couldn't* stop now. How could he? With all Giovanni's machines lined up and ready to go? With Duncan suddenly counting on this thing as he had never done before? How could he pull out on Duncan? Not to mention Teodoro, with the one big *"negocio"* always drifting dizzily ahead of him in the empty air. Even if he did, even if they all decided to stick with what they had . . . how did one really avoid not hearing the words of the promoter, the smart guy from California, "You're not going to lose this opportunity, are you guys?" He who had missed a thousand such opportunities. Still, the words had meaning. The voice in the back of one's head went on to say, "It's a million-dollar business. You know who started it? A guy called Moran, but he quit too soon. Thought he'd stick with what he had. Of course he got knocked out of the race . . ." He could say to himself that he never heard such a voice. That it was superficial, unimportant, not in keeping with the scheme of things, the things he wanted to do with his life. The only trouble was, he did hear it . . . and all the instincts of a hard-driving, gambling, ambitious man said to him, "Now is not the time. Not the time at all."

And so here he hung, as if on a scale with a marker in the middle, waiting to swing one point in either direction. Preposterous, but very real.

The days were getting a little longer now; the sunlight, more intense. He knew that every afternoon when the sun burned hotly, wilting the leaves and bending the grass and driving the cattle into the shade of the *guimbé* trees down by the river, Lia watched the clouds pile up, watched the way the wind stirred the tops of the trees, and thought of rain. Almost every day, as everything sprouted new leaves and clamored and grew with the heat and the rain, a new calf was dropped in the thick deep grass.

If he left Campos before five o'clock he could get home in time, these days, to sit with Lia and the children on the veranda, watch the sun edge those piled-up clouds with brilliant color and watch the calves, tails in the air, leap and sprint across the pasture sparked by the sheer joy of being alive. It was a compulsion of his to get home now before the sunset. That was why he'd gotten rid of Wayne Merkelson from Des Moines, Iowa, as quickly and subtly after lunch as possible. It wasn't worth it—no, not at all— to allow himself to be delayed a minute too long.

He speeded even more than usual, over the hill where the white church on its crest, called "Capela do Alto," marked the final stretch home. Lia might be watering the garden at this cool hour, or simply standing, leaning on the fence watching the cows and calves as they set out from the salt box toward the stream. But she was doing neither. Even the dogs had not come out in a rush to greet him as they usually did. There was a curious silence over everything that somehow made him breathe and move at a pace just short of a run. Then a small, high voice at the door announced, "Daddy, Paul's been hurt!"

CHAPTER 35

She was inside, of course, with Paul, where she had been ever since the doctor had announced that there seemed to be no reaction to the tetanus shot and she and Jacob could take him home. When an accident is survived, the first thing one says is, "We were lucky." Ridiculous. But one cannot help it. And so there she was, feeling relieved and lucky that the gash, deep and long as it was, had not been a worse one; that Jacob had been there to drive them into town, with the boy, his wound held together by torn sheeting, between them. When he was sure that Paul was all right, Jacob had gone.

He had arrived early in the morning, having subjected himself to one of those all-night drives up the mountain, as if to what? Reassure himself of his strength by testing his endurance? Sometimes it seemed so. At any rate, he had walked into the house looking fresh and strong and none the worse for the wear, his eyes bright with an almost childish enthusiasm, saying, "I've come to get my buffalo."

"No business before coffee," she'd said sternly, trying to contain an excitement at his appearance that left her slightly breathless. She'd set bread and honey and steaming coffee and milk before him and seated herself. "Can't I interest you in some Santa Gertrudis bulls instead?"

"Not for my hot, marshy lowlands."

"Very well. Finish your coffee and we'll ride over to see Ari Gomez." The smile she gave him reminded him of something encased in plate armor, and then, as if remembering they held some sort of truce, he said, "I'm already stocking my pastures, that's pretty good, isn't it?"

"Very good," she had said with the same overdone enthusiasm. "I'm so glad."

There was no one in the *coxeira*. Gardenal had already gone in search of a cow whose bawling from the direction of the ravine suggested she had lost her calf. They had saddled the horses themselves and ridden out. Ari Gomez' Fazenda Santa Ana was the one that could be seen from the high place, with its buffalo lakes that mirrored an ever changing sky. The way to it lead through the valley along a road bordered by old eucalyptus trees whose trunks were thick and gray and mottled with age, and whose branches reached upward and out of sight. The wind roared in those high branches constantly, but they were so high that the sound was a faint, lulling murmur. Down below, along the road, the sun cast stripes of shadow and light between the trunks of the trees and the leaves that fell to earth sent up a rich aroma of menthol and herb.

They had ridden in silence for a long time, glad of each others' nearness and yet troubled, knowing that things had not been the same since that day in the orchard. The old rapport was still there, that caused them to think alike about so many things; about music and books, the mountains and sea and the wild country that man could possess if he put his mind to it. About the shortness of life and the need to do what one loved best because there was so little time . . . all that. They had talked so much, gazing upon each other as they had, with such brave innocence. But it is difficult to keep up the brave innocence forever. The old rapport was there that had troubled her and made her agree with Jacob in silence from the first time he had argued with Josh about the mountain. But now it was complicated by a desperation growing beyond limit. A longing that touched every word, every gesture, giving all a double meaning. At length because she could bear the silence no longer, she had said to him:

"What next, Jacob, now you've got your trees begun and you're stocking the pasture?"

"Oh, the house, I suppose. I meant it when I said it was spartan. I'll admit, I'm a bit of a loss." Then, as if he could bear this patter no more, he reined in his horse, forcing her to do the same. When he spoke again, his voice was low and urgent, the voice of the day in the orchard, begging recognition, release from pretense. "Remember what I said about time and circumstance? Lia, did you ever think how it would have been if we had met before?"

"Before we created the lives we now lead?" She tried to keep her voice calm and reasonable. "There's no use in thinking, Jacob."

"None? That's what I tell myself, with great good sense and reason. But then myself comes back at me, saying, Is it my fault that I didn't know? And suddenly all the great plans I have seem meaningless. And I feel desolate and robbed."

"Stop it," she said. "You are going to destroy the only possible thing we can have."

"Oh yes, I know. Our friendship." He answered with a searing bitterness. "Well, I'll tell you, I don't give a damn."

She could have said, longed to say at that moment, "Nor I." But instead, she kicked her horse into a gallop.

They crossed the valley and came to a rise beyond which lay the wider valley of the river and the buffalo lakes. The lakes lay gleaming and placid in the morning sunlight. As they approached, a flurry of small wild ducks took flight and settled again amongst the tall cattails on the water's edge. On every side, low hills covered with thick, gray-green *caatingeiro* grass sloped toward the lakes. When the sun was high, the buffalo would lumber slowly down toward the water like black dhows in a sea of grass. Now they stood motionless, swaybacked, their great heavy heads lifted, noses stretched toward the wind. Beyond them, on a hilltop, stood the coxeiras and the house of Ari Gomez surrounded by ancient *Jaboticabeiras*, their feathery leaves sheltering the clusters of black fruit that covered their branches in the mid-summer season.

Ari Gomez stood by the corral. Lia saw him with the relief of one being rescued from drowning. "Oh, Ari!" she called to the large, heavy man who stood in a white shirt, bombachas and scuffed boots speaking to a milker who stood bucket-in-hand by the corral gate. The milking was evidently done, for the calves had been turned loose with the cows. The corral was in a state of confusion as the calves milked and milked, sometimes four on a cow. The cows stood stolidly about, indifferent as to whose calf was whose.

"Good for communal living." Lia laughed as she dismounted and embraced her friend.

"*Pois é*. They're crazy, these animals," Ari said with delight, "not possessive like cattle at all." He was a handsome man with the boyish face of one who seldom worried, who enjoyed the very simple life he led. He had inherited this land of low hills and abundant water, and it was because of all the water that he had begun to raise buffalo. With time the strange, coarse-skinned, waterlogged black beasts that were not cattle, but a race apart, had become his passion. It was said that he knew and loved each and every one as much as he loved his own children. He seldom ever left the fazenda, and when he did, it was to make a yearly pilgrimage to the Amazon in search of new bulls.

"You have water?" he said to Jacob, once the introductions were over. "Because if you don't, it's no good. There's no fence will hold them. I don't even consider selling my animals to a customer unless I am perfectly sure—" He looked at Jacob as if he were sizing him up. "You sure?"

"Oh, I've plenty of water. Marshy lowlands."

"Good water, not brackish?"

Jacob nodded effusively, beginning to wonder if he would be permitted to make the purchase he'd come for. "My lakes are fed by mountain streams."

"In that case," said Ari Gomez, his prerequisite apparently filled, "shall we suck jaboticabas?"

"With pleasure."

For the next half hour they stood under the great old trees doing exactly that, sucking the white, sweet fruit from its bitter black skin, spitting out the seeds and between sucks and spits, talking buffalos. When it seemed at last to Ari that Jacob was sufficiently versed in the preliminaries, they set off once again toward the corral. They were thus, leaning on the fence, watching the vaqueiro turn the cows out to pasture to make room in the corral for Jacob's choice of bulls, when they heard the sound of galloping and saw the boy Ken approaching on his mare.

Something in his furious riding, the way he scarcely slowed the horse until he was nearly on top of them, gave Lia a warning. Then she saw his face, as he bent toward her over the horse's sweating neck, pale beneath his ruddy skin, eyes wide with alarm. "A cow got Paul," he gasped, "his leg—it's all hanging open. Come, will you?"

Ari, father of seven, veteran of countless disasters, was the first to act. "Leave the horses," he said, "my jeep is there, take it."

Lia didn't remember whether she answered or not. In an instant she was in the jeep. If anyone moved faster than she, it was Jacob, who was already at the wheel.

Paul and Gardenal had found the cow and the calf which had fallen into the ravine and it was necessary for one to climb down the bank, tie the calf with rope for the other to pull from above. Paul, being the stronger, had elected to pull, once the old man had done the tying. Everything would have been all right had not the cow, a wild-eyed demoness of a range cow, elected to kill Paul on the spot. With her first charge, she knocked the boy flat on his back. With the second, she gouged him, ripping open his thigh with her devilish, pointed horn. The force of will is, at times like these, everything. The old man, who no longer had the strength to haul a calf out of a hole, leapt out himself with the agility of a boy and flung himself at the cow with the fury of a wildcat. Her surprise lasted long enough for Paul somehow to drag himself under the fence and the old man to roll under after him. Panting and cursing and praying, he draped the boy over his shoulder and somehow got him up the hill.

It was Jacob who ripped open Paul's pant leg with a knife and first inspected the wound, a gaping, jagged gash some two inches deep on the inside of the thigh and ten inches in length. Miraculously the horn had missed the artery, so the gash was oddly white and near bloodless. "Tear up a sheet and we'll tie this together." His voice, Lia would always remember, low, steady, imperative. Once they reached the hospital Jacob had had to go in search of the doctor. So she had helped the nuns, talking to the dazed boy, as they stretched his suddenly incredible length on the operating table, gave him a sedative and a cloth into which he could set his teeth.

When it was all over and the doctor had done his sewing, twenty-five stitches inside and out, they'd rolled him into a room to sleep off the drugs and wait out the effect of the tetanus shots. It was then, with the door closed behind them, that Jacob took Lia into his arms. She relaxed against him, her face pressed into the hollow of his neck. Horror, fear, anxiety, receding from her

at last in the strength and peace and then the rapture of his nearness, she was scarcely aware, at first, of the kisses with which he
touched again and again her forehead and hair.

They waited out the boy's sleep, sitting silently in the breathless atmosphere of the room with its shutters closed against the
glaring afternoon sun, faces in the shadow, waiting, saying
nothing.

When the doctor assured them that there was no more danger,
Jacob carried him to the jeep and they took him home.

She would remember again and again later on, every action,
every glance as they laid the boy on the sofa, supported his band-
aged leg with pillows, and covered him with a heavy blanket, for
he was cold, in spite of the heat of the day. This done, Jacob had
stood over her with a crestfallen expression that had made him
look painfully young. "Do you know how I hate to leave you?"

"Yes," was too difficult to say, so she nodded and said instead,
"You must get Ari's jeep back to him. Besides, he's still waiting to
show you the bulls."

"Everything all right?"

"Oh yes . . . everything."

The boy stirred and asked for a glass of water. And she turned
away to fetch it, glad that he could not see her face.

A few moments later the other children and the dogs were all
about, hovering and peering anxiously at Paul, who lay smiling
faintly, feeling the first warming sensations of heroism. By the
time Josh arrived, he found a joyous tribe, happily recounting the
details of a danger that was past. Only Lia seemed too quiet and
distant, as if she had no emotion to spend.

"What in hell happened?" Her impassiveness made him want
to shake an answer out of her. He had never seen her so.

"It's as Kenny said. He and Gardenal were trying to haul a calf
out of the ravine. The cow charged—"

"What was Gardenal doing?" Josh said angrily.

"The best he could." Suddenly her voice exploded upon him in
anger and passion. "If it hadn't been for him, Paul would be dead.
They were alone. Just the two of them—"

"And I suppose that's my fault."

"You can't be everywhere." She could scarcely believe her own sarcasm. "But we managed. Thank God, Jacob was here."

Josh said nothing for a moment, thinking bitterly and not knowing quite why, "Jacob, with his perpetual labor and sacrifice and goodness." At last he said aloud, "Good he was here. But you'd have made out all right alone."

"Yes," she answered, her face once again curiously empty of expression. "Yes, I'm sure I would have made out all right alone."

CHAPTER 36

When the stitches were removed from Paul's leg, Lia went with the children to Malachai's house in São Sebastião. Swimming in the sea, said the doctor, would be a fine way to relax and exercise the damaged muscles. It was the summer holiday, at any rate, and Clea had long been counting on their coming.

Josh was to have gone, but in the end it was impossible. "You *do* understand, don't you? Teodoro is up to his ears in '*luvas*' and '*calças*' and Duncan and I have got to play the earnest entrepreneurs a little longer."

"Be careful you don't turn into one."

The fine lines of humor had crinkled around his eyes. "No need to worry about that," he'd said with irony. "If I were, we'd have a *real* balance sheet, not just a funny one. I'll miss you, though." He'd looked suddenly almost childishly lonely, reminding her of the few other occasions on which she had gone away for any length of time. The look had always managed to make her feel a ridiculous pang of guilt every time.

She thought of it. But later on, as she wandered along searching for shells, or sat by the hour watching transparent fish darting around in rock pools high above the sea, she thought, "He hasn't the patience for this. That's the difference between us." And she had tried to avoid the other thought that, no matter what the difference, the real guilt had to do with the fact that this time when he had said he could not come, she had felt as though she had been set free.

Eduardo da Silva was there, whose fine, all-Negro play, *Agora Nos Vamos Cantar*, was receiving a somewhat distorted acclaim in France.

"Why France?" Malachai, sitting in his wicker chair under the low tile roof of his veranda, had wanted to know.

"Funny that *you* should say that"—Eduardo's mournful Negro-Indian features had looked askance—"surely you know the routine. The French fall all over themselves because it is Negro and, therefore, chic. The Brazilians, on the other hand, won't accept a Negro play unless it has first been to France. Not so?"

"I am impatient to see it," said Francisco, though his words, like everything he said these days, had a particularly hollow, forced sound.

Since Delia's imprisonment, he had given up all ideas of the river and, even though he could visit her but once a week, had confined himself entirely to São Paulo, the great city he had so often left with such abandon before. Then he had gone for the love of his work and been half glad she had not seemed to miss him. "Let her be a fanatic if it keeps her busy," he had often said laughingly. Now the memory of those words pained him and even his work seemed to give him little solace. It was as if his only comfort was in staying in the city, as close to her as possible, sharing her suffering as much as he could.

Malachai had understood this and had reprimanded, "You will accomplish nothing for her by hiding yourself from the sun."

To which he had replied, "She is allowed into the yard now and then to take the air and sunlight. But by the time it is her turn it is late in the afternoon. For three months she has not felt the warmth of the sun, but only seen its light cast upon the wall."

Even here, he inadvertently sat in the shadow, as if the brilliance of the sea pained him. Clea's straightforward, generous heart knotted at the sight. She tried to sound encouraging. "Thank God they can cook for themselves. I hear they've got it all organized, a common store, everything."

"Delia was always good at organizing." He smiled ironically. "That's probably why she is where she is in the first place."

"Any news about a trial?" Lia dreaded asking.

"Ah yes, they finally caught up with the girl who left the suitcase. She admitted having left it without Delia's knowledge. They are saying she may possibly be released for lack of evidence of any real involvement."

"Thank God," said Lia. But Francisco shrugged his shoulders

with the look of one who had abandoned optimism because of the repeated pain of its betrayal. The very despondency of his gesture touched them all, so that here on the terrace of this old fisherman's house that Malachai and Clea had made so pleasant with a tiled roof, hammocks and potted geraniums, each in his own way felt troubled and ill at ease. Each found his own mind repeating to him, "Why should it be? Why should it be?"

"I'm knitting her a sweater," said Clea, and then immediately sucked in her breath at the fatalistic connotation of her own words.

In the silence that followed, the air seemed still and dark and oppressive. A storm was building out at sea and clouds had momentarily covered the sun that Francisco chose to avoid. The appearance of Jacob Svedelius, standing on the edge of the terrace, looking overworked, undernourished and far from unhappy, was a relief to everyone.

"What's this," Malachai wanted to know, "a provincial holiday?"

"Of sorts." Jacob smiled cheerfully. "It's the buzz saw again. Parts missing. I've decided to send my *tractorista* up the hill to get them, however. So the holiday is only for me." His eyes swept over the terrace, taking in everyone and coming to rest at last on Lia. "So you came?"

"Obviously."

"And the children?"

"They are waiting for me right now to go and hunt for mussels. Who wants to come?"

"Don't expect me to cook them unless *you* clean them," Clea said warningly.

"Are you sure you didn't throw a wrench into that buzz saw yourself?" said Malachai.

No one else, it seemed, had the inclination to search for mussels on the jagged rocks at the end of the beach but Jacob. Nor, for that matter, did anyone else seem to care much for walking endlessly in search of shells, renting a fishing boat for the day, or scaling the rocks, climbing till one was breathless and then stopping to sit for hours with one's feet in the rock pools.

Jacob loved such pastimes. It was as he had always told her in those brief moments on the fazenda, when she had allowed herself to stop for a moment, rest and talk. "Books and music I crave, but I couldn't live without a wild place to walk in. I must have some time like this every day."

There were countless such places along this rugged shore. Countless rock pools where they could sit for hours watching the tide rise and gradually change the waters from placid mirrors shot through with transparent ghosts of fish to raging worlds of destruction, beaten and torn by the strange marriage of earth and moon.

It was easy to lose oneself in such a marriage. This was not life. Life was contained. It was saying to oneself, "It's not worth it. Too much is involved." But the very fact that one had repeated these words in one's mind again and again seemed to make them more difficult to heed. Here where one was so alive with the sun-warmed rock beneath one and the salt spray flying all around.

She remembered the first time Jacob Svedelius had come to the fazenda, when Josh had brought him home and they had sat by the fire talking about the place on the mountainside. She remembered how the things he had said had been so disturbing to her. And how later on she had known that it was not just the things he said, but himself, so stubborn and resolute, yet so absurdly gentle. She had thought, "It would be very easy to love such a man." And this thought she had put in its place to be kept and considered only with objectivity.

Perhaps it would have remained so, had he not returned again and again during the long days of her doubting and loneliness on the fazenda. When it had seemed to her that her life was one and Josh's another and the land a half-forgotten, childish dream.

But he had come and talked as he had on that first day in a language that she had never really heard before his coming, but it seemed to her she had always understood. She should have said, "Don't come any more, Jacob. It's too subtle a game you're playing." But she'd never said it. She wondered now how she must have looked when Josh had said, "I can't go. It's impossible." Ridiculously blank, no doubt. As if she couldn't believe she was being cut loose, set adrift to be caught up like the tide between the moon and the sea.

One moment she had considered herself safe. The next, she had broken trust, permitted herself the impermissible, to pursue herself into her own unspoken wonderings, to risk everything, to accept a look, words for what they were.

"Everyone is leaving on Monday but you, Lia. Come up the mountain with me."

"But the children."

"Maria is here. You needn't worry. Say you are going to visit a friend over in the town—say anything. It can't be *that* difficult—"

"It can."

"Not if you want to come. Don't say you don't want to come. I can't believe it."

And so she went to the house on the mountainside, where one after another had attempted to create paradise in this place halfway between the sky and the sea. Someone before Jacob had built those solid walls, the deep windows, patios, terraces and balconies, the single room at the top with its lone balcony that hung above the trees looking out, far out, over bays and inlets and rock-strewn, jungle-clothed islands. Standing on the balcony, looking out over the treetops, it was almost possible to believe that there was nothing else, but this mountain, these islands, the sea.

It had been left alone for a long time, this house, for no one for many years had been enough of a dreamer to be able to see it as it might be, or had the audacity to try to make it so. So the walls had faded to a blue tinged with green and lighter than the sky. The vines had clambered over the balconies and lifted the tiles from the roof and, in the patio, the roots of trees had broken through the cracks in the walls, making room for moss and ferns to grow in the damp crevices.

Jacob had cut back the vines, repaired the tiles, scrubbed the house so that its faded walls and wide floorboards bore an air of monastic cleanliness and industry. And at the same time a curious haunting sadness. Because it was too late. Jacob had come here too late to discipline this jungle as a man must do if he is to survive in its midst. It was all too late, even his falling in love.

Still, as he wandered with her through the gardens, half redeemed from their jungle overgrowth, the patios, with their ferns and mosses, telling her of his plans, saying, "This will be," and,

"This will be," she allowed herself for a while to be caught up in the enchantment. If he had played the game alone before, she joined him in it now with the abandon of a romantic heart that had all its life been disciplined and contained.

On the wood stove, where in the evening he had heated many a solitary meal, she cooked for him as she had done many times before; but never for him alone, with all the world shut away. And then they had climbed the stairs to the single room at the top, with its balcony high above the trees, and watched the dazzling sunlight give way and the islands become shadows in a silent sea.

Though she had never been here before, the room with its shadows of jasmine and bougainvillea against a moonlit wall was familiar to her. She knew it as she knew how the lovemaking of this man would be: gentle, unearthly, seeking that part of her that had always been so distant and inaccessible. That she had kept from the time when she was still a child and Josh Moran had walked in, roughhewn and "unacceptable" and alive, to offer her, if not romance, an adventure. It was a part of her that Josh had never known. Perhaps because to Josh it would have been a myth. But to Jacob it was real and so it revealed itself to him alone.

She never really slept, but lay very still while the shadows of the vines deepened, then faded as the moon faded into the gray emptiness that preceded dawn. Beside her he breathed deeply, evenly, his arm stretched toward her possessively, unaware that she had already slipped from his reach. She was glad he was not awake, for she did not want to talk to him. Instead, she looked at his face, the fine lines of which she was sure would change little with the years, the skull beneath being too strongly made, the flesh too finely molded. Too civilized. It was the face of a man ahead of his time, always and forever, for no time would ever exist in which one so persistently gentle could survive.

"This will be," and, "This will be."

"Oh no, Jacob. It could never be."

She wondered if he realized as he lay here sleeping so peacefully that he was already beaten. That this splendor and beauty above the sea was not a part of life at all, but only a magnificent deception, heartless and indifferent, upon which one could spend all one's dreams. She wondered if he would realize when he awakened that, just as she should never have come here in the first place, she would never come again.

The light from the window was changing now, coloring with the first pale yellow of day. A fluttering of shadow against the wall warned her that there was no more time. She dressed hurriedly, silently, afraid that he might awaken, for she did not want to see the look in those haunting dark eyes. And then she crept downstairs, through the empty rooms, across the terraces and patios and ruined Portuguese gardens in the shadow of the great brooding trees and was gone.

CHAPTER 37

She sped. It seemed to her that the road down the mountain was even more rutted and curving than it had been the night before. Still, she took the curves at an impossible speed. She had to get there, somehow, before the children awakened to hear Maria, diffident yet smirking inside, say, "Your mother will be back soon. I'm sure."

There was no time to think, to see her feelings for what they were, not now. There was only this terrible urgency to get back onto the straight level highway that led toward Malachai's beach, toward life; her life. If she could only get there in time, so that Josh might never know.

She pulled the car in under the shed and walked toward the house through the grove of coconut palms. The house was silent, no sign of activity, and she thought, "Thank God the sun and sea tires them so; they're not up yet." And then she saw Josh Moran. This lean, tough unsympathetic figure upon whom she had always relied, sat in Malachai's chair smoking a cigar and watching her as she came. The coldness in his eyes made her feel weak.

"Good of you to get here before breakfast. Where were you?" His eyes were still cold, but something in his voice begged her to give another answer. If she could have lied, she would have. But she had not accounted for the fact that she had never really lied to Josh before. There was no carefully built structure of deception between them. One could hardly begin now.

"With Jacob Svedelius," she said.

"Damn you." He stared at her a moment longer, as if to force himself to be convinced. Then he rose to his feet and, taking the terrace steps in two long-legged strides, set off in the direction of the beach. She neither called after him nor tried to follow him. What would have been the point? What else is there to say when with a few words, one has made everything seem as though it has never really been?

I must go inside, she thought. I must see that breakfast is ready and call the children. And at the same time she dreaded these simple, satisfying actions; thinking how ironic, how grotesque their performance had suddenly become. She was standing thus on Malachai's terrace when the sound of the telephone penetrated her thoughts sharply, intrusively and without mercy.

The connection was just what one might have expected of a few drooping strands of wire strung along kilometers of road winding through a jungle. Faintly through myriad cracklings and buzzings came the voice of Ricardo Soares. At least they *thought* that was who it was, though the voice faded and returned and faded, as if playing some capricious game. She was about to tell him to try for a better connection when, as if virtually willing it, he managed to get the unbelievable message across.

He had been trying to get through to Josh all night, he said, but the phone office in São Sebastião was closed down from ten-thirty to six in the morning. Yes, Josh was to get to São Paulo immediately. Why? Because on the way home from the center of town last night, Duncan Roundtree's car had been assaulted and Duncan had been kidnapped. A message had already been discovered in the poor box by the sexton of the Church of Nossa Senhora de Consolação, the distant, wavering voice continued its tale. Money and an exchange of political prisoners had been demanded. Among those on the list indicated for exchange was Delia Cavalcanti.

Stunned, all thoughts of a moment before erased from her mind, Lia hung up the receiver and ran down the beach in pursuit of Josh.

So it wasn't only friends with their cakes and Francisco with his vigilance who remembered Delia Cavalcanti. There were others. The foreign press romantically called them Robin Hoods, but some, like Dorval, who taught Caroline to play the guitar, knew that it was not quite that simple.

When in the course of development, class distinctions have disappeared and all production is concentrated in the hands of a vast association of the whole nation, public power will lose its political character. . . . In the place of the old bourgeois society with its classes and class antagonisms, we shall have an association in which the free development of each is the condition for the free development of all. [Karl Marx]

How pure, how noble, how absolute, this manner of thinking that has made slaves of so many people. Of the young and innocent who seek justice and are impatient; of the old and narrow who began when they were very young, with a curious, twisted discipline to train the mind to see only that which it is convenient to see. These latter are extremely effective. They have trained themselves well and are good teachers. They speak of freedom of intellect but accept no freedom but their own. And this they use to offer a cause to which disciples can be wholly dedicated without having to consider the desires of others or contend with the obstacles that life puts daily in every man's way.

It is so much simpler to believe in the absolute. So much simpler to be convinced that once the world is turned upside down, all will be well. And once one believes this, to rely on bandits to cut through the obstacles of everyday life in order to hasten the day that, otherwise, would certainly never arrive. Few of the dedicated ever have direct contact with the bandits. It's better to read about their actions than actually see some "obstacle" be cut down in the street because he happened to be in the way. Then, when the bandits, in their turn, die, they may be thought of as heroes. And others will rise up to take their places in the struggle for absolute change.

Heroes? It all depends on how you look at it. Dorval had looked at it in one way in the beginning. A poor young student from the Northeast who gave guitar lessons to help support his studies and still had time to perform his mission of enlightening and indoctrinating factory workers. A tireless young man from a place in which hunger and injustice were everyday facts of life; where political positions and spoils were still fought over with guns. Where far out in the dusty towns of Euclides da Cunha's sertão, the rich cacau lands of the *reconcavo*, the immensity of the jungle and the rivers, the *coroneis*, who had ruled since the beginning of everything, might themselves possibly rather die than conform to the rules of modern times.

Dorval was impatient. It would have been difficult not to be. The only solution for the people of his overcrowded, hungry corner of the world that he had ever encountered, was to pull up stakes and come South. And what sort of a solution was that, to be crowded into the great cities to live in shanties built of packing cases and old tin cans?

The fact that no previous government had ever tried so diligently to reverse the suffering of the Northeast and yet so many still suffered, only served to heighten his impatience. Truly these roads and dams and agricultural and economic programs were too slow. There had to be a quicker way. As a member of the Movimento Revolucionario Popular he set about seeking it.

At the university the course that inspired him most was that of philosophy taught by Delia Cavalcanti, who, with her warmth and intelligence and dazzling manner, would have been an inspiration no matter what she taught. All manner of political philosophy was explained in her course, but Marxism was the "natural outcome of all the others." And Delia, too, was impatient. She belonged to no political organization, but she openly sympathized with those who dedicated themselves to "the cause"; and she would never refuse money or shelter or aid to those who needed it.

Sometimes, shyly, with the excuse that he needed advice about a paper, Dorval would go to Francisco and Delia's apartment. Delia was direct, open, spellbinding. Once the "advice" was taken care of, Dorval would remain and they would talk eagerly for hours. And though she belonged to no organization herself, it was Delia, more than anyone, who inspired him to take action and join the MRP.

For a time it was an exciting, heady life he led. Studying, teaching, talking, indoctrinating the workers. He had little contact with the terrorists and their leaders. That was not his department. And perhaps, like so many, he would have avoided being deeply touched by the truth concerning these heroes had it not been for the killing of John Winslow.

The story was in all the papers, of course. On the morning of

August 21, 1969, Winslow, an American Army captain, veteran of Vietnam with a Fulbright Fellowship to study political science at the University of São Paulo, was preparing to take his son and various other boys to a boy scout meeting at the American School in Morumbi. Calling back to his son, not to forget to close the front door, he walked to his car, which was parked in front of his house in the old and fashionable borough of Pacaembú. As he unlocked and opened the car door he didn't see what his son saw; a Volkswagen coming out of a side street, its passengers armed with machine guns. He never did see, because by the time his son screamed he was slumped over the car seat, riddled with bullets—dead. A message was left near the body as distorted as the thinking that went behind it, accusing Winslow of being a spy and a war criminal and declaring that justice had been done.

Perhaps there comes a time in everyone's life when he is confronted with more than he can swallow. At such a time he must either change his thinking or be dishonest with himself. And surely for the latter, the ever increasing need to make up excuses is part of what makes a fanatic. This time Dorval could find no excuse for what had happened. He had known Winslow at the university, argued with him, sometimes violently, on political matters. A blustery fellow, not given to discretion, too outspoken for his own good. An Army captain on a scholarship to study political science who couldn't resist a shouting match. CIA? Dorval doubted that anyone so vocal and obstinate could have been chosen for such a discreet service. He had made a good propaganda target. That was all.

Dorval couldn't get the thing out of his mind. The face of Winslow—expressive, pugnacious, so alive in his memory. The photo of his body, slumped over the car seat, bleeding to death. The same man. Worse than that, he thought he knew one of the individuals involved; a thin, high-strung boy named Mario, who, when he didn't avoid your gaze, looked at you with such a penetrating, inhuman stare, you felt compelled to look elsewhere yourself. The day after the killing Mario did not turn up at the university. He was never found again.

This time Dorval had been close enough to see and to remain haunted by the faces of two individuals involved in the drama. A sensitive boy, intelligent, gifted, a musician, Dorval realized with a pain as deep as his former impatient, blind dedication, that he was a member of a group of cold-blooded murderers who had shot down a man before his son's eyes in order to tack on him a bloody label.

It was then that Dorval decided to quit.

Unfortunately, as history has related again and again, it is far easier to *join* than it is to *quit*. He knew he was being watched, probably from both sides. It affected his studies, upset his work. A cold stare from some colleague in a classroom could cause his mind to blur, everything to go out of it except fear, leaving him at once cold and suffocated.

On the day he had no classes at the university, he gave guitar lessons at a fusty, pretentious school in an ancient Victorian house on Rua Libero Badaró. One morning he awoke with a premonition that if he left his room—like Winslow—he would be killed. Nothing he could tell himself to the contrary could convince him to rise, have his coffee and bread and step into the street. He was, of course, dismissed from his job. Delia was too perceptive not to be aware of a change in the behavior of one of her finest students. She saw his distraction in class, noticed the pallor of one who is overtired, has worms, is under an incredible nervous strain—or perhaps all three. When he failed an important exam, she asked him to stay and speak to her after class and then recommended that he see a doctor. But he said he would rather see her. He must talk to someone, and so she said, "Of course. Come to my home—now, if you wish."

"No," he'd said with a furtiveness that made her smile, "I don't think we should leave the university together. I will come later, alone."

"Very well. Sr. Francisco is off in Paraná again, trying to get the dam finished before the rains sweep a whole year's work away and he's blamed for it. He should appear tonight and I shall be up, waiting . . ."

There was not that much to tell. Simply the disgust and the fear that was grinding into him, wearing him down. She listened quietly, smoking and watching him with her great eyes that could hold such fire or such sympathy.

"So you haven't the stomach for such occurrences as the death of Winslow," she said at length. "But did it ever occur to you how many who are loyal to the revolution have suffered too as a consequence of this one act?"

"But don't you see?" Dorval said desperately. "How can you expect such fanaticism not to cause reprisal? Must it go on for ever and ever?"

She made no answer to this, as if indeed it were useless to do so, but simply said, "If you cannot accept it, then by all means you should get out. It is not easy, I know. You are like the carrier of a disease now, wanted by everyone. I think nothing will happen to you. But at all cost you must hold firm—you must not run. That *would* be dangerous. You've already lost your job and you needed that money, didn't you? Well, we must see, perhaps we can do something about that."

So that was how he came to give guitar lessons in private homes, recommended by Delia, who knew so many people in so many different kinds of worlds. Most of his pupils were pretty little girls whose mothers had them on a frantic schedule of activities to keep them "occupied" between the ages of puberty and marriage. The natural music in them far surpassed Caroline's. They'd instinctively moved their entire bodies to a samba beat ever since they could walk. But their knowledge of music was nothing, their taste, evolving from the Brazilian desire to be "modern," tended toward gut-twisting Brazilian aberrations of rock music. Besides that, they didn't practice. For Caroline, the introspective, strong, disciplinist, every note was the result of grim determination. But she knew music. And she believed this *"bossa nova,"* with its poetry and subtlety was a unique moment in Brazilian music, a happening of human spirit. She wanted to catch it all. And so on Caroline's afternoons, they sat and pored over the best of Baden Powell, Vinicius de Morães, Dorival Caymmi, Jobim, Chico Buarque, getting down notes and chords, testing, listening —delving so that at times he felt like a musical archaeologist, a discoverer, an historian. It was exciting, elevating. Unconsciously he began to look forward to this moment during the week as a bright spot of forgetfulness in the long dreariness of protracted anxiety.

In a sense, Caroline had broken a spell that had been cast over him, he could scarcely remember how long ago. Perhaps it had begun when others, seeing his growing preoccupation with his country's ills, had begun to convince him that everything of importance was political. That there was no means of serving his country except through radical self-denial.

The idea had clung. Even after the death of Winslow had convinced him that those people were wrong, he had not grasped his own imbalance, but floundered along, thinking then, "There is no solution at all." And this state of mind had continued until the moment when, to put an end to his brooding stare, Caroline had said with utter indignation, "Look, in this room during this hour, anything but music, including politics, is just one big waste of time," thus suggesting that he was on entirely the wrong track.

More than anyone or anything, Caroline awakened the musician in him. And without discussing any of these things, for she hadn't the time, she had suggested to him that between total dedication to a cause, and existing in a vacuum, there was something else that was called "living." It had to do with contributing to the world by developing your own talents to the fullest.

So it was not a sin, when others suffered, to enjoy, to live, to think of oneself. In spite of his anxiety he began to live as he had not lived since the spontaneity and indifference of childhood. He began to see his country, his people as he had seen them then: alive, colorful, richly inventive. Did he not come from the Bahia of candomblé and crumbling churches, white lace in doorways, *acarajés* and *quitutes* sizzling over cookstoves on street corners, of jangadas that braved the seas daily, blessed or cursed by the Goddess Yemanjá? Had he not left that poor and wondrous city dozing in the sun and come to São Paulo, crude and vital, full of ideas that needed brains? And every step had music in it. As they learned together, working over the music, it would have been difficult to say who was teaching whom. Dorval offered talent, skill, a natural genius. Caroline, knowledge, discernment, a civilized and scholarly discipline. He learned to look for many things he had never looked for before. He began to compose.

His anxiety didn't leave him. Indeed, the greater became his grasp on life and all its rich meaning, the deeper became his fear that, one day, because of what he knew, it could all abruptly come to an end.

Then Delia was arrested. It was Caroline who told him. She, who was not interested in his politics but in his music, flung it at him accusingly. "How can it be? In this country?"

And he had answered despairingly, laconically, as if some truth had just been conclusively ground into him. "We have made it so."

Yet something in it didn't make sense. He thought of this fiery, intent and brilliant woman who nonetheless had so much heart. He thought of their conversations, and of her advice to hold firm, not to run. They had found the evidence. It was there in her apartment. Yet somehow he couldn't believe it. How often the conviction came to him, during classes, walking the streets, that he must go, immediately, speak to someone, tell them it must be a mistake. Delia Cavalcanti involved in these tactics? She spoke. Oh yes, she said what she thought and she was willing to listen—to sympathize; but act in this way? Take part in a robbery? Endanger life? Several times he, who feared for his life, barely escaped losing it, stepping heedlessly into the surging traffic—his mind possessed. But always in the traffic, or lying awake listening to the deep, untroubled snores of his roommate in the Republica, he came oddly and sickeningly to his senses, thinking, "Who in the police would you go to? Who would listen?" And when you told them these things, who would not say, "Is that so? And what do *you* know about it all? Tell us." He had heard of others who, fed up with running and hiding, had given themselves up and actually been given another chance, let off with a reprimand. "The recuperables," they were called. Why put *them* through the mill? It was worth their gratitude to give them another opportunity. But he had lived too long with his fear buried deep within him. He had succeeded too well by simply "holding firm." He couldn't bring himself to take the chance.

"Hold firm." Sometimes he saw her large, dark eyes, bold and assertive, mouth turning up at the corners in a smile at once defiant and reassuring. At other times he imagined her thin and hollow-eyed, a mockery of her own words, looking at him now from the depths of some living grave.

He lived in two worlds, one teeming, lively, filled with ambition and hardship—the extraordinarily compelling world of hope. The other world, the one he feared, was one of dedication to something total in which he no longer believed but which pursued him still . . .

CHAPTER 38

He had never dealt directly with the bandits when he had been a member of the MRP. But one day, about the time when Duncan convinced Giovanni to make the machines, and Josh sold his first herd of bulls to a *fazendeiro* in Mato Grosso, and Teodoro made his first "*grande negocio*" selling the land of a politician's mistress to the *prefeitura* of Campos for an art center, and President Medici distributed the first land grants to Nordestino settlers along the Amazon highway, Dorval came face to face for the first time with the terrorist leader, Julio Bandeira.

It was a fellow student, by name, Shinishi, who brought him the news that Bandeira himself wished to speak to him. Dorval knew about Shinishi and even during the time of his own "dedication" had wondered how this son of zealous, hard-working Japanese immigrants could be involved. But then, he had always reminded himself, it was not only poor Nordestinos but the most remarkably diverse individuals who became inspired by this vision of "remaking the world."

When his own "inspiration" had died, he had often caught Shinishi watching him, felt his narrow eyes upon him with a curious look of disdain and—worse—pity that had made his stomach turn watery. Then one day Shinishi had approached him after class.

"I?" Dorval could feel the nervous sweat from his armpits pouring down his sides as Shinishi repeated the familiar code name, and the instructions as to where to go. It was as if he had been there before, perhaps in a dream. "I'm sorry. I have nothing to do with that any more," he had said as convincingly as he could.

"You had better go, all the same." The pitying eyes had become curiously cold and adamant. "He does not like us to change our minds."

The face of Marighela, Bandeira's predecessor who had been shot in a battle with the police, had been that of a bandit whom, in other times, one could imagine riding out of the gulches and caatinga of the sertão with a marauding band to terrorize the towns. Peasantish and brutal. The face of Bandeira bore no such characteristics. It was darkly handsome, the features thinly ascetic. He had endured much, yet his body was not made for enduring. One wondered how such fragility could survive. The sight of him caused men and boys to admire him for his courage and women to want to cherish and protect him. One at least, had committed suicide on his behalf. He had another now. There was always another. The very thinness of his fine Moorish features made the impression of his eyes that much more intense. They were black and deep-set in darkly shadowed sockets. Their gaze was arresting, persuasive. It occurred to Dorval as he sat before this compelling stare, that Bandeira could make one believe in the reasonableness of anything.

"It is not anyone in particular we care about. Why should we? Why should our hearts bleed for one any more than another? We can only weep, think in terms of the entire unjustly enslaved world, can't we? Where would we be, indeed, if we thought of this one or that one? At present we are thinking of Meneghel. We all know he shot Winslow, that is not the point. The point is, he was my guard. He knows everything. He is insanely brave and stubborn. He has said nothing yet. But if he is tried, he will be condemned for thirty years. Not even Meneghel can keep quiet that long. It is imperative that, before the trial, we get him out."

"Why are you telling me all this?"

"Because"—the steady, reasonable gaze became coldly cynical—"we believe we can trust you." He paused only a second to let that sink in, and then went on, "Of course, you realize one name on the list of prisoners is not enough, especially one like Meneghel. There must be others to counterbalance, to bargain with. Names that are unimportant, but perhaps would be embarrassing to them if they turned up in Mexico or Algeria; names such as that of Delia Cavalcanti."

"Delia Cavalcanti." Dorval had been certain the name was coming, yet when he heard it he felt a scream growing within him, one that nevertheless came out in a desperate whisper, "I have heard they can find nothing on her, no new evidence. You must know, it's possible she will be released."

"All the more reason to get her out now, *não é?* What's the matter?" Bandeira smiled innocently. "I've heard she did much to help *you* during some 'difficult' period in your life, don't you want to help her?"

"Not into exile." The whisper became a bellow of rage.

"Shhh. *Calma.* Even here we must speak silently. It's too bad you don't want to help her, because you'll have to." Bandeira took out a cigarette, put it slowly to his lips and lit it, at last, avoiding Dorval's eyes. "Because, as I've said, we trust you. We know how loyal you have been, the good work you've done, the way you have kept things to yourself, even"—he turned again toward Dorval and winked—"during this difficult period." The wink was out of character. It didn't go with the asceticism which was almost saintly. More than anything Bandeira could have said, it brought him down, created in this musty hiding place with vines trailing under the roof, an evil, inescapable darkness. "And so for the same reasons you had then, we would not expect you to betray us now."

"What could you do?" Dorval did not shout this time, but raged in a low, hoarse voice, a boy suffocating, scratching against the walls of darkness.

"Surely you know." Bandeira gave him a remonstrative schoolteacherish look. "Didn't you learn our lessons? Don't you believe what we say?" Then gently, encouragingly, he went on. "It's not much we'll ask of you. We are aware of the degree of your courage. We wouldn't want to test it too far. It is simply that due to various former embarrassing situations, we feel that diplomats are a little too well guarded these days. Therefore we have been thinking, a businessman, an American—the director of a prominent bank. Oh, we don't expect you to *kidnap* anyone, you may rest at ease. We'll do that. It's only that we must know a few more details about the comings and goings of Sr. Duncan Roundtree. Is he a creature of habit?"

CHAPTER 39

He was not, actually, never had been. One of his great pleasures in life had always been to do things on the spur of the moment. One of the few things he did do regularly, however, was take the car downtown on Friday. It was an "escape the city preparation" that made it possible for the Roundtrees to be ready before sundown, the car greased and checked and waiting to leave. Sometimes they went to the fazenda, sometimes the sea. They knew every beach, every *caiçara* village from Ubatuba to Angra dos Reis, having visited them all on the spur of the moment. The thing was to be ready to get out, for after the incredible mayhem of its work days, São Paulo was depressing, almost sinisterly empty on the weekends.

This evening he drove with Teodoro beside him, following his usual course, taking certain side streets to avoid, as much as possible, the crush of Friday night traffic. Driving up the unavoidable Conçolação amidst thousands of desperadoes all bent, like himself, on escaping to the fazendas and beaches, generally brought out his worst manic-depressive tendencies. But tonight, he felt for once happily oblivious to the traffic. This afternoon, too much had turned out miraculously as he had wanted it to for him to be able to feel otherwise. Too much that suggested that this entrepreneur game that he and Josh and Teodoro had been playing might just possibly turn into something big. That one day he might just be running his own show. Might? It had to turn into something big. As of this afternoon the capital of Frango Frito Limitada, the miserable pittance they had grandly called "initial capital," had been doubled. Ricardo Soares' Banco Nacional de Investimento had bought in for 49 per cent, leaving the reins in the original owners' hands. It was up to them to make it go. If they didn't, it was easy to visualize a huge tidal wave smashing everything—feed business, real estate, fazenda—flat. But they would make it go.

So, sitting in the car, with Teodoro beside him, heading for home, he couldn't help smiling to himself as he thought back over the afternoon and the show they'd put on for Investimento's Board of Directors. To Duncan, at any rate, it had resembled, more than anything, a magic lantern scene illustrated with some impressive-looking graphs and charts and a balance sheet that he himself had pieced together from the most erratic information, but which these people, used to doing business in the jungle, were willing to accept. They had all looked their parts. Duncan, conservative, knowledgeable, good credentials; Josh, solidly determined, capable of bearing up under great strain; Teodoro, eager, earnest, immaculate, respectful. It was a mark of Teodoro's genius, Duncan thought, that he could look like the bus conductor who had made good without inspiring an air of patronization or irritation.

All in all the show had gone well. It had given the directors a chance to look them over to see if the three partners' shoes were solid-looking and their collars not unsettlingly threadbare. To frown at the charts, look knowledgeable and say, "Now, what about a cash-flow analysis?" Indeed if they had been of a mind to force Duncan to produce one or, like Stanley Heimowitz, demanded an accounting of every centavo spent or to be spent over the next five years, the whole thing would have fallen through. But, as Malachai had thought to himself, sitting under the trees on the fazenda so many months ago, it was a matter of the moment and the individuals involved. At this moment there was a feeling of confidence in Brazil, that anything would succeed, given the right people to run it. If the abortive negotiations concerning International Bankers had been of any practical use, it had been that of giving Ricardo Soares the opportunity to come to know Duncan Roundtree very well. That, in itself, had done more to convince the board of directors of Banco Nacional de Investimento than all the balance sheets and cash-flow analyses they could have put together. Then there had been numerous business lunches during which everything but business had been discussed till it was time to serve the cafezinhos, but which had given Ricardo Soares ample opportunity to gauge Josh Moran. Then finally, the lantern show. The business over, they had gone to the Cambridge bar to celebrate. Later, Josh, dreading the thought of returning to an empty house, had gone to spend the night with Ricardo Soares and his family; and Teodoro had joined Duncan, to stop a moment at his house before the Roundtrees headed for the coastal village of Angra dos Reis and Teodoro took a night bus back to Campos.

They drove together in silence, each thinking his own thoughts, immersed in their own dreamings of investment companies and real estate firms, scarcely aware of one another for the time being as Duncan followed the route carefully planned to avoid as much traffic as possible. The route he inevitably took on the one day he drove the car downtown—Friday. They had reached Pacaembú, where the relative quiet of high discreet walls and great leafy trees reminded him of a kind of oasis. Home was but five minutes away. They had only to turn left and then left again. Then, out of one of those winding streets that converged upon Rua Julieta, a Volkswagen surged forward, cutting across their path. Instinctively, Duncan slammed on the brakes, cursing. The Volks swerved and stopped in front of him, blocking the way. "Damn fools," he was thinking. "Hell I didn't even hit them and I don't want to waste time arguing, I just want to get home."

And then he felt Teodoro's hand on his arm and heard him say, softly, cautioningly, "*Cuidado, fique quieto.*"

At first he couldn't believe what he saw. By the time he could, it was too late. They had machine guns and hoods over their faces and held the guns as though they were the actors in a B movie. "Just do as we say and you won't be harmed," one of them was saying. "Get into the Volks, quickly." The voice was high and nervous, the voice of a boy frightened, yet, because of his fear, all the more frighteningly determined. For an instant, Duncan thought of simply surging ahead, but the Volks blocked the way and when he looked back he felt the nuzzle of another gun on his neck. There was nothing to do. In another moment they had him in the Volks, hooded, and on his knees. He thought he heard the other car's door open, some shuffling and then a thud accompanied by a grunt. He remembered later thinking, "Teodoro." And then began the cramped, dark, weaving, interminable journey to nowhere.

Teodoro was agile—as agile as he'd ever been as a boy, running in the streets, playing futebol or dodging the waves on the beach in Rio. If his eyesight had been anywhere near normal, he might have been able, as he had intended, to knock one of them down by flinging open the car door, and then he could have grabbed his gun. As it was, Teodoro's poor, rolling eyes misjudged the distance. The victim in question was too far to be struck by the door and close enough, as Teodoro lurched forward, with all his force, to be able to strike him a resounding blow with the butt of his gun. Teodoro fell unconscious, back across the seat. His attacker shoved his feet inside, slammed the door and was gone.

When he came to, floor, ceiling, mirror, windows, trees, walls, streetlights, houses, whirled in the darkness before his eyes. Trying not to panic, he forced his hands to explore slowly the seat, the floor. Finding nothing, he reached for the door handle and, opening the door slowly, gently began to feel the gutter. Beyond the gutter, bordering the pavement, he could barely make out clusters of flowers and thorns called bride's bed. He shuddered in despair but then something glittered. Reaching toward it, he stabbed his finger on a thorn. The glasses disappeared. He plunged his hand in after them, scarcely aware of the scratching and tearing of thorns. Then, putting his glasses on, he realized there was not much to be happy about. Only now did he notice how his head was throbbing. Inspecting it with his fingers he felt a lump and the warm stickiness of coagulating blood. For a moment, he thought he'd faint, so he sat down again, his head making a spot of blood on the back of the car seat. God knew how long he'd been unconscious, it was just dusk when they'd struck him, now it was dark. The street was entirely deserted. Even if someone had passed this way he would have hurried by, thinking to himself, "A drunk," or, "None of my business." In a big city people only stop to look when there's a crowd. Gradually the feeling of weakness and emptiness began to recede. He leaned forward, holding his watch to the light and saw that it was seven-thirty. Even as he did so, he realized, with horror and disgust, what had happened to Duncan.

"I must get to a telephone," he thought, his mind now working clearly, with urgency. He scanned the houses about him with their high walls and iron gates and rejected them all. There was a bar at the end of the street; much easier, quicker, even if he had to walk a little, than getting one of those gates open and explaining his way to the telephone. As he hurried toward the bar, he thought of whom he should telephone first and decided on Josh. Didn't he say he was staying at the house of Ricardo Soares and would probably go to the beach in the morning to tell Lia the good news? Didn't he say he couldn't stand another night alone on the fazenda?

His expression was polite, nonchalant as he asked permission to use the phone. It was only once he was already dialing that someone noticed the lump and the blood on the back of his head and people gathered close around to hear the conversation.

It was Soares himself who came to the phone. Josh, it turned out, was no longer there. They had tried to persuade him to stay overnight, but he was extremely keyed up, full of energy after the profitable events of the day. Yes, he had decided not to wait till morning but drive down that very night to the beach to tell Lia about the deal.

"Jesús," said Teodoro, his head suddenly twinging painfully. Then he tried to sound plausible to this near stranger and at the same time tell in as few words as possible what had happened. When he had finished, Ricardo Soares' voice came back filled with shock and anger.

"*Escuta*, did you get their license?"

"They knocked me out."

"Never mind. They've probably changed cars by now anyway. Look, I'll try to reach Josh. You get on to the police and call me later."

By the time he'd gotten through to the DOPS and spoken to the chief of this organization, for which he had always borne a suspicious distaste, but to which he spoke now with a sudden, trusting eagerness, the crowd in the bar had closed in, blocking the way, their faces curious, avaricious for the spice of disaster. "*O que passa, que passa?*" They pressed closer.

"A kidnapping." And while they digested that, always correct, always polite, he said, "*Com licença*," and pushed his way past them into the street.

He didn't bother to go back to the car. He couldn't see to drive in the daytime, let alone at night. Duncan's house, at any rate, was on the street below. There was a *ladeira* that cut straight down the hill between the houses, making it much closer than if he followed the street. He found it, a high wall on one side smelling of urine, an overgrown lot on the other. He sprinted down the ladeira, his feet barely touching the steps.

Caroline was good and mad. She'd had everyone dressed and ready, the bags and baskets ready to put in the car for over an hour. Finally she'd given up and put the children to bed. It was too late to start on the long trip to Angra tonight. They would have to fight the Saturday morning traffic or not go at all.

She could see Duncan and Josh and the rest sitting in some bar, drinking, placing Frango Fritos in outlandish places all over the map of Brazil . . . Piruibi, Passo Fundo, Caruarú, Fucks, the German town in Santa Catarina . . . ho, ho, ho. "Fuck you, Duncan Roundtree." Her eyes filled with tears of rage.

Then Teodoro appeared, panting and gasping and telling her to be calm, that everything was going to be all right. And the more he struggled to begin, to prepare her, the more she was certain something terrible had happened, something evil and beyond conception.

"*Pelo amor de Deus*"—she seized his arm at last as if to shake it out of him bodily—"tell me!"

He took a deep breath at that and then said as gently and calmly as he could, "Someone held us up on the way here, Sr. Duncan and I. They hit me over the head, Dona Caroline. When I came to, Sr. Duncan was gone."

"Duncan."

She was very glad of his hand, surprisingly strong for all his meagerness, that had held her steady, guided her to the sofa, sat her down. It was all so frightening, so senseless, so difficult to grasp.

"Teodoro. Look, is this a joke?" For an instant her eyes blazed angrily, hopefully.

"It is not a joke. They are serious, Dona Caroline. They will do anything." He spat out the lowest thing he could think of, "*Espíritos de porcos*." He hurried on, aware that he had already wasted precious time. "I have already called the police." Then he couldn't help smiling with an odd sheepishness. "I know this is a joke with you people, but I *do* have a brother-in-law in DOPS."

"In DOPS?" She stared wonderingly. At any other time she would have laughed uproariously, but now it was suddenly serious, this "joke" of a brother-in-law.

"I am going to call him again as soon as I have some more details." Teodoro straightened and focused his eyes upon her intently. There was in his look something almost professional, the gaze of a walleyed DA. "Has there been anyone here? Anyone aside from your good friends, asking questions about Sr. Duncan, his comings and goings?"

"Of course not!" she blurted. "Who would care?"

"Think a little more," said Teodoro. "Someone wanted to know, someone cared."

And then, with the bitter sensation of one betrayed, she thought of Dorval, the musician.

CHAPTER 40

Traveling at night on an unfamiliar road always makes a journey seem twice as long as it actually is. Imagine then, traveling at night blindfolded on one's knees, facing sidewise while one's mode of transportation moves in apparent figure eights and circles with the nervous rapidity of a water bug gone mad. At one point, as Ricardo Soares predicted, Duncan's captors did exchange the car they had stolen for another, possibly their own, hustling him roughly from one to the other, making certain with the cold nozzle of a gun, nudging the back of his neck, that he made no attempt to shout or break and run.

By the time they reached their destination his legs, in their position of kneeling, were agonizingly cramped. His head ached for any number of reasons: fear, anxiety, the nauseating sensation of being whirled from nowhere to nowhere in the darkness. It took all his concentration not to vomit over the seat, the knees of his captors, himself, and this in itself was a blessing, probably, because it kept his mind from fully considering his plight.

They got to where they were going at last, if he could but have known, not far from the place where he and Teodoro had been waylaid in the first place. Like so many in São Paulo, it was a house built into a steep hillside with a garage underneath. When they pulled into the garage, and hauled him out, he wondered at first if his cramped legs would carry him. But then, as they hustled him, still blindfolded, up a flight of stairs, his legs and back at last unbent, he couldn't help feeling the most ardent relief. Though it was only temporary. He felt himself being guided through a door and heard the door close behind him. A light was switched on and the black hood that covered his head was removed.

The two figures who stood before him still wore the hoods they had used for the assault. He would indeed never see anything of their faces but a certain gleam through the most diminutive eye-holes imaginable. Looking at them this time, he was appalled by their slightness. Neither one of them reached in height above his chin and their bodies were not muscular. They were, in short, like any number of young Brazilian men who had never done a lick of physical work in their lives. Hand to hand they would have been pushovers, but there was between themselves and Duncan still, the all too dominant power of a gun.

"Where," the most useless of questions began to formulate it-self on Duncan's lips. But no one was in a mood for conversation, it seemed.

"Keep still and keep quiet and you won't be harmed." The words came in a high, excited voice from beneath the black hood nearest him. In the next moment, backing out, his captors closed the door behind them.

Duncan heard a key turn in a lock and then something that sounded like an iron bar being lowered into its slot. In his mind, he could see the bar and the slot. Many doors, even window shut-ters in old Brazilian houses had such arrangements. He'd often wondered, in this modern world of big cities and eternal petty crime, why such a means of barring the enemy had been aban-doned for fancier, far less effective devices. Well, his captors had known a good thing when they saw it. Only a battering ram could force such a door and he had nothing larger than a ball-point pen.

The house itself must have been an old one, only slightly restyled to suit the times. For the room in which he found himself now was one of those *alcovas* that Lia had found so repugnant in the house on the fazenda and converted into bathrooms with skylights. No one, however, had made a skylight here. Only four windowless walls and a high ceiling provided a perfect place for holding a prisoner who was not to be heard or seen. Against one wall was a narrow bed and underneath it, a chamber pot. The sight of the latter reminded him that the need to urinate was growing uncom-fortable. But having been in jail on other occasions for such child-ish activities as drunken driving and disturbing the peace, he was immediately reminded that the most unattractive feature of prison cells was the smell of stale urine. So he decided to hold off a while longer. The room would have been oppressive enough in cold weather, but now it was hot, so that, added to the feeling of absolute helplessness, was the miserable sensation that he might slowly suffocate. Once again, he felt a ridiculously exaggerated sense of relief as, looking down, he noticed that the door was unevenly hewn so that there was a space at least half an inch wide at one end between it and the floor.

He would spend a lot of time in the next few days, watching that space for a passing shadow, bending his ear to listen for a sound. Now, flinging off his jacket, and tie, he sat on the bed, elbows on his knees, his mind in a turmoil. He had had no doubt from the moment they had seized him and thrust him into the car, that this was a political kidnapping. They were common these days the world over, and yet he had never expected it to happen to him; perhaps because he had long ago ceased to think of himself as an alien, or as representative of anything, really, except himself. But now, of course, he realized that what he considered himself to be was of no importance to these people. They were interested in a figure whom they could use as a pawn with which to pressure and embarrass the Brazilian Government. As representative of one of America's most important banks, he was as good a pawn as any. There his stream of thought branched off, diverged along numerous paths, most of them leading to agitated thoughts of Caroline, alone and wondering, her fear mounting as she telephoned one likely spot after another until there were no likely spots left to phone.

Or had Teodoro gotten away? If he had, at least he could get to Caroline. It was better knowing the worst than not knowing anything. Other than that, what could Teodoro do besides phone the police, get in touch with Josh? What could any of them do? What possible clue could they have to his whereabouts and even if they did, what use could they make of their knowledge? Very little. That was why kidnapping was the most effective form of extortion, its outcome depending upon what value those involved placed upon a human life.

Robin Hoods? Jesus Christ. He wished they'd kidnap the representative of the UP sometime. No, on second thought, he wouldn't wish this on anybody . . . this position of absolute helplessness. His head throbbed and his eyes burned. Removing his glasses, he closed his eyes and leaned back against the wall. Exhausted and keyed up at the same time, he fell into a fitful doze.

He was awakened by the sound of the bar being lifted and the door once again opened. Shuddering slightly, he adjusted his glasses to take in the thin hooded figure who entered, followed by the other with the gun. "In twos, like nuns," Duncan thought. But for the presence of the gun, he could find nothing fearsome in these individuals, there was something so amateurish in their deportment, even in the way the guard clutched his gun as though it were alive.

The first held a simple block of cheap writing paper in his hand and a ball-point pen. It was the one who had ordered Duncan in high, sharp tones to "keep still and keep quiet." Now his voice was oddly conciliatory. "Would you like a glass of water?"

"A scotch on the rocks would do me a hell of a lot more good," said Duncan sincerely.

"We don't keep liquor around here." The boy's tone became uncomfortably righteous. It brought sharply to mind something Duncan had remarked again and again upon reading about these people. No drinks, no drugs . . . nothing to shore them up but an abnormal seriousness. If their physical appearance was not frightening, this seriousness was. It was increased by the fact that one could see nothing but the indistinct glitter of the boy's eyes. The thought that he could so veil his feelings, if he had any, aroused in the presently vulnerable Duncan a profound sense of outrage.

"You know, this all may seem very heroic to you, but I don't like being here one bit."

"*Sim, compreendemos.*" The boy sounded conciliatory once again. "*E tambem sintimos.* But unfortunately, it is necessary. There are people in prison who must be released."

"Perhaps—but I'm not responsible for their imprisonment. I have a wife and—"

"The system is responsible," the boy cut him short. "You are a part of it, are you not? We consider no one innocent." He repeated, as if for emphasis, "No one."

"*Bom,* I'm glad to hear that." Duncan's mouth twisted sarcastically. "I always thought you fellows had a corner on virtue."

"I wouldn't make jokes, if I were you." The boy's voice became once again high-pitched, suggesting again the intensity of his own nervousness. "I am here to tell you something. You had best listen." Duncan could sense the boy's trying to gain control as he went on. "We have no desire to harm you. I repeat, we have been forced out of necessity to bring you here. You are being held until the Brazilian Government and your employer bow to justice"—he cleared his throat—"to the just demands of the Movimento Revolucionario Popular as set down in a manifesto about to be delivered."

"Might I ask," Duncan interrupted him, "what demands they are?"

"I was about to mention," the boy said sharply, "so that you may know, and know as well who is responsible if they are not complied with. Our organization is in need of money to carry on the revolution. Therefore we have asked of your company, one of the largest and richest in the world, a contribution of $500,000. It should not be so much, should it?"

In answer, Duncan's eyebrow went up ironically.

"Our other demand is the release of twenty prisoners," the boy went on, "among them Ignacio Meneghel, whom we believe, due to the ill treatment he has received, to be close to death."

"Meneghel," Duncan repeated the name softly and with a terrible, fatal sense of awe. "The one who shot Winslow. You must be joking!"

The boy's shrug was eloquent. It seemed to dispel the arrogance of a moment ago. When he spoke again, Duncan was reminded of a medical assistant from whom the patient had forced a reluctant truth. "Our chief is Bandeira, he does not make jokes." He stepped forward, thrusting the block of paper and the pen at Duncan. "Perhaps you would like to write something to your wife?"

Duncan took the block and sat for a moment, helplessly wondering. What to say—how to reassure her, of what? How did one reassure and warn at the same time? He found himself thinking of the words of the American ambassador, the Japanese consul, messages printed in the newspaper to their wives. Brief, furtive, loving words.

I am sitting in an alcova like a Donzela, being well treated. Try to influence those responsible to respond favorably to the demands. These people are deadly serious. Don't be afraid—it won't do any good. Be tough.

I love you,

Duncan

The boy took the message, began to read, frowned and shook his head. "The first sentence will not do. Surely you know there are only a few houses left in São Paulo that have alcovas."

Duncan *did* know, but there'd been no harm in trying. The boy gave him a new sheet of paper and he wrote the message again.

When he handed it to the boy this time he said, "How long do you give them?"

"Three days," said the boy, "perhaps more, it depends. Sometimes there have to be substitutes."

"But not for Meneghel," said Duncan.

"No," said the boy, "not for Meneghel."

CHAPTER 41

By the time that Josh and Lia and the children reached São Paulo on that most memorable of mornings, a number of impressive and terrible events had occurred. The first of these was Teodoro's expedition in search of the musician Dorval. Having already contacted the political police, he had subsequently gotten in touch with his brother-in-law, an officer within their ranks, and together they had set off for the Jogral. It was still Dorval's habit to perform there on weekends. Often now, he played songs of his own composition. He came on regularly at ten o'clock, for he was the favorite of a select number of music lovers who squeezed themselves into that tiny hole-in-the-wall, like toothpaste back into a tube, for the sole purpose of hearing him. But though it was nearly eleven when Teodoro and his brother-in-law arrived, the proprietor, with an expression of profound concern, informed them that he had not yet appeared. "It was not like him." He had never failed to come before. No, he hadn't a phone, but the proprietor gave Teodoro Dorval's address, frowning and shaking his head as he did. "I hope nothing is the matter . . . a strange young man, *não é*? But very talented."

The Republica, which Dorval shared with a number of other students from various regions of the interior, was an old house among countless others on one of those peculiar streets that was neither commercial nor residential, but a little bit of both and a great deal more. The house was a bar downstairs. The students formed one of two *republicas* that occupied the five rooms on the second floor. Upon inquiring, Teodoro was informed that Dorval's roommates both lived in the little town of Tietê, an hour's distance, and had gone home for the weekend. Whether Dorval had gone out or not, the proprietor did not know, but Teodoro was welcome to climb the backstairs and see.

When there was no answer to their persistent knocking, Roberto, the brother-in-law, hauled out the appropriate tools from the brief case he carried and forced the door open. The figure lying on the bed, embracing his pillow, might have been simply asleep after a long hard day of study. But both the men who entered the room had had enough experience to recognize, even before touching the body, the rigidity of death. Beside the bed on a table was an empty bottle of Seconal. Beneath the bottle was a folded slip of paper. When Teodoro unfolded it, he saw that it was addressed to Caroline Roundtree. At first, being the discreet and sensitive person that he was, he hesitated. But Roberto, discreet, but less sensitive than practical, protested. "If you don't read it, you fool, I will."

So Teodoro did, and in doing so, was filled with a profound and terrible sense of anguish.

If it were not for you, I would not bother to explain my action, for who would care? But, having done what I have done, I cannot allow you to believe for the rest of your life that it was an act of malice. Better that you know it was the act of a coward who, backed against the wall, hadn't the courage to speak out. Caught between two alternatives, I chose to betray the two people who meant the most to me. Dona Delia and yourself, who gave me faith in a talent that might have succeeded greatly if things had only been different.

I was instrumental in the kidnapping of your husband, Duncan Roundtree. I do not expect you to forgive me but I hope you shall feel more at ease in your heart, knowing that my act was not out of hatred but the weakness of one who could not face the circumstances that surrounded him on every side.

I know nothing of Sr. Duncan's whereabouts except what I managed to overhear during one unguarded moment. The house must be an old one, for the room in which your husband is being kept, is an alcova de Donzela.

I pray for your safety and that of your husband. Dorval.

When Teodoro finished reading the note, he handed it to Roberto, who, in turn, read it and exclaimed triumphantly, "You see, what did I tell you? How many houses are there still standing in São Paulo that are old enough to have an alcova?" Because Teodoro could say nothing, he answered himself, "A very few," and already imagining the headlines, *"Primeira Pista Discoberto pelo Tenente Roberto de Oliveira,"* he immediately set his mind to considering the *bairros* in which such an "ancient" type of house might exist.

The death was duly reported and the necessary activities for the removal of the corpse set in motion. And while Roberto set off to DOPS with his precious information in hand, Teodoro returned to deliver the note to Caroline. When he did so, there was still an ache in his throat. Probably he would never be able to remove from his mind the memory of the pale, sensitive face of the dead boy whose message he had just read. How many boys like that had he known? He had been one once himself, young and poor and determined—full of dreams. But for an accident of fate that had made him see life and the world in a different way, this Dorval could well have been himself.

"I know it is not very appropriate for me to say so at this moment," he said as he handed her the note, "but I hope you will not think too badly of him."

"Badly!" She fairly wrenched the note from his fingers and glared at it, her sleepless eyes bright with outrage. But when she had read a few lines, her expression changed and when she had finished, she sat down and stared at Teodoro, the tears streaming down her face.

It was 7:30 A.M. when the sexton of the Church of Nossa Senhora de Conçolação opened the poor box, as it was his habit to do every Saturday morning at that hour. As he turned the large, old-fashioned key and lifted a lid as aged, recalcitrant and creaking as himself, he discovered within, atop the crumpled, dirty cruzeiro notes, two folded pieces of notebook paper with messages upon them that fairly made the wispy fringe round his bald pate stand on end. As he had done on every alarming occasion for the past thirty-five years, he rushed with his discovery to the priest, who, already in a bad mood because it was Saturday and there-fore there was an endless stream of weddings and baptisms to perform, frowned acidly over his spectacles and declared the thing an unsavory joke. The sexton would not be appeased, however. When the American ambassador was kidnapped, had the first note not been found in the poor box of a church in Rio de Janeiro? He had been waiting for a similar occurrence to happen to him ever since. He persuaded the priest at last to allow him to call the police.

By nine an emissary had been dispatched to Caroline with the messages and the promise that everything within the power of the Brazilian Government would be done to secure her husband's safe return. Through diplomatic channels, International Bankers had been informed of the ransom demand and their response was expected at any moment.

In the meantime, Ricardo Soares had telephoned to say that he had gotten in touch at last with Josh, who was already on his way. This last bit of news was more reassuring to Caroline than any other. If there was one other person besides Duncan in whom she had confidence in this world, it was Josh Moran. Somehow everything seemed in a state of suspension until he should appear to set it all moving. As Duncan had admonished her in his note, she had determined to be tough. A member of the police guard who had been assigned to permanent duty around the Round-tree house had been requisitioned to take little Andrew to kinder-garten. The police, he had been told, had come to take care of them while Daddy was away. He had gone off quite happily, hold-ing the policeman's hand. Then, the baby trailing behind, Caro-line had gone about her usual duties, automatically, busily compelled to move and act lest she be paralyzed by panic. Around ten o'clock she usually took up the guitar for an hour. Everything else she had been able to do with relative, if numb, success. But when it came to going upstairs and taking the guitar from its corner in the bedroom, her knees felt oddly weak and something told her she simply couldn't do it. "I must do some-thing else," she told herself sharply—anything but sit in a chair and stare into space. "I'll make bread." It was a command she made to herself totally without inspiration, for want of anything else. She was about to turn her steps forcefully toward the kitchen when the doorbell rang, loudly, shatteringly in the silence of a house at this hour generally filled with music.

On the threshold stood Clea, the lack of her usual theatrical make-up emphasizing even more a gray look of distress. One of the guards stood beside her, a hesitant arm on her elbow. "Will you tell this creature to unhand me?" Her voice was low and harsh.

"*Pode deixar.*" Caroline gave the guard a commanding look that left no room for questioning. He backed off, allowing Clea to enter. She looked at Caroline wild-eyed.

"I'm at my wits' end. They've arrested Malachai—"

"Malachai?" For a moment Caroline stared blankly at Clea as if this last was too much, impossible to absorb. Then she said dully, "When?"

"An hour ago. You know Delia was on that list. They suspect him of having something to do with this . . . horrible thing that's happened."

"Then why not arrest me too?" Caroline came to herself suddenly and with a vengeance. "The idiots. Of all the damn fool useless things." She seemed ready to storm outside, or to the telephone to let loose on someone—anyone—all the aching wrath and despair within her. But then she saw Clea sink into a chair, her head in her hands.

"The poor darling." She began to weep. "All his life he's been expecting something like this to happen. All his life. And he's such a coward."

Caroline sat down on the edge of her chair and put her arm across Clea's shoulder. "It's a mistake," she tried to say encouragingly. "When something like this happens, lots of people get hauled in. He'll be released in no time." Then, because Clea seemed none too comforted by this, she said, "They let Duncan send me a note. He told me to be tough. I think it's best, don't you?"

At that Clea straightened and, taking a handkerchief from her purse, blew her nose. "Fine thing, my coming over here with my troubles." Her tone was deep and steady now, the English in the Crimea, London during the blitz. "At least I know where Malachai is. In jail."

Caroline couldn't help smiling. "I'm glad you came, Clea. You would have come anyway. So please stay. No need for either of us to be alone."

It was thus that Josh and Lia and the children found them upon arrival. Caroline got coffee for everyone and they sat down, with the curious air of strategists in a war, to decide what could be done.

Clea, it was decided, should definitely stay with Caroline, not only for the sake of company, but for the obvious reason that, his wife's sharing the same roof with the wife of the victim, might possibly cause the truth to dawn among those responsible, about Malachai's innocence. Further, Teodoro would return to DOPS, where, enlisting once more the aid of his resourceful brother-in-law, he would look into what could be done on Malachai's behalf.

Josh himself was to set out immediately to discover what was being done officially to effect Duncan's release. Just as Caroline had expected, even though no one knew of Duncan's whereabouts or whether anyone was making a sincere effort to find out, somehow Josh's arrival made her feel less hopeless.

"You give a damn," she said in a small, high voice, trying to hold back tears. "I know you won't give up, don't you see?"

"Of course I won't give up." He hugged her tightly for a moment and then placed his hand under Clea's chin. "And we won't give up on Malachai either, do you hear? It's not everyone has a brother-in-law in DOPS."

Lia took her leave, promising Caroline she would return as soon as the children were safely deposited with Gardenal and the fazenda set in motion for the next few days. If there was an odd formality between herself and Josh, the others didn't notice it, so absorbed were they in thoughts of the safety of those they loved.

CHAPTER 42

It was a weird world in which all those involved existed during the next few days. A world filled with odd meetings and strange conversations made heavy with the thought that each conversation was concerned with bargaining over a man's life. The advantage, of course, was clearly on the side of the kidnappers, for the life was in their hands.

The American consul, Mr. Berkly Parks, was unable, though he tried, to cover his consternation over the fact that Duncan Roundtree, a private businessman, had "managed," as he put it, to get himself kidnapped. For this set a new precedent which would in turn complicate even further the already nightmarish rigamarole of international security. What move to make? How far should one go? Mr. Parks seemed paralyzed.

"I hardly think 'managed' is the proper word," said Josh dryly.

"Very well, but you must admit, Mr. Moran, there are certain precautions a man in Mr. Roundtree's position could have taken, such as putting in an alarm system, periodically taking a different route home, not to mention checking on the background of his wife's music teachers."

"He was aware of the background of his wife's music teacher."

The consul threw up his hands. "You see? But then, when something happens like this, who is left to pick up the pieces?" He gave Josh a martyred look. "I cannot describe all the means, Mr. Moran, but I assure you our government is doing everything within its power to secure Mr. Roundtree's safety. The money, as Mrs. Roundtree has been informed, is already in our possession, ready to be delivered, if necessary. Even *that* was not the easiest thing in the world. The legal department of International Bankers seems to be looking into the possibility of suing the U. S.

Government for lack of protection. Would you believe it? The other part is not so easy," Parks went on. "This Meneghel."

"He's already caused one unnecessary death." Josh looked steadily at the consul, who looked back this time with a sudden grave appreciation of reality.

"Let us hope," said Mr. Parks, "that the Brazilian Government looks at it that way too."

Driving to the headquarters of Colonel Silveiro Amaral, who had been detailed to deal with the terrorists in this case, Josh found himself alone with his thoughts for the first time in hours. He thought of Duncan somewhere in the city, waiting while the hours—all too few of them—ticked by. Did the time seem frighteningly short, or interminable? He wondered if Duncan thought there was anything he could do besides try to gauge the intent of the negotiators, try to make things as easy for Caroline as possible. That was it. He had, in short, never felt so incapable in his life—even when the plane was falling from the sky, he had had the controls in his hands. And something else, there had been Lia. Now when he thought of her it was like having all the wind knocked out of him, all the assurance and strength and zest for life gone. He couldn't think of her now. He wanted literally not to think of her ever. Forcibly he thrust her out of his mind.

In his present state, it was almost a tonic to try to imagine the colonel with whom he was about to meet. In the back of his mind he carried a far from encouraging image of another Colonel Ramiro Bastos, whom he had met at a cocktail party just at the time when the Japanese consul had been kidnapped. The colonel, who also had had something important to do with security, had his ideas all safely organized, as if to him they were security itself. "We are at war," he had said with a stuffy finality, "and every diplomat should consider himself a soldier."

"In other words?"

"Bargaining with criminals only leads to further crimes."

It must be wonderful, Josh remembered thinking at the time, to be so positive of one's position. To him it had always denoted nothing so positive as the proof of a profound lack of imagination.

Happily, Colonel Silveiro Amaral did not strike him as a man of carefully categorized thoughts. Still, it occurred to Josh, as he came forward to meet him, that this man could be, if the situation so demanded, politely, reasonably, intransigent. He was tall and erect, his iron gray hair brushed back immaculately from a jutting forehead. On either side of a nose of Cyranoic proportions, his dark eyes were deep-set and searching. His approach was at once solicitous and reserved. "It is lamentable, what has happened. These people are ruthless. I hope there is something we can do. Please sit down, Sr. Josh."

Josh clasped the hand held out to him and then seated himself upon the chair indicated by the colonel. A young man in military dress brought a tray with cafezinhos. The gesture seemed somewhat bizarre, but the moment Josh lifted the hot, steaming cup to his lips, he realized that he was very grateful.

"I wish to assure you"—Josh felt a mad desire to repeat along with the colonel these words that were growing so familiar—"that our government is doing everything within its power to secure the safety of Sr. Roundtree."

"I am aware," said Josh, feeling oddly formal and diplomatic, "that that has always been the Brazilian Government's policy in these cases."

In answer, the colonel's eyes became veiled. He seemed to be watching Josh from their very depths. "A rather unusual case. We are informed that Mr. Roundtree was quite well acquainted with this person, Dorval, who assisted the kidnappers and then took his own life."

"Dorval was Dona Caroline's music teacher. I have the impression from the note he left," said Josh, "that what he did was against his will."

"Sim"—the colonel nodded thoughtfully—"there are many of that kind who feel themselves trapped. We would give them a chance if they came to us, you may believe that, Sr. Josh," he said emphatically. "It would be to our advantage, but how are *they* to believe it? And so they become pawns. Bom"—the colonel shrugged—"we can do nothing for him now. But he has provided us with a track—not much, but, all the same, a track."

"The alcova?" said Josh.

"Exactly. The areas where such old houses could possibly exist can be narrowed down."

"And if you should find it?" Josh suddenly sat forward on the edge of his chair.

"We would watch for an opportunity." The colonel regarded Josh gravely. "You must know that trying to rescue a kidnapped individual by force is a very dangerous business. Only in the last event—"

"And what would the last event be?"

"Sr. Josh." The colonel's expression was very serious. Pay attention, it seemed to say, for I am laying this on the line. "We try to make bargaining as easy as possible for our opponents, so that if there is the smallest chance of give and take, they know it is available. But remember, they have a different set of rules. For them, the end justifies the means. The consequences of being caught, even if it means death, are always weighed against the advantages gained by their cause: money, an aura of unrest and insecurity, publicity—"

"Publicity?" Josh felt the bitterness that had been burning all this time within him, come to the surface. "What do these people want, the whole world to hate them?"

"Do you think they care?" The colonel suddenly looked impatient. "Don't tell me Senhor is one of those who think they are trying to convince the world to *like* them." He shook his head wearily and then leaned toward Josh with a look of appeal. "Why is it so difficult to comprehend, Sr. Josh, that popularity is not their game? That their purpose is to prove that in the face of their determination, a government that tries to play by the rules is helpless? Then, if they succeed"—he smiled bitterly—"they will call it the force of history."

Josh gazed in amazement at this military man whom he had expected to despise, whose comprehension, like that of the colonel who had said, "We are all soldiers," he had expected to be a blank wall. "You put your point across very clearly," he said. "It is not difficult to comprehend, but because of where it leads you, difficult to face."

"But necessary, or else they *shall* win." The urgency and conviction with which the colonel said this made Josh feel oddly cold.

He tried to sound collected as he said, "And so this brings us back, Colonel Amaral, to the original point. What would be the last event, in which you would find it necessary to try to rescue Sr. Roundtree by force?"

The colonel frowned, took a deep breath and looked hard at Josh. "Most of the people on the list presented by the MRP are negotiable. They are political prisoners, involved in the National Security Code. Delia Cavalcanti, for instance—"

"Sim, Delia." Josh was about to say more, but the colonel held up a warning hand.

"We are concerned with securing the life of Sr. Roundtree, are we not? So, please, let me continue. There is one on this list who, I am afraid, is set apart from the rest. Meneghel is a killer. You know his history. We have never been asked to release such a man before. You must also admit that in view of what I have just told you concerning the aims of the terrorists, this would be a very dangerous precedent."

"So he is not negotiable," Josh said very quietly.

The colonel continued looking straight at Josh. The intransigence of which Josh, at first glance, had suspected him to be capable, hung heavily between them.

"I understand that this is difficult for you, Sr. Josh, but let me ask you one question. What would you say about our position if you were not personally involved?"

Josh's eyes became veiled. It was not difficult for the colonel to guess that he was considering strategy, thinking, "At this moment, no matter what I think, I must not agree."

"But that's the difference," he said at length, "I *am* personally involved."

The colonel nodded, and not without a certain amount of sadness, he said, "Yes, that is always the difference."

CHAPTER 43

Once out in the street Josh walked slowly. He felt a dreadful need, though there was no time, to calm down, catch a breath of normal air, if only between the Military Headquarters and the corner where the car was parked. For the first time he felt the strange sensation of walking in another world; the everyday world to which he had belonged so short a time ago, in which the immediate preoccupation at the moment was how to get across the street in the non-stop traffic. The everyday world in which all but a very few were busily, healthily, normally preoccupied with ordinary problems. It was still difficult to believe that he should be among the very few faced with an incredible catastrophe. But that, of course, was exactly what the colonel had meant when he had spoken about personal involvement.

"We are trying at this moment to locate the twenty people on the list. To make sure, among other things, that they actually *are* in prison. We haven't much time." The colonel had risen abruptly. "The instant we have something to report, we shall let Mrs. Roundtree know and we know she will do the same."

Now the thing was for Josh to report back to Caroline, tell her that he had been favorably impressed with the colonel. That he had found him intelligent and comprehensive; that indeed he had given him a clearer insight into the intentions of terrorists than anyone ever had before him. But then he wondered if he should also admit that, for this reason, there was no hope of the colonel's turning loose a murderer.

Nor was there only Caroline to report to. Any number of times he had considered speaking of Malachai. But each time he had realized that in this game, where the slightest misstep could erode the will to bargain, there were no favors to be asked. If Malachai was to be helped, it must be once the business over Duncan was concluded, whatever way it came out. Until then there was nothing to be done except through Teodoro's brother-in-law, the Tenente Roberto de Oliveira. He hoped the hell this Roberto had as much "jeito" as Teodoro claimed he had. Poor Malachai, whose only desire in life was to live and think in peace. Perhaps one shouldn't think. That was probably it.

He found the car and, pulling out, headed up Conçolação toward the back street which was the shortest way to Duncan's house. It seemed an eternity since Duncan had gone that way and not returned. An eternity in which he, Josh Moran, who had always been able to find a way, had accomplished nothing.

He found the two women playing cards with Teodoro and could tell from the generally relieved expression on Clea's face that something good must have happened on behalf of Malachai. Clea confirmed it with an approving sidewise glance at the third contestant in the game of *burraco*. "Remember you once told us, never try to live in a country like Brazil without knowing a Teodoro? Well, you're right, my dear. This brother-in-law of his is simply fantastic."

Josh looked at Teodoro, who gave him a modest smile and thrust his thumb upward before launching upon an explanation of how knowing bigwigs in the police force was perfectly useless. In a scrape it was the underlings who counted, who could wander around effecting little miracles unseen. "There are high category suspects and low category suspects," he explained. "When they were sorting them out, Roberto happened to be there and saw to it that Sr. Malachai was escorted to the lowest group of all." He shrugged and made a disparaging face. "*Gente sem importancia.* I have little doubt, in a matter of days, he'll be out. Besides, Roberto managed to get near enough to him at one point to let him know he was Teodoro's brother-in-law. He was very white—he turned the color of a Dutchman. *Juro por Deus, Dona Clea.*"

Josh's eyes met Caroline's. "No new messages?"

She shook her head. Her gaze was questioning and direct. Josh could see that she was bracing herself with every fiber in her determined being. He'd thought of a number of ways to make his report sound more encouraging, but he felt somehow now that none of them would work.

"It's Meneghel they're going to fight over, isn't it?" she said.

"So it seems. I was favorably impressed, Caroline. He is no fool, this Amaral."

"Still, they won't give up on the murderer, not even if it means—" She bit her lip and swallowed hard.

"They have to take a position somewhere."

"Why? Goddammit, why?" Caroline threw down her cards, and stood up, the control she had managed during the past hours giving way suddenly to a terrible and true anguish. "Let them have their bloody murderer—send him to Algeria for Christ's sake. What difference can it make, put against an innocent life?"

"To us, in our position, none. Nothing can be so important. That is what I told him."

"And?"

"He is aware of it—as aware as any man on earth. And he is Brazilian—remember that."

"What does that mean?" Caroline said warily.

"It may mean nothing. He is also a human being in a very tough position. But somehow at this moment, I am glad he is not, say, a Paraguayan or an Israeli or an Argentinian. Do you know what I mean?"

Caroline lifted her chin and stared hard at Josh and nodded.

"Have you had any rest?" said Josh.

"Not much."

"I suggest she take something to relax a little," said Clea. "I'm full of *calmantes* myself. Feel like a bloody half-wit."

But Caroline shook her head. "I'd rather fall asleep from exhaustion than wake up any more depressed than I am." She gave a little twisted smile. "It's an insane world we suddenly find ourselves in, isn't it?"

"And you know," said Josh, "everyone lives on the edge of it all the time."

No one slept that night except in brief fits of exhaustion. Certainly no one retired to the solitude of a bedroom. It was better to stay together and talk. Better for Josh, who, left alone, sensed himself overwhelmed by the absence in spirit as well as body of

Lia. Better for Clea, who in the presence of Teodoro could almost believe in the efficacy of Roberto de Oliveira's protection. Better for Caroline. Ah, for Caroline, though she often lapsed into silence, anything was better than spending the hours alone. They talked, even joked about how, without the saving graces of booze, Duncan would most likely come out dry and indoctrinated. Hadn't the American ambassador emerged admitting somewhat coyly that he had found his captors articulate and intelligent, and that they had indeed had some interesting talks?

"Which makes you wonder," said Josh, "if he had to get kidnapped to discover the facts of life, where he'd been up till now."

"In a lovely, protective vacuum," said Clea disgustedly. "Ah, diplomats and priests. They're all of the same pixy world. Then when they stick their feet in hot water and get scalded, everyone says, 'Imagine doing *that* to a priest?' Bananas." She made the appropriate gesture, at which Teodoro's eyes rolled out of sight as he suffered an inner explosion of laughter. Not long after that he rose and excused himself, saying that, now Sr. Josh was here to take the place of a man, he would be off to see if his brother-in-law had anything new to report. If, by chance, he did, Teodoro would be back with the news that very night. "I wish I could take a written message." He regarded Clea sympathetically.

"Never mind," Clea said brusquely, "just have the tenente tell him to put on the extra socks I sent him. We musn't have him catching cold, must we?"

Once he was gone, Clea sat smoking and staring at the window as if he had carried with him whatever reassurance she had felt. Her brief euphoria at knowing that Malachai was "without importance" was gone. Dread rose again, like the pain of a wound when the drugs have worn off, making her mute.

They tried to talk of other things. But how, when your entire life is suddenly held in suspension, can you get away for long from the cause of your distress? Better to talk about it than around it, and so they did, Clea beginning again with the gloomy comment, "Remember what Malachai said about the Dark Age that comes periodically? I think it is descending now."

"What's the Dark Age to you?" said Josh.

"Why," said Clea, "obviously the willful destruction of everything that is of worth—that has been painfully built. As if it had no value at all. What do you think?"

"Maybe more than anything," said Josh, "it's the destruction of honor. A man's word." And he told of what the colonel had said to him that morning about the terrorists' indifference to what people thought of them, their determination to destroy the ability of governments to play by the rules. "Every time they make a move like this one, they score. People who ought to be locked up are set free. Others who are innocent"—he looked more intently than ever at Clea—"get thrown into jail." He spread his hands helplessly. "You have to fight on their terms or not at all."

"That's interesting," said Caroline in an intensely sardonic tone, as if someone had just revealed a hitherto unmentioned, but fatal symptom. "If there's no honor, no keeping their word with them, how do we bargain? What's it all for?" She tried not to let fear creep into her voice as she said, "Why, how can we believe they'd *do* anything they *say?*"

"I'll tell you," said Josh, sorry to have alarmed her so. "Because this is not a one-time shot for them. Unless they stick to the bargain, kidnapping will have no meaning for them the next time." And then, thinking of Meneghel, he wished he hadn't said that either. He felt of a sudden as if he'd trapped himself in a lie.

Caroline sensed this and felt sorry for him, for Clea, as much as for herself. "I've no more Schimmelpennincks," she said, "and I could damn well use a smoke."

"How about a Chico?" Josh reached into his inside pocket and brought out the small slim cigars rolled by exiled Cubans in the Canary Islands.

She lit it with a few strong, determined puffs and looked at the others through the smoke. "Remember," she said, "the big arguments we've so often gotten into about the meaning of happiness? We always act so worldly wise, but it's all so simple. The only thing is you only know what it really is when you don't have it." She took another deep puff and looked around her, but no one in the room seemed able to take her up.

Who knows how the silence would have been broken if the doorbell had not rung? Josh moving anxiously to open it, found the guard and, just behind him, the tall, bent figure of Francisco Cavalcanti.

As if by some unspoken pact, no one had mentioned him, though everyone had been awaiting his appearance all day. No one had wanted to suggest that his silence was strange, or to speculate aloud upon what his behavior might be in reaction to Delia's being on the list. It was almost too much to face the tormenting knowledge that exile for Delia would mean exile for him as well, because he would never stay without her. It was like a breach of faith to consider—though it was such a strong presence in their midst—the fact that other prisoners on other occasions, confronted with exile, had chosen not to leave. All very well, but if a prisoner refused to leave, it also seemed, in past dealings of this kind, to have been a matter of honor that a substitute be found to leave in his place. That word again, "honor." One moment it was to be destroyed, the next, it was so obviously indestructible. And in the slow, agonizing interim which could end as no one wanted it to end, what if a substitute could not be found?

What a powerful mixture of feelings was aroused then, as stepping into the room and coming toward them with an impossible air of cheerfulness, Francisco said, "I've been meaning to get here all day. But have any of you ever tried to explain to the passport authorities that your wife is leaving jail tomorrow and you must have your papers in order to meet her in Mexico?"

CHAPTER 44

For a long time it had seemed to Delia Cavalcanti that she had been through everything there was to go through. The interrogation had been as others had told her it was, though she had never wanted to believe it. She had always wanted to believe that Brazilians were gentler. And they are, and more tolerant. But there are certain circumstances under which men become beasts. Not all men, but those who would be beasts in the first place. Such men exist among all people.

She had screamed and cried like the rest, but there was no information she could really give them, because there was nothing she really knew. She had known the girl with the suitcase, but the girl with the suitcase was gone and Delia knew nothing about where she was.

The place where she was imprisoned had, during the early days of the empire, served as quarters for slaves awaiting sale in the market. It had not been much changed since then, a huge cell with a high, barred window through which there filtered a feeble light. At the far end, in a corner, was a kind of improvised pissoir boxed in with wooden boards, and a sink with a faucet. The inspectors from the health department must never have been here, for obviously the installations would not have passed regulation 195730.

When they led Delia through the corridors of the prison that had been added to this place, she was at first relieved because the interrogation was over. And then it seemed to her she was being buried alive.

But a woman of her spirit could not remain totally dejected for long and gradually she began to think and to hope. She quickly made the acquaintance of the other prisoners, of whom there were forty-nine, and began to accommodate herself to the routine. There was much, she discovered, that could be done to make prison life more tolerable and this, in itself, became a kind of challenge. If they had the money, the prisoners could provide themselves with whatever amenities they desired, as long as they passed security inspection. Therefore there had been established in the opposite corner from the latrine, a kitchen and a storeroom which consisted of shelves made of packing cases and a bottled gas stove.

A fund was established for the purchase of disinfectants, which were used in large quantities, and the purchase of food. Those who could afford these things provided for those who could not; for it was not in the Brazilian nature to sit in the same room and eat roast beef with someone who was eating a kind of stew highly seasoned with saltpeter. It was one of the few instances in which the edict "from all according to their means to each according to his needs" actually functioned.

A television was set up at one end of the cell for those who wished to watch Chacrinha, Ebby Camargo or American films in which all the actors had the same voices and people's lips moved interminably, though what they'd had to say seemed to have consisted of an unenthusiastic two words. As on the outside, the futebol games were really the only thing worth watching. Delia confined her entertainment to books, the censorship of which was as erratic as the knowledge of censors. Sometimes the stuff was as bland as Donald Duck, sometimes it could have inspired a revolution. Except that by now, most of the people who read it, had had enough of revolution.

Since fifty people required fifty bunks, space was something of a problem. Bunks lined the walls and stood in rows in the center of the room. Many of these were covered with neat little curtains and became the only havens in a world where privacy was otherwise simply a state of mind.

In this crowded, inauspicious atmosphere, Delia spent much of her time marveling at human nature. Some of the women imprisoned with her were middle-aged, women who had communist records dating back to the early days of the young hero Luiz Carlos Prestes. But the majority were healthy young creatures, skittish and full of life. There was a considerable amount of horseplay, and yet Delia could not help but marvel at the remarkable display of self-control. Promiscuous behavior was all but non-existent. An occasional explosion of temper, the culmination of inner grief and desperation, was somehow attended, quietened, prevented from causing irreparable damage. Yet many of these girls had brandished machine guns, manufactured bombs, held up banks and armored cars. How could all that boldness and fire be contained? Perhaps fear of being removed from what at least was familiar had something to do with it. Perhaps, too, it was the necessity to distinguish themselves from the common prisoners across the way, whose raucous, tragic noises disturbed an already fitful air at all hours of the day and night.

Was it tolerance learned at last in this well of despair, or the determination to survive? She would never know, but she pondered it much, just as she reflected deeply upon how they had gotten here in the first place. They were so young. What could they know? What people like herself and others more adamant had taught them, she answered herself, before experience could teach them anything. So that their only experience was the brief romantic moment of fanaticism and the grim reality of prison.

More and more, as this reality lived and breathed and suffered before her eyes, there arose in her mind the simple terrible phrase, "What a waste." Her sleep was troubled by thoughts of the times when many of them had come to her, and, rather than tell them to enjoy themselves, dedicate themselves to their studies, to love, life, a quiet but persistent pursuit of knowledge, she had with fire in her eyes, abetted them.

Among the books that the censors allowed, out of ignorance or laziness, to slip by, was a volume containing the writings of Albert Camus. Delia had delved into Camus before and cast him aside as an ineffectual sentimentalist, incapable of the positivism necessary to effect real change. Now, as she read his words during these wasting days in prison, it seemed to her she was reading them for the first time. And after reading, she passed them on to one and then another. In particular, those words with which he referred to rebellion, wherein he spoke of men striving in an imperfect world. And of the danger of believing there was such a thing as perfection except as an objective perpetually to be sought but never reached. In these writings, the plea was for a rebellion that was constant but never definitive; that rejected falsehood and distortion but never sought one absolute truth. That made of the rebel a perpetual challenger, but not an annihilator.

All this, in turn, led her often to think of Malachai and the many times he had spoken to her gently and with sadness in his eyes. When he was the only one among those friends—ah, Francisco included—with whom she could bring herself to speak about what was deepest in her heart.

It was not that she had changed her mind concerning her beliefs. She was convinced, as a *religieuse* is who will not allow her fundamental precepts to be questioned, that another system could, if not dispel greed, lessen it. And her belief in this system, she would defend as doggedly and readily as Josh Moran would defend his, or Francisco would refuse to defend any. But during the long hours at night, kept awake by the conversation of her cellmates, the shrieks of hideous welcome that meant someone new had arrived in the common blocks across the way, she had come to reject one very vital concept: That the end justified the means. Not when the means led to the death of innocents, the wasted effort of good minds, wasted lives in prison cells, brutality in answer to brutality.

All this she thought during the months when there was little else to do but think. Still perhaps, despite the efforts composed of cooking, maintaining order and spirit, prison life and the speculations it aroused would have been intolerable had she not known that Francisco was somewhere nearby. That on the day of visiting, he would be there with his bundles, and books and goodies from friends and his impractical but unbroken dream.

It was of the river he spoke, winding across the sun-baked plain. Shining waters, white sand, wind and sun, the thorny caatinga, the vast enigmatic sertão. He spoke of the dusty towns and the strange handsome people, parched and brown as the earth, alert and half wild, mystic and fascinating beyond all people he had ever known. "Our people, Delia, and yet we do not know them. There is so much they need to learn; simple, practical things that are common knowledge to us, but to them, the unknown! Ah, the valley would become green if someone could teach them. Wouldn't that life be more satisfactory than—"

"I must admit, my dearest, it would be quite different."

"Teaching, Delia," he pressed on, "no matter what level it is. Men have to have knowledge so as not to be treated like fools. Knowledge they can put to use. Out there the *tecnicos* teach them how to regulate their irrigation and they teach the tecnicos how to test the humidity of the soil by clenching it in the palms of their hands. Who is teaching, who is learning? It's a constant exchange. For us, the 'educated,' a constant revelation."

So he spoke to her in the fleeting moment during which they sat and, barely touching, drank one another in with their eyes, while the guard stared embarrassedly at the wall. Oddly enough those brief, inadequate meetings, overshadowed with the dread of parting, were in many ways more satisfying than any meeting in the past. For they had come together before, loved passionately, selfishly and gone their own ways. Neither had given much, though love demands such giving. But now, Francisco refused to leave the city, though the possibility of his performing the job he most desired, became more distant with every day.

"Don't worry, there will be other jobs on the river. Engineers are needed for everything."

"But *that* job, Francisco—"

"It doesn't matter half so much. I only want to know that you will come with me."

"I will come with you."

The dream became their life. Everything. But sometimes it seemed nothing but a hideous mockery. The great cell was so chill. It was not a coldness you could alleviate by putting on three sweaters and two pairs of socks. It got into your bones first, and then into your soul. "Imagine the earth without the sun." She had never forgotten her fourth-grade science teacher's vivid description, designed to shock the children into understanding the earth's dependence. She thought of this description often as she walked in the prison yard, seeing the sunlight on the farthest wall, yet never feeling its rays. One day she said to Francisco, with an exaggerated lightness, "Why don't you calculate, just for the hell of it, so that I will know just where to stand and what day?" So just for the hell of it, he had. And the conclusion of his calculation had been that, in that yard, there would never be a day when she would feel the sun's rays upon her skin, rather than see them upon the wall. When he went to tell her, he found himself unable to speak.

The sun was somewhere else—burning and parching the sertão and shining on the river. And she began to feel, despite everything he told her, that the world had forgotten all about her. After all, how many people knew or cared in the first place? Perhaps it would be better if she died. At least he would be free.

And so, on the day that the guard came to fetch her and ushered her into the office of the prison's director, it had seemed that she had gone through everything already; there was nothing more.

CHAPTER 45

The prison director was an unimpressive individual who, from time to time, had called her in to allow her lawyer to inform her of his progress or lack of it. She had grown to loathe his patronizing insouciance, the air of Pilate, that seemed to say, "Well, you got yourself into this, didn't you? I haven't enough pity to spread it so thin."

It was not the prison director, however, who came forward, with a certain unmistakable deference, to shake her hand and ask her to be seated. It was not a man of coarse, indeterminate features, but one who bore a look of good breeding, strengthened perhaps by country life. The very nose, large and sharp, spelled character. The deep-set eyes were stern and commanding, yet there was in them, though she dared not allow herself to trust it, that humanity she had hoped for in other days. When he introduced himself as Colonel Silveiro Amaral, she knew immediately and with sudden sense of fear, who he was. Intelligence. What had turned up now? What, indeed, was there? Who could say?

He began with a strange admission. "Your record has been brought to my attention, Dona Delia. It should have been, some time ago. And so, in a sense, I should apologize. But that's rather useless, isn't it? Better to say, we are living in a difficult time for which we are not fully prepared."

"Perhaps," said Delia, some of the old fire coming into her eyes, "it is better to say nothing at all."

"Perhaps," the colonel conceded, but with a look that said at the same time, enough of apology. "I am here for a very important reason, Dona Delia. As I have said, your case has been brought to my attention. From the testimony of those involved, it seems possible that your involvement with the terrorists which led to the evidence left in your apartment on the fourteenth of March, 1969, was one of sympathy rather than collusion. I shall not go into the details here, there simply isn't time. However, I feel it is my duty, before anything else, to inform you that within a week you are to be released, pending your trial."

Delia held on to the arms of the wooden chair in which she was seated. She felt very cold, as if indeed the sun had been gone too long and she could not withstand being told. She could think of nothing to say . . . she sat staring rather stupidly, unable to take her eyes from the colonel. Then, as she did, she realized with a curious, indefinable apprehension that he was not finished.

"It was necessary to give you this information first, so that you might evaluate it in the light of what I am about to say." His eyes were incredibly grave. "There has been a kidnapping." Delia sat up rigidly at attention. "In exchange for the life of the victim, there has been presented a list of prisoners, one of whom is yourself."

"Myself, but why, if—"

"The kidnappers are not aware of your status, nor do they care." The colonel went on steadily, as if he must come to the end of his tale. "The victim is an American banker and, I am informed, an acquaintance of yours, a Sr. Duncan Roundtree."

"Duncan Roundtree?" She felt a sudden hysterical desire to laugh at this man before her, who each time he opened his mouth, seemed to have something more absurd to say to her. It was too much, she had the strange sensation that she could not possibly be sitting in this chair, that it was not Delia Cavalcanti but some illusive figure in a nightmare who was at once herself and not herself. She would awaken any moment.

"I know this is extremely difficult for you to absorb," the colonel was saying now, not unkindly, "but you must. He is an important banker, a prominent man."

On the edge of her hysteria, Delia smiled foolishly. "I had never really thought of him as such—"

"Nevertheless, he is." In an ever more urgent attempt to help her see, the colonel went on. "There was another acquaintance of yours involved . . . a music teacher, Dorval Ribeiro."

"No." She shook her head. What was this, some kind of new, refined torture? But even as she thought this, the name, pronounced slowly, distinctly, brought everything piteously into its proper place. The effect was to make her fairly shout at the colonel. "And so, if I am on the list, exchange me. What are you waiting for, what?"

"Be calm," he said sharply. And then in that voice that demanded absolute attention, he added, "Only this. You must listen carefully and you must decide. You see, Doña Delia, the authors of the ransom note make their stipulations extremely clear. The twenty prisoners to be exchanged are to be put on a special plane and sent to Mexico. Naturally, it is in our interest, as well, that none of them remain here. Any exchange, any dealing we do with these people is merely in an effort to save an innocent man's life. If they go, they are exiled for good." He paused and said with even greater clarity, "There is no possibility of their returning to Brazil."

"I see." She looked in front of her at nothing as the idea sank in. Exile. In all her wildest imaginings she had never thought of it.

"However," he was saying in the same quiet, uninterruptible tone, "there have been occasions such as these when prisoners have asked for a substitute—someone to be sent in their place. Of course you realize that this is not easy. The substitute must meet not only our requirements, but those of the terrorists. In the meantime, to say the least, every minute for the victim is agonizing and dangerous."

All the while he had been speaking, ever since she had entered this bare, unhospitable room that smelled of prison, he had been watching her and thinking. One could not help but be arrested by such a woman. If anything, the pallor and thinness of prison served to intensify the fineness of her features. And in spite of a weariness that traced heavy circles beneath her eyes, there was an intransigence in the thrust of her lower lip, a deep burning expression in her eyes that reminded him that there was such a thing as an indomitable spirit. Oddly enough, the reminder often lifted his own spirit in some indefinable and contradictory way, just when it was at its lowest. At the same time, right now, it warned him. This one, though she had been classified as such, was not among those who could be considered "recuperable." She had not belonged, no. But she believed and she had used her influence, worked, talked, convinced, provided the fuel from which others had made the fire. Once she was out in the sun again, she would begin again. He did not know how, but he was sure of it. And yet for some time he had sought her release, and to find every means for her to stay.

As if she were reading his mind, she regarded him now with dark, angry eyes. "So you think I am among the 'recuperables.' Is that why you make me this offer?"

He did not answer her directly. "It's part of my business to know what is going on within the prison. I know, for instance, that you have been reading Camus and passing it around."

A look half of fear, half defensive, crossed her face which caused him to add, "Censorship to me is ridiculous. It generally causes what it was meant to prevent. As for Camus . . . if every man could see as plainly—"

She cut him short, "But that is not the reason, and we are wasting time."

"Very well, among other things we know your husband's desires concerning the future. He is a brilliant engineer. Perhaps the best. We can hardly afford to deny him to ourselves." His look became once more almost unendurable in its intensity, "Nor should he be denied."

"Ah." Her mouth twisted bitterly. It seemed to her that now he was playing a cruel game with her indeed. "So now you come to that conclusion. If only you had arrived at it, say, five months ago. How much time is there?"

"A few hours at the most," he said. "Beyond that we can take no more risk. So"—he rose, pressing a button as he did to call the guard who stood outside the door—"I must ask if you have an answer for me?"

"But of course," she said clearly. "If you know everything about me. If through some eavesdropping insect of a guard or through some device, you have listened to all my conversations with my husband, you must know my desires as well as those of any. But Duncan Roundtree is my friend. And even if he were not, let me tell you, this is what I have learned from Camus. I want no innocent man's life endangered because of me."

He dismissed her then and she went, a small, erect figure, turning her back on him, giving him no quarter as the guard led her through the door. For a moment afterward, Silveiro Amaral sat very still, knuckles pressed against his eyes.

CHAPTER 46

Sometimes when he sat thus an old vision appeared behind his lowered lids of the place in the distant stark mountain country of Minas Gerais, whence he had come. Where most of the time it was so quiet one heard nothing but the high wind in the trees or the voice of a lean black Mineiro, talking behind his mule. There had been a great house of blue stucco with a wooden terrace across the front called the *passarella* from which the *padrão* had looked down to watch the coffee being turned again and again on the square brick terreiro below. A great house with many children. Too many. The girls had stayed at home. The boys had been dispensed like chessmen: one a doctor, one a lawyer, one a priest, one to the Army, one for the fazenda. He hadn't particularly wanted to go to the Army, but he'd craved learning and they had not been wealthy by any means. Or so his Mineiro father had said.

The vision faded, swallowed up in dust and wind and distance and time. There was no returning. The place was no longer there. Nor did he really want to return. What he really sought more than anything was rest and peace. Unless one was inhuman, it was what anyone would seek before long in this job. And he was not inhuman. It was one of the reasons why he had been chosen. He had a great imagination, a way of gathering bits of information, putting them together and seeing in them what others could not see. He was seldom wrong about human nature. He had an uncanny knack for gauging pride, stubbornness, greed, compassion, fanaticism, all those ingredients involved in the performance of desperate acts. And it was for this reason, too, that he had been chosen as opposed to, say, Colonel Ramiro Bastos ("We are all soldiers") to do the bargaining. But he was deathly tired—no one could imagine the degree of his weariness, and the more tired, the greater his sense of hopelessness.

Whatever way Amaral's mind turned, it stumbled against the poor, vengeful, tragic figure of Meneghel. A child of the wind-swept plains of the South. Son of a whore, trained as a solicitor. A laughingstock, he must have been, so ugly was he with his bush of black hair, low brows meeting at the bridge of a large curved nose, small black eyes set so close that, even though they weren't, they gave the impression of being crossed. Pugnacious in his ap-proach—"Want to know a good woman?" They couldn't help laughing and pitying him. But who wants to be pitied?

His mother died, drunken, covered with sores. He was taken in by a doctor who, in exchange for his keeping the yard, cured his syphilis, fed, clothed and sent him to school. He must have looked old and funny in his school uniform, there amidst the first graders. The doctor felt sorry for him, but he was impossible to love; diffi-cult even to take seriously. When he became a mechanic's assistant, the doctor was glad to be rid of him. There wasn't much me-chanical to fix in a bleak little border town in Rio Grande do Sul even in the late fifties, but there was only one mechanic, who be-came moderately prosperous letting Meneghel do all the work and paying him next to nothing. There was no one really to blame for his hard and lonely life, but it is almost too painful to put the blame upon the misfortune of being ugly and unpleasant.

One day in the winter of 1962, Brizolla, the governor, came to town. He was one of those orators who make up for lack of quality with quantity and volume. He had someone to blame for every-thing, but mostly, and with the usual lack of imagination, blood-sucking American capitalists. It was because of their grip on the country that the Southerners could not compete with imported wheat, or afford expensive imported machinery, or even machinery made in American factories in Brazil. And people like Meneghel who worked on cars and tractors and trucks from morning till night could not afford to own even a bicycle. It stood to reason. Everything was drained, like blood by a leech, and sent up there to feed the great war machine. Meneghel became, of all things (Amaral's head hurt when he thought of it), a Brizolla fanatic. And when the Communists planned their first of May takeover in 1964, Meneghel was to have been a member of one of the trusted "*grupos de onze*" who were to occupy the key positions of the town and "justicize" its leading reactionary citizens. At the top of the list for justicization was the doctor who had sent Meneghel to school.

However, the first of May takeover never occurred, because the revolution which took the government out of the hands of Goulart happened in March. Meneghel didn't get his chance until later.

When he finally stepped in front of Winslow and pumped him full of machine-gun bullets, he probably did believe he was eliminating a war criminal, an enemy of the people. Certainly when he was caught some months later, he said as much. But that was all they could get out of him. He would talk about no one and nothing. One had to admit grudgingly that there was something heroic in his stubbornness. This swarthy, bestial, valiant creature who defied his interrogators to kill him. But they wouldn't. They kept him in solitary confinement. Watched him carefully and anxiously awaited his trial.

He was watched anxiously from without the prison walls as well as from within. The MRP didn't want him to be tried and sentenced. They wanted him either out and exiled in some country from which he might never find his way back. Or they wanted him dead. Each time Amaral in his endless maneuverings for the life of Duncan Roundtree, came up against this unsurpassable stumbling block, he found himself wishing more and more that Meneghel would indeed find a way to do one or the other.

"Meneghel is a murderer who shot a defenseless, innocent man down before the eyes of his son. To protect the life of another innocent man, we have conceded to all your demands but this one. On this demand we are unable to find any reason to justify our giving in." Thus he had written in his final message delivered at 7:00 A.M. to the radio station indicated by the MRP to broadcast their messages and the government's response.

It was now 9:00 A.M. and no response had occurred. He wondered if the kidnappers were aware that, thanks to the track provided by the music teacher's letter, the house had been discovered and was now being watched. And if they were aware, he wondered what effect it would have. There was no time to think of that now, really. He put it in the back of his mind and did his best to concentrate all his efforts upon the matter at hand, as once more the guard opened the door, and ushered in Malachai Kenath.

CHAPTER 47

His clothing was rumpled, his face gray beneath two days' stubble of beard. He walked with the hesitant step of one who has lost control of actions and events. It frightened him, Amaral had seen that fear before, and this was a man of no great bravery. And yet when he raised his eyes to meet those of the colonel's, there was a dignity in them that bore a greater effect than all those qualities which the colonel had seen at first glance. Up to that moment, Amaral had thought of any number of ways in which he might persuade this man to do his will. Lying, intimidation . . . Now all these were swept from his mind.

"Sr. Kenath, sit down, please." And once more he found himself apologizing. "It is unfortunate, the ordeal you have undergone. When something of the magnitude and urgency of a kidnapping occurs, sometimes people are suspected who should not be. There is so little time. You were listed as a close acquaintance of Delia Cavalcanti's, one who tried more than once to secure her release."

"She was in trouble," said Malachai. "I tried to help her. I didn't know what she had done, I still don't." His face sank into an expression of weariness. "I have always tried to keep out of these things, observe from a distance. That is one of the reasons I came to Brazil twenty years ago. Because I thought, here, no one cared; there would be peace."

He shrugged his shoulders hopelessly and again something touched the colonel and caused him to say, "Twenty years ago no one *did* care. Brazil was a joke. It almost makes you wish it still were." He knew he should not have said that and he knew it was weariness that had allowed him to. That and the resigned, listening attitude of this man before him that was almost hypnotic. He hesitated, thinking what next he must say.

In that moment, Malachai, straightening abruptly and drawing upon a none too reliable fund of courage, said, "Sr. Colonel. Am I to understand that you realize my imprisonment is a mistake and, since that is the case, that I am to be released?"

The abruptness of the question took the colonel by surprise, like an unexpected sword thrust. There was nothing left for him to say in answer but, "Yes. Yes, that is basically so. However, that is not why I had you brought here—"

Malachai held his breath, watching intently, feeling the train of events moving once again, uncontrollably forward, hardly realizing that the colonel at this moment was feeling strangely out of control himself, carried along by the same tide. Now, at last, he heard himself explaining to this Malachai Kenath, almost as if he were telling a friend an incredible story, the situation of Delia Cavalcanti, his certainty that she did not desire to become an exile. The pressing need to find a substitute. When he came to the end of his explanation, Malachai was still gazing at him, his hands quietly in his lap. But the look in his eyes was no longer mild and resigned. It was as if suddenly within Malachai Kenath, a dam had broken and something that had been building for only God could know how long, burst forth in a high-pitched roar of indignation.

"And you are asking me? No! Does that answer you? Delia Cavalcanti is a fool, she deserves to be exiled. If it were a matter of Duncan Roundtree's life, but no. I've been imprisoned for nothing and now— Look here"—he leaned forward, wagging a trembling finger at Amaral, who sat staring—"I am not a terrorist, nor have I ever any intention of being. If a cause must be supported by kidnapping and killing innocent men, there is something wrong with that cause. How many times did I try to explain that to Delia? But she would not listen and now she expects me—"

"Not she!" the colonel broke in, aware of a straw in a raging torrent. "Not she, by any means. She has no idea that I am proposing *you* as a substitute. Nor must she. Nor is it so much for herself that she desires to remain, but for her husband." He took a deep breath and said slowly, "You are aware, Sr. Kenath, that Francisco Cavalcanti is a brilliant engineer. Perhaps the most brilliant in the country."

"I am aware," said Malachai unbendingly, "that I have been

done an injustice. One becomes, after many centuries, weary of injustices." He said this almost as if it had taken his last bit of strength, but his jaw set with an astonishing firmness, once he had said it.

"*Muito bem.*" The colonel bowed his head a moment and then looked up again. "It will take until afternoon for your release to be 'processed,' as they call it." He pressed a button and once again a guard appeared.

The guard had taken Malachai halfway down the corridor leading to the cells for political prisoners of minor importance when Malachai seized the guard's arm and shouted, "Wait!" In the scramble that ensued, it was a miracle that Malachai was not shot by his sentinel, who could only imagine he was attempting an escape.

CHAPTER 48

It was Monday. For most people, the beginning of another week of traffic, smoke, noise, faulty telephones, deals that were always just pending. For some, however, the end was drawing near.

In his strange day-to-day dialogues with the colonel, which became each time less like anything than simple hypothetical exertions, Josh suggested that perhaps the exchange of Meneghel would be more expedient than he thought. For this was not a diplomat, but a banker, and if a foreign businessman's life were sacrificed, what foreign business was going to risk its investments, let alone its employees' necks? To which the colonel countered with an equally valid argument—that if kidnappings were so successful, for what reason should they not continue, endangering lives and investments even further?

From these two lines of argument that annulled each other and still do, the two men sat regarding one another and thinking of the killer, Meneghel. His image remained between them, unfortunate and evil.

"The worst," said Josh, voicing his thought at last, "is that at this point, his own people have as little use for him as we."

"Do you suppose I don't think of that?" said the colonel. "Unfortunately"—he looked steadily at Josh—"it brings us no closer to a solution." His answer made Josh ashamed.

"What he was saying, and what I was thinking," later Josh expressed his shame to Caroline, "was that he could have Meneghel wiped out with one sentence. But he won't."

"And you call that justice?" Caroline reminded him of a creature in pain for whom there was no help. "That Duncan should die so that that murderer should live?"

"Do you think he's wrong?" It was like giving Caroline a rag to bite on. She leaned back in her chair, closed her eyes and shook her head.

The house in which Duncan was a prisoner was, in fact, not far from the center of town. One of the last of a number of heavy, imposing, pseudo-Victorian *palacetes* built toward the end of the great coffee era. It had survived because its former owner had wanted it to. A stern matriarch, a woman of will and tradition, she had been born in it, married, raised her children, become widowed and was in the process of raising her children's children within its dark labyrinthine confines, when she died a natural death. Her descendants, released at last from the sentiments that had forced them to share this bastion of brooding tradition with *vovó*, had been only too eager to move out and rent the place to a private language school, O Instituto de Idiomas Praticos, until it might be knocked down and forgotten forever. Regular students preparing for entrance exams for the city's faculties had their lessons in the front of the house. The back was used for extra-intensive courses. Nobody questioned of what these courses were composed, nor did it seem strange to the neighbors—especially since the house was surrounded by those indifferent species of dwellings, apartments—that the special courses continued on even through the long summer vacation. In this world where one seized one's education when and where one could, students cramming through holidays, was no great exception to the rule.

However, since it was a particularly old house, built in the time when fathers still felt it expedient to shut their daughters in windowless rooms, it had come within the criteria of Dorval's letter. Further investigation had singled it out as "the house." Whether they were aware of the discovery of their whereabouts Duncan could not know, not being aware of it himself. But certainly, as time went by in this infernal eternity of hours, their behavior became increasingly neurotic and desperate. The behavior of creatures trapped themselves.

In the beginning, after the first shock of having succeeded in bringing him where he was, and after the first message had been responded to "submissively," as they put it, they had become temporarily confident, even cocksure. The part about Meneghel was only a question of time. The spineless Brazilian Government could not risk offending the Americans with the sacrifice of International Bankers . . . Duncan would see. Had any kidnapping victim lost his life yet in Brazil?

"That should be a credit to your government."

"*Puxa sacos dos estrangeiros!*" the boy who stood in the doorway replied. And added, "Look, I thought you might like something to read." It was the one who had had him sign the message. His voice was very young and easily impassioned. Duncan couldn't see his face, of course, but he was certain it bore acne from nervousness and adolescence. The book was A *Compendium of the Thoughts of Chairman Mão*, Portuguese translation.

"Listen, uh—don't you have anything a little more interesting, a little more true to life, like maybe some Hemingway?"

"True to life? Hemingway?"

"Have you ever read him?"

"He never expressed himself on anything important," the boy side-stepped.

"You mean politics, of course," said Duncan. "But he was good on trout fishing, bullfights, wars, what people were like. Not what he wanted them to be."

"The product of a degenerate system," the boy continued in the same vein.

"Oh, Jesus." Duncan felt the hair rising on the back of his neck. He waved his hand toward the "Mão Think" which lay, abandoned, on the bed, looking as absurd as the hoods, the machine guns, this entire insane situation in which all of them were involved. "Look, I've read some of that stuff. Did you ever really think about it? I mean, do you guys really think that by changing a system, you can change human beings?"

"By removing the evil of competitive capitalism—"

"*Que merda*." Duncan shook his head pityingly. "That's like saying money is responsible for what men do with it. What I can't see is what in the name of God you think you're going to accomplish."

"In the name of God, no." The boy's voice became vehement, obsessed. "In the name of decency. You think we are alone, but we are not. This is only part of a great effort. We have friends, in Cuba, Chile, Uruguay, everywhere, who will supply us when the moment comes."

"Supply you." Duncan shrugged. "And someone else will supply your enemies—whoever you think they are. Then there'll be a big shoot-out and who do you think will benefit? Some guy in Little Bavaria, Illinois, or Lyons, France. Whoever makes the arms. Listen"—Duncan's voice became almost fatherly—"didn't anyone ever tell you men are a bunch of greedy bastards no matter how you look at it? The thing is to learn how to beat the racket, whatever racket's going. You might even end up doing something worthwhile."

"Such as?" There was a sneer in the boy's voice, also a tremor.

"Why, any number of things—like screwing some rich, beautiful '*filha de industrial*' who'll then finance you to discover a cure for chagas' disease. How in hell should I know? Use your imagination." He looked around him at the high narrow walls that enclosed them both. "I'd think anything was more worthwhile than painting yourself into a corner like this."

The boy made no answer, but stood very still, tensely poised as if he were at a loss as to what to say or do. Of a sudden, Duncan was seized with the sensation that the boy was indeed suffocating, that it was all he could do to keep from tearing the ridiculous hood from his head and looking at Duncan, face to face. It made him feel like shouting himself, "Go ahead, take that thing off, you poor helpless son of a bitch." The silence in the room was becoming more suffocating than the room itself. If only to break it, he heard himself saying, "Look, ah, I've got to go to the bathroom. I wonder if, just this once, you might not trust me alone—"

It was enough, apparently, to do the trick. The boy straightened, recovered himself, resuming the role assigned him—that of the outlaw, the zealot, tough and unyielding.

"What do you think this is," he snapped, "some kind of kindergarten?"

"No," said Duncan, "I'd just like to take a shit in private." But it was no use, even in this matter. If he'd had any desire to take a shit, he'd lost it. All the same, since he'd asked, he stood up to be escorted to the bathroom, resigned to being constipated until the day of his release or his death.

CHAPTER 49

Perhaps only Meneghel knew exactly how it happened, and he would never tell. The rest could only be a matter of conjecture, and there was plenty of that. From the day of his arrest three months before, when they had found him at last in a small inland town of the Vale do Ribeira, he had been kept in solitary confinement.

He had scarcely known anything but suffering from the day of his birth. The suffering of humiliation for his mother; of his ugliness and taciturn nature; the bitter suffering of being pitied but never loved. Then he had known the exquisite suffering of the fanatic, dedicated to a cause, and that, in turn, had become his passionate devotion to the "hero" Bandeira. Bandeira had never pitied him. He had needed him and he had used him to kill a man whom he had never known and upon whom he could place no personal blame, but whom Meneghel had shot down in cold blood, blaming him for the misery of the world.

He had shot him with all the hatred stored up in his soul and out of the feeling closest to love he had ever known, his devotion to Bandeira. In prison he had suffered greatly, beyond the endurance of most men, to keep Bandeira's secrets. Perhaps he was simply weary of suffering. Perhaps somehow, in spite of, or because of his guards, he had gotten the message that Bandeira was bargaining for his release, but that it would never be effected. And that, even if it were, he would be sent away, no longer useful.

At any rate, alone in his cell on Monday night, Meneghel had torn his rough prison shirt into strips, wound it together into a sturdy cord, attached this to the grate in the ceiling through which from a skylight in the roof there shone a pale reflection of the moon. Adjusting the thing around his neck and swinging from the edge of his bunk, he had successfully ended his life.

As soon as the discovery had been made, Colonel Silveiro Amaral received the message over the closed line with which he maintained contact with the prison. After a night of fitful sleep he had fallen into the deep oblivion with which the mind defends itself at times like these from breakdown. Awakening to the urgency of the tenente's voice over the phone was rather like plunging out of oblivion into the routine of nightmare. The conscious and the subconscious contested, blurred, became one as Amaral struggled into his clothing. In the next moment, as he hurried downstairs and poked his head into the kitchen to hurry the cook with the coffee, reality rose to the surface. It was like a prayer answered. "Though," he reprimanded himself, "one doesn't pray for such things." Indeed, he had not permitted himself to order its occurrence. And yet . . .

The cook, grumbling over the fact that Sr. Colonel was arising earlier each morning, placed a tray with steaming coffee and milk on his desk in the study. Sipping the coffee, he sat very still, trying to absorb the news, calculate the impact it would have upon the terrorists. The last message broadcast over the radio at the demand of the terrorists had stated once more that all requirements of the kidnappers had been filled. The prisoners listed had been located and were now quartered at the Army Air Force base of Cumbica, from which an army transport plane would deliver them to Mexico City, where they had been promised asylum by the Mexican Government. The prisoner Malachai Kenath had been substituted for the prisoner Delia Cavalcanti—this substitution having been approved by both the Brazilian Government and the negotiating committee of the MRP.

Only one request had not and could not be fulfilled. That was the release of the prisoner Sergio Meneghel, who was to be tried on the thirtieth of the month for first-degree murder. A sum of $500,000 matching that demanded of and delivered by International Bankers Corporation was being offered by the Brazilian Government (he did not add, and guaranteed by the United States Government) as a substitute for the release of Meneghel. He had finished in the usual way, soliciting consideration in the name of decency and humanity and the life of an innocent man.

Amaral had gone to bed last night, certain that the answer would be negative. If the response was what he expected, he would give the order for the police who had been watching the old house to close in. It was a desperate, highly dangerous, last resort and he had lain awake that night thinking of the wife and children of Duncan Roundtree.

But now, perhaps desperation would work in another way. Meneghel, the tool, had become, in prison, Meneghel the obstacle; the knowledge of what he knew giving Bandeira no rest day or night. Perhaps now, with the obstacle removed, the terrorists in their own desperation to get this hideous thing over and done, might consent. It was what he had resisted, but what had lain in the back of his mind temptingly, reasonably for the past three horrendous days, and now it had happened without his doing. Hoping to heaven that the people in the old house were not aware that they were being watched, he set his mind to wording a final message.

The response seemed agonizingly long in coming. The reason, of course, was that Bandeira had to be contacted and this, as on all other occasions, took a combination of murky telephone calls and footwork that only the logic of the perpetually hunted could design.

On edge as anyone, Duncan's captors kept him in his alcova de Donzela with two seated outside the door instead of one. Commotion, muffled voices came to him through the cracks in the door. When it was opened at last and the boy with the pimply face beneath the hood stood before him breathing heavily, legs apart, he thought, numbly amazed that it had at last arrived, "This is it. I'm dead." But instead, the boy said in a low, excited voice,

"Do you know what they've done? Meneghel is dead."

For the first instant, Duncan could feel nothing but relief, as if a great weight had been lifted. "Jesus, that changes everything," he gasped, but the boy shook his head and said as if it were a curse,

"*Tudo depende de Bandeira.*"

"Bandeira," Duncan started to shout as the boy turned his back, "screw him." But the boy only shut the door in his face and, for the first time, the full meaning of the power of Julio Bandeira struck Duncan speechless.

Caroline, too, had received the news, after a sleepless and despairing night, with a wild sense of hope. But as the day had worn on, the euphoria had worn away with it. Exhausted, nerves strained to what in someone less stubborn would have been the breaking point, she sat near the radio in a trancelike state. Vaguely she heard in the background Clea quieting the baby, George, while Lia and Analia, the maid, prepared the children's supper. Without any sedation, she was drugged by the long emptiness, the hours of dread, hope, disappointment. It seemed as though she could absorb or feel no more, and then the announcement, righteous and humiliating, came once more from the station designated for this exchange.

Regardless of the safety of the American capitalist Duncan Roundtree, the Brazilian Government has consistently refused to free the prisoner Meneghel in exchange for his release. Last night, unable to withstand any longer the rigors of imprisonment, the cruelty of his interrogators, the hero Meneghel, faithful to the last to the great cause of the Movimento Revolucionario Popular, took his own life.

Roundtree is a criminal like all those who serve the cause of repressive capitalism. In retribution for the life of Meneghel, he should be justicized. However, to secure the freedom of the nineteen heroic individuals who had suffered imprisonment and now await exile from a country that could not support their struggle for justice, the exchange will be carried out as agreed. As soon as the members of the Movimento Revolucionario Popular are reported safe on Mexican soil, the American capitalist Duncan Roundtree shall be released.

In the delirious excitement that followed, everyone noticed the look of sudden desolation of Clea's face, and everyone heard her say, "I can't stand it any longer, I'm going to find out for myself." But no one followed her as she threw on a jacket and went out the door, except Teodoro.

The journey to Mexico City via Brasília, Manaus and Caracas, in an army transport plane is a matter of twelve hours. At sometime around 5:00 A.M. on Tuesday, Duncan Roundtree, having ridden sidewise on his knees for something close to half an hour, found himself standing on stiff and aching legs in a deserted side street not far from his home. One of his captors kept a gun trained on his back so that he might not turn around while the other removed the hood from his head. Then they released him and were gone. They never returned to the old house, and, of the five who had kept him and themselves prisoners there, they were the only ones who got away.

The air that morning was heavy with the sulfurous smell of a city that could not quite believe the number of smoke-belching industries it had created in the past twenty years. But to Duncan, it was the fresh, sweet air of freedom. He took it deeply into his lungs and then began to walk rapidly—he had been told not to run—toward his home. Within the space of ten minutes he had kicked the front gate open and, with dogs and children leaping and dancing wildly around him, he was holding Caroline tightly in his arms.

Josh somehow managed to fend off the reporters until 7:00 A.M. But at that point, it became impossible to inhibit the rights of the press any longer. Duncan didn't really mind. How can one mind anything, after all, when, quite by chance, one's life has nearly been taken and then again, quite by chance, been restored? He rather enjoyed sitting in his living room with a cup of coffee and Caroline by his side, holding court with the press. Particularly with Zach Huber acting as the principal interlocutor.

"I suppose, Mr. Roundtree," he said with a formality meant for his colleagues, "in view of the circumstances, you'll be making plans to return to the United States?"

"On the contrary. If this kind of thing is going on everywhere, why not stay here, where I've already been kidnapped. Has to do with the tightrope theory . . ."

"Ho Ho, very clever, very amusing. In a more serious vein, can you tell us something about your captors? How did they impress you?"

"Young and ignorant as I was at their age. And trapped." Duncan's expression became thoughtful. "I mean, where do they go from here?"

Zach hesitated slightly. "That's a good question. Now let me ask you another. Did you have much opportunity to talk to them? I mean, really converse, during your days in that room?"

"From time to time. They were just as scared as I was."

"And during those talks, did you find at any time, any reason to sympathize with their position?"

"That this is a stinking world?" said Duncan. "That people on top take advantage of the ones below? Of course."

"So then you can actually express a certain admiration—"

"Like hell!" Duncan zeroed in. "Look here, young man. Have you ever been snatched off the streets and kept with the threat of death hanging over you for four days? Some people have been kept for months and died at the end of it. For what?"

"Got it." Zach Huber nodded like an army private being dressed down by a sergeant. Duncan had to grin. It made way for the next question, which, since Duncan seemed in the mood for parrying, was calculated as something of a thrust.

"In spite of your feelings concerning such individuals, Mr. Roundtree, it seems that a number of persons directly or indirectly involved in this kidnapping were personal acquaintances of yours. The guitar instructor Dorval Ribeiro, the prisoner Delia Cavalcanti, who was to have been exchanged, but at the last moment was replaced by the prisoner Malachai Kenath."

"Malachai Kenath!" Zach had expected a reaction, but not quite so intense as the look of incredulous shock on Duncan Roundtree's face. "What are you saying? What's going on?"

Duncan seemed to be looking from one to another in the room, in search of an answer, but every face seemed to be as shocked as his. Every face that was, but that of a slight, pale mulatto with thick glasses who had been sitting in a corner, doing his best until now, it seemed, to make himself as inconspicuous as possible. It was to him now that Duncan addressed himself in a sharp voice that cut through all the murmurings of the others in the room.

"Teodoro, *que aconteceu?* You look sick."

CHAPTER 50

It was only after the press was finally and protestingly dispersed, that Teodoro, recovered, and reveling somewhat nervously in the ardent attention of his audience, allowed himself to give the details of the disappearance of their friends. Of how Clea, upon reaching the delegacy, had been given by the colonel a letter addressed to her from Malachai. And how, upon receiving it, Clea had enlisted Teodoro's and the colonel's help in getting her safely aboard a plane, making them swear to secrecy until after the moment of her departure. Even to the point—didn't they remember? —of his calling in, sometime around midnight, to advise them that Sr. Malachai was safe and well and Dona Clea had gone home to her apartment. He had failed to add that she had gone home only to gather together a few of her most important belongings.

Later on, though correspondence with the exiles was strictly forbidden, somehow, as things happen in a country where there is always a way, each friend in his turn received a letter from Malachai. Francisco received his in Juazeiro, where, immediately following Delia's release, he had offered his services to THE COMPANY on an irrigation project that would water some fifty thousand hectares of heretofore parched and useless land. Delia was teaching young people who had not had the opportunity in earlier days, to read and write and do arithmetic. Fifteen- and sixteen-year-olds in the first grade whose endeavors to accomplish the written word were no less earnest than those of her best university students to grasp the theories of Kant, Marx and Spengler.

Perhaps the most curious thing to relate concerning these two was that Delia could have had her position back at the university, had she wanted it. But quite sincerely she had not. In answer to Malachai's letter she had written:

The first thing we did when I was released was to take the trip on the river. Francisco wanted me to do this before we decided once and for all what we would do with our lives. It was all as he had described it, that shining river, those strange people living their predatory lives in a vast, abandoned wilderness. For the first time I saw those people whom I had described so many times to my students, hinting, suggesting, preaching revolution. And so for the first time I saw their real needs.

So we are here now, beginning at the beginning. If you could but imagine the intoxication one feels at having the ignorant daughter of an illiterate caboclo approach one with the heretofore totally unfamiliar word "why?" It means, my dear Malachai, nothing less than the fact that she has ceased simply to accept.

When Malachai read these words, he rolled his eyes heavenward with a look of apprehension.

He wrote a letter of congratulation to Duncan in São Paulo, where, since the bank had demanded that he remove himself to less vulnerable surroundings, he had resigned and was now, somewhat more precipitously than he had expected, establishing himself as a private investment agent. Tough, since he was far from prepared financially to take this leap; but "the moment" had not been kind enough to await the proper preparation. How seldom those moments are.

Josh received his just before noon on the twelfth of February, the Sunday of Carnival. It had always been the habit of all of them to come to the fazenda for Carnival. In the little town of São João de Barra the high school youths with their floats depicting spaceships, scenes from Arabian Nights, Greek Tragedies; the Negroes with drums and jawbones and *cuiquas*, dressed in bright satins that became more redolent with the passing of the days, were somehow more alluring than all the spectacles a great city could offer. To give oneself over to the drumbeat, joyously dancing, spinning, weaving in the pressing heat of the "*clube*"; to follow the Negroes into the street, down along the rain-freshened, steaming pavements to the diverse and magical beat of their *batucada*. To behave thus every night, and on Ash Wednesday to fall into a sleep as profound and innocent as that of a child, had, in a strange and vital sense, the effect of casting off the weariness and disappointment of a year gone by and beginning anew.

And so the friends had come each year to join in this simple, childishly joyous ritual of washing away sadness and starting anew. And this year, as every other, they had danced all night, followed the *escolas de samba* in the streets, slept all day until, once again, as the stars heralded a break in the inevitable summer storms of Carnival, they could hear the drumbeat in the distant town. Even Francisco and Delia had come the long journey from the Northeast, for, as all agreed without saying, it was the perfect time to brush aside differences and do away with what Malachai had once called the "illusion about arrogance."

Only this year it could not help but be different, for they had all had their brush with the "Dark Age," and all that resulted from it, the cruelty, the agony, the separation, the waste. It was not something they had read or heard and talked of in objective tones, changing the subject when things got too complicated. It was something that had happened to each in a different manner. Though they laughed and were, perhaps, more alive than ever, it was a lot of sadness to wash away. And then, too, there was the absence of Malachai and Clea.

Malachai was not there, bobbing along in the crowd that followed the Negroes, or dozing on the veranda in the Austrian chair with his hands over his middle, or here, under the pines. But when Josh opened the letter, it seemed quite natural that he should read it aloud. And as he did, it was not Josh's voice the others heard, but Malachai's, the high, thin voice with its rolling *r*'s, at once fatalistic and gently rational.

"So here I am, and even now I cannot help stopping from time to time to ask myself, as if a different answer might turn up, 'what happened?' I, the aloof and distant observer who obviously observed too much. But then I suppose it is quite impossible, if one cares enough to be interested, not to become involved in the events and lives one is watching.

"I must tell you that, despite that country's rude behavior toward me, I really had no desire to leave it, and I said as much to the colonel. In fact, I turned my back on him and walked away. I suppose this is because, despite my cynical view of the world, born of two thousand years' experience, there are certain hopes I cannot keep my obstinate mind from clinging to.

"For instance, did you ever notice that civilization may be arrested, but it is never lost? The Romans picked it up, in the end from the Greeks and during the Renaissance, the Europeans returned to seek again among the ruins for Phidias and the things which Herodotus and Euclid had to tell. Not to mention the stern rules the Jews have carried wearily from continent to continent and back. I sincerely think that perhaps I could not live if I did not believe that civilization and struggles for power are separate entities. The conquerors never create a civilization. When they still their bickering and men can breathe again for a time, then people with a mind for such things, pick civilization up and go on.

"So in the end I suppose what made me turn around and accept the colonel's bizarre proposal was Francisco. I know that he is one of those people who create civilization. He cannot look at a piece of landscape without wishing to change it, carefully and thoughtfully, for the better. He cannot see rock and steel and cement without wishing to build. Civilization has need of such men as he. It even has need of such as Delia, with her fiery intelligence that will not accept palliatives. Where Delia goes wrong is in allowing herself to believe that there is some magic means to make mankind what it isn't. Perhaps she will learn, perhaps she has learned it already, that such faith in the absolute goodness of some new kind of man, is as dangerous as the cynical assurance that in the *old* kind of man, corrupted by profit, there is no good at all. Profit does not corrupt man. It is not an extraneous element, but part of his nature. The *new* and the *old* are one man. We must keep manipulating within the confines of what he *is*.

"All this I have thought out during damp, cold winter evenings in London, with careful logic, reasoning with myself as much as anything to make the whole thing easier to bear. But it was not this, of course, which caused me that day in December to suddenly seize the arm of the guard and say, 'Wait.' I could not have thought of it all then. It was this:

the sudden, absolute knowledge that I could not do this to Francisco. I could not send him into exile from a country he loved.

"Because of the desire for power and the Dark Ages that come each time man attempts to impose his beliefs, I have been an exile all my life. A man without a country who nonetheless believes it is good to have a country and love it. It is a strong combination. Perhaps the strongest. Francisco could build dams and bridges anywhere, of course. The world is crying for his services. But for him it would not be the same. For he would think always of the place where he should be, where he belonged.

"There are few countries in the world at this moment which inspire love. For all its defects, Brazil is one of them. Perhaps it is only for the moment. Men forget, become disillusioned, allow their dreams to go to pieces. A country is, after all, only a reflection. But while it lasts, this love, it is an experience which, like a real love for a woman, no man should be denied.

"Obviously, each of you shares this experience in a way. Duncan may joke all he likes about the relative security of remaining in a place where the odds, having struck once, will probably not strike again. But he has given up the security of a paying job in order to remain. Why?

"As for you, Josh. You came, by chance, to seek a piece of land. It could have been anywhere and you would have adapted to it, the land, above everything. But now that you have it, I know that this experience that is Francisco's is yours as well. A part of the country and of the moment, you could never bring yourself to leave now.

"As for myself and Clea, I have news from the colonel that there is an absolution in the air. No proof, so to speak, of my involvement in Duncan's kidnapping or any other terrorist activity. But the question is, Should I absolve them? How far can a country go in combating the Dark Age without becoming a part of it?

"But then, that is what this game is all about, isn't it?

"Do I dare to be as much of a dreamer as you and hope that Brazil will be 'different' enough to win?"

CHAPTER 51

There was another part of Malachai's letter that Josh did not read aloud. Instead, he handed it to Lia, saying gruffly, "Maybe you can make something out of this."

She didn't read it then, but waited until she was alone, lying under the same pine trees later in the afternoon.

> I know of your trouble with Lia and I know that, despite the sophisticated attitudes of our times, it is a trouble no man bears easily. Especially one as unbending as you. But let me say this; that of all of you, with your schemes and projects and fantasies, perhaps Lia alone has all these years lived in a mythical world, which is different from a dream, for dreams are based on reality. If things have turned out as I expect they have, I believe she must know that now. And if such is the case, it would be a pity if this truth were lost to you, now that it has at last been discovered.

They were true, these words of Malachai's. Lia understood them perfectly. Her understanding drifted back in memory to the girl seated in a bookstore, reading Salinger and feeling trapped. It recalled the tall, lean, unpolished and unacceptable young man who had offered her the possibility of escape from ready-made dullness into a world of her own creation. The fazenda as she—they—would have it. And so it had been a thing of their own creation, and yet something had always been missing. She had not known it was her own sense of reality until the day she returned to the fazenda alone.

She remembered so clearly the kind of day it had been: hot and sultry with clouds piling up in the northwest corner of the sky—

that place from which the rain always came. A faint breeze had cooled her cheeks, coming from nowhere, hinting of the great wind, the storm that was to come. How she had always loved such storms as they came sweeping down the valley, bending the grass and trees, filling the sky with wild, untamable flashes of light. And then the long, steady, all-night rain beating on the tiles of the roof, soothing the parched earth. But that day she hadn't cared for the coming of the storm, or for anything.

She had gone through the day mechanically, walking down the long rows of coffee where the men were hoeing in the rich, leaf-strewn earth beneath the trees; watering the garden that had been neglected, left to wither in her absence. The old man Gardenal had been waiting for her as she'd driven into the shed—outrage, pity, morbid curiosity all alight in those piercing blue eyes. "Who would believe it, Dona Lia? Sr. Duncan never did any harm to anyone. The spirits of pigs. They ought to be hung up and cas-trated." He'd licked his lips. She had felt repulsed by the inveter-ate, low, human lust for blood and had not wanted to go on with it.

"I don't care what happens to them. It's Sr. Duncan who mat-ters," she'd said, perhaps a bit too curtly. "The thing is not to give up."

"*Pois é.*" He'd nodded accommodatingly and said with an awk-ward righteousness, "May God guide them." Then he'd gone on to tell her about the new calf born in the lower pasture and how the cow had cleaned out and the calf was sucking on all four tits —but he hadn't had time to cut the cord yet. He would have gone on forever, but she hadn't wanted to hear him; hadn't wanted to make the usual everyday responses, ordinary and reassuring, that he expected of the *patroa.*

So she'd cut him short. "Get me a horse, I'll see for myself." And she had gone, the dogs trailing behind as she'd ridden to the high place, crossed the ravine to the pastures where Josh's grass grew thick and deep.

The storm had come with a vengeance. A post had snapped on the power line, plunging everything into darkness. She had taken the child Christina to bed for company. It was not fear that had prompted her, for even in that moment of terror in which Duncan Roundtree had been enveloped, she could not have associated such an intrusion with this place, this world in which she lived. Rather, it had been a growing, aching loneliness that had prompted her to take the child to her bed and then, blowing out the candle, lie silently as the child slept, her thoughts punctuated by the flashings of the storm. How often she had lain thus with Josh beside her, their heads toward the foot of the bed, watching the streaks of lightning in a distant sky until Josh took her to him, always wanting her more than she wanted him. Herself forever withdrawn, hidden within a part of her being to which no one had access. But that night she, who had always been so used to this solitariness, had felt intolerably alone. So much so that she could scarcely wait for daylight and the chance to be gone.

After the trouble with Duncan was over and they had returned to the fazenda together, the feeling had not changed. The fazenda that had been to her everything, had become an alien territory which she tread without sensing the strength and goodness of the land beneath her feet. Oh, it was simple enough now to see the reason why. The life in it was not simply the grass, trees and earth, the shadowy land itself beneath the shifting clouds that hovered over the high place. The life in it was Josh, with his scheming and struggling and his bent for gambling but never sacrifice. It had been there all the time, though she had never allowed herself to be aware of it. Instead, she had lived narrowly in an exacting, mythical world.

Thoughts of that world had led her to the house on the mountainside to lie in the arms of Jacob Svedelius. And it had all been as she had known it would be, but for the fact that she had never wanted to return there again. For it was there that she discovered that myths exist too. But only as long as you keep them in your head and don't try to make them a part of your life.

So deep in thought had she been that she hadn't heard Josh approaching, had only realized he was there when he had seated himself in one of the green wooden chairs. Putting his feet on the table, he lit a cigar and leaning back, sat smoking quietly, waiting for her to speak. Or so it seemed. It had been a very long time since he'd asked her anything, after all. He looked to her suddenly, incredibly tired of being alone. The sight was almost unbearable, like watching someone in pain and not being sure you had the right medicine. Lifting the letter from her lap, where she had allowed it to fall, she broke the silence with, "Maybe you should tell me if you can make something of it."

"Oh, I can," he said.

"Then it would be a pity, wouldn't it?" she went on.

He shrugged, a little smile, half sorrowful, half derisive hovered about his eyes.

"Josh." She sat up and looked at him with a sudden sense of exasperation that seemed to say, enough of this. Enough of martyrdom. Where is it getting us? "Listen," she said. "I'm glad this letter came, because there are things I must say. And if I don't say them, as Malachai puts it, they will be lost to us forever."

"Then say them."

"All right." It was strange how bold she felt now, like a gambler putting his cards on the table with everything to lose or gain. She felt no longer ashamed, but compelled, forcefully, to speak. "I have wronged you. Not just that time, but for many years. I was so certain of what life was and what I wanted from it. But now I see what Malachai means by the difference between myths and dreams. I have neither now, and I am lost."

She paused a moment as if to clear her thoughts, and went on. "Do you understand me, Josh, when I say that if you took me back now, my feet would touch solid earth as they have never done before . . . But you would have to take me back in every way."

"Is that a command?"

"Oh, Christ! It's the truth! If you don't stop being so goddamn laconic, I'm going to scream." There was an old defiance in her voice that somehow warmed him and made him want to laugh.

"Okay," he said, "I'll stop being laconic. I know it's the truth and I believe it. And I suppose I seem unwontedly cruel as usual. But it isn't that, this time. Other times I've meant to punish you, but not this time. It's just that I've been wounded and it hasn't healed. Sometimes I guess such wounds don't."

"So there's nothing to do but wait, is there?" she said quietly.

"I guess there isn't."

"But not forever," she said. "That wouldn't do either. We would come to hate each other."

"No," he said. "Not forever." He rose then and, leaning over the hammock, kissed her with an unusual gravity and gentleness, and then, calling the dogs, he set off across the pasture.

She didn't follow him but remained where she was, feeling oddly grateful. He had not taken her back yet. Perhaps he never would. Yet it seemed infinitely good to know this person to whom things made so much difference.

It was hot and still now. She lay back in the hammock, looking up into the high branches of the pines, watching the birds. There was an astonishing variety, robins, wrens and sparrows, steel blue *sanhassos* and yellow *Bem-ti-vi*; hummingbirds that darted like black and turquoise streaks of light and the foolish cattle birds, fussing and quarreling eternally over their heaps of eggs. Birds that had migrated to this particular place because instinct had told them they would not be harmed, here in these trees on this land.

Down on the lawn, she could hear the voices of boys, yelling at one another in a game of futebol. It was hot and still and there was a hint of storm in the air. As the cool breeze from the north-west touched her face, she found herself longing for the storm as she had not done in a long time.